WOLF
SHADOW

JANE WADE SCARLET ...
... was born in Essex, and moved to Wiltshire
when she was twenty-two.

Over the years she studied to become a librarian,
a bi-lingual secretary and a graphic designer.
Now she is a writer, living in Dorset.

Jane's previous novel, Wolf Wind, was longlisted
for the Yeovil Literary Prize 2015, and the
Dorchester Literary Festival Writing Prize 2018.

WOLF SHADOW

JANE WADE SCARLET

Published by Scarlet Mermaid

ISBN: 978 1 9998220 2 6

To Dangerous Dave,
who has always believed in me

SUMMER'S HEAT *was failing,* *but the chill of leaf fall* *had yet to come.*

The seasons were in balance, as was the man seated on a boulder that held his body as if moulded from his shape. His horse stood close by, resting from four legs to three as the time passed – as had every other horse he had ridden since the palomino. Once a wayward silver-grey had stamped on the hillside, once an angry chestnut and a sharp-eyed bay. Now a black stallion tossed its mane over loose reins as it waited for the watcher on the rock.

He was still a young man, the colour of his horse darkening as he matured; as he grew from wildness to responsibility. He sat easy. His back was straight, his head was high, and he gazed with eyes that saw beyond. Clouds swayed overhead and told him things; the wind fingered his hair and told him things; a bird flew high with a cry that told him things. And when the man spoke the black horse listened.

Then after a while the watcher stood from the rock, tall enough to see even further, tilting his hat to the ground as the wind rose, lifting dust. Curving its neck, the stallion high-stepped from his approach. He pulled at the reins, pulled the animal close and murmured to the flattened ears. That was all and that was enough.

The horse was appeased and the man took to the saddle, guiding it down the slope to the levels below. The hill withdrew, other hills around it stretched wide and the sharp peaks softened with distance. When he gave the stallion its head, the hooves drummed inside the man's chest until his heart was full.

ONE

TREMORS SHOOK the yard when the black horse stamped in from the valley. The woman scattering feed for the fowl bathed in a float of air as the rider kicked stirrups free and dismounted. He grasped the stallion's muzzle to ease its mind from the wild where it had once run with mares, and the woman came forward to brush a streak of earth from his cheek.

'Night Dancer is learning,' she said.

'He is a clever horse.' The man nodded, still with his hand to the animal's head.

'That may be so.' She leaned back to see his eyes, searching for the gold that was sleeping inside. 'But I believe it has more to do with his clever teacher.'

The gold awoke when he smiled. Lines from the corners of his eyes were hidden by his hair, for it was longer now that he had fledged from youth to man. Although bleached by the heat of summer, its corn-pale colour was combed with darker streaks that pronounced the father's blood in the son's veins.

'The wind is growing stronger,' he said, his gaze following the words to where he had been cross-legged on the rock. 'A storm is coming.'

He knew this because of the gusts that had shivered his back as he sat there; that had added strength to speed, as though he had a mind to outride the weather.

The woman peered up to the track that led away from the farm, chasing curves until it met the town. 'Colt is still out there.' She bit into a fingernail. 'Should we look for him?'

'Colt is in no danger from a storm, Sage.'

The boy has knowledge of such things, he might have added; but there was no need, for the woman knew it also.

Chickens scattered from the corral where the man unsaddled the stallion, rubbing its hide with dry grass. The horse stood tethered by the soft voice and the magic winding through its ears, until the connection was broken by a slap to its rump. It kicked the ground in protest, and farm horses from the second corral stamped their disquiet and drew away.

The saddle a warm weight against his chest, the man crossed to the barn, stirrups making their own music as they tangled with the bridle. The woman waited at the threshold, stroking the residue of chicken feed from her apron. The wind whisked it into her face as she watched him slipping harness over posts on the wall. She knew what was coming, and when it did he froze, hands falling from the leather.

In the unearthly light that told of the encroaching storm he shrank back into the cub who had spent his days in her father's fields, and his nights locked behind darkness in the barn. But it was only a moment, a glitch in time; and when it was over the cub had given way to the wolf. And all seemed to be well with the man who came out to the yard.

The woman took his arm as they walked to the house. Rain began to fall, beating crazy patterns over the pond. The angry wind was left at the door and the room beyond, where once colour had died. But whitewash and tapestries had brought new life. The floor had been scrubbed and woven with rugs, and furniture gathered before the hearth where the fire's fodder was waiting for the flame.

Martha Madison turned from the stove, bearing a steaming dish in thin, strong arms. Elderly before her time she shuffled to the table, the cooking cloud circling overhead. Savoury smells enriched the room and ignited a run of saliva in the man's mouth, for he had not eaten since rising that morning with the early birds, sustaining himself with a hunk of corn bread dipped in milk. He had been trained by deprivation to cope with hunger, but the smell of the stew that the old woman had made was good. He went outside to sluice his hands at the pump, and the rain washed dust from his hair.

They were at the table now – Martha and Sage; and the little girl who had appeared from nowhere, as though conjured by some magician. She was perching at the end where she would not be touched. Round-faced and serene, she gazed up at the man with eyes that were his eyes – earth-brown with a core of gold. She drank in his image to store in her mind, and as Martha scooped stew onto her plate she picked up a spoon and began to eat.

There was nothing to read from the child's face, but when hoofbeats thumped through the yard the man learned from the widening of her gaze that she too had recognised the rider's distress.

A boy came in through the porch door and the storm came in with him. It rampaged around the room, grabbing at pictures on the walls and pulling skirts before it was shut away, leaving the sound of rain dripping from the newcomer's clothes. The boy beat his hat against his leg, sprinkling the rag rugs with silver drops that glistened before disappearing.

'You are late home, Colt.' Sage stared at him over the little girl's head. Her eyes were bright because she had been worried, but now she was relieved.

'I'm sorry.' He said it quickly. The patches of colour on his cheeks could have been sparked by the storm, but the man knew that the cause was something else. He went to where Colt was standing, unsteady, as if awaiting permission to move. He touched the boy's shoulder and felt him shaking.

'Dry yourself and then you can eat,' he said, and Colt nodded, turning from the small pool of rain by his feet.

'And find something to wipe away the water,' the man called out, and when the boy looked up there was chaos in his eyes.

The meal was swiftly eaten and the table cleared. The little girl had already left the room, disappearing unnoticed. Outside the wind was fierce and the storm dashed rain like tiny stones against windows as it rumbled overhead. Sage heated water on the stove to clean the dishes and Martha brought to table the dough that she had left to rise. She began kneading with clever hands, closing her eyes to hear the music in her head. Loose flour rose up to meet her as she worked.

Colt's hair was almost dry, he rubbed it as he made to leave and it fell around his face in dark strands. He heard the man following and turned like a small animal cornered by danger.

'Help me check the horses,' the man told him, plucking waterproofs from hooks. Hood up and head down, he strode through the rain to the corrals; the boy's footsteps were reluctant behind him.

They stood together by the fence, but Colt sought his own distance. Hide gleaming, the black stallion huddled under the shelter beside the enclosure. The three horses in the other corral posed in a triangle of bay, dapple-grey and chestnut. The grey shook its head and a lace of raindrops shivered from the mane.

'Do you have something to tell me?' The man spoke quietly, but the boy could still hear over the downpour.

'No. Nothing.'

'I know that is not true,' the man said. 'And you know that I shall keep on asking.'

There was a hush in the middle of the storm and Colt scuffed the ground with his foot to fill it. 'How long will you keep on asking?'

'Until you trust me enough to talk about it.'

He looked down at the boy, remembering the days when his own trust had died and all he had left was the will to survive.

Back hunched, Colt turned away, stepping through puddles to the little bay mare. The other horses bundled together but he paid them no heed. He lifted a hand to the pony's crest and began to speak.

The man waited, but the words were not for him. He crossed the yard to the house, passing walls that had once been bent and broken, crumbling like a feast for the earth. It had taken him ten years to make them strong again. Ten years since the cub had been released to a boundless world. He could have gone anywhere, done anything, but he chose to stay, to rebuild what he had tried so hard to escape.

There were still days when the wolf questioned the sense of it.

The little girl knew the man was outside her room, for pictures in her head showed him coming from the corral. Showed the boy with his rust-coloured pony, keeping to himself the things that were troubling him. She had seen shadows in Colt's face as he sat at table with a plate of stew. She had searched for the secrets in his mind but they were hidden behind mist and she could not break through. The man, however, was hiding nothing. He was strong and familiar, gazing through her window with the clearest eyes.

She crawled across her bed to reach him. She crawled across Martha's bed when it got in the way, and placed both hands flat on her side of the glass. The man placed his hands on his own side, and it was as if his bigness wanted to eat up her littleness.

If there had been no glass between them she would have been trapped like a fly in the web of his thoughts, smudged with memories of the time when he had been young.

The memories that came with his touch would not let him go, no matter how hard he tried to throw them off, and she hated them. They made her cry, and when she cried she could not stop until he went away and took the past with him. But his mind was free now, filled with pictures of her as the baby birthed six years before; born on the morning of midsummer with no wailing to greet the start of her life. The quiet child who lived within herself. Who understood him, in the same way that he understood her.

Wet air sprinkled across the sill when she opened the window. It danced around her room and the man's scent came with it – that smell of leather and horse, and the wind from the hill that was clutching his hair.

'Where is Colt?' She clamoured, as if she had lost him. 'I want Colt!'

'Hush now. Colt is with Vixen.' The man reached out to her flaxen hair, and she stepped back, only slightly but far enough. 'Come and see the horses with me,' he said.

The little girl moved away from the glass. He watched her fading into the shadows until only the pale moon of her face remained, and the two dark eyes that mirrored his own.

'Come and see the horses, Clove,' he said, knowing that the words were just an echo and the child had gone.

But not too far, for she watched him leave, misshapen under the waterproof wrap. Pinpricks of rain spat in through the open window and landed on her hand. She held it in front of her eyes, and the man's figure disappeared and reappeared between her spread fingers until the weather had swallowed him up.

TWO

THE ROUTE between farm and town had remained indifferent to change as the years passed, but the landscape had been altered by incoming homesteaders laying down footings. With a year's grace between them, two dwellings had grown on either side of the track, not far from the Madison homestead. The wolf was known well by the Hockadays high on the left and known badly by the Wellersons sloping to the right – as far as they could from his sinfulness. But that afternoon their contempt mattered little to the rider of the black horse.

Joanie Hockaday was busy in her yard. She looked up at the clatter of hooves as the man came near and beckoned for him to stay a while. The stallion fought him as he reined it in. The daughter of a rancher through whose hands many wild animals had passed, Joanie recognised Night Dancer's temperament.

'Come over and see us when you are not occupied with this animal,' she said. 'Emmett might be getting his hands on a rare wild beast that needs putting in its place. He would welcome your expertise.'

'I can do that, ma'am.'

He could do that, because that was what he did. His name had travelled further with every horse he had tamed to bear a rider, and his heart had filled each time he was asked to prove it could be done.

'That is good of you, Wolf Shadow.'

Joanie Hockaday smiled, her cheeks dimpling, because he was a fine-looking young man.

'Why not make it an evening?' she said. 'Bring Sage and the children. I'll put together some supper.'

'Thank you, ma'am.'

Wolf eased his shoulders; muscles tested by the stallion. Night Dancer had more need of tuition, and the man might take him out that night to let him run. He might ride without a saddle, for the full moon promised to paint the land silver and the way ahead should be clear. Without the leather on its back the black horse would taste liberty again, and Wolf Shadow would remember the courage of another stallion and its wild strength between his thighs.

Further along the track, the Wellerson holding was silent and unfriendly, but he paid no heed to the glare of eyes as he rode past. He had learned quickly since the day that Maria Wellerson recoiled from his Indian blood, leaving her pasty-faced husband to order him off their property. The distant hills were keeping pace with the stallion's speed and Wolf gazed at them instead, with the familiar tug in his chest for the ride to freedom and the lost beauty of a golden horse.

Oasis appeared out of the dust, rowdy from saw and mallet, and builders shouting by the roadside. Bordered by wooden walks, the town had grown since the man was a child; previously nothing more than a dirt track, now the main thoroughfare was hard-packed and solid. Stores were crushed together like a mouth with too many teeth, and the sheriff's office had been squeezed narrow by new neighbours.

Dr Ryker's residence was no longer at the very end of the street, the place where the wilderness began. It had been incorporated into the heart of the bustle; in much the same way as Daniel and Lucy, and the twin daughters born to them five years since.

Wolf Shadow too had known change. Once roundly scorned as the bastard son of a drunkard, now only a few tightened their lips and looked elsewhere as he rode to the doctor's house, where the original picket fence had been replaced by a post and rail structure mighty enough to enclose trees that had grown tall with the years. Wolf dismounted beneath their shade, spending a moment with the stallion before following the path to the bell-pull. Night Dancer shifted beside the hitching pole and settled in the wake of the young man's words.

The little maid who opened the door was gawping at her feet. She wiped a hand across a well-floured apron, pushing powdery residue into the folds of her skirt from where it shimmered to the floor. The man waited for her to look up, and when she did she saw pale hair and dark eyes, and a strong body fitting well within its clothes. His smile, when it came, sharpened creases at the side of his mouth, and her face turned pink beneath its dusting of flour.

She didn't move until the woman had approached from the kitchen, heels ringing on the tiles, her peacock blue dress in bright contrast with the girl's dun-coloured garb.

'Thank you, child, and away you go,' the woman said. 'And come back with a brush for the mess you have created,' she called loudly as the little thing made off with downcast eyes, scattering white ghosts in her wake.

Taking a moment to smooth the front of her dress, the woman turned back to the door.

'Well, here you are, Wolf,' she said. 'And what an unexpected pleasure.'

'Daniel wanted to see me,' he told her, stepping across the threshold as she closed the door and shut out the busy town. The tick of the parlour clock was the only sound, until a sudden clatter protruded from the kitchen.

'Dear Lord,' the woman groaned. 'Esme still has need of instruction. But she is such a sweet girl I think I should employ leniency.'

She glanced up at him. 'I believe it would be wrong to dismiss her so soon and make life more difficult for her family. They are quite impoverished.'

There was a creak of boards from the floor above, but she didn't appear to notice. She was holding the young man's gaze slightly longer than was necessary.

'You are looking well, Wolf Shadow,' she said, and only turned away when the footsteps had reached the top of the staircase and brought her husband with them.

'Good of you to come so quickly,' Daniel Ryker called down before descending the stairs. The narrow passage was instantly constricted by bodies, and the woman stepped aside.

'I'll have Esme bring some coffee to the office,' she said on her way to the kitchen, lifting her skirt clear of white smudges on the tiles; or something that no one else could see.

Her reprimand for the little maid was strident through the closed door, followed by hush and the parlour clock. Ryker did not seem aware of anything untoward in the raised voice, but the young man had heard excitement.

Ten years had not greatly altered the doctor's office; it still smelled of dark wood and polish, overlaid by something sharp and medicinal. The couch resided in its customary position, the leather dipped and dulled by use, and the same desk hugged the wall even though the chair parked beneath it was a replacement.

Daniel Ryker sat there now, elbows on the chair's arms, hands joined in prayer by his waist. There was grey lurking in his hair and far more streaking his neat beard, but the dark eyes were as indomitable as the time before, when the cub had lain semi-conscious on the couch, his back scoured by beatings.

Ryker began to speak, but hesitantly, as though what he was about to say would not come easily.

'I... I have a friend. A good friend, in fact, whom I have known for many years.'

He stared down at the hands that were still clasped at his stomach. 'A friend who has the misfortune of finding himself in a bit of bother,' he said. And then he said nothing more.

Wolf waited. A man accustomed to lengthy periods of solitude in the place where hills rose and the grass lands were stripped to bare rock, he was no stranger to the suspension of time. But the doctor's shoulders were stooped now, as though the silence was becoming too heavy to bear.

When Ryker looked up his eyes had taken the strain. He blinked in the light, and turned his gaze to a spot just to the left of Wolf's head; perhaps to hide his thoughts.

'He is a very good friend,' he repeated, as if that hadn't been made clear. 'And I need to help him. Just as I helped you ten years ago.'

He jerked as the door opened, hiding what seemed like relief when Esme backed into the room with a tray of coffee wobbling in her hands. Wolf took it from her before the cups should fall, finding a space on the small table that bore nothing but a lamp, trimmed ready for nightfall. He did not see the girl's glance, darting from beneath scraps of hair, and the new blush that was more obvious on her freshly washed cheeks.

The doctor took a long breath as she closed the door very carefully behind her. 'Lucy is training her, you know,' he said. 'She might do well to start with knocking before entering a room.' He barked a laugh, but there was little mirth in it.

Wolf handed the man a cup of coffee and took the other one for himself. The drink was strong and black, as he had grown to like it. He settled back on the couch, and still he waited.

Ryker shook his head. 'Now I am turning you into a servant, Wolf Shadow.'

The young man sucked a mouthful of coffee before he looked up. 'Is it not my service that you need?' he said, and the doctor placed his cup on the desk before turning back. He deliberately met Wolf's eyes.

'A strange thing, this wisdom of yours. You had it when you were still a boy. And possibly before I ever knew you.'

'I learned young.'

'Yes.'

A sudden wind picked up in the street and somewhere a door slammed. Neither man paid it any attention.

'You were telling me of your friend,' Wolf prompted. Ryker shrugged.

'I was not talking about a friend. But I expect you already know that.' The doctor bent forwards; hands tightly clenched as though to bind himself together. 'It was of myself I was speaking. It is my bit of bother.'

The young man nodded. He swallowed more of the coffee and stared through the window at the busy street, until the new silence had smothered some of the disquiet in the room. The tall trees outside the house were still clothed with the late summer foliage that helped to hide what went on in the doctor's surgery from passers-by. Or maybe to hide Dr Ryker himself. Wolf wondered if that might be so as he leaned back on the couch.

The leather protested, and he sent out his thoughts to check for restlessness from the black stallion.

Ryker eased his shoulders. 'Forgive me,' he said, 'for that deplorable display of weakness, but this thing has been preying on my mind for a while and now it shortens my sleep.'

'Will you tell me what it is?'

'Indeed, there is nobody else I can tell.'

'Not even your wife?'

'No.' The doctor huffed. It was the sound of a man who had known better days. 'I have no wish to give her an excuse to seek an end to our marriage,' he said, lifting his head. 'There you have it, Wolf, another confession off my chest. But now I see that I may have shocked you with it.'

'It is your business and none of mine,' the young man said. He tucked a thumb into his belt, where Daniel Ryker's old hunting knife still slept in its sheath. 'But you and Lucy are my greatest friends and I am sorry for you.'

It was rare to see emotion pass Wolf's face and the older man smiled at him. The bonding of years was behind that smile; years that had introduced him to a tattered youth, and all that had followed the doctor's decision to help the cub escape a brutish life. And then later, to help him escape the noose as well.

There were over twenty years between the two men; enough to make one a father and the other the son. But there were fewer than ten between Lucy and Wolf Shadow, who had been little more than a boy himself when his own son was born.

Spare of build but powerful, muscles shaped by his determination to restore the dilapidated farm, Wolf was still some years away from thirty. The proud bloodline bequeathed by his late father was strong in the set of his head. Daniel Ryker had silvering hair and walked with a stoop, but his wife was still young, still vivacious.

Still vibrant and hungry in bed, lying with a man who was too beleaguered by foreboding to be of much use to her.

Lucy often alluded to Wolf's ability to conceal what he was thinking behind his eyes; sometimes with a catch of breath, and a flash in her own eyes that her husband preferred not to see.

Ryker looked at the silent young man before him and felt an old man's envy. He thought of the way Lucy stood when Wolf was nearby, as though she wished to spring from her everyday life and run with the horse whisperer.

I will fight you for her, Wolf Shadow!

The doctor recoiled from the words in his head and the fading fire of dislike that had burned with them.

He felt ashamed, because was Wolf not a friend? He had grown from a hungry boy to the consort of a lovely young woman and the father of two fine children. He had brought a dying homestead back to life with his own hands, and he was the only one that Daniel Ryker could approach with the story he was about to tell.

He spoke swiftly to have done with it.

'I have been involved in a business I would prefer to keep private, but that with misfortune has now been exposed,' he said. 'The one who has brought this about is threatening to tarnish my good name and ensure that I am not fit to be the doctor of this town. And if I cannot pay for an end to his revelations, I may also find myself imprisoned.'

There was nothing in the young man's face to show what he was thinking, but Ryker had been stripped bare.

'I have to prevent this man from talking. And I need to know if you will help me.'

Wolf blinked slowly, as though capturing an image and storing it at the back of his mind.

'I will give you whatever help I can,' he said. 'But your wife…'

'Lucy would leave me if she found out about this,' the doctor said. Then after a moment he tried to laugh, as though that might have been a joke.

'I have always believed your marriage to be steadfast, Daniel.'

'Once I believed it also, but we have moved on since and things are not quite the same.'

And was that a glimmer in the young man's eye? Was he calculating a move on a lonely woman whose marriage was no longer steadfast? Was he planning a way to help her too?

Such miserable thoughts; Ryker tried to scatter them, but they remained as though planted by some demon. They would take root and grow, and he did not know how to stop it happening.

It might make him feel like half a man, but he had to ask. 'Are you really my friend, Wolf Shadow?'

'Of course. Why should you question it?' The young man frowned. 'I am friend to both of you.'

I know what she feels for you, the doctor thought. And it is more than simple friendship.

The muted tick of a clock could be heard through the wall, but the silence between the clunk of seconds was pure. He had not spoken aloud; he had rubbed his face and taken his thoughts away with his hand, and they had dissolved.

'I seem to be questioning everything these days,' he said, his voice as distant as the sounds of life trickling through the window.

Movement was intermittent out on the street, townsfolk passing between branches of the protective trees where leaves hung limply under the heels of a blowsy summer. The doctor's office gleamed in the late afternoon light, but all that Wolf could see were the chores awaiting his return to the valley dip. He wondered how much of the work his son might have shouldered already, for Colt did not turn aside from hard toil.

Rather like Wolf himself at a similar age, although the taste of the whip would have allowed him little choice. And oftentimes, he was given the taste as a reminder.

'I will help you, Daniel, as far as I am able,' he said. 'But the evening is close and I need to get back.'

The doctor looked up. 'Of course. I had not noticed the time.' He hesitated. 'Lucy would expect me to have asked you to stay for supper. But another time, maybe.'

Or maybe not, he thought as Wolf followed him to the house door, his pale hair lifting in the breeze before he could tame it with his hat.

'When everything is ready,' the young man said, 'I shall ride with you to tackle your discoverer.'

He spoke quietly, so that the words should not reach the doctor's wife who was mothering the twins in the parlour. A rudimentary song was being tapped from the piano to the accompaniment of childish voices out of sync – Dulcie Ryker commanding the tune with modest Bella two seconds behind.

And beyond the fence Night Dancer snickered, as if he was trying to join in.

Wolf fished a titbit from his pocket, a sweet treat to hold under the stallion's nose. He slapped the black neck, speaking for a while to soothe the horse so that he could climb to the saddle.

Dr Ryker caught the soporific words from where he was standing at the house door, domestic life carrying on behind him as if it was another world. The young man's voice was full of charms; he saw them bewitching his wife just as they had bewitched the horse. He saw Wolf casting spells in Lucy's ear. He saw her raising her head to him; parting her lips.

And then he closed the door so that he should not see anything more.

THREE

THE ANGRY crowd was gaining on him and he didn't stand a chance…

Until he woke to find himself safe under the eaves, and Sage lying with her back to him, her hair spread over the pillow like a horse's mane caught in flight. Strands drifted across his skin when she moved, and he drew them between his fingers. To bring calm again. To keep the dream at bay.

After a decade of comparative civilisation, a bed was still an oddity and an inconvenience. A body accustomed to the hard ground below and the cool night above had trouble sleeping on softness. Sage, however, had been tranquil for hours.

She smiled as she slept – his woman, the mother of his children, who had not been much more than a child herself when they first made love on beds of straw. The rapture of that loving and its gentle afterglow had been overwhelming and tender, and it still was.

The air from the open window was chill, but Wolf didn't feel the cold. He smelled the yard, the horses in the corral, the late flowers that Martha tended behind the house. He smelled open spaces where he wanted to be. He cupped the woman's breast and rocked to the beat of her heart; when he left the bed she rolled into the warmth that remained. She didn't wake. She never woke in the middle of the night, when her lover abandoned her for the dark and the wild.

Wolf stepped outside to wetness. The rain had ceased falling a while before; there was none left on the roof to drip from the eaves. But the house was surrounded by a shallow moat that would be gone come daybreak, sucked away by parched earth and the residue of a dry summer.

The scent of fresh water lifted from the small pond, it was sweet and delicate, and Wolf held it at the back of his nose as though it might ease his own thirst. But it was not enough to feed the hunger. Only the stallion could do that.

Night Dancer was ready by the corral fence. The man could see the pricked ears, the toss of the head. He blew a breath and a trickle of words, and the horse came closer as though roped by language, whickering a reply when the gate opened. Wolf grabbed a hank of mane and mounted. He took the stallion towards the track that led to the town, and everywhere that was beyond the town; keeping to a walk, pulling away to the rough ground.

It was very dark; moon and stars tucked behind a blanket of cloud. The Hockaday house was a solid black shape, although Wolf espied a sliver of paleness, as of a light being struck and placed in a window.

There were other homesteads further ahead, closer to Oasis but still separated by the land, the rocks and wild brush and all that had yet to be tamed. One day they would reach the town, joined to fellow houses by their own rules and behaviours and a barricade of fences. Out here where Wolf rode, the land was still wild and still free.

Beneath him the stallion shivered, scenting the plain and the creatures in hiding. Night Dancer was ready to run but the path was not yet clear. The rider curbed the horse with his knees and his tongue, and it settled into a lope, keeping pace with the rising falling shift of words.

Wolf relaxed, one hand flat against the broad rump where muscles bunched and eased and bunched again. His mind brought him pictures of the man who had taught him to ride under a sky-blue canopy, riddled with holes where the light played. Faded memories, like paper left out in the sun. One day none would remain of the Indian who had fathered him and died from a rival's bullet, and Wolf would have no more need to step into the past.

Except that the past had never left him. It returned in the shape of dreams, like the one that had woken him that night to darkness in the window and Sage asleep beside him. A dream that often came to plague him, sparked this time by the memory of Colt standing near his pony in the rain, with the worry that he was holding inside painted across his face.

Night was on the wane, opening up to a new dawn. Wolf let the stallion run. His shoulders still ached from the battle to restrain, but now the air was wild in his face and there was nothing to hear above the singing of speed. Civilisation fell away and all he could see were the hills. He knew how it felt to crest the summit with pain in his thighs and rocks in his chest. He knew the spread of land rising to the next peak, falling to the next hollow, leading to the end of everything.

Once he had crossed to the other side, but now he was haltered by a conscience and a sense of duty. Now wrongs had been righted and life was better – at least that is what he told himself. Although a little of the magic still remained, a shred of memory that might never be erased. Occasionally it clashed with his every day, sending him miles out into the wilderness with the black horse before he met the invisible wall that stood between what was then and what was now.

But there would be no ride to freedom that night. The wind itself was a barrier, hindering progress and driving him back. Night Dancer objected to the decision; head down, kicking out, getting nowhere. Wolf recognised the ache of its hunger. He gritted his teeth as he managed the horse, and it took a while before they could leave the wildness behind them, unexplored.

He returned to find Sage outside the house, her white gown flapping in the dawn breeze like an angry ghost. Her hair was loose and the gusts blew it around her face as she crossed over to the barn, disappearing inside and emerging again.

Leaving the stallion fenced and furious, Wolf found her at the back of the house, in the garden of straight furrows that her mother had raked across the earth. The ground was limp now, denuded stalks and a few flowers all that remained of the summer's abundance, but Sage was aware only of the soft folds of land that led to the horizon. Her shoulders were high but she was very small. When he reached her she clutched his arm; even through his buckskin sleeve her hand was too warm. He couldn't see her eyes, but he knew they were burning.

'Did you find him?' she said. 'Did you see him, Cub?'

She stared at him as though the ten years had never passed; as though it wasn't the man she was addressing but the boy he had been, in the days before she felt their son stir in her belly. Distressing days. She had stumbled then and she was stumbling now. Wolf shook her gently until her mind cleared and she knew him again.

'Why is Colt not with you?' she said.

'Where has he gone, Sage?'

'How can I know? I did not hear him leave.'

24

She pointed to the corral, where the chestnut and the dapple-grey were standing watchful of the stallion and its tantrum. 'He's taken Vixen.'

'Where is Clove?'

Sage frowned. 'It was Clove who woke me. She came straight from her bed and told me that Colt had left. She sees things, Wolf.'

'Yes, she sees things.'

'But she cannot tell me what has happened to him.'

'Then she does not see everything.'

He used to have difficulty keeping a smile on his face, but it had grown easier after ten years of better days. He smiled at her now, and she leaned towards him as though to feed on the reassurance.

'Try not to worry, Sage,' he said. 'I think I know where he might be.'

Still unforgiving, Night Dancer tussled with the man who dared to mount a second time, fighting the calming language as they headed for the valley road. Light was stronger now, distances clearer, but there was no other rider out where the land twisted, clutching rocks worn smooth by storms.

Trees circled shrinking ponds, leaving dregs and fallen leaves. The stallion ran through gathered water, fanning Wolf's legs with a fever of spots as they rode for the cluster of slopes where he had once sought refuge in a cave. That dark morning when the farmer had died, and the sheriff had hunted the wolf cub with a loaded gun at his belt.

The hiding place was tucked behind overgrowth, still reeking of the creatures that sheltered there and bore their young. It had been a few years since Wolf had shared knowledge of the burrow with his son, and now Colt had taken his father's sanctuary for his own. It wasn't far to go on a swift horse, and it wasn't long before he sighted Vixen searching the ground for food.

Alone and riderless, the little mare was following the incline towards juicier grass, and Wolf Shadow slid from Dancer's back and began to climb as well. The lair was halfway up the slope; a bite out of the hillside, its mouth hidden under a net of foliage. Wolf pulled the fronds to one side and picked up movement in the shadows where the earth walls met. It was only when dawn light slipped in through the opening that he caught sight of the boy's face, and the glint of tears.

'I shall wait for you to come out,' Wolf said. 'I am not going away.'

He sat outside the animal's lair with his back against a rock. Night Dancer was clattering the loose stones below and little Vixen snickered into the grass above. It was peaceful and calm in this place, where the paths had once rung with the sound of angry hooves and angrier men, and Cub's heart had been as hollow as the canyon where a horse lay with blood in its mane.

Concealed behind sullen cloud, the sun was hovering above the horizon, but it had already begun its slow climb by the time Colt emerged from the cave through a curtain of stalks. The boy squatted on the ground a few feet from his father, and Wolf waited, until his son had edged closer and closer still. After a while they were sitting side by side, their backs against the rock that reared towards the top of the hill where the pony was busy feeding.

'Vixen seems content,' Wolf said. 'But Night Dancer is being called by mares.' He picked grass blades and stared ahead, but he knew he had his son's attention.

'Will Night Dancer run, Pa?'

'No. I will not let him.'

'How can you stop him?'

'I can speak his language, Colt.'

Wolf Shadow glanced at the boy, the earnest brown eyes, the dry streaks on his face that told of his tears.

'And so,' he said, 'can you.'

The child looked away, it was sudden, like breaking a connection. 'No, I cannot. Not any more.'

Wolf shook his head. 'Why do you say that?'

'Because it is a curse.'

'It is a gift, Colt. From your grandpa. He passed it to me when I was small and I am passing it on to you. And when the time is right you will offer it to your own son.'

'No! I will not!' The boy began to struggle to his feet, but Wolf stopped him with a hand to his shoulder.

'Tell me what is wrong.' The child whimpered but fell back to the ground. 'Tell me now, Colt,' Wolf said.

'They call me a filthy bastard.' His voice rose with every word and he hid his face in his hands. The pain in his crying twisted something in his father's heart.

'Who are they, Colt?'

But maybe he already knew.

The boy looked up. 'Korky Kendall.' His voice broke. 'And Jonah Wellerson.'

Wolf nodded. He turned and peered down the hill. The black stallion was still there, its head raised, nostrils flaring as the breeze brought scents across from the plain where mustangs roamed.

Colt breathed deeply, staring at his father's profile: the straight nose and the curved brow, the ruffle of pale hair scattered around the collar of his jacket. The man's stillness crept into the boy's head and it was soothing. But what he was about to tell him caught in his throat, and he had to swallow before he could find the courage to say it.

'They call me a filthy Indian whore bastard, Pa. And they call you a murderer.'

His father stiffened. But he did not speak.

'They said you killed Grandpa Madison.' Colt started shouting. 'Did you kill him, Pa? Did you stab him and leave him to die…?'

'No!' Wolf turned towards him. His eyes were ringed with gold. 'No, I did not.'

His outline shimmered, as if he was disappearing, and Colt shouted even louder for the fear of it. 'They're going to hang you, aren't they, Pa?'

Wolf hesitated. He shook his head with the weariness that had crept into his bones. 'No one is going to hang me, Colt.' He tried to laugh, but the sound was so forced that the boy winced. 'Except for your ma if I don't get you home soon.'

'I hate them, Pa. I hate school… I can't…'

'Quiet now.' Wolf Shadow stood, dusting the ground from his pants. He looked tall and proud and brave, but when Colt had stood as well he had become his normal size again. The boy wanted to hug him, to keep all that was proud and brave safe inside, but his father had already started to walk away.

'Fetch Vixen,' Wolf said as he went down the hill to the black stallion.

FOUR

SAGE WAS waiting for them in the yard, fully dressed now, the wind playing with her skirt. She was outwardly calm but her fingers were busy, clenching and unclenching at her sides. Her mother stood by the house porch with Clove, Martha's clothing the same colour as the shadows that made them both difficult to see.

For the second time that morning Wolf led the black stallion to the compound, sweeping sweat from its hide with his hands. Colt was still sitting on Vixen's back, as if reluctant to meet the ground. He acknowledged his mother and his grandma. For a moment he locked eyes with his sister. And then he dismounted.

Sage put her hand to his shoulder, up where his neck sloped so that she could touch his young skin. 'Go in the house, Colt,' she said. 'Warm yourself at the stove.'

'First see to the horses,' his father told him. 'Vixen needs to be rubbed down. Night Dancer also.'

'Your son needs to go in to the warm, Wolf Shadow.' Sage stood in front of him. 'He was not dressed for riding in the cold.'

'It was Colt's choice to ride without his coat, but not the horses' choice to ride as well,' Wolf said. 'They have worked hard for his sake, so he must give time to them first. After that he can go in to the warm.'

Sage's eyes told him nothing. He turned to his son.

'Do as I tell you, Colt.'

The boy nodded. 'Yes, Pa.' He led his pony across to the barn and unbuckled the cinch, but his fingers were too cold and he fumbled. His mother sighed, and Wolf shook his head.

'He will come to no harm, Sage.'

'He has already come to harm, Wolf Shadow, and this morning he tried to outride it.' She looked up at him. 'Tell me what he told you.'

Wolf indicated Martha at the porch, and the child who was with her. The little girl was staring at her father, her eyes rummaging. Her mind was a turmoil of thoughts; he could almost hear words in the jumble.

'When we are free to talk, then I will tell you,' he said, and Sage nodded, drawing closer to the scent of leather, walking with him to the house.

Her son was conversing with the little mare. There was nothing articulate in the soporific language, but Sage had heard the speech so often from his father's mouth that it almost made sense. Soothed by the sounds she gathered together her daughter and her mother and made entry to their home.

Clove slipped away, as she always did, finding space in the corner of the room. She drew a length of knotted string from a pocket in her pinafore and began to form creatures' cradles with her hands, humming something at the edge of her voice. It sounded gentle, like chanting.

Wolf heard the horse language in its lift and fall from where his daughter was sitting with her back against the wall with the web of string at her fingers. And then Sage's mother stood in front of him, peering high to reach his eyes. She had to stretch her neck back a little further now, for every year she seemed to grow closer to the ground.

Once she had been taller, rearing over him with sharp

words and dislike, but not even her husband's brutal handling had stunted much of the young boy's growth, and there had come a time when he had seen across the woman's head in his turn. Now he was the one who needed to bend to her height.

She took his hand and stroked it as she might a kitten. There were no sharp words left to speak for they had died along with Haine Madison; the dislike had been forgotten and respect had taken its place. Martha had learned to live again, and the boy she'd dismissed as her husband's bastard was now her daughter's spouse in all but name.

'You could have left me to cope alone after that man died,' she told him. 'You could have gone away and taken my Sage with you, just as I had woken up and seen her wholesome again, without the taint of the devil and his poison in the air. That is what you could have done when Clay Russett let you go. But instead you came here and offered me your help.'

She stopped abruptly, and it seemed as though she had been battered by some emotion that even after ten years was still a novelty. Wolf read the thoughts from her face and saw himself again, set free from the sheriff's cell to follow the valley road back to the farm.

He had passed Daniel Ryker on his way out of town that day. He had told the doctor where he was going, the words pressed to his tongue by a compulsion he couldn't see and still didn't understand.

'I needed your help when you were a boy,' Martha said. 'And now that you are a man I offer you my help in return. In any way that I can.'

She let go of his hand. It took a while for her warmth to fade from his skin, and by that time she had wandered to her bit of land at the back of the house, where Wolf had helped her plant the garden that bloomed richer and riper as each year passed. There was the late summer growth to be harvested, the dead stalks to tidy, the soil to prepare for another time. She picked up tools and set to work, and a few moments later Clove came out to join her. The child was bending in turn, working the ground like her grandma. Keeping her own counsel with the earth.

'I have offered him my help,' Martha said, speaking half to the garden and half to the little wraith who was copying her movements. 'But I know you want to help also, don't you, maid?'

Clove was silent, then after a while she started to hum.

'Will you tell me now?'

Wolf didn't answer. The room was still dark and his eyes were covered.

Her mother and her daughter were safely behind the house and Colt had taken himself to the barn. 'We are alone, Wolf Shadow,' Sage said, grabbing his arm, 'and free to talk about our son.'

He picked her hand from his sleeve and held it in his own. 'He has found trouble at school.'

'Much as I thought you would say.' She stood back and turned her head, as though searching for a clue. 'Who brings this trouble? What form does it take?'

'Other boys. They call him names and they give him labels.'

'Well?' Sage looked up at the man again. She wanted to see his eyes, the golden spark deep inside the brown that held his spirit, but his sight was still hooded. 'What names, Wolf; what labels?'

'The ones that are in your head.'

He glanced at her and looked away again, as though

he was to blame and knew that she thought the same.

'How can you see what is in my head?' She was almost shouting. 'All I can think about is that Colt has found trouble, and it is so bad that he should try to escape it before the day is awake. I need to protect my son, Wolf, and I cannot do that if you keep trying to protect me.'

Sage had not grown much beyond the years of her youth, as though living through her father's oppression had kept her slight for speed and slender for the need to hide. But anger always raised her; high enough at least to reach the eye of the storekeeper who charged too heavily for flour, or the Sunday school teacher who had once mistaken Clove for a dunce. Or with the man she had chosen for her mate, who was gesturing for calm before he would tell her the names and the labels.

'They call him an Indian bastard.'

Filthy Indian whore bastard; the words were branded on Wolf's brain.

Sage slumped; she turned away.

'Are we never to escape it?' Her voice was weary, as though she was still recovering from a sickness that had lasted a whole decade. 'People will always see what they are used to seeing. Then they pass the knowledge to their children, and so it goes on.'

She walked away from him and he didn't try to follow. The need to run was powerful. Muscles twitched in his thighs as though they were already wrapped around the stallion's flanks and the farm was disappearing behind him. He grabbed his hat and went out into the freshening day. He reached the corral before he realised what he was doing, his hand raised to the catch and Night Dancer receptive, ears pricked for messages.

There were jobs to complete: repairing a breach in the field fence, easing the cart's wheel that had seized in mid-turn, picking up the feed from Kendall's store. Actions requiring more from him than the riding of a horse. But even so, it was a struggle not to open the gate, for this was no ordinary day.

The equilibrium had been disrupted by old fears. Fears so entrenched that they had become part of his life, the legacy of a dead man who had governed by the whip.

Wolf left the catch alone and turned away. The black stallion whinnied, a forlorn sound. The horse was calling the man back where he belonged, and he felt torn. His skin crawled as if he was in the wrong body, being forced to live the wrong life.

The life he wouldn't be living at all if it were not for Lucy Ryker.

Lucy Ryker. He thought of her again in her blue dress, the colour almost luminous against the shaded walls of her house on the day that he had listened to the doctor's confession.

'You are looking well, Wolf Shadow,' she had said, but there had been another message behind her eyes, a confession of her own that had been prevented by her husband's appearance at the top of the stairs. Maybe she was waiting to tell Wolf what he didn't want to hear, or maybe she was thinking twice about opening her mouth.

Maybe he would open it for her…

The earth shook beneath him. He made a sound, and heard it a second later. And Clove heard it as well. The horrible sound that was making a tangle of her grandma's garden, until there were no neat rows left.

Martha worked on, aware only of the hidden places where weeds were lurking, the holes left after the slither of worms, rainwater puddling areas untouched by the sun. But she looked up when the small spade fell, and there was Clove, going towards the house; patting the wooden wall six times to make everything right again. Because very little was right about the way her father was standing between the corral and the barn.

He knew she was there; he saw the corona of golden hair, the pale sun of her face. He tried to smile, but it only reached his mouth. The rest of him was in another place, a murky place, and Clove didn't like it.

A bucket full of weeds in her hand, Martha arrived to tempt the child back to the spade and the digging. She noticed nothing untoward, except that Wolf seemed so very still in the middle of the yard.

'Dreamers, the both of you,' she told the little girl.

'Dreamers, the both of them,' she told her daughter as she came from the house, the strangest look on her face.

'Whatever is the matter, Wolf?' Sage touched his arm. It was like an empty sleeve. She grabbed it tightly, feeling for his flesh, and shook him hard enough to hurt. 'Where have you gone?'

Wolf's lips were too dry, he had to lick them before the words came. 'I am still here.' He smoothed the skin that was puckering her brow. 'Where else am I likely to be?'

Where else?

Sage was still holding his arm where the muscles were clenched. No longer an empty sleeve, it had been filled with rocks. But at least it was warm.

'Colt will stay off school today,' she said.

Wolf nodded. 'If he stays off school, he must help me to mend the field fence.'

She raised her head. 'He is reluctant to face you, Wolf, for the words that he spoke.'

'They were other people's words. Why should he fear me for that?'

'Our children do not fear you, husband.' Sage needed to see that there was life in his eyes, but it was still hidden. 'They revere you. You have no need to feel shame.'

The shame in him had another reason, but she must never know that.

'Take Colt with you to mend the fence,' she said, 'and later we shall drive into town and speak to schoolmaster Jackson, and then this trouble will be done with and all will be well again.'

All will be well? Was that a wish she was making? Just like the ones she used to make as a small girl. In the evenings when her father came home to the mangy yard, belly tight with the day's whisky, eyes wild under a dusty hat, and hands reaching for the whip.

FIVE

EVEN AT this time of year, when the night encroached like a hungry coyote and dawn was reluctant to rise, the sun could still show its teeth. After just one day the ground was dry again, as though it had never been so rain-sodden that a necklace of little lakes had circled the land.

Wolf drove through the main street where earth was packed hard, and a fan of dust rose from the wheels to make a shimmer of the woman beside him. Sage bent her head as if she would prefer to hide, but her coyness was unnecessary, for those who trod the sidewalks were intent on their own business and not much heed was paid to the rattle of the cart or the family it was carrying into town.

Colt sat between his parents. He was frightened. Wolf could feel him shaking.

'Aren't you scared, Pa?' the boy had asked him earlier, as the dapple-grey was harnessed to the cart, and Wolf had hunkered down to test his repair of the troublesome wheel.

There had been another wheel once, bending like a fractured limb on unforgiving rocks. Wolf remembered the pistol-shot sound of wood cracking, and a group of travellers coming together to help with the mending. He remembered splinters in his fingers, dust in his eyes, and all the tribulations that had followed.

'I have been scared many times, Colt,' he said. 'But never of the empty words put into a child's mouth.'

'You are the bravest man I know, Pa.' There was such awe in the boy's words that Wolf had turned away. His son needed to stay strong and telling him the truth would only bring weakness.

He steered the cart along the street to where Kendall's store beckoned through its gaping door. The smell of paint was still fresh across the new extension that Kester Kendall had erected after his father Tobias handed over the reins.

The replacement sign was swinging in a sharp breeze above the sidewalk, and Kester stood beneath it for everyone to see the "& Son" half of the concern made flesh.

Arms folded across his growing belly, the storekeeper watched the young man climb down from the cart. Wolf stood by the sidewalk and Kendall gave him a nod, his mouth fixed on the impression of a smile that was going nowhere.

'You have a face that looks like it means business,' he said, rocking on his heels. 'And I sure hope it's for something that I'm keeping on my shelves.'

'Yesterday I would have been satisfied with the feed I have ordered,' Wolf said, looking up at his eyes and ignoring the mouth and the painted smile. 'But today I need answers as well.'

'Do you so?' The portly man wove thumbs through the straps holding up his pants. 'Although I guess that all depends on the questions you wish to ask.'

Wolf lifted off his hat and stepped up to the sidewalk. In the sun's glare his hair looked white, albeit flecked with darker lines where the light could not reach.

'The questions are for Korky,' he said.

Kendall was shorter now that he and Wolf stood together, and his thumbs seem to have become trapped behind the suspenders. 'You are a grown man,' he said. 'And with a face like that, you want to ask questions of a nine-year-old child?'

'I am starting with your son, and then I shall go on to ask questions of others.'

The storekeeper was sleek, and growing sleeker each month on the profits from his business. The wooden boards creaked as he came closer. Almost close enough to share breath with the young man who was now as still as stone.

'Well then,' he said. 'You must go through me first.'

'I see no problem with that,' Wolf said. 'Since you are the one who will have given Korky the words he passed on to my son.'

Kendall's smile had gone before it had a chance to appear; his thumbs, set free, were now wrapped around his fists. 'I'm not sure I like the tone of your voice,' he said. 'In fact, Mr Wolf Shadow, I'm not sure that there's anything about you I like at all.'

Quivering from jowl to fleshy thigh, the tradesman took a step forward and emptied his voice into the young man's face. 'What right do you have to question me or my son, you miserable half-breed?'

There was a red mist inside Wolf's head, and it was all he could see. He stood with legs wide and muscles hard, and his fingers closed on the knife at his belt.

'No!'

The word, sharp and high, came from the woman in the cart, her arm around the shoulders of the boy beside her. 'Wolf Shadow!' she called, louder now, and the sound thundered into his brain.

Hair tumbling from the coils around her head, Sage was glowing in the sun. He read the warning in her eyes, as he had read every warning over the past ten years in a place where minds were small and memories vast. And then he saw humiliation on the face of the child at her side.

Footsteps came to a halt behind him.

'You need to break this up now.'

The command was followed by a jangle of spurs when the speaker stamped his foot. Spurs like those worn by a fox-haired man in a town called Liberation, where Wolf had once faced a sheriff's gun.

But there was a different sheriff standing before him now, raising a fist that came close to Wolf's jaw but did not touch. 'Break it up,' he said, the star on his chest flashing back a reflection from the window of Kendall's store.

He nodded to a group of women watching from a spot by the wall as though unsure whether it was safe to proceed any further into their afternoon. 'There is no need for concern, ladies. For either this man is about to walk away,' he turned to Wolf, 'or the next place you find him will be inside my jail.'

'Leave him be, Sheriff Parnell.'

Wolf hadn't noticed Sage descending from the cart, but he felt the flick of her hair as she came to his side. 'You leave him be,' she said. 'My husband has wronged nobody.'

'Not yet, maybe, but give him time.' Parnell looked down at her from his greater height, and then he rocked back a little from the look in her eyes. 'Well, all right, Miss Madison. But if he and Kester want a conversation it must be kept at a decent volume and in a private place, or I shall be involved.'

40

He glanced up at Colt, sitting rigid on the bench seat.

'And you have your boy here. Surely you wouldn't want him listening to this?'

Colt jumped to his feet and the cart rocked. He stumbled but did not topple. Filling his chest, he pointed at Kendall with a finger so piercing that the man winced.

'Korky Kendall has been telling everyone that my pa is a murderer.'

There was a buzz of excitement around those who had gathered outside Kendall & Son, all eyes assessing the man standing motionless on the sidewalk. The store owner was in front of him and the sheriff one pace behind, but Wolf paid them no heed.

'And are we not all mindful of the lie in that nasty little rumour?'

Projected from the opposite side of the road, the voice was loud. A group of horses tied to the hitching post jostled, bumping together as they tried to escape the noise, and the white-haired man pushed their rumps out of the way and squeezed his bulk between them.

'That is, those of us who were here at the time and are not too decrepit to have mislaid our memory,' he said, crossing to the cart where the dapple-grey mare stood white-eyed and trembling. He eased her distress with a hand to her neck, allowing himself a moment to catch his breath.

'I for one have a very clear memory of those days,' he said, mounting the sidewalk. His beard bristled as he nodded. 'And so does a judge called Gerald Hopgood.'

The lawman raised his eyes. 'Thank you for that, Clay. But your intervention here is not required.'

'Oh, is it not? Well, now, Sheriff Parnell,' the older man said, adding some spit to the title, 'it must be obvious to everyone that my intervention is exactly what is required, before any more foolishness occurs in the middle of the street on this fine afternoon.'

He twisted his lips, as if there was something he didn't like about the sheriff's face. 'And don't call me Clay. My name has been Mr Russett since the day you acquired my badge and my position.'

The lawman bridled, raising a hand to the holster at his hip, as though the gun would be too easy to draw.

'You are going to have to stop hindering.'

'Hindering is it?' Russett threw him a look, and then took the look away again as if it was hardly worth the bother. 'It seems to me that the only hindering here has been perpetrated by Mr Kendall.'

'Certainly not.' The storekeeper rocked on his heels. 'I have been no impediment at all, and yet I was virtually attacked by this…'

He flapped his hand towards Wolf before his thumbs found their way back to the suspenders. 'And I have witnesses to prove it,' he said, twisting his head from side to side.

But the curious had already wandered away, followed after a while by the sheriff, and a while later by Kendall himself.

'I believe it is time to make a move,' Russett said. 'Or we may turn into a bottleneck, and our friend Parnell will come back to arrest us for obstruction.'

'I still have questions for Kester Kendall's son,' Wolf told him.

'You may well have questions, Wolf Shadow, but perhaps right now is not the best time to ask them.' Russett nodded briskly, exciting what was left of his bush of hair, for it was more of an outline than a nimbus after ten years had brought him to the age of sixty. 'Just let me tarry here a while, at least until Kendall has supplied you with whatever order you might have made, and maybe I can gather some of the answers you require. Would that be acceptable?'

He stared at the young man, eyebrows raised, but Wolf turned away. 'There will be nothing to learn from closed mouths,' he said. And then he faltered, his back prickling, because Lucy Ryker was standing behind him in a turquoise dress and her perfume was filling his mind.

His first thought was of her hair, glowing in the sun as if it ran with honey. His second was how it would feel like velvet against his lips.

His third was whether she could read what he was thinking from his face.

She didn't even look at him, too busy conversing with Sage like friends who had just met in the street on a day when all was well. Although clearly it was not. Decked in identical pink dresses, curly heads bonneted, Dulcie and Bella had been deliberately positioned in front of their mother on the sidewalk, and the little girls' intervention was keeping everyone at a distance.

Kendall's workman came out of the store, weighed down by a sack of feed. He acknowledged Wolf before heaving it into the back of the cart. The shiny paint on the walls winked at his image as he went away for the next load. It didn't take him long to deliver the whole consignment, for he worked at speed.

He hesitated before leaving, reaching out to shake Wolf's hand. It was sudden, the decision of a moment. 'Not all of us are guided by Kester Kendall.' He spoke quickly, as though criticising his employer was not the wisest thing to do. 'I just thought that was something you needed to hear.'

Wolf nodded and the workman stepped back, casting a glance towards Kendall & Son's complacent façade. 'I know a little about Korky,' he said. 'He's Kester's only child, which would explain a lot. But the kid is basically stupid, and that is a dangerous quality in a bully. He feeds on the bounty that spews from Kendall's mouth like manna from Heaven.'

He gestured towards Colt. 'He will be fine, your boy,' he said. 'Looks like he can stand up for himself. Just like his pa, so I hear.'

Hands in pockets, he returned to the store, where late afternoon customers could be seen through the door, milling from shelf to shelf. Kester Kendall had planted his bulk in front of the counter, a plump and preening bird with the smile smeared across his lips.

And down the street floated the doctor's wife with the little girls trotting beside her, their bonnets in a fluster as they tried to keep up. Wolf watched until the turquoise and the pink had merged into one colour, and then he turned to find Sage standing on the sidewalk, shining in the sun. Staring at his face.

SIX

NIGHT HAD fallen under streaks of cloud cover, and remnants of the day's warmth were drifting up from the corral fence to a deep sky that sparked with stars. The air had grown gusty, rumbling and restless above the yard, and Wolf Shadow wondered if it was the same where the land rose in jerks and canters to the hills, or whether the wind up there would be sweeter and the clouds more scattered across the hidden moon.

Hiding was easy, but not the answer. Kester Kendall sheltered behind a strong veneer: storekeeper, pillar of the community, third generation Oasis-born. And from that position of power he had denounced Wolf as a miserable half-breed, and the young man had hidden from the shame of it.

Wolf kicked the fence post; it shifted in its socket but was too deeply grounded to tilt. He knew of the fence's permanence for he had buried the posts himself, but his toe winced from the kick and branded him a fool. Resting nose to flank, the horses in the corral jerked away from the noise, but Colt's little bay stood her ground and stared.

Wolf didn't need another horse's judgement. He'd driven back that afternoon with silent passengers, and the grey had been skittish, picking up their unease. It had tried to nip him as he pulled off the bridle, but the young man had no time for soothing words. He had slapped the dappled rump, sending the mare packing through the compound gate, and his son had filled Vixen's head with the words instead. He talked to the pony because his father would not listen and his mother could not hear.

They had returned from the Kendall confrontation to find Martha stirring something flavoursome at the stove. The house had been rich with the smell of it. Clove was sitting cross-legged on the floor with her back against the wall, weaving cradles from the string around her fingers. She took little notice of the cart's arrival, burdened by sacks of feed and the silent trio sitting at the front, but she had felt the strain from the dapple-grey as it dragged heaviness into the yard.

Her brother was staying outside, sharing his problems with the red pony. From the beginning of the day he had been weighed down by bother and nothing about that had changed, however some other discord had come home in the cart with him, as though it had stolen a ride from town. Clove caught the swamp-thick smell of it, masking whatever was inside her grandma's cooking pot. A storm cloud had gathered, and while it was hanging dark over her father's head, her mother's face had been awash.

Clove started to sway, backwards and forwards, her shoulders knocking at the wall. She struggled to her feet, hands over her ears, mouth open on a silent cry. Sage made to go towards the little girl but Wolf had stopped her. Although he did nothing to stop the child who was running from the room to the place where she shared nights with her grandma. Because that was where she would feel safe; where bad things could not touch her.

Martha had glanced up at the commotion, her spoon raised in mid stir. 'Well it's a big bee that has just flown into her bonnet,' she said, before she caught sight of the strain in Sage's eyes and Wolf's struggle not to show anything. They had both been holding something inside, and it was hurting because they held it too tightly.

She turned back to the stove, where the food was waiting to be served, but nobody seemed ready to eat. 'I have been teaching Clove to knit,' she said, her voice falsely bright. 'She is so supple with her hands, making those fairy cradles the way she does, that I knew she would pick it up real quick.'

Sage had started to spread cutlery on the tabletop. Martha was cheered to hear it drawing her daughter away from the tussle in her mind, if only for a time. But Wolf Shadow had been too quiet, and the old woman felt a fierce desire to beat words from him with her spoon.

Wolf was not even in the room; he had gone to check on his daughter. He listened for a while outside the bed space, but the child was attending to her own peace, and gave her father nothing to hear. Kendall's sacks needed to be stored in the barn before the light failed, and he heard that reminder instead.

He had slipped away from the house, and if Sage and her mother noticed him leaving they were too absorbed with their own thoughts to pay him any heed.

Wolf shouldered the first sack and the cart creaked. The noise was too loud in the empty yard. The door of the barn gaped and the space beyond had been full of the past. Weighed down by the feed he made his way to the threshold, and couldn't move any further.

The smell of the place was always the same. If he had experienced a cushioned childhood it might have nudged him with nostalgia, but it made him sick instead.

There were ghosts inside the walls: a frightened boy wrapped in darkness; a man standing in the doorway,

47

back-lit by a sour yellow haze like something dragged up from hell.

But there were other memories here as well, of the girl who had come to lie with him on beds of straw when the dark had taken sight and left them alone with touch. He thought of the way the morning light had painted youth and beauty across her face; the final kiss before they parted. The sweet moment when Colt had been conceived. The love.

He had never stopped loving her, all through the ten years they had cleaved together, remaking their lives in this haunted place. Building new from old and ensuring that Colt and Clove would become good citizens of the honest town of Oasis. And all that time Sage had trusted him, believed in him, and loved him back with a passion that had never dulled.

But as Wolf Shadow stood in the yard later that night, attacking the fence post and worrying the horses, he knew the balance had tilted and that he was to blame.

He sucked in air that was cold to his lungs. The scent of horse was pleasing, and just as familiar as the woman's perfume that had made an idiot of him on the sidewalk that afternoon. The woman who had fought for his life with a circuit judge. Who had even helped with the birthing of his children, goddam it; wiping blood from his son's face as if Colt had been her own newborn.

She was a friend. She was the wife of a friend. But Wolf had once seen a patch of desiccated grass set alight by the sun, and he knew that Lucy Ryker would burn if he touched her.

The night was vast above him; the wind blew chill and messed with his hair. Even in the dark he could visualise the distant hills.

Alone in the other compound the black stallion was

restless, because there was something unsettling about the man by the fence. The horse challenged him, kicking the ground. It tossed its head, scything the air, but the snap of mane was a sound from another time, the anger of another stallion, the one that had carried him almost to the end of it.

Wolf Shadow struggled up to the present, spat out some bile and swallowed the rest as he stumbled across to the corral, fumbling the latch with dead fingers. Night Dancer frisked to and fro, playing catch-me-if-you-can, but the young man had no patience left. He filled his hands with mane and leaped, his shout drowned by the stallion's scream, and the big hooves pounded wounds in the ground as the horse dashed from the yard.

Wolf turned his back on the town that lay in darkness, and all the good citizens who turned their own backs on those that didn't belong, and the drum of the gallop wrenched Colt from his sleep. Battered by a dream of thunder the boy woke stupefied. He searched the night from his window, but there was little to see for the black horse was barely visible. The wild rider, however, was of a denser darkness, as though something had made away with his soul.

The empty yard was clattering with the ghosts of all the other horses that had carried Wolf Shadow away at night, painting the backcloth of Colt's life. The sounds of adventure and excitement that had accompanied his childhood, the exodus from common sense and the blind ride to freedom. The expectation that there would come a time when Wolf might take his son along with him.

Up in the roof space, where the bed was corseted by rafters slanting from apex to floor, Sage lay listening to the hooves running free, the thud of the hard-packed earth and the jangle as the horse breached a rise of rock, then the thud again. She listened until the noises faded into the night, and all that was left was the mournful howl of the wind.

If he couldn't sleep Wolf Shadow went riding. If a worry was biting the back of his mind, that was when the darkness called him. In the very early times, when he was still the wolf cub and before the baby in her womb had grown too large, he had taken Sage behind him on the back of a stallion, lulled by his smell, her cheek pressed to his heartbeat. They rode until the night was on the wane, seeking a place to lie with each other, their bodies making music for the rising sun.

Once the power of their love had been pure, but now it was like milk left too long in the jug. Soured by the doctor's wife with her beautiful hair, her fine dresses, her gracefulness; and her two-faced friendship.

The bed was too big without Wolf Shadow beside her. Sage stroked the dip in the mattress where he had been lying before leaving her for the stallion. The sheet was cold, as if the empty bed was the premonition of a future still waiting to happen.

There was to be no more sleep for her that night.

SEVEN

RECENT RAIN had raised the level of the pond. The breeze wrinkled the surface, and from her reflection it seemed as though Clove was dancing through little waves as she stood watching her brother saddle Vixen over by the barn.

It was morning, a school day, and Colt was angry; tightening the cinch so fiercely that Clove could almost taste the red pony's distress. Not having felt Sage's scissors since the summer's end, the boy's hair was grazing his collar, and the back of his head was all that the child could see. But she didn't need sight of his eyes to know what he was thinking. And she wanted to help. She could set at rest his turmoil of thoughts if only her tongue would find the right words.

Harnessed at last Colt mounted the little mare, but his shoulders were sinking as they turned towards the town. Clove stayed by the pond, kicking an easy foot through the water until the click of hooves had faded.

She liked the way the drops scooted up at her and the rainbows they painted as they fell. The colours made her think of the knitting that was waiting for her on the cowhide trunk by the stove. Her grandma had shown her how to hold the needles, how to turn the wool into a new stitch, and Clove wanted to see that stitch growing into a row, and the row ending and starting a new row to weave into something amazing.

The little girl left the rainbows drying to nothing on the ground and hop-skipped back indoors, and if she registered the depth of silence inside the house it didn't show on her face.

Her father had already ridden from the homestead. He had clapped a bridle on the dapple-grey mare early that morning, departing long before reluctant Colt had reached for Vixen's saddle. It was her mother who stayed behind, clothed in the silence; the empty sleepless hours having robbed her of the ability to speak.

Wolf's return from his hard night's ride had been heralded by the black stallion's cough beneath Sage's window, but he had not bothered to share the remains of the darkness with her. She'd heard him reach the foot of the steps that led up to their bed space, but then there had been a second of hesitation, and that second was all it took for him to turn away. She had wondered whether to slip from the covers and seek him out, but if he had no intention of coming to her then there was no reason for her to pay him any heed.

They had spent what was left of the night within mere feet of each other but parted by miles.

Sage was wearing the silence like a hair-shirt, and her mother knew from the prickles that all was not well. Martha stood in softer air beyond the porch door and gazed towards the far hills; just as she had gazed as a bride when the man she had married turned coarse and callous. When the wonderful new life she had expected became that view of velvet grass, trees like fur on a dog's back, the gentleness of distance.

The old woman was fatigued. Her granddaughter had been restless most of the night and Martha was a light sleeper, even though she had not heard Wolf leave the house in the darkest hours, or the clatter of the stallion as it cantered from the steading. It was the wind-moan in the chimney that had kept her from sleep; the sound that she would always associate with unhappiness.

It was unhappiness that had been keeping Sage awake as well. Martha knew about it, as though she had peered through wooden boards into the eyrie that the wild boy had fashioned. The wolf cub had laid a new floor and raised a ladder in the days when the daughter had been content and the mother had discovered that it was possible to look ahead. But now the seasons were turning and the way ahead was muddy. Martha recognised that something was very wrong, and that maybe there was more of the wrong to come.

Wolf Shadow recognised it also; he had known it since the night of the storm when Colt had been late home bearing trouble on his shoulders.

He could see the Oasis road from where he and the dapple-grey were waiting. The mare had been spoiled by an adherence to feeding times, and she was letting him know of her hunger. Wolf spoke the words that would tame a wild stallion to bear a rider, but the grey wanted more, and got it with a jerk on the bit.

Stretched thin by insomnia, the man had no patience left for a horse's ill temper. He needed everything to be still so that his son, on his way to school, should not know that he was watching from behind the cover of trees near the track. And because everything was still, Colt did not notice his father as he trotted past on Vixen with his eyes to the horizon and his thoughts contained, following the dip in the road at the place where the Wellersons dwelled.

Hiding near the house, young Jonah Wellerson was also unaware. He did not realise that Wolf Shadow was above him when he urged his chestnut pony after the little bay, chasing the clatter of Vixen's hooves. And when Wolf urged his horse forward the boy had no idea that he, too, was being stalked.

Jonah kicked the pony to a canter and drew level with Vixen, the chestnut clashing with the little mare's rump so violently that she skittered sideways. Colt lost his stirrups and clung to the saddle horn. The Wellerson boy pushed him to the ground and he landed awkwardly, rolling away from the stamp of hooves as Jonah came at him again.

Wolf drove the mare between them, shaking the chestnut's rider from its back. His muscles tightened as the anger took control. It was a dangerous moment that would have brought consequences, if he had not waited for a count of seconds before dismounting the dapple-grey; sidestepping the Wellerson boy who was sprawling in the dirt, cradling his arm and whimpering.

Colt was on his feet now, and all he could see were his father's eyes – black under the brim of his hat as he stood over Jonah Wellerson.

The man came from nowhere like a charging bull, and Wolf was tossed sideways. He skidded across the road and the man skidded with him, clamped to his body. Squeezing the younger man's arms until they were numb; setting him free with a thrust to his back. They fell apart, straddling the track, but Wolf was the first on his feet, facing his attacker in a puma's crouch.

Moses Wellerson's colourless face was distorted by loathing. He swayed as he stood beside the boy blubbing on the ground. He snapped a look at him; snapped it back at Wolf. 'Get up, Jonah,' he said, his eyes never leaving the other man.

The boy didn't move, lying heavy as though he had

been felled. 'He broke my arm, Pa,' he whined, through twin streams of snot. 'It hurts real bad.'

Wellerson reached down and dragged him up by his good arm. Father and son, they stood side by side with the same look about them, the same meanness as they glared at the pale-haired man.

'I saw what you did, you filthy half-breed.' Wellerson raised his hand and aimed a finger, stepping close enough to stab. 'I saw you attack my son.'

Wolf stood firm, jerking slightly with each jab, and there were shutters over his eyes. He didn't speak; he didn't react to the finger that was leaving bruises on his skin.

'The sheriff's gonna lock you up for the longest time.' There was a sheen of spittle across the man's face, and he wiped it off with the back of his hand. 'Yessir, Andy Parnell is gonna put you in his cage.'

Wolf raised his head until the light reached him. 'Your boy and Kester Kendall's boy have been troubling my boy,' he said. His voice was calm, but there was a crack in it. 'And I have already dealt with Korky.'

Wellerson grabbed his son, shaking him until he rattled. 'Is that true, Jonah? I'll strip your hide if you say it is, but if you say not, I'll strip the Indian's hide instead.'

Hanging from his father's grip, the boy choked on the words. 'It's not true, Pa. I ain't done nothing. I swear.'

Wellerson pushed him away. Jonah recovered quickly, hiding behind his father's back to watch the men standing eye to eye, bloodshot to steady and dark. Too steady; too dark. Wolf seemed to have grown in height, his body was so taut.

'Your boy's nothing but a liar, half-breed.' There was farmyard stink in the man's breath. 'And so are you.'

The probing finger was back. Wolf made no move to

avoid it, but the muscles in his arms were rigid. It took a while for him to realise that Colt was standing beside him. He could feel his feverish warmth. He glanced down, and his son stared up with a look of such fear in his eyes that the pain of it was a stab in the chest, far deeper than the irritation of Wellerson's pathetic assault.

He asked Colt if he was all right. He asked in thought, not with his voice, and the boy nodded as though he had heard what was in his father's mind. But the fear was still there.

Wolf didn't see Wellerson drawing back his fist. He was unprepared for the blow that knocked him flying. He blacked out, but only for a moment, and then the sky floated above him with the sound of thunder, with voices yelling, and thudding on the ground under his ear which was from scuffle, not from storm. He could see two men fighting by the side of the road. They swam away from his sight and he shook his head to bring them close again.

Moses Wellerson stood surrounded by trail dust and Emmett Hockaday stood before him, his arms raised to pacify. His back was turned to Wolf, as though he was shielding the young man. 'What the hell do you think you're doing?' he was saying, preventing Wellerson's movements with his bulk and his greater height. 'Moses, this has to stop.'

Wolf Shadow got to his feet, stretching until the aches subsided. He went across to where his hat was lying in a nest of scrub. He took his time banging away the seed husks and fitting it with the brim over his eyes, and then he sniffed the air. He could smell the rain that was bringing chill from the north. It reminded him to sort out the horse rugs when he got back to the Madison place so that the animals should be protected.

The two boys were standing together, watching the

men brawling in the dirt. Wolf stepped towards them and Colt jerked away as though snapped by a rope.

'Leave Jonah be!'

Wolf barely heard Wellerson shouting, because everything inside him had frozen. He was conscious only of the men breaking apart, kicking stones aside as they came near.

'Keep away from my son, half-breed!'

Wellerson was close enough now for Wolf to feel the spit on his face. He was aware of Emmett Hockaday beside him, but nothing else registered. Nothing but the terror he had seen in Colt's eyes.

And then the scene changed. Only Emmett remained. Wellerson was heading home, throwing threats back over his shoulder. Jonah followed his father, one hand to his pony's neck and the other clasped at his waist like a broken wing.

There was a lingering wisp of vitriol after they had gone and a buzzing sound in Wolf's ears. Emmett had asked him a question. He knew he was expected to answer; he opened his mouth but couldn't find anything to say. Emmett asked again, and his voice had risen. The man's eyes pierced like a blade in a sudden shaft of sunlight.

Wolf stumbled along the track to where the grey was searching scrub for fodder. He urged the horse into a canter before he had settled in the saddle, leaving Emmett Hockaday standing by the roadside, staring at the ground.

He realised that he should have thanked the man for something, but it would have to wait. All that mattered was that his son had already disappeared. He had ridden away so fast there was nothing left to hear of the red pony's hoofbeats.

EIGHT

THERE WAS a big stallion in the corral; dark grey, nose slashed by a patch of white hair and eyes red with rage. Wolf Shadow watched it from the yard.

The animal screamed through jagged teeth. It loped to the far side of the pen and kicked the fence when it could go no further. A malicious attack, but the posts were strong and the boards reinforced. They needed to be for they were often assaulted by the horses that passed through the young man's hands; passed through his voice with their ears awake to the language he spoke.

Ranchers, farmers, wealthy men and trappers, they all brought their wild and wicked stallions to the Madison smallholding. From far and wide they had heard stories of the curious man with magic in his voice, and such flair with the feral that he could train the most fearful of beasts to nuzzle food from his palm.

Unlikely tales were told of the time when, little older than a boy, he had tamed a stallion to bear a rider without the aid of ropes, whips or restricting harness; using in fact nothing more potent than the sounds from his throat. After a decade it had become just as preposterous as a folk myth and those who scoffed would watch Wolf Shadow from behind the fence, ridicule at the ready, only to be trapped by the words that were trapping the wild horses they had brought to be tamed.

The big grey in the enclosure was more than wild, it was savage. Those sharp teeth had already left their mark on the owner's skin, and now it had a taste for blood. Wolf moved through the gate and fastened it behind him. He began to walk; only a few steps before the horse came to life, spinning on its back legs and clouting the beleaguered fence until the wood rang hollow. The boards remained upright and the stallion screamed in fury. It charged the young man who was standing unprotected; it reared over him, hooves ripping the sky. And Wolf Shadow began to speak.

The stallion dropped to the ground, trying to shake away the words that were coming and coming; trying to chase them out of its skull. But it was already ensnared by the voice that swooped across the corral like a bird's flight, higher and lower, and closer and closer, until Wolf was there by the horse's muzzle, lifting his hand to the white diamond that blazed between its eyes. The grey tossed away, then came forward again with teeth snapping. But they snapped at air, not the fingers that stretched towards them; as though an impenetrable barrier had risen around the young man's body.

Wolf Shadow stood still. Words vibrated through the air as time passed, and when enough time had passed the stallion bowed its head and came nearer, big hooves pounding close to the young man's feet. Hooves that could cripple; but Wolf did not move.

He felt the ground shaking as the stallion stamped and snorted, wetting his face with its breath; and after a while his voice was the only sound that remained.

The buggy rolled into the yard, and Sage waited for it to creak to a stop before she went over to greet the driver. She smiled at the tall man, for he was a friend. She smiled more freely than usual because this time he had come without his wife.

'Good day to you, Sage,' Dr Ryker said, slipping off his hat.

'Good day to you also, Daniel.'

She touched his arm with affection. Once he had helped to save a boy's life, and for that she would always be grateful. Ryker squeezed her hand where it rested on his sleeve, but it was done distractedly for his attention was elsewhere. He was looking around the yard, through the porch and into the house.

There was something not quite right about him, she thought.

'Is Wolf Shadow at home?' he said, and his voice didn't sound right either.

'He works in the enclosure today. Just follow the scent of horse,' Sage said, watching the neat suited man as he crossed the yard, and followed the scent of horse.

Ryker slowed as he approached the compound. There was something mystical about what was taking place between the young man and the big grey stallion. It was almost a union of two tempestuous minds, and the dark-haired doctor felt like an intruder.

Wolf was unaware of the onlooker by the fence. He appeared to be unaware of everything but the horse that stood before him with its head lowered, ears alert now, flickering towards his voice as if hungry for the sound. And it kept on going, the rise and fall of words, the breathing of the horse; the occasional interruption of birdsong and the little wind that was dancing through the late summer grass.

The doctor was soothed, as though the magic had filled up his empty spaces and was making him complete. But that was an illusion, because it would be a long time before he felt whole again.

Wolf had noticed him now, waiting mournful-faced by the fence. He smoothed back the grey's mane with a palm, and the horse stepped away from him as though it had been dismissed. The young man watched it for a while, and then he walked towards the gate, barely lifting his feet from the ground.

Daniel Ryker had seen it before, this crushing fatigue that followed fierce concentration – for it required a deal of strength to hold a wild horse steady with words alone. There had been times when Wolf used himself so hard that he simply collapsed, and the doctor's care had been summoned.

But not this time. This time he came through the gate upright, although Ryker wondered if it was perhaps an unnatural rigidity, manufactured for his benefit.

'Wolf Shadow,' he said. 'I think you are hurting.'

There was a flash in the brown eyes, a glimpse of the gold that was lying deep inside. 'Just tired.'

'No, man; you are exhausted.'

Wolf nodded. 'You may be right, Daniel, but I shall recover. I always do.'

They stood together watching as the grey sucked deep and steady from the trough. The whisperer and the horse were like two wild creatures, resting after the fight.

The words struck Ryker as having some relevance.

'You need to know about Moses Wellerson,' he said, his eyes on the stallion and his ears attuned to the young man beside him. Wolf stiffened slightly when he heard the name, and the doctor shot him a glance. 'He was in Sheriff Parnell's office, claiming that you assaulted Jonah and broke his arm. The fellow has a loud voice when he opens his mouth.'

'Then perhaps it would be better for everyone if he

stopped opening his mouth.'

The doctor made a noise in his throat that could have been agreement, or warning.

'He brought his son to see me,' he said, 'with a bruised shoulder.'

There was a pause.

'But not a broken arm.'

'Not a broken arm. Although it was difficult to tell at first, for the wailing of the boy. He has inherited his father's loud voice.'

Wolf studied the ground. 'The sheriff should know that Emmett Hockaday was a witness.'

'No witness will be needed, rest assured. Parnell may be swift with his mouth at times, much like brother Wellerson, but he is no fool. He has heard too many empty accusations from Moses before, and this time it appears he sent him on his way with a pat on the back.'

Wolf was quiet for a while, staring ahead but seeing nothing. Then he turned to his friend, and Ryker was struck by the unhappiness in the young man's face. 'Colt has not spoken to me since that morning,' Wolf said. 'Not once.'

'Colt is very young.' Ryker thought quickly, hunting for words. 'Perhaps too young to know what to say.'

'No.' Wolf shook his head. Some of the pale hair fell across his eyes, and he left it lying there as though it was a wall behind which he could vanish. 'His life is twice troubled now, and it is because I tried to help him. I could not forgive either, when I shared his age.'

'When you were Colt's age you already carried the burden of a grown man three times as old,' Ryker said. 'Your son is still a child, Wolf Shadow. Something I don't believe you were ever allowed to be.'

Although Wolf could still recall how it felt to be borne

on the shoulders of a black-haired man, through thickly growing trees, across grassland enriched with spring flowers. A time from long ago, more fantasy now than memory.

'I am sorry that you have these worries, Wolf, and I regret having to add to them.' Daniel Ryker paused. 'I think you already know what I am saying.'

'You are saying that the hour has come to face your discoverer.'

'It has.' Ryker thought of the communications he had been receiving, almost every other day now. So far they were addressed to him alone, but he knew, for he had read the threat on the single sheet of paper, folded twice and sealed down, that soon they would be addressed to Lucy as well. And he had to do something to stop that happening.

'Are you still willing to help me?' he said.

Wolf shrugged, turning swiftly to look across to the house that was resting peacefully beyond the yard. 'Away from here is somewhere I need to be,' he said. 'Just tell me when you want to leave, and how long until our return.'

Ryker followed his eyes to the house. It was looking friendly now in the afternoon light, but he remembered when the place had been sucked down by wretchedness. In the days when Wolf Shadow had been a boy with no proper life, but burning inside with a spirit that no amount of bullying had ever managed to extinguish.

The older man thought of the task that lay ahead of him, and envied Wolf that spirit.

'I need us to leave as soon as possible,' he said, 'and it will take as long as it takes.'

Wolf nodded as if he was pleased with the answer. 'I will let Sage know that I shall be away for as long as it takes, and I will ask Emmett Hockaday to keep charge of my land, and Joanie to look out for my family.'

He smiled. It lifted his face, but didn't quite reach his eyes.

I have good neighbours, Daniel,' he said. 'As well as good witnesses.'

NINE

THEY HAD been dressed for the season when they left Oasis, daybreak being as cool as an autumn dawn can get. But now the sun was rising steadily, bringing its heat with it, and their backs were sticky with sweat.

Ryker slipped off his jacket and strapped it behind the chestnut's saddle. The sudden chill was delicious on his skin. He stretched until his body creaked, and sporadic puffs of wind lifted hair from his forehead.

So far on the expedition they had climbed as high as they needed, and it was a beautiful place to be. The hill slopes swooped away behind them, curve rolling into curve, gathering trees and falling into thickets of scrub and hardy bushes. There was late green everywhere, and the russet and gold of weeks to come had already begun to spread across the ground.

The sky was cleared to a shimmering blue, as though some giant hand had pushed the clouds to the other side of the world, and the doctor's heart billowed.

It was a feeling to relish for a man so worn down with worry that he believed his core to have shrivelled like a dried nut.

'This is spectacular,' he said, and the breeze carried his words to a stony elevation some feet distant, where the young man was standing.

Wolf gave no indication that he had heard. He was

not looking into the same panorama that had made the doctor's soul sing, but staring out instead to where the hills were sharper and closer together, and the few trees that grew there were hanging by tenacious roots from the sides of ravines.

Dr Ryker turned to follow the other man's gaze, although serenity still lay behind him and he welcomed its pull. It was helping him to face their destination, but even so he had to take a deep breath to calm the anxiety that had begun to jump in his belly.

'What can you see, Wolf?'

The young man lifted his head. 'I see a long day's journey in front of us,' he said. 'And rough terrain for the horses.'

This was inevitable, and Ryker nodded. 'Although it appears to me that we have already travelled a goodly way,' he suggested.

'We are doing well. And we will continue to do well.'

The doctor laughed. 'There are many reasons why I asked you to accompany me on this quest, my friend, one of them being your ability to shorten a lengthy ramble with a few well-chosen words.'

Another of them, he thought, was to keep you out of range of my wife.

It was a loud thought, and it shocked through his head until his scalp felt squeezed. Wolf knew nothing of it; he was looking out towards the folds of land again, but his shoulders had lifted slightly as though he had heard, and Dr Ryker felt chastened.

Lucy had arisen from their warm bed to watch him leave that morning, bringing with her a lamp to clear the rooms of darkness. Her glossy hair was hanging over her shoulder and it glinted with light and movement when she breathed.

She kissed him at the doorway, a pucker of the mouth from a long-married wife. He kissed her back, touching her lips with the tip of his tongue. Although it was slight, he didn't imagine her recoil. It made him feel less guilty about the lies – the fabrication of a medical convention in the town of Malachy Rise, at which he claimed to have been asked to speak.

'Too far to travel in a day,' he had told her. 'It will mean a couple of nights in a hotel, but I shall be home again before you know it.'

'Remember to bring back some gifts for the girls.' That was all his wife had said. Perhaps she was just as relieved as he at the prospect of a short separation.

The children, however, were another matter.

'Bring me a little dolly, Papa,' Dulcie had demanded, her cheeks pink with excitement. 'I want a little dolly from Malky Rise. And Bella will want a toy farm, with animals and hay.'

'Is that really what you want, honey?'

He had been perching on the edge of the twins' bed, close enough to his daughters to smell their clean hair and the lingering scent of babyhood on their skin.

Bella had sat up as straight as she could, slapping the coverlet with her hands. 'Not a toy farm, Papa.'

Her eyes were a dusky green, and they had been shining like circles of moss. 'I don't want a toy,' she said. 'I want the real thing.'

My God, so do I, Ryker thought now, watching as the young man jumped down from the ridge and climbed into the stallion's saddle. Standing tall in the stirrups, calculating the distance of the route ahead, stretching until the muscles in his back were tight.

The doctor observed the width of Wolf's shoulders and the leanness of his hips, and then he looked down at himself. He was forty-seven years old, greying and going soft. But once he too had been a young man; dark-haired, straight and strong, and Lucy had been proud to hold his arm when they strode along the main street.

Those had been the days of the real thing, but now it was difficult to remember the last time he and his wife had done anything real together.

With a creak as his knee protested, he settled back into the saddle and followed Night Dancer towards the long day's journey. The black horse strutted between an outcrop of rocks that bowed as Wolf Shadow passed beneath, as though he was a prince of some kind – fair-haired and vibrant, and as wild as his steed; but when Ryker took his turn the rocks were menacing instead.

He heard the clatter of a loose stone falling close to the chestnut's rump. It sounded like a warning.

Towards the end of the afternoon they had reached the last peak, and finally the country was sweeping away from them in gentler folds, almost like a reward for hard work. And it had been hard work crossing the cuts and creases of Wolf's rough terrain. An underworld sharp with hills and steep with gullies that had made a nonsense of the doctor's spectacular landscape.

Thirsty and saddle sore, with trail grit between his teeth, Ryker felt twisted; he had been on a fairground ride for so long that his body might never be straight again.

His merciless mind took him back to his comfortable home: the padded armchair, the savoury aroma of supper cooking, a rich red glass of wine in his hand and the children playing at his feet.

Lucy sitting opposite, body tense, lip caught between sharp white teeth, fingers tapping the cover of a book she was pretending to read, as had become her wont on most evenings now.

The doctor shook his head. He knew he was getting old, and that he had become too accustomed to a soft life which made him more privileged than some. Unfortunately, none of that had prepared him for the prospect of sleeping under the stars.

He studied his companion, seated on the black stallion just ahead.

Wolf Shadow had brought them here. A half-Indian scout, he had directed them towards the easier passages between cliffs and caverns, and all the comforts that they had encountered were down to him. Just like the doctor he was grey with dust, but it transformed him into a statue instead of a tired old man.

'For pity's sake,' Ryker called out. 'Please may we stop sometime soon? Before I become one with my saddle?'

Wolf glanced back swiftly, as though he'd forgotten that he was not riding alone. He pointed ahead, but his companion found it difficult to see much beyond the waves of land.

'We shall set up camp when we reach the flat ground,' the young man said, kicking the stallion away once again, and Ryker followed, every movement of his horse's legs echoing at the base of his spine.

The discomfort was as jagged as glass, and it continued even after they had finally come to rest; a dull throb which had been set up to remind him that his saddle would only be empty until the morning. He moved stiffly to unharness the chestnut, and everything seemed to weigh twice as much, and maybe it had something to do with the miles of empty land that surrounded them, and the boundless overhang of sky.

Wolf had already laid a brushwood fire, and the flames were jumping up the sides of a cooking pan as though they wanted to feast on the canned stew that it contained. It didn't take long for the mess to bubble, and he stirred it with a bent-handled spoon.

For some reason, the scrape of metal on metal set Ryker's stomach rumbling, and he realised with a start that he had not eaten since breaking his fast with toasted bread that morning.

'This might be nothing but a potful of tasteless mush,' he said as he settled himself, carefully, on the ground, 'but I believe I shall make short work of it.'

'Maybe I shall catch a rabbit tomorrow.' Wolf glanced up; the jumping flames caught his eyes and gave him a devilish look. 'There was no time today for the hunt.'

The other man nodded and looked at the ground, his face hidden by the angle of his head. 'I fear there will be no time for anything until this undertaking has been completed,' he said.

Wolf stirred the pan, flames following the spoon as though they had a taste for that as well.

'There is still much I do not know,' he said. 'And a lot I need to learn before we are to meet the man whose words you wish to stop.'

The doctor jerked, and looked up. Wolf's face was stroked in turn by darkness and wavering firelight, but his eyes were fixed on Ryker, and they weren't about to let him go. And when he spoke it was with the quiet power that he might use on a horse with a mind of its own.

'I have come on this quest with you because I am your friend, Daniel. But I have come under a blindfold and now I need to see.'

'Then I will tell you,' Ryker said, and nodded, as if he was eager to talk. But he drew back a little from the grip of Wolf's scrutiny.

'It began one day, a while ago, when an Indian woman

came to my door. I asked her if she was ill, if she wanted to come in, but she wouldn't move from the path. It was as if she was afraid of entering my house, or any house for that matter. She was certainly afraid of something. She had huge eyes.'

He stopped for a moment, recalling the day that the woman had stood before him. She had been wearing a heavy skirt and a shawl that crossed her chest, the ends fastened loosely behind her back. She wore the colours of the earth; he remembered that now – green and chestnut, and red as dark as dried blood.

He imagined that it must have taken courage to come to his door, because it was clear that she had no desire to be there.

'She told me she required my assistance, but not for herself,' Ryker said. 'She required it for another. She asked me to go with her to see this person.'

He hesitated. 'No. She didn't just ask, she beseeched me.'

Aged somewhere in her thirties, the woman had been worn down by years and seemed older, although her hair was still rich and glossy. She had a hungry look, her head too big for her gaunt frame, and her eyes, her huge eyes, had been unsettling.

She had turned up at the doctor's house in the middle of the day and there was no one else to answer her knock, for Esme the maid had yet to be employed, and Lucy had taken the children to play with friends who lived at the edge of the town. It was just Ryker's good luck that she hadn't taken the buggy as well. That it was still in the yard waiting to be yoked to the mare. Waiting for the two passengers and the excursion they were about to make.

'Now tell me your name,' Ryker had demanded as the woman climbed to the bench seat, but she had said as much as she was going to at his front door, and now that they were on their way she had become as silent as a ghost. She only moved to lift the shawl over her head, but it was an unnecessary disguise for she had drawn too far inside its hood for anyone to catch sight of her face.

She appeared to be praying, but if that was so it must have been a prayer for anonymity. And it seemed to have worked, because nobody gave the earth-coloured clothes a glance. He might have been taking the buggy for the pleasure of a trip in the countryside, except that he was driving at speed; invigorated by the aura of desperation that was emanating from his visitor.

When the town disappeared behind them she allowed the shawl to slip to her shoulders, and it was then that her strong profile revealed the fortitude that Ryker had suspected. The only movement she made was to point in the direction she wished him to take. He obeyed her guidance blindly, perhaps stupidly, but it was compelling, the sense of urgency that radiated from the woman's rigid body.

He swung the buggy around the rugged land that followed the line of distant hills, and the further they travelled from Oasis the more hostile the ground became as it lurched towards Indian territory. And the doctor began to wonder if he'd make a mistake.

As if startled into alertness by his apprehension, the woman turned to him. She didn't speak, but her silence was reassuring. He sensed that she was not a threat; she had not travelled those miles to Oasis just to lead him into danger. And it was incredible, the distance she had walked from her settlement in order to find help.

It may have been a lively place once, but when Ryker's horse stumbled upon it the Indian woman's village was pretty well deserted; just three tepees with an open fire, that had been started and then abandoned, lying between them. There was a meagre collection of cooking pots strewn close to the dead hearth, empty and dry as though no food had been prepared for some time.

The whole place was overshadowed by a sense of dilapidation, and initially the doctor thought that he was to be guided straight through and on to somewhere that made more sense. But the woman stopped the buggy, simply by cutting the air with her hand, and Ryker pulled the horse's head back so abruptly that the wheels skidded across the ground and left ruts.

The silence that followed was sudden and eerie, but it was eliminated by the sound of a cry as weak as a kitten's mew. It was coming from one of the tepees, the least shabby of the three, and it galvanised the woman as if she had been brought to life.

She jumped from the bench in one movement, landed like a cat and ran to the tent, lifting the hide flap at the opening before remembering the man in the buggy. She gestured with vehemence and disappeared inside. Ryker grabbed the medical bag stowed behind the seat and climbed down to follow.

The light inside the tepee was the colour of sepia, and the air churned with the smell of animal skins, stale food and human sweat. A collection of objects lay around, mostly baskets and boxes with contents neatly packed as though this was merely a temporary dwelling, soon to be abandoned.

And in the centre of the space was a shallow bed of furs and a young girl lying on her side with her knees drawn up to her chest. Her eyes were closed and she was making the kitten noise in the back of her throat.

The woman kneeled on the ground, stroking the girl's brow, crooning words that were intended to bring calm.

Words in an unknown language, but Ryker translated the meaning from the rise and fall of her voice: I am here now. I have brought him. All will be well.

She looked up at the doctor, her eyes fierce. 'You will help,' she told him.

It was not a question.

'Who are you?' he said. 'What is wrong with her?'

The woman took a while to answer; she seemed to be battling with just how much information she needed to impart, but the doctor wasn't having any of that. He had been through too much mystery already, and enough was enough.

'If you want my assistance,' he said, 'you must answer my questions.'

The woman pulled him down; it was done so swiftly that he fell to his knees before he could be surprised by it. She spread her hands in the air above the black leather bag, as though worshipping what it contained.

'You help her,' she said. 'Take baby away.'

'A baby?' Ryker looked around, but there was no sign of one in the half-empty tepee. 'Where is the baby?'

'You take her baby away,' she said.

She began to croon to the girl lying on furs, combing back the straggle of hair so that Ryker could see her face for the first time.

She wouldn't have been more than twelve years old, and she had the same huge dark eyes as the woman. He didn't need to ask to know that the girl was her daughter. He didn't need to ask any more questions at all.

'So, you've brought me all the way from Oasis to carry out an abortion,' he said. And felt the tug of hairs rising on the back of his neck.

TEN

THE NIGHT was as black as the underside of a blanket. Even the air felt heavy. Wolf lifted his arm to move it aside so that he could see the man sitting across from the dying fire. Quiet now, the doctor was a hump on the ground; flames had carved light into his face but the rest of him was in darkness.

'And that is what you did?'

Wolf felt around for something to put in the fire. The earth was hard and deathly cold, and all it would yield was a gnarled stick, the torn root of a bush that had perished under the summer sun. It would do. He slipped it to the heat and the flames licked, but sluggishly. Even the crackle of burning was off key.

'There was little else I could do,' Ryker's voice came from the hump. 'I had no choice.'

Wolf huffed, but it didn't sound much like laughter. 'You always have a choice. That is what Sage would tell you.' The dark shape across the fire jerked, and the night was agitated.

'She was a child, Wolf Shadow. She had been raped.' There was a harshness to the doctor's voice. 'So just tell me about the choice I should have made.'

'I cannot answer that for you, Daniel. I was not there.'

'No. You were not there.'

'Just you, the woman and her child. And the man.'

Ryker clambered to his feet too swiftly to care about the aches of the day. He skirted the fire and drew closer to Wolf, but the young man had not moved. He sat with his legs crossed and his spine straight and watched his friend; saw the threat in him that he might kick, because that was the time when he needed something to kick.

The doctor hesitated, like somebody poised on the edge of a cliff. And then he turned aside, exciting the weary flames so that they danced around each other for a while before taking hold of the piece of root.

'Yes. The man,' he said, his voice muffled, as though he was being whisked back to the past.

It was so dark beyond the fire that losing sight of the present was easy. Just as easy as it was to remember the deserted village, the musty tepee, the young girl and her mother; and the choice he'd had to make.

To remember the silence in that abandoned place, and how quietly he had asked, 'Where are your people?'

'My people too afraid to stay.' The Indian woman had raised her head, and her fierce eyes, to answer him.

'And they left you here on your own?'

How could anyone do that? It had felt inhuman then, and it still did.

'They come back.' She had been staring up at him, sharply enough to hurt, and then her face had softened when she saw his concern. 'When wrong is put right, they come back.'

The woman had stiffened when Ryker got to his feet, as though she was afraid that he might leave. He had certainly been considering it. The day had been lengthy and problematic, the journey from Oasis exhausting and his patience was thin and ready to snap. He had no desire for the dilemma she was offering him.

'No more riddles.' He'd almost shouted the words. 'If

you want my help then just tell me the reason why, or I will not stay another minute.'

She had waved her hand as though to draw him closer, dispelling the distance between them, tightening the leash so that he would have no option but to stay. He sensed her power, but by then he felt angry enough to break the pull. The woman had turned swiftly to face him. To do battle, maybe.

Her daughter cried out at the sudden movement, and Ryker was grabbed by the child's helplessness. She had been curled up on her side like an infant, and for a moment he had seen Bella lying there on the meagre fur bed; just as weak and just as vulnerable.

The woman moved towards him. He tried to back away but the leash she had fashioned was wrapped around his heart, and she stood there, holding him with her eyes. Her slightness had bothered him; she looked as feeble as a sapling, too easy to snap.

No. There had been more to her than that – muscle and sinew and determination. She was a fighter, staking him steady, filling him with her story.

'White men came with guns. Took what they wanted, destroyed what was left. They killed…'

There she had faltered, but only for a second.

'They killed old men who could not run, young men like fools who tried to fight them. All dead.'

Ryker gripped her arms when she stumbled, to keep her from falling. Her whole body had shuddered at his touch.

'Big man seized me. Daughter took knife to him. He seized her instead.' The woman had stared over the doctor's shoulder, seeing only the invaders, and the evil they had brought to her village.

'Daughter screamed for me but I could not help her.

Other men – stopping me move. When big man finished, he held knife to her heart.'

Those words must have been difficult to speak, for she could only whisper the rest. 'Better that he killed her.'

Ryker had waited for more, but she'd said what she had to say. Nothing else was needed to paint the picture of the big man, the small girl, the atrocity.

'What happened after that?'

'Men went away. We buried our dead.' She paused there for a moment. 'We lived.'

'But these men have broken the law.' The doctor had been outraged. 'They should be punished for what they have done.'

His declaration had struck her as amusing. 'White men; white man's law. Who would punish?'

And that was when Ryker looked at her. Really looked at her for the first time.

'Where did you learn English?'

The woman jerked, as if the question had opened something inside her. When she answered her voice had been higher, younger. 'My man was scout for soldiers. Was good teacher.'

The doctor had been pleased to hear that. 'Your man would tell you that the law is for everyone,' he said, peering around the tepee for the good teacher. 'So where is he now? Why can't he help you?'

'Is dead.' She spoke with strength, with anger. 'He was young man. He was fool. We buried him too.'

'I'm sorry.' Ryker was a fool as well, it seemed.

'Be sorry for daughter.' It had been more a demand than a request. 'Take away baby, take away shame, and my people come back for us. If do nothing, they cast us out. If cast out – we die.'

The final two words had clinched it for him.

There had been just the three of them in the Indian village, hidden behind rocks and the land where nobody lived. Dr Ryker had taken off his coat, and with it his knowledge of what was right, because he could find nothing right about the situation. He had opened his leather bag for the instruments he would need, he had performed basic sterilisation with flame and alcohol, and the woman had cradled her young daughter's body as he worked.

The operation was completed as evening arrived. Ryker's face had been wet, the sweat stinging like tears. He'd rubbed his sight clear with a sleeve so that he could watch them, mother and daughter, gazing at each other with their hearts in their eyes. It was an image that had stayed with him since that memorable day, and it still made him feel that he had done something honourable.

When he went out to the buggy the shadows were long and flat to the ground, pointing his way home. The air cooled quickly as the sun came down. The woman had brought his coat out from the tepee, but even as he slipped it on he wondered how long it would be before he was properly warm again.

Her face had seemed younger in the evening light, as though portraying the person she had been before the destruction of her home and the massacre of people she loved. In a moment of camaraderie Ryker had given her his name, advising her to seek him out if her daughter was in further need. He regretted the words as soon as they left his mouth, but it had been easy back then to dismiss the likelihood of ever meeting them again.

He remembered floating with relief when he left the damaged village behind for the journey home. Because what was started had been finished, and what had needed to be done was done.

…And Wolf Shadow must have allowed the fire to go out because the night was dark again, despite the gash where clouds were parting over a freckling of stars. They looked like points of ice, and Ryker shivered. 'Can't you get that fire to roar?' he said.

'It roars already, Daniel.' Wolf's voice was distant. 'But you are too far away to feel it.'

The doctor turned around. He was out on the edge of the open space where they had stopped to camp; the shapes of rocks surrounded him and the trees were so close he could hear wind rustle in the branches. The fire was beyond; it took his sight, sparks of light shooting towards the broken clouds. Wolf sat beside it like a red-gold effigy, twisting the knife between his fingers.

Ryker shivered again and came out of the wind, stumbling on chilled legs. 'I must have wandered,' he said. 'And I wasn't aware.'

He offered his hands to the fire until they were wrapped in its heat, but the cold night was still there behind him.

'You were telling me what had happened with the woman and the child.' Wolf poured coffee into a tin mug and held it out. 'And you did not need to be stopped.'

Ryker took the mug and settled on the ground, not too far from the blaze. His body reached out for the warmth. 'Now you know it all.'

'Not all. We are only here because there was a man.'

The doctor was nudged by disquiet. 'Yes, there was a man. I had no idea he was there. God knows where he was hiding.' He swallowed a mouthful of coffee, seeking some comfort in its heat. 'He saw everything.'

'What was he doing there?'

'Christ almighty.' He slammed the mug on the ground and hot coffee slopped over his hand. 'I don't know,

Wolf Shadow. I don't know how he got there. I don't know anything about him.'

But that didn't stop him imagining what it would feel like to have the man's neck between his hands.

'I have been sent messages,' he said. 'The first wire only told me that someone was at the Indian village that day, and that person must have seen me perform the… operation. I chose to ignore it, and when there was nothing further it began to slip from my mind. Until the second wire arrived with a stronger message.'

He shook his head, picked up the mug and threw the rest of the coffee into his mouth. He needed its strength. 'And now the sender is threatening to rip my life apart.'

'What does he want?'

'Money, of course. He wants money. And the amount he wants grows higher with each message.'

The young man dipped his head; firelight blazed in his hair, painting it gold. 'Why have you waited so long for my help, Daniel?'

'Why do you think, Wolf Shadow? It is because I am guilty. And I am ashamed.'

The doctor stared at him, belittled once again by his youth and the life burning through his veins. Lucy hovered in his mind; she was holding out her hands, but not for him. Never for him, her husband.

'I broke the law, because I felt I had no other choice. And I have no wish to go to prison for something I had to do.'

Wolf looked up again. 'That is all I need to hear,' he said. 'You will not go to prison, Daniel. And tomorrow we shall make sure of it.'

ELEVEN

DOCTOR RYKER struggled to stand the next morning. The ground had been an uncomfortable bed, the saddle an unforgiving pillow, and the depth of night had chilled him to the bone. He felt ill and old, and envious of his companion, for Wolf had slept through the hours. His breathing had been easy at first, and then it changed to ragged and Ryker knew that there were dreams webbing the young man's mind – and perhaps those dreams had not been so easy.

But Wolf treated the new day like an old friend, and had even found a slick of water in a rock hollow to dash sleep from his face. He was already brewing something up in the pot over the fire by the time the doctor came scowling through the morning mist.

'I cannot even contemplate another night of torture like that one.'

He spat the words, massaging the small of his back where the aggravation was most insistent.

'If we find today what we have come here to find, then perhaps you won't need to.' Wolf spooned food into a dish and offered it. The doctor scowled at that instead, receiving it as though it was his last meal.

'What is this? Or is it indescribable?'

'It is the lining of a bull's bladder, with pig eye juice to help with the taste.'

Wolf stirred what was left in the pot and started to eat, but Ryker could only stare, dry-retching each time the young man swallowed.

'Daniel, it is cornmeal mixed with last night's gravy.' Wolf looked up and smiled.

'Well, I didn't know you had a sense of humour, Wolf Shadow.'

'There is still a lot you don't know about me, Daniel Ryker.' He wasn't smiling now. 'And perhaps you never will.'

He finished the small meal and swallowed the dregs of his coffee. 'I will saddle up; you deal with the rest,' he said, kicking earth into the fire.

He went out to where the horses had walked to the ends of their long tethers, his footsteps fading into hush, and Ryker was alone with the splutter of choking embers. The mist danced above the ground and combed wet fingers through the doctor's hair, and all else was still.

The horses were frisky-fresh after their night's rest, and the men rode them hard across the stretch of country that curved from the rough hills. It was good riding, but there were holes hidden under the scrub, and the dry scars of dead water courses that fell away without warning. Ryker followed the man who knew the land and the black mustang that knew the wild, because it was safer that way. Because he was confident that Wolf was leading him towards the town where he would do what he had to do, even though he was still unsure what that might be.

He was glad to have the young man with him on this journey, but what he had said that morning still rankled. The doctor thought he had learned all there was to learn about the boy Wolf had been and the man he had become. He had helped to secure the freedom of the former and formed a bond of friendship with the latter, and he would have trusted him with his life. But perhaps there were things about Wolf that he still didn't know, and probably never would.

Dirty clouds rolled in from the north and the sky grew dark. The two riders covered the ground swiftly but they could not escape the sleet that came at them with ice in its bite. They lowered their hats and lifted their collars, and the hard rain fell in front of their faces like curtains, so that they had galloped over the threshold of the town before they realised they had arrived.

Wolf reined the stallion back, but the doctor had travelled further, and was halfway along the main street before he could do the same with the gelding. The people taking shelter under shop-front awnings stared at the stamp of water and the squealing chestnut, and then at the black horse that pranced in its wake. Groups of women huddled beneath bonnets, shaking their shawls and frowning; clusters of men, thumbs hooked behind belts, hats nodding, boots tapping. All staring.

Wolf took no notice of them. He guided Dancer to the hitching rail and the stallion snorted, half rearing as he dismounted. He brought the animal to rest with a mutter of words and waited for Ryker to walk back with the gelding.

'Word of our arrival is already spreading,' the doctor said.

Wolf slapped his hat against the post, and water freckled the wooden boards beyond. 'We will not be here long enough for them to remember us.'

'I sincerely hope you are right.'

The telegraph office had been squeezed into a side alley off the main street. The rain didn't seem so heavy here; like the narrow building it too had been forgotten.

Hidden at the back of grain stores and haberdasheries, the interior of the office was dark, and no lamp had been lit to cut through the murk. Daniel Ryker walked straight in and Wolf lingered at the door, as though there was someone in there that he had no wish to meet. But the place appeared to be empty.

There was very little furniture: a cluttered desk, some cabinets for paperwork. A large map was displayed on the board that hung from a picture rail, and a few chairs had been arranged for the benefit of customers.

The doctor leaned on the counter that formed a short partition close to the entrance. He hit the bell three times to no avail, and then three times more. The sound rang impetuously around the walls and sank through the half open door to a room beyond, and there was a lengthy pause before the man turned up, his footsteps fussing along before him.

'All right, all right,' he snapped. 'A morsel of patience would not go amiss.'

Despite the gloom the telegraph operator's forehead was glowing, and a scattering of reflections jumped across the lenses of his spectacles. He peered through them as if the shine was a distraction, and saw a tall, respectably bearded gentleman waiting at the counter. He raised his head, shaking back shoulders as if standing to attention.

'Is there something I can do for you, sir?' the operator said with a sycophantic smile.

And then he caught sight of the younger man by the door, and the welcome slipped from his face, leaving him strangely naked.

The fellow must have seen something that disagreed with him, but when the doctor turned around he could only find Wolf Shadow standing there. Ryker frowned.

'Is anything wrong?' he said, but Wolf barely glanced at him, and it was the operator who spoke.

'Are you both here together?'

Ryker looked at the man, the face grown surly, eyes staring across the room as though Wolf might be about to spring like the animal after which he was named.

'In answer to your first question,' Ryker said, 'there is something you can do for us.' He fished a piece of paper from an inside pocket of his jacket where the rain had yet to soak. 'I'd like you to tell us where we might find the sender of this communication.'

The operator leaned closer, his back unnaturally bent from the hours he spent transferring words to taps on the telegraph machine. He studied the piece of paper and the message it contained.

'Well now,' he said, straightening up as far as he could. 'I'm not too sure that I recognise this.'

The truth in his eyes had been practically obliterated by spectacle-shine, and so Ryker tried to find it another way. He lifted out some coins from the same inside pocket. 'Not even if we make it worth your while?' he said, rattling the money in his fist.

'Ah. That is a different matter altogether.'

The man liked the melody of money; he dipped his head to hear it better. His hand opened under Ryker's nose, and a smile opened with it as the doctor dropped coins into the calloused palm. This time the smile also embraced the one who was standing by the door, but Wolf Shadow appeared to be too fixated on the slowing rainfall to pay much attention to what was happening behind him.

The telegraph operator picked up the piece of paper again, jabbing it with a pointed finger nail.

'Now I come to think about it maybe I do remember

the gentleman who dictated this message,' he said. 'He's been in here two or three times over the past month.' He wrinkled his forehead until his eyebrows disappeared behind the gleaming lenses. 'Always with the same type of wording.'

He peered up, sharp-eyed, like an animal scenting blood. 'Are you in some sort of trouble, Mr…?'

The name he wanted was on the telegram before him and he read it out too slowly. 'Doctor. Daniel. Ryker.'

Wolf left the doorway swiftly and in silence, and the operator jumped back from the counter as if he had been stung. 'You have been paid for a service and we are still waiting,' the young man said, pointing to the money in the other's hand. 'Tell us where we can find the sender of messages.'

The small man began to wriggle. 'Well, I'm trying to think. You see, he's not from this town, he's only kind of passing through.'

'A month is a long time to be passing through.'

'Well, yeah, I mean… how do I know where he lives? I can't keep track of everyone who calls in here. This is a busy place. I'm a busy man.'

'A busy man who works hard for a small wage.'

'You got it there, fella; right on the button.' The telegraph operator banged the counter with his fist and held out his hand again, palm open. 'There's always room for more,' he said.

Wolf leaned across the counter, grabbing the man's wrist before he could move. He twisted and the operator yelped, bending back against his captor's grip, beginning to fall, but Wolf held him upright and held him tight.

'Take that up with your employer,' he said. 'But first, tell us where we can find the one who sent that wire.' He spoke softly, as he might reason with a jumpy stallion that needed to be put in its place. 'Then we will leave you alone.'

'Wolf Shadow.' Ryker looked at the operator, cringing with pain; looked at the young man whose eyes were too dark to see in the gloomy room. 'You're hurting him. Let him go.'

Wolf ignored him. He shook the man like a hound would shake a rabbit, and the doctor grabbed him and dragged him back from the counter. Wolf blinked until the blackness had cleared from his eyes, and the little telegraphist fell away clutching his arm.

'You'll find him in a cabin, down by the river,' he yelled. 'Follow the road out of town and go north, past the three pegs of rock.'

His voice was practically inaudible, gabbling words as if there were too many for his mouth. 'You'll smell him before you smell the water.'

He sobbed, backing away until he hit the bank of filing cabinets by the wall, and the doctor hesitated. 'I'm sorry,' he said. 'Let me look at your arm…'

'Go! Just go!' The man's eyes were white-rimmed and terrified. 'Take your animal with you!'

But Wolf had already left.

And Ryker followed.

TWELVE

TREES GREW wild down by the river, stretching into the water as if they were on their way to the opposite bank. Late summer hardwoods, they were already dry and brittle from heat and the onset of leaf-fall. There was yellow amongst the green in the high canopies and the weight of shrivelled fruit pulled at the branches until even the trunks were groaning.

Disquieted by what had taken place in the telegraph office, Dr Ryker had ridden hard on the tail of the black stallion, and the young man whose back was too straight. The day was progressing but it hadn't taken them long to find the three pegs of rock. The vegetation here was thick enough to choke; the horses sank to a halt and stood wheezing, foam dripping from their muzzles.

Night Dancer pranced for a while before searching for grass, his shoulder shivering away a fly, but the chestnut was dulled by the ride and had no wish to wander further. Ryker left the reins loose, peering back at the rock formations that rose from the ground like alien growths – a triangle of stone pillars carved into sinuous shapes by wind and weather. The doctor felt far from home.

He glanced across at his companion, but Wolf seemed to have forgotten that he had not come there alone. He had already set off for the cabin that was sinking towards the river as though it had given up.

The young man was silent in his walking, and the trees covered the sight of him, except for his hair that seemed to float above the ground like a strange yellow bird on the hunt for foolish little animals; or the even more foolish telegraph scribe who had no idea that he was about to receive visitors.

Ryker lifted off his hat, hitting it against his leg to eject renegade twigs that had fallen from boughs. He replaced it with care and, with a mix of moods that pushed and pulled, followed the trail that Wolf had laid. His body felt almost too cold to move, but his face was burning.

Wolf had reached the cabin; he was standing by the wall, away from the window that looked back to the three graces of rock; away from the rough plank door recessed into shadows like something that needed to hide. There was no sign of the fight that had entered his body at the telegraph office, or the hardness that had blackened his eyes as he twisted the operator's arm. That strange iniquity had been left behind in the unfriendly town, and the man that the doctor had always trusted was with him again.

There was a roan mare at the side of the dwelling, secured to a post that was trying its best to hold up the sag of roof. The horse whickered as Daniel Ryker drew near. The call was not loud enough to be heard, and yet an answering sound came from inside, like chair legs scraping across the floor.

'He is at home,' Wolf said, as though to himself, before looking up at the hesitation on the doctor's face. 'Are you ready?'

Ryker nodded, as if he meant it; and together they approached the door. It was opened before they could reach it, and there was a man standing on the threshold.

Jacket-less, vest gaping over thick black suspenders; a pipe with a dark wood bowl in the cup of one hand, the other empty but wavering, as if it had been occupied a moment before – with a news-sheet perhaps, or another note for the telegraph office. Or maybe the occupant of the cabin had been oiling his palm for the money he was expecting.

Wolf got to him first.

The man took a step backwards from the Indian with the pale hair, and another from the doctor who was standing by his shoulder. He bolted out of the door and ran for the roan, dropping the pipe and scattering ashes on the ground.

Wide-girthed and heavy of limb he was not built for speed, and Wolf caught him with ease before he could raise his foot to the stirrup. There was a struggle, but it was a token resistance. He lashed out with his weight behind the attack, and Wolf ducked beneath the blow and came up swiftly, felling the man with a quick punch to the head.

Ryker could see him properly now, the discoverer. Belly bloated from lack of exercise, skin sallow from lack of sun, he was an indoors dweller who perhaps made a point of preying on lonely women and young girls. One who liked to make money from another's misfortune. And Wolf was standing over him, hunched like a bear about to pounce.

'What do you want me to do with this, Daniel?'

'I think,' the doctor turned the young man around with a hand to his arm, 'we should get him inside so that we can talk to him.'

Wolf Shadow's eyes were night-black. Ryker couldn't see his spirit there, and he was chilled. 'Help me take him into the shack,' he said, shaking his friend's shoulder fiercely to bring him to life.

The interior of the cabin was subterranean dark under waves of vegetation and an encroachment of earth across the floor. There was a second window looking out over the river. It made the flimsy building feel like a boat, square and rough-hewn.

A boat that was anchored to the ground and going nowhere.

The gloom lifted as eyes grew accustomed, and what had appeared as inconsequential objects before turned into items of mean furniture: a couple of stools with ill-formed back supports, a table made from a door on bricks, a thin mattress pushed up in a corner where a rusty stove huddled.

The stove was dead, so choked with ash that it might not have seen a match for quite a while. There was even a small, dusty pile of cut wood nearby like a gesture towards a better time.

The man had crept to the far wall as though he might hide behind the shadows that spread there. He stood with his head turned away, loath to face his visitors in a room from which there was no escape.

Wolf was guarding the exit. He was not a tall man nor heavily built, unlike the one he was overseeing, and there was a silence about him as his mind reached out to the thoughts that filled the cabin. He seemed unnaturally still; it was a stillness that spoke of something leashed. Wolf was an adversary, and the man who had squashed his stoutness against the back of the cabin knew this.

But even so, he was going to fight.

'Who are you?' he said. 'What do you want?'

For a big man he had a thin voice, pitched high with alarm. It scratched Ryker's eardrums. He gritted his teeth and winced.

'I think you know who I am,' he said. 'And what we want is to talk with you.'

The man's eyes were naked with fear; they flicked to where Wolf was motionless at the door. 'Keep him away from me.' His voice was shrill, and it broke in the middle when he grabbed his skull and shook it like a ball. 'He's trying to get inside my head.'

He stumbled; his shoulder knocked the wall and the hut shivered, flakes of dry wood dropping from the roof. Ryker could see lines of light between ill-fitting planks and edges softened by rain. He could smell the river as though it was about to rise up from beneath the crumbling floor.

'Sit down,' he said, indicating one of the chairs, but the man was already there. He sank into the seat, and the wood groaned as though it was unable to bear his bulk. Ryker stepped across to the other chair, dusting grime from its surface before testing its dubious stability. He and the man sat half-turned towards each other, like acquaintances who were taking time out of their morning to catch up with the news.

Wolf Shadow stood in stillness. A gust of wind rose outside, slicing between the boards behind him. It pushed his hair across his eyes, but he made no attempt to clear his sight. He could already see as much as he needed.

'Tell me your name.' Ryker leaned back as far as he dared, and the chair shuddered. The man looked up, looked away. He didn't speak.

'It would be a courtesy, if nothing else,' the doctor said. 'You already seem to know my name and where I live. You have taken it upon yourself to correspond with me. You have threatened my family and my livelihood. You have made it necessary for me to travel this far to find you. And here we are now, sitting together like old friends, yet I have no idea who you are.'

The man hadn't moved but his fingers were busy, gripping the edge of the chair until the tendons on the backs of his hands were rigid.

'Let us begin this conversation,' Ryker said. 'Tell me your name.'

The shack was full of sound: the slither of something that had landed on the roof, the mournful sigh of wind, the rumble of water through the window, and the harsh breathing of the man who didn't want to speak.

'Very well.' The doctor rubbed his beard, fiercely, reluctantly, as though he had arrived at a decision that had been difficult to make. He got up, stood behind the chair with his hands on the back. 'If your will is locked, then maybe my companion here can persuade you to set it free.'

He signalled to the young man by the door, and Wolf came forwards as if he had been released. The fat man squealed, bending to his knees as far as he could, his arms crossed over his head.

'No! I'll tell you, I'll tell you. Just keep him away.'

Ryker raised his hand, but Wolf still came as though no power was going to stop him. He reached out to grab the man, but the doctor was there between them. Years of hard work had made the young man strong, and the doctor had to use all his might to push him away.

'For pity's sake, Wolf Shadow, leave him be!'

Wolf looked into his eyes and out to the back of his head, and Ryker felt as if a knife had gone through him.

'Let me put an end to his unworthy life,' the young man said.

'That's not what we came here for.' But the doctor wrestled with the thought of it.

'Then why are we here?'

'For answers. For clarification.'

'You would have your answers, Daniel, if you let me finish him.'

'I don't want that.'

'Who would know?'

'I would!' Ryker shuddered.

He searched inside the young man's eyes for the glimmer of gold, the spirit that lived within him. It was still there; it was smouldering like a dying ember, but he could see the promise of the wolf who had grown from the cub.

'I would,' he repeated. 'And so would you, Wolf Shadow.'

Wolf looked down at the man in the chair, still folded over himself with his jowls quivering. His legs were squeezed together, but they could not hide the wet stain spreading in a fan from his crotch. The smell of urine was sharp in the air, and Wolf turned away with his lip raised in disgust.

'Only I can decide that, Daniel,' he said, going back to the shadows that were collecting by the wall.

The man in the chair raised his head and watched as Wolf opened the door. The scents of river and trees and earth swarmed into the room, and their memory remained after he had closed it behind him, and all that had been outlined inside the shack by the light of freedom had dissolved again under the murk.

'He would kill me,' the big man said.

'I guess he would.'

The doctor took his seat again and nodded, as if he was privy to whatever was happening inside the mind of the man whom he had once believed he knew better than many. He felt weighed down with disappointment.

'Hooch.' The man wriggled. 'Hubert Woodard is my name, but friends call me Hooch.'

He looked up. His eyes were naked, and ash-grey in the gloom. 'I may be down on my luck, but I am a good man, Dr Ryker.'

Ryker suddenly thought of his wife, living through her day back home in Oasis. She might be spending money in Kester Kendal's store, or instructing little Esme on the preparation of a midday meal. She might be playing with Dulcie and Bella; hitching her skirt and scrabbling over the parlour floor like a child herself – until one twin or the other would look up and ask Mama if she knew what Papa was doing at that moment.

Papa was sitting in the squalor of a dilapidated hut with a man who had brought him almost to the brink of insanity for worry. A good man? No, Hubert Woodard was a slug, and at that moment Ryker wanted to kill him.

'Tell me what you were doing at the Indian village.'

'I was looking for stuff.' Woodard blinked slowly, as if reaching back into his memory. 'Stuff that I could sell.'

'You were stealing.'

'How can you call it stealing? The Indians had already cleared out.'

'What about the woman? What about the girl in the tepee?'

'I'm telling you no one else was there. There was only stuff…'

'Belongings.'

'… left behind. How was I to know…?'

'Boxes and chests. And the bed. The bed with the girl lying on it.'

'… to know they were coming back for it? I didn't see a girl, just a bundle of rags.'

'And the woman.'

'There was no squaw until you brought her with you on your buggy.'

And there it was again – the twist of fear that had curdled the doctor's belly as he drove the woman out of Oasis, on the Samaritan quest that was about to change his life.

He remembered believing that she could be trusted; that she was not knowingly leading him into danger. He remembered the silence in the middle of that deserted village, sudden and eerie as though there was something lurking behind the two skeleton tepees, or lying in wait inside the one where a child cried with a kitten's mew.

'I saw what you did, Daniel Ryker.'

Woodard's voice dispersed the memories, its scratchy falsetto digging claws into Ryker's head.

'I watched you inside that tepee with your doctoring tools, performing ungodly operations on that native girl.'

The voice was grinding through his skull now. An ache had started at the back of his scalp where the skin was prickling.

'I know all about your crime.'

Ryker saw the Indian woman again with her thick glossy hair, gaunt with hunger but fierce with love for the daughter who had taken a knife to the white man when he came with his gun.

They went away, she had said. We buried our dead. We lived.

'Was it you?' Ryker stood suddenly and the chair scattered. He heard something splintering as it fell to the hard-packed floor. 'Did you rape her?'

Woodard slithered from his seat, leaving his reek behind. He backed away, the thick suspenders squeezing black channels into his belly. 'No. Not me.'

'She was only a child.' A child who had suffered for

her mother's protection.

'I didn't do it.' The voice was as thin as a blade, and Ryker flinched in pain.

He made fists, fingernails gouging his palms.

'I didn't do it,' the fat man repeated, 'but I saw who did. There was a whole group of them went down to that village, a couple or so months back. They were shooting guns and killing. Boy, did they make a lot of noise.' He shook his head and smiled at the memory.

They killed the old men who could not run, the young men like fools who tried to fight them. That was what the woman had said, swaying as if she was about to fall from the horror of it.

The doctor had held her steady and she had shivered as though he was tainted with the same disease.

'And you tell me that you are a good man?' He took a step towards the smile and watched as it faded from the pudgy face.

'I'm ten times holier than a baby-killer, Dr Ryker.'

'You were there, that day, and you did nothing to help them.'

'I was also there the day you committed your crime, and if you want me to keep silent about it then you're going to have to pay.'

Woodard held out a hand as though he was already feeling the weight of money in his palm. It was the only action that truly described his character, and it was his last mistake.

Ryker leaned forward and punched him in the chest before the man realised he had moved. Woodard landed hard, and the noise he made thudded back from the walls as if the wooden boards were applauding. He lay stupefied, too confused to avoid the kick that landed somewhere around his ribs, cushioned beneath blubber.

He screamed, an ear-piercing sound, and the final straw. By the time Wolf had burst through the door it was practically too late to pull Ryker away from the man on the floor, eyes as protuberant as eggs from the grip the doctor had around his throat. Even so Wolf had hesitated; for a couple of seconds.

'Let me go, Wolf Shadow.' Ryker struggled but Wolf's hands were accustomed to the tug of a wild stallion, and his hold was certain.

'You are not the one who should do this, Daniel.'

'I want to kill him.'

'You are a physician. You save lives.'

'Not this one.'

Wolf shook his head, and then he shook the doctor, half dragging him out of the cabin, away from the stink and the fat man who was sitting up now, his backside solid on the hard earth and his hands to his throat as if he was strangling himself.

Ryker hauled in lungfuls of air like someone who had been rescued from drowning. The cold tang of the river was cleansing the sour heat from his blood, and he could see clearly now, straight up through the clack of branches to where the sky was hanging serene and silver.

The grip on his arms relented as Wolf felt the man coming back to himself, and then the doctor was released, standing alone and steady, with the warmth fading from his skin where his friend had held him.

'There is nothing more I can do,' he said.

'Then we are leaving?'

'We are leaving, Wolf Shadow.'

'The problem has not yet been resolved.'

'No.'

Ryker sighed. He turned to where Wolf was waiting before him, broad-shouldered and straight. The gold in the young man's eyes had been caught in the light, and it seemed as though his soul was burning.

'What will be will have to be,' Ryker said; but Wolf shook his head.

'Let me do the resolving for you.' He spoke quietly, lifting his knife from its sheath and balancing it in his palm. And after a moment the doctor nodded.

But Woodard struck without warning, hurling himself through the open door, propelled by his bulk towards them. He was making the squealing noise in the back of his throat; it was huskier now but still pitched high, and its momentum was carrying him forward.

He would have crashed into Ryker's body but Wolf was quicker, dropping the knife and shouldering his friend aside.

They landed in a heap together by the hitching post, sending the tethered roan into a craze. Wolf was the first to get to his feet, and he was the one who watched as the fat man smashed blindly into the riverbank trees.

The shattering of his skull was sickening. He slipped through an opening between the trunks as if they had spread aside for him, and sank headfirst into the water.

It was elegant and soundless, like the dive of an otter.

THIRTEEN

SAGE WAS in the yard at the place where chickens might peck, but the chickens were hiding from the dog. The dog was tied up at the hitching post by the porch; it had been tied there all night and now it was hungry. And Sage wanted Emmett to come and take it away.

It was still early; early enough for Colt not yet to have left for school. He was on his way to the red mare with a saddle in his arms. He was going to be late if it took him any longer, but he had been caught by sight of the dog and now he was standing too close to its mouthful of teeth.

At least that was what his mother was thinking.

Sage lifted her skirt and moved towards him, her hand raised to stop the teeth from biting her son; but Colt was talking and the dog was listening. The speech shone from the boy's mouth and shivered hairs on the back of her neck, as it did when Wolf used the same words to quieten horses in the corral.

There were times when he would whisper them in bed at the top of the house, holding her close and chanting into the dark until her whole body was shivering. The language was all his own and meant nothing to her; these were words that rose from his heart and floated in the air to be frittered away by the breeze.

This was how it always seemed, that the breath of the

man Sage loved was frittering away words that he spoke to the wild and wicked horses. And Colt had inherited the talent from his father. Although at that moment he was also a young child in range of a big dog's fangs. His dark head bent towards them and he was laughing, as though he could see something comical about the beast and not the threat of meanness and muscle that his mother could see.

But now her daughter was there as well. She was standing in the porch, and the danger had been doubled.

Sage called as she hastened to reach her. 'Stay where you are, Clove. Go nowhere near the dog.' Be aware of the power of hounds, she thought. Be afraid, like me.

The little girl shook her head, as if settling something that was slightly out of order.

'The dog is hungry, Ma,' she said. 'I see meat in its mind; small animals running; the dog chasing; the dog catching. I see it eating all the little animals, Ma.'

'Hush now.' Sage folded the child to her skirt, hiding her eyes from the things she could see. 'Mr Hockaday will be here soon to take the dog away.'

'Mr Hockaday is bringing the small animals with him,' Clove said, with her fist to her mouth. 'He is riding his horse along the track.'

And then Sage could hear it as well, the shlop shlop of hooves as her neighbour rode into the yard, dismounted and came forward, tapping the brim of his hat to the woman and the little girl. Grabbing the dog's neck-scruff with more force than was required to drag it away from Colt's attention.

His roughness bothered the stallion in the nearby enclosure – the big dark grey that was becoming a liability to anything that crossed its path, including a bulky hound with sharpened teeth.

It gave Emmett Hockaday grief that Wolf Shadow had upped and left in the middle of cultivating that half-tamed animal. The stallion had mean eyes and a tendency to bite, and the young man was going to have a great deal of work to do when he returned, for the horse would need quite some hours of persuasion before it might dance to any mind-shifting tune.

Which was something that Emmett found doubly aggravating, because the newly-acquired mustang in his own corral was doing nothing but fill its belly and kick the fence as it awaited Wolf's ministration.

'If everything here is where it should be, then I shall take this hound away,' he said, slipping the rope loose from the post.

The dog started to pull, as if it could already see the small animals that Clove had prophesied. Sage tucked the child tighter against her skirt, and the man noticed the strain in her face.

'Do you know when Wolf will be back?' He put a stop to the dog's shenanigans with a tug, and Sage jerked, as if she too had been haltered by the rope.

She said, 'I do not.' Because before riding away on the black stallion, with the rudiments of survival strapped to his saddle, Wolf Shadow had barely told her anything of the trip he was about to take.

Hockaday hesitated, as though he had to steady his temper before he could speak again. 'You know that you can depend on my help, Sage, but my resources of time are limited.'

'You have already given us as much as you can spare,' she said, 'and I am grateful.' She pulled her daughter closer, until they seemed to be joined by more than just blood. 'But I have no knowledge of where Wolf has gone, or why.'

Her neighbour's eyes were as clear as a sky in full sun, but bleak with concern, for he was a kind man. 'I shall bring the hound back again towards evening,' he said. 'He is a good guard; he spooks well when spooking is required and his bark is loud enough to carry along the track to me. You have nothing to worry about, Sage.'

'Emmett,' she said, looking as small as the child she was holding. 'The worry will stay with me until Wolf has returned.'

Hockaday could see a woman who was young, brittle and alone, and his heart twisted.

'Joanie will be over later,' he said, fiddling with the dog's rope as though it was a plaything and he had all the time in the world. 'She finds she has a glut of vegetables from the garden, beans and green stuff, some roots, and all the like of that. It would be a crime to let it go to waste, and she would be obliged if you'd take it off her hands.'

He moved away before Sage had a chance to reply, and a chance to refuse the generosity of a friend who only wanted to help. Although it was not in her mind to refuse when the kitchen cupboards were groaning like an empty belly.

A wave of anger rolled through her, followed on its heels by one of apprehension, as though the anger might bring bad luck to the man who was missing from her life. But Wolf would return – at least this is what she told herself. He had been absent from the household before, sometimes for a length of days, and yet he always came back.

'Wolf Shadow would never leave us like this,' she called out to Emmett Hockaday as he walked the hound across the yard, scattering clumps of earth with his big feet. 'Not unless he has good reason for it.'

The man climbed to his saddle and urged the horse towards the track that would take him home. He turned at the entrance as though he had a reply to make, but his sight had shifted to the prancing stallion that was wasting everybody's time in the compound.

Emmett worked his mouth in irritation, shaking his head like somebody who didn't need to be pulled into an uncomfortable conversation. He left without looking back.

The two men had parted company a while since: Dr Ryker to head towards Oasis and the innocence of his children; Wolf Shadow to make for the Madison place, and the responsibilities he had put aside in order to help his friend.

There had been no words between them on the trek back from the hovel, where Hubert Woodard was being stroked by weed tresses at the bottom of the river.

They didn't talk about how they had lingered on the bank by the trail of blood spots and the place where the big man had fallen into the water, or the improbability that Ryker's discoverer would emerge again, brandishing his threats and reaping payment for his silence. But even so Wolf had waited with the knife in his hand, and his arm tensed ready to use it if the round face were to blubber to the surface.

He waited until the breeze had dropped and the trees stopped moving, before slipping the blade back in its sheath. His fingers were stiff with expectation and he flexed them, staring up through the cradle of branches to the sky.

There had been no conferring; the men had simply checked around the empty cabin and taken away all the evidence of their short visit. Before they were mounted and ready to leave, the doctor had tidied the bankside and used river water to wash away the blood.

He loosened the roan mare from the hitching post so that she should find her own direction. She had followed them past the three standing rocks, but they didn't notice when she scented sweeter grass and left them to ride alone.

They had found somewhere to rest a few hours after night had fallen, when it would have been foolish to go sightless through unknown territory. The coffee Wolf had brewed up over a small fire had been sufficient, for there was no hunger in them. With little inclination to sleep they had settled back on the hard ground, sinking into the swathe of darkness as the horses slumbered. Their voices were subdued over the crackle of fire, as though to speak loudly would have been tantamount to meddling with things that were best left undisturbed.

'None of this,' Ryker had said, 'is to go back with us to our homes.'

Wolf didn't reply; he remained silent for so long that Ryker thought he might have yielded to exhaustion. The Lord alone knew that the doctor was himself exhausted to the point of oblivion. There was just his mind keeping him awake, continually rewinding every action that had taken place at the cabin by the river.

But Wolf had not been asleep; he was looking up to where the stars were spread like petals on a black field, as though it might be preferable to fly up there and leave the world behind.

'I guess none of this ever happened,' he said. 'If that is what you want.'

It was Clove who first heard the sounds that signalled the black stallion's return. Yet they were not hoofbeats that she heard, but the heavy wheeze of Night Dancer's breathing and the harshness of fatigue in its throat at the end of the long ride. She felt the creak of the saddle and smelled the sweat on her father's skin. She swallowed the uncomfortable mess of thoughts that were swirling in his mind, and it made her belly ache.

'Pa has come back,' she told her mother, who was in the process of squeezing out two loaves of bread from the last of the heavy flour.

Sage looked up abruptly and pale powder scattered over the table edge when she jerked her hands from the dough mix. She listened, but there was nothing yet to hear. Her daughter's ears were attuned to the whistle of wind in far trees and the calls of wild creatures out on the plains, and what sound she had heard was still to arrive at the homestead tucked in the valley cup.

Martha appeared at the porch door, flushed from a morning spent in the fresh air of her garden. She pushed back the bonnet so that her face was clear.

'There is a rider away up by the hills, I can see the dust climbing,' she said. 'It might be that Wolf Shadow has returned.'

Sage rubbed the last of the sticky dough from her fingers and went to join her mother by the door, so that they together with the child could go out to watch the rider approaching; to recognise the black horse and its cloudy wake.

Night Dancer was making heavy weather of the final slopes, and Wolf kicked the stallion on because he could see the three of them waiting at the place where the yard opened up. He felt their minds probing as he came nearer. He felt hope, and then he felt shame. A mixture of light and dark, one repelling the other like oil in water.

The closer he drew to his home, the easier it was to

discern the lines that creased Sage's forehead. She was trying to smile beneath the worry, and that piteous attempt twisted his heart. Martha was standing by her side, frowning her displeasure at his temerity to have left and then to return on a whim. Little Clove, slightly apart, was alone in her own world.

His daughter's eyes pulled at him; he could feel her stealing away snippets of knowledge that should have been locked inside his head, but it was only the weariness that was leaving him so exposed. He struggled to obliterate the journey to a town where the telegraph office cowered like an afterthought; the truths that Daniel Ryker had divulged; the discovery of the doctor's discoverer beside three twisted pillars of stone that stood like a portal to Woodard's unnatural life and awkward death.

Wolf emptied his mind and Clove felt a buzzing, like insects in her ears. The strange images that had slipped into her thoughts vanished, leaving a vacuum that was filled with the sudden impression of a mysterious form. Still far away but coming closer. Bringing blackness.

She whimpered, but nobody else could hear over the commotion that had arisen with her father's return.

Sage reached for Dancer's bridle, and the stallion was too spent to fight capture; bending its neck as Wolf slipped from the saddle.

'Husband,' she said, with her hand firmly at his arm. There was relief in the word, and reproach; and there was also love. Her hand was hot and lingered for a while seeking the bare skin under his shirtsleeve.

'Was it worth it?' Martha's voice was quarrelsome. 'Taking yourself away like that to go we know not where and do we know not what.'

She was shouting now, leaning into his face with fury

in hers. 'I hope it was worth it for you, because it surely was not for us, left on our own with no idea if you would ever come back.'

There was a time, long past, when Martha Madison had punished him for forsaking his daily chores in order to gaze at the freedom of a bird. Once he had resented her hold on his life, but now Wolf turned away from her condemnation so that she would not see his debasement – the urge to twist a man's arm until it snapped; the compulsion to kill that had filled his throat like vomit.

He had not found rest since Hooch Woodard's death by hungry water, and he was too weary for Martha's stridency when the need to sleep was so seductive.

Although a sickness had settled in his stomach and it would take a while for him to close his eyes, and just a while longer before the dreams began.

Martha huffed at his stubbornness; she stormed off to rid her garden of weeds and Wolf scanned the yard for his daughter. Maybe Clove would allow him to rest in her silence and quench his fire with her serenity.

But while Martha was lecturing him the little girl had disappeared as quietly as ever she did, and Sage was the only one left waiting. She came close, pressing her body to his body and her lips to the base of his throat, where his heartbeat was thrumming.

He lifted her from the ground, she was so light. It was good to hear her laugh.

'Emmett has been bringing his dog to care for us. He tied it to the post each night and told us that its loud bark would protect us from spooks,' she said, stroking the hair on his chest. 'But I believe that we would have been the ones spooked if we had heard that big dog's bark in the middle of the night.'

'I am sorry,' he said, breathing in her sweet smell.

'Are you sorry that we were guarded by a big brown dog?'

'I am sorry that I had to leave you alone in the guard of a big brown dog.'

Sage filled her mind with the scent of him: the fresh sweat and the hard ride, leather and horse, and the essence of Wolf Shadow. 'And why did you have to leave us, husband?'

His sigh shivered across her scalp. 'I cannot tell you.'

'Oh? Why can you not tell me?' She frowned, feeling the chill when he lifted his head away. 'Is it because you are ashamed?'

She glanced up at his silence. He was staring into the heart of the yard, but she knew that he was looking far beyond the clods of cracked mud. 'I cannot tell you,' he said, 'because there is nothing to tell.'

But Sage could see that his eyes were filled with the image of a honey-haired woman in a rose-pink dress, and maybe she had caught the drift of Lucy's perfume from his clothes.

'Well,' she said, hardened now, twisting away from his arms. 'If you have nothing to tell me, I need to see to the feeding of your children.'

She began to head towards the house, but then she returned to stab a finger into his chest; into the place where she had kissed him just two minutes before.

'Because there are more important things in life, Wolf Shadow,' she said, quietly and fiercely, 'than the wearing of fancy gowns and the scent of lemons.'

And finally she walked away, straightening the narrow back that had borne so much for him. He watched her go but did nothing to stop her.

All he could think about was her breath on his skin, and all he could do was curse Daniel Ryker's innate sense of decency. Because the cement that bound Wolf's family together had been cracked apart by an Indian mother he would never meet.

And he didn't know how to mend it.

FOURTEEN

EMMETT HOCKADAY had been correct in his claim that the dark grey stallion needed work. Wolf had left in the middle of the taming to hunt Ryker's discoverer, and what had been assimilated by the animal's brain had eked away with inactivity. The outing had been an unnatural vacation, and an expensive one, for it meant that Wolf would have to begin the battle afresh.

Colt had cared for the horse well in his father's absence, as he had cared for all the animals of the smallholding; but although it had been kept fed and watered, the grey was crazed by indolence. The sturdy enclosure fence bore the evidence of that; bitten and kicked by the demented animal, but still proud and strong and upright. Much like Wolf Shadow himself.

He had been standing by the gate for a while, watching the stallion in safety, and now his hand was on the latch. Maybe he was ready, maybe not, but too much time was passing and he dared not waste any more. He could feel it, like a warning deep in his gut. He didn't yet understand why – but soon he might.

The horse was prancing. Eyes white-rimmed and ears flat to the skull, it lurched closer and stamped away. Wolf waited until it had chased its shadow to the far side of the pen, and then he entered, closing the gate behind him. The grey roared its hostility, and as he started to walk forwards the horse stiffened, all four legs hard-muscled. It began to step backwards. Its rump hit the fence and slithered on the wood, and Wolf stood completely still in the centre of the enclosure.

Something was not right. He could smell the rankness of the horse's fear. The animal had caught a little of what was inside the man's head, the trouble that lay there like a sickness; and it was terrified.

It charged. One moment it was trying to squeeze through the solid fence and the next it was galloping. There was not much time to shift out of the way, but Wolf was already attuned. He twisted from the stallion's path and the heat from its hide hit him as it went by. It was too close, and Wolf hadn't moved quickly enough to avoid the slash as the horse bucked.

The edge of a hoof sliced across his forehead and he was immediately blinded by blood. He swiped his face with the back of his hand, but the blood kept coming. He ripped off his shirt and wound it around his head, and now he could see. The grey was pawing the ground; small explosions of grit kicking up around its legs. It pulled back its lips and screamed, and those teeth were jagged and wanted to bite.

Hardening his concentration, Wolf tried to reach the animal's mind. His thoughts seethed like a storm wind, but he fought for composure until his heartbeat slowed and his body was still. He stared at the furrowed ground. He did not raise his eyes higher, and the animal stayed where it was, scuffling the dirt into hoof holes until it had kicked enough. Wolf could feel it watching him for weakness. The wound was sharp and his head was throbbing; the grey's legs swam in and out of vision, but he was not going to fall.

He tried to compose himself; the strain was fierce, but

his mind was clearing. The troubles that cowered there were not going away, but he could lock them out of sight until time brought darkness, and another sleepless night; which had been the way of things since his return from the shack and the riverbank, and Woodard's otter dive into the water.

The stallion tossed its head, scattering muzzle foam; the rumble in its throat more an expression of bravado than warning. And then it turned away. Wolf took a step forwards, for the horse seemed almost harmless now, looking out over the fence and across to where the plains began. It ignored him but the ears were snatching at the sound of his feet. He stopped moving then, because he didn't know whether he was going to fall and he had to wait to find out.

The shirt turban was too tight, and there were other discomforts: a twinge in his leg where the muscle was rigid, the deadweight of insomnia behind his eyes, chilled air across his naked back. Wolf breathed deeply and started to speak, unsheathing the language that flowed across the compound. All that he could see was the grey horse, its head lifted to attention, nostrils inflated by the scent of blood. It stood waiting, tail shaking like a flag-crack as the young man came closer.

It was a difficult afternoon and the hours passed slowly. The sky had shifted from light to shade as Wolf Shadow worked, but he didn't notice. All he knew was that a few more sessions would be needed before the stallion could be allowed through the gate without a rope trussing it to submission. And the thought of it all was wearying him to the core.

The blindness was back. He didn't see Sage clinging to the fence; her hands bone-white on the top rail she was gripping so hard. There was blood in Wolf's nostrils now, and for a while that was all he could smell. The shirt wrapped around his head was wet and as hot as fever. He dashed the sightlessness from his eyes as he walked, using the binding to wipe away the mess. He felt her hands on his arms as he staggered through the gate; her hands by his head, taking hold of his own. She had cool hands; and a voice heightened by dismay.

'Come with me into the house, Wolf Shadow,' she said. 'There is so much blood, I cannot see the wound.'

He allowed her to lead him across the yard, and all sound dulled when they reached the porch, as though the world had been flattened by a lid. He smelled sweat and heat in the enclosed space, and the reek of gore.

'Clove must not see me like this.'

'Clove is in her room,' Sage said. 'Ma is having care of her.' He could feel how close she was. He would always recognise the woman he loved by the scent of clean skin and the kiss of her breath on his face.

She left him sitting at the table while she collected what was required, settling beside him with the clunk of china and the trickle of water. 'What were you thinking? The beast could have killed you.' Her voice was quiet, but her mind was shouting. She dipped a cloth in the bowl and began to clean the wound.

'The stallion would not have killed me.'

'You may believe that you are beyond harm,' she said, pressing harder and sending a shock of pain into his head, 'but that is not so. You…' She stopped suddenly, and he could hear her swallowing. 'Even you, Wolf Shadow, can be finished by a stallion's kick.'

'It was just an accident, Sage.'

'And you are just a man,' she said, her voice as brittle as ice. 'A stupid man.' She jabbed him with the cloth, knocking him to the back of the chair. 'But you are my man, and I could not…'

She threw the red rag into the bowl, and the water fought like a storm at sea. Wolf's sight had returned now that the blood was cleared, and he met her stare. 'I could not bear to lose you, Wolf Shadow,' she said, with a desolation that chilled his skin. It was as though winter had swept in through the door and set the windows rattling.

Sage saw him tremble and brought a blanket down from the room in the eaves to cover his shoulders. She felt his forehead with the back of her hand, as she would for her children in days of fever. 'You are still hot and yet you shiver,' she said. 'There is a sickness about you, Wolf Shadow.'

'It is the wound; and that is all it is.' He grabbed her hand as she fussed around him. 'Will you bind my head, Sage? There is work I must do.'

'Oh, and must you?' She pulled away as though giving him space to see himself. 'Your head is split and the bleeding will not stop. You need Daniel to stitch you together before you can think about further work.'

He stood abruptly and the blanket fell to the floor. 'Strap me up, Sage. That doctor cannot cure me.' Not unless he could cure himself first.

'How can you be so stubborn?' She leaned close to him, small but fierce. 'Or have all your brains fallen out through the hole in your skull?'

He raised his arms, and then he let them drop. He wanted to push her away. He wanted to hold her so tightly that he would always remember how she felt pressed against his body. But he did neither of those things, and she stepped away by herself and went about searching for a strip of binding for his head, a clean shirt to replace the one that had been sacrificed to his blood.

She discarded the bleakness she hadn't wanted to see in his eyes, so that it could be forgotten and she would not be hurt.

She could do that, if she kept herself busy.

FIFTEEN

THE DARK grey beast had a tough hide that took a while to soften, but finally the day dawned when the horse rested quiet for saddling, and its owner returned to collect. He leaned on the fence boards and watched Wolf riding inside the enclosure, moving the stallion up from a walk to an easy lope.

'By the saints,' the man said. 'You've extinguished all the fire in that creature's heart.'

Wolf halted the grey and dismounted. 'I will not quench a horse's spirit,' he said. 'The stallion still has fire. You will see it in his eyes.'

The owner left a while later, proud and high on the back of his prize, and Wolf closed a hand over the money he had been paid. He nudged his hip bone as he pushed the notes into his pocket. He had trouble remembering when he had last eaten enough to make muscle. The pull of time was more important; it gnawed at him, the knowledge that he had much to do before he could face what was coming.

He crossed to the second compound, where the black stallion had been secured to a post. The whole fence was rippling from its resentment, and the other horses inside the pen had clumped together for safety.

Stubborn and slow to tame, Dancer was throwing himself about as Wolf approached, but the young man had no time for the pranks of the half-wild. He slapped the animal's head away and climbed up to the saddle, pulling the reins so tightly that the horse choked and fought the man on its back. Wolf snarled and the stallion squealed; it was a discourse between two wild creatures, and Wolf wondered when it was that he had turned feral.

Sage looked at him now as though he was a stranger. His daughter took herself away, sitting in the fields where he was not welcome. His son had barely spoken to him since the occasion outside the Wellerson smallholding when two grown men had fought in the dirt like boys. Was it then that he had become an animal?

Or had it been in that unknown town when he had tried to break a man's arm? Had it been the itch to put an end to Hooch Woodard's worthless life?

Even during desperate years under the threat of a whip, Wolf had felt the gentle presence of the Indian who had once carried him high on his shoulders and passed on the horse language as a right of birth. But maybe it had always been in the stars that blood lust would rise to the surface, turning him into Wolf Shadow – the product of circumstance and ill-treatment, and a man whom others would learn to fear.

Gravity was making him heavy. He slumped like a bundle of bricks in the saddle, and it took an effort to wrench the stallion's head towards the Hockaday farm. Emmett was there waiting for him with his next job: a rare wild beast that only needed the words from a young man's throat to be transformed into a horse fit for riding.

For too many years Wolf had been busily moulding obedience from rowdy animals that spent all their time trying to wreck his corral.

His fences suffered and so did he. And now he was about to start the fight all over again.

Emmett Hockaday could see the state Wolf was in as he brought the black stallion to a reluctant halt in the yard. The smallholding was neat; the result of Joanie's care and Emmett's natural skill as a homesteader. There were tidy wooden buildings for equipment, stalls for the fowl, pens laid out for the animals. The smell of beast was clean and their speech was content. But they had started racketing as soon as Night Dancer rode in.

Emmett went forward to catch the bridle, holding the stallion's head steady as the rider dismounted and stood before him.

'You seem discomfited, Wolf,' he said with restraint, knocked back by the young man's appearance: the dark circles under his eyes, the hollows in his cheeks, the long hair that was fingering his jaw bone and sheltering an angry cut across his forehead.

'Wolf Shadow.' Joanie came out of the house and took the three low steps down to the yard. 'My dear, it is so good to see you,' she said; but realised, as she drew closer to him, that she had spoken too soon. For the young man was unkempt and dirty, with pale stubble where once his face had been smooth. And wretchedness was hanging like a pall over his head.

She had never seen him this way before.

'Stay a spell, if you will. I have cooked a chicken, and there is far too much of it for just Emmett and me. You'd be doing us a favour if you would join us at table.'

Joanie realised she was gabbling. Wolf had stepped away from her, as though to avoid the chatter.

'Well, I can see that you are too busy right now,' she said. 'So why not make it an evening? Bring Sage and the children over for a bite to eat, and maybe some music. I know how much Sage likes music. I can hear her singing when she's out in the yard.' And then she realised, with a jolt that left unease in her stomach, that quite a few weeks had passed since she last heard anyone singing over at the Madison steading.

Dull and dark, with no sign of that precious gold to give them life, Wolf's eyes were staring over her shoulder at something that might or might not have been there. It was making her shiver.

'An evening of music, and games for the young ones,' Joanie said, struggling now. 'We did kind of agree such an occasion once. Do you recall? It was a while ago.'

It was before he took himself away from his home without warning, and Emmett had to send the hound over to guard Sage and those small children. And they should not have been left alone, at the mercy of another's protection. It was not in Wolf's nature to countenance such a thing.

But she must have been thinking of the old Wolf, for the one who had ridden away had never returned. The man that had come back in his place was a different matter. He looked wild. He looked as if he needed to be tamed more than the horse that Emmett was getting impatient to show him.

Joanie ignored her husband's tetchiness. She held out her hand, with care as though something that had teeth might take a bite from it.

'I would really like you to come into the house with me. Just for a minute or two. Come inside, Wolf Shadow, and let us talk.'

His neighbour's plump face was lined with worry, and he wondered what had caused it. He tried to smile at her, but it didn't feel as if his mouth could move that way. He took hold of the hand instead, roughened by honest toil but as warm as love.

She squeezed as if she didn't plan to let him go, but

he eased himself away, as though he wasn't worthy of the comfort she was offering. 'They will need your care, Sage and the children,' he told her, sending ice up her spine. 'And I will always be grateful.'

He bowed and backed away, passing the corner of the big barn; following Emmett to the fenced area where the rare beast was pacing.

Wolf could hear hooves tapping the dirt before he rounded the wall. Before he saw the horse dancing as though the wind had lifted its legs. Hens pecked between his feet as he watched the young stallion marching from left to right, its tail flaring as it turned to march some more.

But nobody was watching Wolf. Emmett's eyes were for the stallion, and his mind was for the chores he needed to shoulder once the young man had left. Joanie had gone back to her kitchen where the meal she was preparing required a little seasoning, and perhaps some cornbread to soak up the gravy.

None of that registered with Wolf Shadow. The only thing that mattered was the palomino.

That night the moon pushed out from clouds and reared above the world, stars paling behind its silver light. Everywhere was silent, even the wind had been subdued, slinking across the ground like a scolded dog.

Wolf stood by rock and scrub and crazy shadows, the reluctant air pressing against his legs. The ground curved along the Oasis road and hills bunched together in the distance, swept by ghost light cut with black where the moon could not reach.

He had known this land since childhood, but now it had been vanquished by the new world that was lying beneath the moon. It was like a dream he may once have had, a longing for something better. He could see a path leading to the horizon and it was pulling at him with a stallion's strength. He wanted to give himself up to the way ahead, wherever that might be.

Wolf raised hands to the sky. The silver spun around his body but he was too heavy to fly and the earth was too greedy to release him. He had been wrapped so completely by bonds of metal and wood and all the living things that depended on him, that sometimes it hurt to breathe.

The people in his life believed in his integrity, and he had grown from boy to man hoping that he truly was that honourable. But it had been a worthless honour, as feeble as a brokcn dam. The overflow had begun as hot blood outside Kendall's store, and had surged into a fight by the Wellerson place. And after the sudden demise of Ryker's deliverer the honour had been washed away.

He was torn in two and the good half of him was missing.

The young man stood alone in the night, staring across moon-frost to the hills he had once climbed. His woman and his children were below him, asleep in the valley. Their souls were tied to his and always would be, but to be truly free meant never looking back.

Something nudged Wolf's attention and he gazed up at a shooting star that was sailing the sky in sinuous silence, too far away for its fire to roar. Once he had been as fierce as that star – crossing the hills on foot, taking a palomino from the hands of cowboys, riding the land to the end of it. Although he had never truly reached the end. He had finished with a whimper not a yell; broken not whole.

But now he had been offered a second chance to seal his quest, for the stallion that he thought had been lost to Haine Madison's bullet was at that moment locked inside his neighbour's corral.

Wolf Wind had come back to life; and the hills were up there, waiting.

SIXTEEN

OASIS SEEMED to grow bigger as the days passed, as though only bigger could be better. There had been a time when the town consisted of one main street and three or four side alleys that led out to the dry earth of the plains. Now the main street had doubled in length and the alleys had become roads verged by a sprouting of buildings, and each road had coughed up alleys of its own. Together with an abundance of stores, there was a courthouse, two banks, three undertakers, four saloons, and a railway line that racketed to the edge of the town – everything in the vicinity targeted by smuts from hot engines.

The years had bred an upsurge of newcomers, their strangeness slowly being absorbed by acceptance, and some of them were staring at Wolf Shadow as he rode in from the valley with the chestnut gelding at the end of a rope.

It was as though he was still a curiosity. Still the half-breed boy from the lair of the infamous Haine Madison: the man who had known the saloon like the back of his hand, and known the women who worked there better than he knew his own wife. And one day, according to long-lived rumours, the boy had vanished like trickery, only to be brought back some months later by a lieutenant soldier from a long-lost place near the border.

It had been a time of trouble, as though the air itself was rampant with malady. Death had come to the steading in the valley and wrapped it in a mystery that nobody had ever solved. And before anyone could cast judgement, the dubious boy had taken his own sister to be his woman and the mother of his children.

Tattletales spread the story like germs, but Wolf had grown accustomed to the gawping and it bothered him little as he held Night Dancer in check down the main street. The chestnut's walk was off-balance, but the black stallion's hooves were as certain as drumbeats, heading for the alley where Joel Seneschall was building up his furnace.

Wolf dismounted beside the forge, the fire roaring through the pounding of bellows. He tied the stallion firmly to one of the hitching rails and led the gelding forward. It moved like a wagon with one twisted wheel, and the blacksmith brushed sweat from his brow and nodded.

'Loose shoe?'

'Caught it on a stone,' Wolf said.

The man worked the bellows for a while before stepping away from the furnace to breathe. He crossed hard-muscled arms and stood in the doorway. 'What about the black one?' he said, waving his big red hand at the stallion. 'Anything loose with him?'

'Only his spirit.'

The smith smiled, his face rippling with shine. 'As you say, my friend.'

Wolf settled the hat over his brow and made to move away. 'I shall be back later for the horses, Joel.'

Seneschall nodded and returned to the bellows. Sparks began to fly like the claws of a big cat, but the roaring fell to whimpers as Wolf passed back through the alley to the main street.

The town was busy with the criss-cross of people, and traffic trundling along the road. Carts and wagons and horses, guided by a slouch of riders who took little notice of the pale-haired man, eyes hidden beneath the brim of his hat. Wolf could have been invisible, but only until he passed the front of Kendall & Son, and the shopkeeper who was staring through the window.

Kester Kendall stood to attention and squeezed white fists as he watched the man walking by. 'I am not finished with you yet, Shadow,' he muttered. 'Not finished by a long shot.'

Wolf was unaware of the store, or of the threat that a lingering memory might keep alive, but as he walked he knew he was being followed by someone who would not be shaken off, and he turned around to face the sheriff.

Andy Parnell tugged down the front of his black vest and stood with legs apart as though he didn't plan to move again until he was good and ready.

'Wolf Shadow,' he said, enunciating each word so that Wolf's name grew an emphasis that it never had before. 'I trust there is no mischief attached to your appearance in town today?'

Wolf bent his head until the shade from his hat brim had darkened the look in his eyes. 'I never have mischief in mind, Sheriff,' he said.

'Oh, and do you not? Not since the last time, maybe.'

'The last time?' And then he remembered the last time, and the stout shop owner who had called him a miserable half-breed. He remembered wanting to knock the man's teeth into the back of his head; and he would have done so but for Sage Madison's intervention, and the desperation on the face of his son.

Parnell drew himself up to full height and laid a palm

across the weapon at his waist. 'This is a peaceable town, Mr Shadow,' he said, 'and when it comes to trouble my tolerance is low.'

The lines by the side of Wolf's mouth were sharp when he smiled. 'Then maybe you should carry it higher, Sheriff, so that it might not drag on the ground when you walk.'

Sudden laughter erupted behind them. Parnell's back stiffened, and his hand closed over the gun's grip as if he needed to feel its solidity before turning around to face the listener who was leaning against the door of the cobbler's shop.

'Is there anything I can help you with, Mr Russett?' he said, highlighting the title.

The other man snorted amusement. 'Well I don't believe there is, Sheriff,' he said. 'I am just a humble bystander learning how a lawman should lay down the law.'

Parnell's lips pinched together as though there was an unpleasant taste in his mouth. 'I would be more than happy to teach you.'

'Well, I would be obliged.'

Clay Russett pushed away from the door and took some steps forward until they were facing each other – the tall sheriff and the white-haired man who had twice his years and twice his belly, and a twinkle in his eye that was still as shrewd as it had always been.

'And in return I would be happy to teach you the virtues of consideration and respect,' he said, prodding the chest of the fellow in front of him with one hard forefinger. 'Because I see that those qualities are surely missing from your repertoire.'

Parnell pushed the finger away with force. 'Let me get on with my job, old man.'

Russett flung up his arms and turned around, as if to include the rest of the town in the conversation. 'Which just goes to prove what I am saying.'

'You are saying nothing that I, or anyone else, wish to hear.'

'My, my, Sheriff.' Solemn now, Clay Russett stood still. He held the other's attention with a growl in his throat. 'Don't you still have a lot to learn.'

Andy Parnell opened his mouth, then thought better and snapped it shut. If he caught his tongue between his teeth the pain of it didn't show in his eyes. He raised his head to look down on the older man before walking away, ignoring Wolf as though he wasn't there.

Russett rubbed a palm over his beard and sank for a moment until his shoulders were as rounded as a wagon wheel. 'Andy Parnell wears me out,' he said, his voice creaky quiet. 'He's more like a whirlwind than a breath of fresh air.' He sighed. 'He took over my job two years since, and he's still getting it wrong.'

He seemed about to stumble; Wolf reached out a hand to support him, but Clay shook his head. 'Don't do that, you will just make me feel older than I think I am,' he said, and tottered away on legs that seemed too bowed to hold him upright.

Wolf Shadow watched him go, the strangest ally he'd ever had. Sheriff Russett was the man who had collected a posse and chased the cub to a standstill. He had held him in the jail at the back of his office until the boy had begun to fade. But as soon as justice prevailed, Russett had gladly released him into the rest of his life.

Wolf was swallowed by memory, and it was as if he had gone back ten years, for the touch on his arm seemed like something that he'd felt before. He turned to face the woman who had been younger then than he was now. The woman who had tugged at the bars of Russett's cell as if she had the strength to bend iron.

'You need to make it worth my while to help you, Cub,' she had once told him. 'For if you do not, then I cannot be responsible for what will come to pass.' He remembered that she had held his hand so tightly the blood had surged between them, and his skin had ripped when she let him go, as if she was taking something of him away with her.

And now she was standing before him, clothed in soft grey, a brooch of garnet beads gathering together the ends of the shawl that draped her shoulders. He smelled the scent that she had favoured for as long as he had known her, for Lucy Ryker never seemed to change; it was as if the ten years had passed swiftly enough to have left her youth intact.

There were no children beside her that would need her mothering – today she was a woman alone. A woman with a quiet voice. He had to bend his head to hear her speak.

'Something has happened between you and Daniel,' she said. 'And I want to know what it is.'

The words were snatched away by the town's clatter, but he could still hear the echo, and the challenge. Her eyes had trapped his and everything else slipped into the background.

'Nothing has happened between us, Lucy.'

The hand slid from his arm and left his skin burning.

'Why must men lie? Is it really so difficult to admit the truth?' Though clipped with vehemence, her voice was still quiet.

They were passed by groups of ladies, loosely shawled and comfortably bonneted, businessmen in narrow suits and storekeepers clad in aprons. They all glanced at the couple standing together near the cobbler's shop. Some of them were scowling.

Wolf turned Lucy away with a hand to her elbow. 'We cannot talk here.'

Her hair had been insecurely fastened that morning and it shivered with the movement when she shook her head. 'Come to my house, Wolf Shadow,' she said. 'We shall talk there.'

Before he could reply she had stepped from the boards, picking up her skirt and hastening across the road. It was as though she was running away from him. That is what he thought as he watched her go.

He wavered, just for a few moments. And then he followed, passing Kendall & Son without noticing the stout owner who was hovering in the doorway.

Kester Kendall had seen them coming together on the sidewalk. He had seen the way they touched – the woman's hand on the man's arm; his hand cupping her elbow. They had been standing as closely as two people who knew each other far too well, and Kester recognised exactly what he had to do. It was a moral obligation, more than the chance to get even that he had been looking for.

Lucy had left Wolf's side so fast that she was likely to have arrived already at the house tucked behind trees with wind flap in their branches. He knew she was there waiting for him, but after tramping through fallen leaves to her doorway it felt as though every step had been taking him down the wrong street.

He reached out for the bell pull, hearing the ghost of its chime inside the house. He had expected the door to be opened by the little maid, glancing up with bewildered eyes, flour in her hair and pastry under her fingernails. But Lucy was standing there instead, her shawl discarded and the garnet brooch transferred to her dove-grey bodice. Her eyes were very wide and very blue, and she beckoned Wolf across the threshold before he could change his mind.

He entered with his scalp prickling, and his hair lifted when he took off his hat as though there was a strange current in the air.

The house was so still that it seemed to be lying in wait; there was just the sound of the clock ticking and something like a sigh – but he may have imagined that. He wondered where everyone had gone.

'Dulcie and Bella are making a visit with friends this afternoon,' Lucy said, perhaps reading his thoughts. 'Emma Fitzpatrick's children. She is a great acquaintance of mine; you may have heard me speak of her. But there again, maybe you have not.'

She stared at him for a moment before fluttering her hand towards the parlour.

'Won't you take a seat, Wolf Shadow? And could I offer you something to drink? Esme is not here to wait on us, for I have allowed her the day off. So at least the coffee should taste acceptable.' She laughed; it was an artificial sound.

'Just tell me what is troubling you,' he said, and his voice was too loud. Lucy had turned to face the parlour with its sedate furniture, its correct arrangement of pictures on the walls, its polished floorboards. She was staring through the door of the tidy, respectable room as if she hated it. And then she turned back again, quite abruptly.

'A very nasty accident occurred on a farm last night,' she said. 'A young man was trampled by a horse. Daniel went out this morning to help mend him, but he has been so long away now that I suspect all is not well.' She shrugged. 'Either that, or he has no wish to come home at all.'

Wolf's scalp prickled again. There was a pressure inside his head, as though it had been filled with rocks. 'I do not know what you mean,' he said.

'I did hope that you might know something, Wolf.' Lucy looked up at him, recoiled slightly and blinked twice before holding him with her eyes.

'A little while ago my husband was called away to attend a medical conference at the town of Malachy Rise,' she said. 'And when he returned he was a different man, and I want to know what it is that has so changed him.'

'Why ask me?'

'Well, it happens that I had a short conversation with Sage in the town about that time,' Lucy said, 'and she told me that you had taken yourself away as well, during those very days in fact.' She made an odd movement with her mouth. 'I thought that a strange coincidence, and could only surmise that you and Daniel had gone to Malachy Rise together.'

'No. We did not.'

'Well! What a speedy reply.' She showed her teeth, but it was not quite a smile. 'It tells me that perhaps he did not go there at all. That there was no conference.' She paused. 'A mystery tour, perhaps? Two men out on a trip that might displease their wives?'

She stepped towards him and Wolf stepped away, until he was trapped against the wall. But she kept on coming, close enough for him to feel the heat of her body. 'Tell me, Wolf Shadow. Something has happened, hasn't it?'

'I cannot tell you, Lucy,' he said. 'It is not my place to tell you.'

She was just below him. She had never been very tall; when he was a boy they had shared the same height. Now he was a man, and she raised her head to see his eyes, her face opening like a flower.

'Were you both out lusting after other women?' She was whispering, her voice too intimate for the enclosed space of the passageway. 'Why would you do that, Wolf Shadow? Why go so far away, when the woman you have always wanted is right here in front of you?'

The pressure snaked down his back. His muscles clenched with it. He felt himself crashing; and he didn't care. He cupped the curve of her hips, the point where her waist dipped. He only had a short way to fall because she was already there to catch him.

She wound her fingers in his hair and wrenched back his head. She was kissing the pulse under his jaw, kissing his throat. Kissing the place on his chest where Sage had kissed in another life. But Sage had gone, and for a while all noise receded as well – the tick of the clock, the rustle of clothing, the sigh as Lucy opened his mouth with her tongue.

And then there was the rush of breathing, the scurry of movement, the slender-firm weight of the woman as he lifted her against the wall to accept him.

She had helped him to escape Madison's whip, and when he was returned to face it again she had fought like a wild cat to save his life. Over the years that had passed since those desperate times, Lucy Ryker had followed him with her eyes.

And now she was supported by his arms, her heels were hard against his spine, and there was nowhere else she wanted to be.

The wall shuddered, one picture frame twisted and another fell. Red light flashed from the garnet brooch as

Lucy arched backwards, crying out his name over the shattering of glass.

Her cry faded slowly like an echo that didn't want to die, and she held Wolf tightly, heartbeat to heartbeat. Their kisses were gentle now, their touches soft.

They were unaware that the front door had opened and that Daniel Ryker was standing on the threshold, dishevelled after his long ride. Disturbed by the tale that Kester Kendall had imparted as he came back along the street.

The storekeeper was out there, watching from the sidewalk. He could see the lovers in the passageway, joined so completely it was difficult to separate the man from the woman.

The sight of their depravity filled his soul with the vindication he had been seeking ever since the half-breed had come gunning for Korky.

Nothing was filling the doctor's soul but horror. Wolf lifted his head from Lucy's breast as the light from the street flooded in. He had bitten his lip and his mouth was bloody. Ryker could see his throat gasping as he drew breath and tried to pull away from the woman's body. But he didn't have the strength. It was as though she had sucked him dry.

Lucy peered past the silhouette of her husband. 'You should close the door, Daniel,' she said, 'for I believe that the townsfolk have seen as much as they need.'

Daniel Ryker slammed the door behind him and the street vanished as he tore the young man from his wife. Clothes loose, Wolf skidded across the wall and fell into the parlour, and the doctor was on him before he could get to his feet.

He did nothing to stop the attack, each kick jerking him further across the floor.

Ryker raised his fist high and brought it down twice, three times, but Lucy grabbed his arm before he could do it again. He flung her from him as if she had no substance. She hit the door, and the sound of splintering wood reverberated across the room.

Wolf dragged himself to where she was lying in a crumple of dove-grey. Her husband turned his back, but it made no difference; he knew he would always see them coupled together, he would always hear the sounds they had been making.

He could sense movement behind him, but it was as broken as things could possibly be, and he turned to see the man standing so close to the woman it was as if their bodies were still joined.

Lucy's face was too pale, like a moon stroked with clouds of tawny hair, and there was power in the eyes that gazed at her lover. But Wolf was staring at the man who used to be his friend; and his eyes were empty.

Dr Ryker shivered in the chill, fury dripping away to cracked knuckles and pain in his arms.

'Get out of my house, Wolf Shadow.'

His voice was hollow, as though he was disappearing; and if he disappeared there would be no one left to stop them fornicating again, and again. If this was their first time, he was going to make damn sure that it was also their last.

'Get out,' he said. 'Or I will kill you. So help me, God, I will kill you.'

Wolf limped to the passageway, passing the doctor by the fractured doorframe. There was blood on the back of the young man's shirt, as there had been the first time he had come into the Rykers' lives.

He went out of the house with his clothes torn, with pain in his ribs, with cuts on his face and sweat in his hair. He could see Kester Kendall leering beside the post and rail fence, and the small group of citizens that the storekeeper had gathered together as he waited for sight of the man he hated.

They were jeering, battering him with judgements and obscenities as he passed. Someone threw a stone that chewed another cut over his eye, and a leg was thrust out to trip him. He sprawled across the ground and got to his feet with dust in his mouth.

The black stallion was still trussed up outside the forge; the chestnut gelding was waiting on its four good shoes. Back at the Madison steading were Sage and Clove and Martha, and they too were waiting. He saw them in his mind, but their faces were hidden; it was as though he had already left them behind.

He didn't notice the children who were standing by the school gate, mocking the damaged man as he hobbled across the road; joining in with the crowd that followed him with their roaring and spitting and swearing. Neither did he notice the dark-haired boy who walked alone somewhere at the back, his face starved of colour and his heart filled with such loathing that there was no room left for love.

ROCKS SCULPTED the valley, and the slope where Wolf Shadow was sitting on a sway-backed boulder. Man and stone, set apart as though it was better that way.

He stared up to bunches of cloud passing like grey snow on a black field. He stared out to the gentleness of hills that from a distance seemed as easy to climb as the path back to his home.

If he stood up he might catch lamplight shining from the window of the sleeping space under the eaves, but he did not move because Sage may already have snuffed the flame.

He sat in his own darkness under the rolling sky, waiting for the pain in his side to yield for a while so that he could breathe without a catch in his throat.

The pain in his heart, however, was relentless.

SEVENTEEN

HE HAD left the house without a jacket, but he didn't feel the wind's cold bite. His flesh was burning, as though the doctor's beating had lit a fire inside him, and the fire had reached his head and could not be extinguished.

Maybe it was an eternal blaze, for by the saints he had tried very hard to quench it in the saloon that day, after staggering along the main street with Kester Kendall and his flock bleating at his heels. He had left them outside the swinging doors, and they had taken away the light as they gathered there, until their jeers were swallowed by the off-key piano being murdered by some novice at the side of the bar.

The saloon had been a place of long shadows, where the glow from half-hearted wall lamps played over painted ladies in gilded frames. The subdued glimmer seemed to take the edge off the smell of sharp liquor and the seedy clientele. All eyes looked up as the small doors clapped behind Wolf's entrance, and then some of them looked down again. The rest followed his progress to the bar.

A broken face was a familiar sight in a place like this, and the bartender finished wiping up a spill before he acknowledged the customer. He leaned on the counter as though he was about to tumble over the top, and gave the young man a glance up and a glance down. 'You been in a fight, fella?'

Wolf turned and spat out some blood from his bitten lip, but he didn't reply.

The bartender was persistent, and his voice rose. 'Don't think you can bring trouble in here, because it and you would not be welcome.'

Wolf Shadow stared at the man in front of him; middle-aged and heavy under the eyes, like a poor sleeper. The hair on his head was sparse and greasy, but there was an abundance of grey growth over his top lip.

'I think you might remember my pa,' Wolf said, and his voice seemed to come from someone else. 'He spent a lot of his time in here.'

The barman peered closer through the gloom. 'And who exactly was your pa?'

'Mr Haine Madison, gentleman farmer, and by all accounts one of your best customers.'

'My, my.' The tender slapped the wooden counter with the flat of his hand and disturbed a slick of beer that his wiping had missed. 'You're going back a number of years.'

Wolf fixed the man with his eyes. The fire behind them was starting to burn. 'I am going back at least ten.'

'I remember Haine Madison, right enough.' The man's moustache quivered when he sneered. 'And I remember he had a half-breed kid.'

Wolf leaned on the bar top, lifting himself forward on his elbows. 'That was me – the half-breed kid. And now I am a half-breed man and I want a drink.'

'Sure, sure,' the barman surrendered, lifting both arms in the air. 'I welcome the breed of any money spent in this saloon.' He grabbed a bottle of whisky from the shelf below the counter and poured a glassful. 'This first one is on the house, fella, in memory of the legend that was

Haine Madison.'

Wolf snatched up the glass and raised it in the air. 'To Haine Madison,' he called. 'The best pa any half-breed kid could have.'

He polished off the drink, holding out the glass for whisky to be poured again. After the second swallowing everything started to grow sweeter, and he began to understand why Madison had spent so much of his time wrapped around a bottle.

Breathing carefully, he rubbed the raw skin on his jaw, but the alcohol had already begun to anaesthetise the pain behind Daniel Ryker's assault, locking it away like a stallion behind a fence. The thought made Wolf smile, even though there was nothing left to smile about. His hair fell over his face when he hung his head, and the fingers that came to push it away were cool.

'Oh, honey, someone has treated you badly.' The woman had a smoke-cracked voice that wasn't easy to hear, as though it had been worn away over time, but she was standing so close that Wolf felt every word. She was not young, but her skin looked smooth under the powder and rouge, and her eyes were shining too brightly for the half-light in the room. Her scarlet dress flounced away from a corseted waist, and there was a black rose on the velvet choker around her neck. 'But don't you worry, sugar; I'll take proper care of you,' she said, sweeping more hair off his face. It was not unpleasant, what she was doing.

'What is your name, ma'am?'

'Well now, it could be whatever you want it to be, cowboy, or it could just be plain old Ruby.'

'Mary-Jo.'

Her eyes widened. 'I can be Mary-Jo for you, although I'm guessing that's the name of your sweetheart.' But

Wolf doubted whether Sage's heart would ever be sweet towards him again after that day.

'It is the name of someone I met ten years ago,' he said, seeing again the town where he had joined Christian Faulkner's wagon train, and all the trouble that had come of it. Mary-Jo had been working her trade in the saloon where the wagon-master was drinking. The woman had been clothed in purple and crimson, and she had smiled at the wolf cub as if she meant it.

'Ten years ago, I was half the age I am now,' Ruby said, opening her eyes wide to make it appear true. Wolf nodded as if he agreed with her, but it was only because his neck was weak and his head was loose. He swallowed some more whisky, but it wasn't helping, and when the woman took his hand he abandoned the glass to the counter and let her lead him to the back of the room, where the stairs rose towards bedroom doors. The drinkers at each table they passed turned to watch him stumble.

'I could invite you upstairs to show you a good time, honey,' the woman said, her breath warm on his ear. 'But as I see it, I don't think you'd be capable of obliging me in return.'

'I already have a woman,' he said; and then wondered which woman he had meant.

'Why of course you do; good-looking boy like you,' she said. 'And so do most of my clients, although they don't usually admit to it.'

He hadn't known what love felt like before Sage came to him in the barn where he had been secured like a beast. She had grown from childhood with him, grown close, grown indispensable – but now he had become that beast and she could smell the danger.

'There is a sickness about you, Wolf Shadow.'

Those were her words, pumping like quick fire into his brain. He jerked around, but it wasn't Sage standing behind him. It was Andy Parnell, weaving between the tables with his finger pointing like a pistol, keeping the young man in his sights until he reached the start of the stairs.

'I've come across your sort before.' The sheriff was standing too near; Wolf could hear his jagged breathing, like a dog on the brink of a fight. 'You give off a bad odour, like something inside you is rotten.'

'Hey, Sheriff.' Ruby slipped between them and folded her arms. 'You're intruding into a private conversation.'

Parnell smirked in her face. 'You don't want to do anything private with this one, even if he has already paid you for it.'

'He's been hurt, and I'm going to take care of him.'

The man laughed. 'As only you know how.'

'Ruby… ma'am. Thank you,' Wolf stepped away from her protection to face the sheriff. 'What do you want, Mr Parnell?'

'I want you out of my town, and I don't want to see you back again.'

'I have done nothing wrong.' But that was a lie. Wasn't it wrong to take another man's wife? Wasn't it wrong to lust after a woman who made no secret of her desire for him?

'You said there would be no trouble, and you made trouble.' Parnell pushed Wolf backwards; his damaged ribs shrieked when he hit the wall. 'My tolerance is low, don't you remember?'

'I made no trouble.'

But it wasn't true. He'd left trouble behind in the doctor's house; he had trouble to come in his own.

Parnell grabbed Wolf's arm and hauled him through

the room, knocking chairs aside as he herded him to the swing doors.

'Hey!' The bartender rose up behind the counter, his moustache trembling. 'I want paying for that whisky!'

'Take my money.' The sheriff had reached for a coin in his breast pocket and slammed it down on the bar top. 'His will be tainted by disease.'

EIGHTEEN

HE COULD still feel the vestiges of that disease. A fever had stolen his memory, for he couldn't recall much of what happened after he was jettisoned like any other drunkard through the swing doors of the saloon. It was the end of the afternoon and the town was busy, and everybody had turned to see what it was that Parnell deposited on the sidewalk. He was just another piece of garbage; tattered, bloody and unrecognisable, but an alternative sight for a humdrum day.

His head had been spinning like a compass searching for bearings, and the street had spun with him as he began to walk. People moved aside as though he was tainted; a group of women averted their gaze and sought a fresher scent from their handkerchiefs, a mother hid her child behind her skirts where it would be out of harm's way. He remembered a woman crossing herself as though he was the devil incarnate, and then his mind had mercy on him and closed down, and everything else to do with his exodus from Oasis was blanked.

He knew he must have reached the forge where Joel Seneschall had replaced his horse's shoe. He must have paid the smith what he owed and collected the black stallion from the hitching post, and he must have ridden away with the gelding at the end of a rope. But it had been the action of another; a puppet master manipulating his strings all the way out of town and along the track that was leading him to the farm.

Night Dancer plodded beneath him, the other horse pulled on the rope as though finding it difficult to move, and the whole world was made of sludge. Wolf kicked his feet free of the stirrups and sat loose in the saddle. The way ahead was a tunnel stretching to a black hole, the way back was smothered by cloud, and the young man had come to the end of the ride. He slipped from the stallion's back and began to walk, reins in one hand, rope in the other. The clump of hooves behind him was comforting.

He went by the Wellerson place, lurking in its hollow like something unhealthy. There was nobody around but he could feel the eyes scratching his back and the dislike behind them. He went by the Hockaday homestead, dependable and welcoming on its knoll to the other side of the road, smoke lifting from the chimney in a friendly way.

Joanie was in the kitchen rolling pillows of dough for their daily bread. If she knew of the man leading horses past her home she may have faltered in her work, but she kept behind the table where she would be safe from infection. Emmett was at the side of the barn splitting logs, leaning back with the axe before swinging it hard, and if he knew of the black and the chestnut on the track below it might just have been an aberration and nothing more.

And all that Wolf knew as he passed them by was the pale form of the animal trapped in Emmett's corral. He caught the shake of mane as the palomino's head came up to meet his stare. The stallion twisted around on its back legs and the Hockaday dog started to howl as though something had been set loose. Emmett looked up suddenly from the wood pile, but Wolf had already moved on and there was nothing to see.

The dog's bark followed the man who was following the road into the valley; the place he had thought of as home. Vixen was alone in the corral, red coat gleaming as though rain had been falling. But the ground was hard and dry and ringing from hooves as Wolf Shadow led the horses in: the gelding to one enclosure and the stallion to the other. Night Dancer obeyed him, as docile as a kitten, and the man closed the gate and took the saddle to store in the barn. No ghosts this night, no memories to haunt or claws reaching out from the shadows; everything had been cleansed and Wolf alone was sullied.

The yard was silent; it was as if the chickens had flown and the animals had fled, and no living thing was waiting to give him welcome. Wolf worked the pump and held his head under the splash of water. The bloodied drips rained pink across his shirt. His hat had gone – he had left it behind in the doctor's house or on the path outside, and he could never go back for it. The wearing of it had made him respectable, like a badge of honour; but it wouldn't be needed now.

He pushed his hair away with wet hands and went towards the house. They were all inside, and they looked up as he entered. The fire had not been lit and the room was cold, but Wolf was as hot as fever. It was the sickness in him, the disease.

Sage was waiting by the empty hearth. The children flanked her, one on each side. Colt had his eyes to the floor; he was blinking and trying not to cry, but Clove nestled under her mother's arm, gaping at her father as if she was trying to find a way through the tangle inside his head.

Wolf looked at his son and his daughter, and then he

looked at Sage. Her face could have been made of stone, and even in the shady room her eyes were glinting shards of ice.

He stumbled when Martha hit him. He had not seen her heading for him with something in her hand. She raised it to strike again and again, until it cracked; and he let her do it, his ears ringing. She came at him once more but Sage was there too. She wrenched what was left of a wooden spoon from Martha's grip and threw it across the room. It clattered to the floor, and then everything was still again.

'Enough, Ma,' Sage said tugging at her mother's arm. 'That is enough.'

Martha tried to pull away from her grip. 'I always said that if he ever hurt you, then I would kill him.' She turned to the man she had been beating with the only weapon she could find. 'Because you no longer deserve to live.'

Left alone by the dead fireside, Clove had begun to cry with the sound of a deer caught in a trap. It raised the hairs on the back of her father's neck because there was such loss in his daughter's lament. Martha flapped her hand; holding it to her mouth she hurried to the child, stumbling over feet that were unused to hurrying until she had folded her granddaughter in a hug. The sound went on, and then it faded and stopped; the echo it left was unnerving.

Wolf felt the impact of Sage's eyes. She seemed calm but she was shaking, and her fists were tight, as though she was afraid of her own need to beat him. 'So, it has happened at last,' she said. 'I always knew that one day it would.'

Nothing has happened; that is what he wanted to say. He wanted to hold her so tightly that every fear would be vanquished and she would be convinced. He shook his head because there were words that had to be spoken and he couldn't make them come.

He flinched when she raised her arm, but it was to push aside the hair that was dripping pump water across his brow, and to touch the raw place where the stone had hit him as he walked away from Lucy Ryker's triumph and her husband's wretchedness. It was a gentle touch, filled with love, and Wolf took her hand and held it to his heart. They stood like that for a moment that seemed endless, still joined together as they had always been joined together, and then she eased her hand away from his, leaving a chill on his skin.

'You have to go now,' she said, shadows filling the gap between them.

'Sage.'

She hesitated, on the edge of torn, and then she leaned towards him, so close that he could see her pupils dilating. 'Once you were wholesome, but now you are contaminated,' she said. 'And I cannot bear to look at you.'

She turned her back on him, she walked towards her mother and her daughter. Her son was standing alone – as abandoned as Wolf had been when he too was a young boy, brought to live in an alien place where nothing made sense.

Colt lifted his head, an older head that should not belong on a child's shoulders, and the eyes he raised to his father were burning black.

Wolf Shadow turned around and went out of the house. He did not look back.

NINETEEN

THERE WERE two pillows on the bed, but the night before she and Wolf had needed just the one. His body had been supple and his arms had been strong, and when she came he had held her and kissed her and told her that he would always love her. And she knew he had meant every word.

But was it like that also with the doctor's wife? Did she cry out when she came with him as though the pleasure was as intense as pain? Did he stroke her hair and tell her that he would always love her? Was he on his way to lie with her now in another bed, another life?

Sage stared through the window as far as she could before distance was swallowed by dark. The temperature had dropped swiftly, it was squally and cold that night. She had wrapped herself in a heavy shawl, but Wolf was out there with nothing heavy to keep him warm. His jacket was hanging on a hook by the porch; he had left the house too quickly to take it with him. He hadn't taken anything, not even a saddle for the black stallion. That was still where he had stowed it in the barn after returning bloody from the town.

She'd doused the lamp and tried to sleep, but the darkness had pressed on her eyelids as if it was trying to get inside her head. She wasn't clear about the time, but she knew there were many hours to live through before the sky paled and the sun brought back the warmth. And Wolf must be so cold out there.

Damn Lucy Ryker with her pretty gowns and glossy hair; with her maid and her parlour and her ways of the world! Damn her welcoming smile and her friendship and her help and the constant threat of her hunger!

Sage rubbed her face and her hands came away wet. When she shut her eyes everything disappeared behind a greater blackness, and that was good. Just as Wolf had disappeared that evening, walking away and closing the door behind him so that it was as if he had never been. That too was good.

Wasn't it?

He lost his identity in the dark. He lost his body as well; there was nothing to see when he looked down. But that didn't matter.

There could be no sleep for him that night, the angry weather was going to make sure of it. But sleep would have been an intrusion into what he was planning to do, so that didn't matter either.

The wind rose up and dealt with the clouds, and stars began to emerge from a heartening sky. At one point a mass of light was sparkling up there, throwing some reflection down to earth. The perspective of the landscape had changed, and Wolf could see the roofline of the Hockaday house, still vague, but close enough to reach if he wanted. And what he wanted was for the taking to a man who had lost everything else.

Night Dancer had long forsaken the wind-swept plains of its wildness and was behaving like a pampered pet; chilled and restless, it had become accustomed to a refuge and regular feeds. But many stallions had passed through Wolf's hands in the time that he had made the

Madison farm his home, and Dancer was never meant to be anything more than one in the line. The next one was down there in his neighbour's corral.

Leading the black horse, Wolf followed the slope to the trackway. His shoulders tensed as they drew closer to the farm, but there was nothing to worry about. The clack of hooves had been muffled by the wind storm and everyone at the Hockaday homestead was asleep – even the dog tied up outside the house. The dog that Emmett would now have to tie outside Wolf's house once again so that Sage and the children could sleep safely. Because they would be vulnerable without him. Because the day may come when Sage regretted that they were without him.

The wind was hectic, rattling with urgency, and Wolf was glad of its protection. Beneath its howl nothing would hear the corral gate being opened or the man who stepped inside or the scream of the horse that waited there, head lowered like a bull. Nothing would hear as Wolf stood before the palomino, shielded only by the soft rain of words that dropped from his mouth.

Time passed and the words kept coming.

Clouds stretched and waned and the fight went on.

The dog in the yard was dreaming of meat. It woke once to the sound of pounding and sharp cries, but the wind rose up in fury and whisked the noise away. It whisked away the scent of man and horse, and the hound huffed, falling asleep again with a paw across its muzzle.

Starlight blazed and died and blazed again, and the stallion's pale hide was a blaze of light itself in the hours before dawn. But the horse was at a standstill and the time had come. Near to collapse, Wolf grabbed the mane and hauled himself to the tawny back. Only willpower kept him from falling when the palomino reared.

The stallion was manic. It careered towards the fence, gashing the man's knee on splintered wood. It snapped at his thigh; its teeth caught at cloth and flesh before Wolf could wrench the head around. It reared again and then again, and Wolf Shadow felt himself slipping. He gripped the flanks, hard enough to crush the animal's ribs.

The horse's teeth were yellow in the lifting darkness, nipping at the man's legs – first one and then the other. Tearing skin that had been torn already by Daniel Ryker's boots. Wolf's blood was spotting the horse's hide but he could feel no pain; that would come later, when the battle was over; when one of them had won and the other had been lost.

Wind-howl dropped to a murmur. And the stallion screamed. In the yard the big dog woke, at first confused and then frenzied. It leaped to the end of its rope. The collar crushed its windpipe but still it barked.

A light flickered behind a window in the house and Emmett Hockaday wrestled with the door. But by the time he had wrenched it open the stallion was already tearing away towards the far hills with the man clamped to its back.

The dog whimpered with the pain in its throat, and left behind like payment in return for the palomino, Night Dancer stamped alone in the corral where the gate was still swinging.

Day was born under a caul of cloud, shredded like torn flags. The landscape was unrestrained with burrows and grit, falling away over sudden drops and hazardous with menace. One careless step and a leg would snap as easily as a dead branch, but the palomino was reckless. If Wolf wanted it to survive he had to dismount, but he wanted more than that. He leaned forwards until he was lying flat along the white crest. The recoil trapped his tongue between his teeth. He had to spit out the blood before he could speak.

Breath husk-dry in its throat, the stallion was flagging. Words floated like feathers over its head; some fell away behind but others remained, clinging like Wolf to the chestnut hide. And it was only when the animal began to listen that the ride came to an end.

Breaking free of the horizon, the sun had started to climb. Birds were calling. Little creatures sniffed the air and slipped back underground, although they had nothing to fear from the horse that was standing so still. The wind was failing, sighing as it died, and it was the palomino's laboured breathing that was shaking the dust by its hooves.

The chill breeze was sharp across Wolf's skin, for he was sodden with the stallion's sweat as well as his own. And pain was coming now that the adrenaline had settled, especially where the horse's teeth had torn and the corral's fence had ripped. He moaned as he slid to the ground, leaning against the golden flank as if the animal was a crutch and he would have fallen without it.

He tried again to speak the ancient language that had followed them for the hour of the ride. Or maybe it had been two hours, Wolf had not noticed when the night ended and the day began, for he and the stallion had been joined by something that surpassed time. His voice was made of smoke and wisped away, but perhaps he had no more need of it, since enough magic might already have been sprinkled into the beast's heart.

Now was a good time to rest, and he crumpled to the ground beside the horse's legs – two with white socks and two without. The same markings flaunted by the first palomino he had tamed to bear a rider; the same white blaze as that between the eyes of the stallion he had remembered for ten whole years. But memory was unstable, it floated in wishful thinking and changed shape as the wind blew. Because hadn't that other horse died in a canyon with Haine Madison's bullet in its brain?

Breathing more steadily, the palomino was recovering its strength. Wolf forced himself to his feet, gritting his teeth against the pain. It was time to go now, to ride away on the rare wild beast with its dangerous bite and its taste for blood.

He had coveted Emmett's property. He had stolen a stallion and broken his good friendship with a neighbour, but how long could that friendship have lasted after he had forsaken everything else for a few minutes' pleasure in another man's pasture? Surely the bond between the Hockadays and the Madison farm would be stronger now that the infection had been removed. One day they might forget that he had ever existed.

One day they might also forgive.

TWENTY

THE SUN was not yet fully awake but Sage had been up for hours. That was what happened when the house was tight with the slumber of others and noisy with ghosts and clamouring things. She hadn't wanted to see what the ghosts were showing her over the long and sleepless night, but she was so crazy with fatigue that she imagined movement where there was none; hidden hands touched her face, and the long dead bided their time behind uneasy doors.

Early in the morning she put a saddle on the gelding and set off for town. All were still abed, although noise was rising from the Hockaday homestead. Voices that clashed, wrenched and angry. That was how it appeared, but all sound can be split asunder by the clatter of hooves and the jounce of the ride. And it wasn't Emmett or Joanie that the young woman needed to face that day, not yet, not until she had attended to other needs.

The road to Oasis felt shorter now that the town had begun to reach out from lengthened streets. A sprouting of new neighbours was bringing recognition to the farm in the valley dip; the place that had once been spurned by all who knew of the drunkard and his bastard son.

It was easier to think of that boy, the one she had been told to call kin as soon as he arrived at the farm. Sage had been eight years old on the day her father had ridden an exhausted mare into the yard with Cub sitting before him in the saddle. All that time ago, and she could still remember the first sight of her new brother.

Martha had been staring through the window. She said something under her breath that had sounded like an obscenity, and rushed out to the yard as the flaxen-haired boy slipped from the horse, his sight shrouded and his thoughts with them. Sage had followed, hiding behind her mother's skirts and the mass of hair around her own face.

The boy had stared out at the place where he had been brought to live. His eyes were clear and as brown as a hound's, until the light picked up a glimmer of colour. For a moment it had seemed that there was gold inside. It glinted, like a sudden spark, and then it was gone.

As he had grown so had the shine; but it had always been rare, as gold is. When he looked at her with that light in his eyes it felt as if he was showering her with riches. It had been like that when they were two frightened children living under the lash of her father's tongue, and nothing had changed. She still melted when Wolf Shadow shone his light inside her. She. Still. Melted.

Damn him! And damn the gold in those eyes that had lusted after another woman.

The gelding was galloping now, as fast as Sage's pulse. She brought it to a canter, but the horse was spooked, jumping from imagined horrors at the side of the road. By the time she had ridden into the main street Sage was thrumming with tension; and from something wilder. Maybe the sickness that had infected Wolf Shadow had slithered into her own veins. Maybe she was the daughter of the beast Madison in more than name alone.

Oasis was still quiet, as though the fresh new day had

brought calm. Nothing bad could happen where there were peaceful byways and decent stores and civilised inhabitants. Upheaval came in on the shoes of those who lived on the periphery, and Sage was there to expose the truth of it in the house that lurked behind a railed fence and a blowsy garden, halfway down the street.

There were very few people abroad at that time of the morning. And those who had ventured out stared at the woman riding alone through the town; hair loose around her shoulders and fire in her eyes. But Sage didn't notice anyone who noticed her.

Neither did she see the door of the sheriff's office open, or Andy Parnell taking air on the sidewalk and stretching away sleep before wrapping a gun belt around his waist. She didn't see him, but he watched as she journeyed past – dismounting outside the Rykers' house, shuffling reins around the hitching post, lifting off the sack fastened to the saddle's horn.

Now that leaves had fallen, the trees in the doctor's garden appeared undernourished, gaps between the branches exposing windows where drapes had been drawn. To keep things out. Or maybe to keep things in. From a distance the dwelling seemed peaceful – but any place will look peaceful when it is in hiding.

Sage reached for the bell pull by the door, just as she had on that other morning when the light had not yet risen. When they rode the chestnut into town – she and the boy who had taken one beating too many. And because that morning had been the start of everything, she turned away from the politeness of the bell and banged the door instead, three times with her fist.

The noise was intrusive, and drapes were twitched in casements on the other side of the street. But Sage was oblivious as she waited by the door, staring up at the window where she had once met a woman with a honey-hued braid.

'Just stay there,' the woman had called. And perhaps it was the worst advice to follow, although at the time her only thought had been to protect the boy. But now that he was grown and gone, Sage had a mind to protect herself instead.

The front door opened before the echoes of her summons had shuddered away, and it wasn't the Ryker woman standing there but her husband, turned sepia between the new day's light and the house shadows. He was fully dressed but rumpled, like a man who had slept in his clothes, or had not slept at all. His mouth fidgeted when he saw her on the step, and for a moment he blocked her entry as though he had no desire to deal with her. But Sage was not going anywhere.

Ryker closed the door behind her and the day disappeared – along with the interested parties across the street. It was suddenly darker. No house lights had been attended to since the evening before. And there was a strange mustiness floating in the air, that seemed to carry something heavier than just the spin of dust motes.

The walls of the passageway leaned towards her, but the man blocked her path when she tried to move. He couldn't look at her; his glance neared and then jerked away, as if there was something repellent about the unwanted guest; the young woman with the same wild eyes as his own.

Sage could not wait. 'Where is she?'

'What?' He was looking at her now, but there wasn't much else behind the question, as though he had been emptied.

'Your wife.' Sage spat out the words and they fell to the floor like stones. 'Where is she?'

Perhaps the words had spurred a memory, because he seemed to recover; tugging the front of his jacket, trying to stand straight. 'Lucy is asleep upstairs.'

'Asleep?' Sage laughed. 'I am surprised that she can find the peace for it.'

'My wife has been very tired recently.'

'As have I, Daniel. And as have you, which any fool can see. And yet neither of us has found sleep this night.'

'No. Not this night.'

He turned away again, as though he really had trouble looking at the woman who had come to his house early in the morning to find the same answers that he wanted to the same questions he had already asked.

'Can I assist you in my wife's stead, Miss Madison?' he said.

'Fetch her down, Daniel.'

'I would rather not.'

'And I would rather you did.'

'That might be a problem, Sage,' he said, 'because I'm finding it difficult to be near her at present. Do you understand?'

'More than you realise.'

Ryker shook his head, bumping the wall when he stepped backwards, as though he wasn't sure which way to go. Shadows were creeping towards him, threatening to engulf. Sage reached out and touched his arm so that he should not disappear, but the flesh inside his sleeve had already shrivelled to nothing.

'Dr Ryker, you must come and sit down,' she said, and her voice echoed as though she was standing alone in the shrouds of half-light, talking to the invisible. She grabbed him and tugged. The husk of the man seemed to inflate, and this time her fingers met muscle.

'Did he send you here?'

Sage rocked back on her heels as if she had been struck. 'He did not.'

'Hiding, is he?'

The small corridor was as heavy as the darkness in her head, but there was a half-moon of daylight shining through the glass at the top of the house door, and she gazed up as though it might guide her back to reality. 'Oh yes, I believe Wolf Shadow must be hiding.'

'You believe?' Ryker frowned. 'You mean you don't know where he is?'

Sage started to speak, but she had to swallow the ache in her throat and start again. 'I have not seen him since his return from town yesterday. He returned bedraggled.'

Bedraggled, stumbling into the yard with the two horses, his shirt smudged by blood and dirt, his face torn, the stink of whisky on his breath. Years before it had been her father who had come back to the farm in that state. Perhaps it was to be the condition of any man who took on the mantle of that godforsaken steading.

'I told him to go,' she said, 'because I could not bear to have sight of him.'

She had hit him before he left. She had followed him out to the porch, flailing like a mad woman with no constraints, and he had stood with his hands by his sides as if he welcomed it. She had hurt him in the places where he was already hurt, she knew that by the shock in his eyes, but it seemed to encourage her to greater frenzy. She only stopped when she saw Colt by the side of the house, watching his mother as she fought his father in the yard with murder in her fists.

If Wolf had noticed his son standing there he gave no indication, but he had taken the cessation of the attack as his dismissal and felt his way to the corral where the black horse was fussing.

Eyes mad, Night Dancer had bucked as the man drew near, wicked hooves narrowly missing his face, but Wolf Shadow wasn't going to wait for the stallion to settle. He had thrown himself up to the horse's back, gripping with his knees when it reared, pulling away from the enclosure fence in case the animal should impale itself on broken wood. And he left the farm battling the fury of a stallion so that he didn't have to think of anything else.

'My husband has gone, and your wife is still here, asleep in her own bed.' Sage searched for the doctor's eyes and held him fast with the intensity in hers. 'I have lost and she is still winning. Why is that, Daniel?'

He seemed to shrink, as though his spine was eroding. 'We have children…'

'As do I.' She stared at him. 'But of course, mine are the children of a half-breed and yours the offspring of a higher race.'

'That is hardly fair.'

'Fair?' She laughed; the sound of it scratched her ears. 'Shall we ask your wife to tell us what is fair?'

She stepped quickly towards the stairs and had already started climbing before Ryker understood her intention. He went to stop her, moving stiffly as though he had become an old man overnight, but she stopped by herself, staring up at the twins who had appeared at the top in their night clothes, dolls snuggled in their arms.

Lucy was standing behind them, wearing a primrose yellow dress sprinkled with little white flowers that winked when she moved, and her hair had been carefully brushed to a halo around her head. She was smiling.

'Why, good morning, Miss Madison,' she said. 'It is a delight to see you, of course, although perhaps a touch early for a social visit.'

Sage had started to sway, and Daniel Ryker steadied

her with his hands at her shoulders. He stared up at the woman; at the children she was using as a shield. He wondered when it was that his wife had turned into someone else, and then he realised that she had always been this way.

'I think you should come down and join us, Lucy.'

Her eyes were wide on his. 'Oh, do you now?'

Bella looked down at her father and the lady he was helping to the bottom of the stairs. Mrs Shadow was very pretty; she lived on a farm with Clove. Bella liked to play with Clove, and Clove's mama was nice. But she seemed different now.

She and Papa were holding each other up, and that didn't feel right.

'Is Clove here too?' Bella said, staring at her mother, but Mama seemed different as well, and the little girl felt giddy and held her doll even tighter.

'Go to your room for a while, will you, Bella?' her father called up, his voice gentle. 'Dulcie, go with your sister. Find yourselves a game to play.'

'Mama?'

Her mother smelled nice in her daisy-sprigged dress, but there was a chalkiness about her face that Bella didn't like, and there was more than just a question in the word.

'Your mama has something to do down here,' her father said. 'Why don't you both find something to play with and I'll come up and see you in a while?'

Dulcie turned to go. Bella raised a finger as though she was about to point to what was happening at the bottom of the stairs, but her sister grabbed her hand and dragged her to their bedroom. The slam of the door echoed through the house.

Their mother watched them leave as though she had no wish to be left on her own. But perhaps she realised that it was already too late. She fixed her smile and descended, stair by stair, shiny boots flashing in and out of the yellow hem, all the way to the ground and straight through to the parlour. Brightness jumped into the room when she pulled back the heavy drapes, emphasising the lines on her face.

Sage stood on the threshold, holding the sack she had lifted from her saddle. Ryker placed himself between the two women, but the new light made him appear dusty and insubstantial, and the safeguard he offered was as flimsy as paper.

Everything about Sage was animated by the shine through the window; but standing with her back to the daylight, Lucy wasn't easy to see. 'Is there anything I can do for you, Sage?' she said, and there was a slight echo in her voice as though she was speaking from the other room.

Sage waited a while before answering. 'You have done enough already,' she said. 'You have stolen what is mine and left me with nothing.'

Lucy shook her head. 'You still have him,' she said, with a bitterness that split her sweet mask. Her husband winced at the words, but she didn't notice.

'Not any more,' Sage said. 'Wolf Shadow has gone.'

There was a moment of silence before Lucy could speak again. 'What do you mean, gone?'

'He took himself away. He disappeared.' Sage jerked the words; they became a song, a beating heart. 'We have both lost him, Mrs Ryker.'

Lucy gave a cry like something that was dying. She lifted a hand to her face and her husband saw them again, his wife and the man joined together, her mouth still wet from his mouth; still making those unbearable sounds. He grabbed a chair and squeezed the back until the wood creaked, and Sage pushed past him to stand in front of the yellow dress. She opened the neck of the sack and began to pull out the contents.

'I kept everything you have given me over the last ten years, because I believed that they had the value of gifts from a true friend.' She held each item up to catch the light before throwing it at the woman's feet. 'But now that you have proved yourself worthless, Lucy Ryker, you can have them all back.'

A pair of kid gloves, a richly trimmed bonnet, lace petticoats, a mother of pearl trinket box – they were produced from the sack like rabbits from a magician's hat. A carriage clock, silk ribbons, a silver bracelet hung with little bells that tinkled as it landed.

Lucy stood surrounded by the sad detritus of another life, one that was so broken it could never be repaired. All those little gifts she had brought to the wooden house in the valley dip, in the hope that she might catch sight of Wolf Shadow out in the yard or working by the barn, or weaving around the compound on one of his stallions, bending to whisper magic to the horse's ear – just as she hoped that one day he would whisper to hers.

It seemed paltry now; as tawdry as cheapness always is. The sense of loss began to creep up Lucy's body from the floor, filling her limbs with lead, so that when Sage discarded the final item from the exhausted sack, she could do nothing to stop the ivory-backed hand mirror exploding by her feet, shards scattering like jagged seed heads across the room.

'I have no need to wish you ill luck, Lucy Ryker,' Sage said, looking from the woman in her fine yellow dress to the husband who was holding the chair as though he might never stand straight again. 'For I believe that you already have enough.'

She kicked the gifts aside as she left, and a fragment of mirror glass skimmed across the floor, swathing the ceiling with reflected light like a beam of joy.

TWENTY-ONE

THE CUTS on his face had begun to crust but his muscles were still throbbing from the battle with the palomino. Exhaustion was making fools of his eyes, bringing the ground closer and then pushing it away. It was getting difficult to see where he was going. The only thing he could do was just that – to keep on going for as long as possible.

Bending to its rider's will and the disturbance of his voice, the horse had reluctantly settled to a lope through the new landscape. It had been a slow journey from night into day, shadows starting long and lean and blooming into something portly as the morning passed. The warmth that came with them was welcome. But at noon they began to spread the other way, and the air cooled. Soon it would turn sharp. Soon there would be another cold night with no protection, and the stallion might feel the pull of the wild and scorn the man's hold on it. What would happen when his strength had evaporated, when the beast had thrown him and run? How long could he keep on going then?

Wolf Shadow retched, his throat scorching as though he had been breathing fire. He swallowed to quench the burning, but the tang still remained.

He tasted the smoke before he saw it, puffing soft pillows into the sky just beyond the cluster of broken rocks that collected before him, their steps reaching up to a humpbacked rise. He slowed the palomino to a walk and the animal moved stiffly, wanting only to toss him to the ground. But it was still in thrall to the young man's power; it had no option but to follow his voice to the top of the climb and the view that opened below.

The pillows of smoke were rising from a fire of broken branches and a man was sitting beside it, swaying as he stirred a savoury mess in a battered pot. The smell of food rose up, hitting the back of Wolf's nose, and he gulped as though he already had it in his mouth. The palomino stamped. A scatter of loose stones escaped, chasing each other like children over the ground, and the man looked up.

'Who is it?' His voice was clear, and carried easily to the one on the horse, but he was peering through the haze as if searching for something he had lost. 'Who's there?'

Wolf raised a hand. 'I mean you no harm,' he called. 'But I would like to share your fire for a while.'

'Is there anyone with you?'

'No. I am alone.'

The man tipped his head; he could have been listening for guidance. Perhaps it was favourable, for he nodded. 'You are welcome to share my fire,' he said. 'That at least is free.'

The stallion baulked when Wolf urged it forward, as though it could sense that its rider was weakening. Maybe the language from a cracked throat was no longer a strong enough tether. Wolf was losing power, but it was the earth's power that was helping him now, for the ground had grown treacherous with broken stones and the horse stumbled.

It lost its footing and slid to the bottom of the slope,

rearing, biting the air, and the man by the fire got to his feet. He seemed dangerously unconcerned about the flail of hooves and the hungry teeth.

'Can you get that animal to the trees just yonder?' he shouted, pointing in the direction of a spinney, barely visible through the campfire smoke. Hidden by nature and its own colouring, Wolf could see a cloudy grey mare, chewing from a nosebag.

He nodded. The palomino was fighting his decision and he swore as he wrenched the horse towards the trees. But the man was there first. He had moved fast.

'I believe you might need this,' he called, and threw Wolf a coil of rope.

It was just long enough to make a tie, and to hitch the stallion to a tough trunk, scarred by the teeth of creatures that had chewed its bark for insects. The palomino chewed in its turn but didn't like the taste. And then it fell quiet – under the grey's influence, maybe. The old mare shook her head as though she had seen it all before, and stretched for titbits at the bottom of the bag.

Wary of the pain in his ribs, Wolf eased himself down beside the fire. The heat caressed his face, making the cuts sting even as it was soothing the ache in his bones. The man had a coffee pot bubbling at the edge of the blaze, and he poured some into a dented mug. Wolf nodded his thanks and drank it in four swallows; then he waited until the bitter dark taste and the burn had subsided before he could breathe again.

The man passed over a dish of the savoury mess with a hunk of bread and took the mug away to pour some coffee for himself.

'It is a curious thing to see,' he said, nodding over to the trees, which had already started to vanish into the twilight. 'A man riding the land on a wild stallion.'

Wolf finished eating and returned the plate, wiping his mouth with the back of his hand. 'As curious as one who camps alone.'

'I guess so.' His companion smiled. 'Although I have no trouble being alone, whereas you are building up more trouble than you need with that beast.'

A burning stick had fallen by Wolf's feet, and he kicked it back into the blaze. 'You may be right.'

'So what is the story behind it?'

'Why do you think there is a story?'

'Because it is a curious thing. And I am a curious man.'

'You have your business and I have mine.' Wolf got to his feet. His ribs crunched with pain and he winced.

The man looked up at the sudden movement. 'Where are you going?'

'I am grateful for the food, but not the conversation.'

Wolf tried to walk, but something had gone wrong with his legs. He crumpled to the ground like a baby. The last thing he knew before the darkness came down was the man standing over him with a blanket.

He was awake before he opened his eyes. The ground beneath his body was unforgiving, but the blanket had kept him dry despite the dew. There was something wrapped around his head, covering the stone gash he had received outside the Rykers' house.

He was lying close to the campfire, and that was the first thing he saw, smouldering in the morning damp, its heart alight and shining on the face of the man who crouched above it. The coffee pot was still bubbling at the edge of the blaze, and its aroma enriched the air when the man filled the tin mug and held it out.

Wolf sat up slowly enough to ease the pain in his back,

stretching carefully until his ribs warned him against it. He touched the bandage by his temple and took the mug, allowing the contents to cool slightly before drinking. 'Thank you,' he said as the coffee's heat spread its pleasure inside him.

The man shrugged. 'For a bite to eat and a mouthful of coffee? No need to thank me.'

'For those things as well,' Wolf said, and tried to stand, but the man stopped him with a hand to his shoulder.

'Where do you think you're going now?'

Wolf shook his head and looked over to the slope down which the stallion had slithered the evening before. He had been too feeble to hold the horse then, but he was stronger now. He knew that. 'I have to leave,' he said, but made no further attempt to move.

His host refilled the mug for himself, crouching by the fire. 'Are you running from the man who wants to kill you?'

'I am not running from anyone.' But there was Sage, watching him from the yard as he rode away; there was Emmett Hockaday, who had been a good neighbour to a horse thief.

'You are bloody, my friend, and your ribs are cracked. That has either been done by a man who wishes you ill, or maybe you were trampled by the stallion.'

Wolf stared over at the bunch of trees which were clearer in the daylight, but still mottling the coat of the grey horse that rested there. And then he saw the gold shifting between moss-green trunks.

The man had followed his eyes. 'The wild horse is still with us. I don't know why, or how.' He looked back at Wolf with a tilt of his head. 'Do you?'

'I thought he would have run, found his own way.' He

spoke softly, as though to himself.

'Maybe like you, he doesn't run from anyone.'

'Maybe not.' Wolf looked at the man, properly this time. He saw dark hair, already greying at the temples, and kind eyes in a narrow face; eyes that seemed to shift a little as though searching for focus. Wolf quietly raised his hand and moved his fingers.

'I know what you are doing.' The man smiled and the eyes fell into a crinkle of skin. 'I can still see movement, but not much beyond that.'

'I am sorry.'

'And I have grown accustomed to it, therefore I cope. I seem to have developed another sense where there used to be sight.'

'Like curiosity?'

'You could label it as such. But it is strong, my friend, and it tells me that you are in trouble.'

Wolf shrugged. 'The ribs have already told you that.'

'Yes.' The man frowned and the planes of his face fell into shadow. 'But this trouble is greater than cracked ribs.'

The breeze lifted and Wolf shivered in the sudden chill. He stood up to get away from the man's words, and they dropped useless to the ground. It was then that he saw the hills, purple on the horizon, pulling back like a frozen wave. Once they had been the only way ahead for him, and ten years later they still were. His next life was out there, on the other side of the rise and fall.

The man had also climbed to his feet, and it was as if he was watching Wolf as Wolf watched the distance. 'Before you head out on your journey will you tell me your name?'

'Wolf Shadow.' He had no real name when he was a boy, and now he was standing straight and proud at the sound of it.

'Indian?'

'The one who fathered me was an Indian.'

'Is he?'

'He died.'

For a moment the man didn't speak, but his hesitation had seemed to last much longer.

'I am called Shev Deeley,' he said. 'I should like you to remember that, Wolf Shadow.'

His voice had sounded strange and Wolf frowned. 'I will remember that.'

They left the fire chattering to itself and went together to where the horses were tied. The palomino stood on spread legs, grunting a warning as Wolf came near. But it did not try to pull away. The grey mare raised her head, whickering softly as though she approved.

Wolf began to talk as he unfastened the stallion's tether, and its pale hide quivered at the rub of his hand. He led the horse into the clearing, grabbing the feathered mane to pull himself astride.

The other man was suddenly too close.

'Take care! The stallion…'

'The stallion will not hurt me, Wolf Shadow.'

And he was right; the palomino had not moved. It was as though it couldn't even see him standing there, holding up the blanket that had covered Wolf in the night.

'Take this; it will protect you from the cold, if nothing else,' he said, and stepped away. 'Until we meet again, Indian.'

Wolf wrapped the blanket around his waist and turned to thank him, but Shev Deeley had already gone back to his place by the fire. He was sitting there as comfortably as a man in his own home, pouring a dark stream of coffee into the metal mug, raising the drink to the air as though saluting something that only he could see. His eyes were closed, and he was smiling.

Heat from the campfire and the coffee stayed with Wolf like a good memory as he rode the palomino across the land, but after a while the wind rose to sweep hair from his face and the memory went with it, along with the loosened bandage. Only the blanket remained, warm around his body, and the rope that he had fashioned into a halter.

He could ride with ease now that the stallion's fury had dissipated. The terrain was civilised, offering slight resistance as it rose and fell in big waves on an ochre and green sea, crowned with rocks like broken whitecaps. Even so, the hills remained distant, further than Wolf had ever remembered; they seemed to pull away more than they came closer. But it was of little consequence to the man on the wild horse, for this time there was no sheriff on his scent to drag him back to a vicious regime and a coiled whip.

He was no longer a ragged boy known as Cub and his mount was not the stallion Wolf Wind, but nothing else had changed. This was still a ride to freedom, and Sage was still the one he had left behind, just as he had left her before.

Pain squeezed his gut when he thought about her. Maybe she was thinking about him as well, all those miles away. Sending out a silent call as she stood amongst the piles of ordure that gathered in the yard.

TWENTY-TWO

ANIMAL MUCK, mud from the fields, implements that had not been stored after use – it was all strewn across the open space between the rough wooden house and the barn. It was reaching up to the corral where the horses had gathered, and the other one lying empty behind a closed gate where once mustangs had danced to Wolf Shadow's tune as though he controlled their passions as well as their behaviour.

The pond was now little more than a slick of water across the ground, bringing comfort only to the short-winged birds that stayed long enough to drink before flying off to find somewhere better. Sage stood by the slime that was left and wished that she was one of those birds; to lift into the air and forget what it was she was flying from. It seemed so easy for them, so why not for her?

It had always been easy for Wolf to fly. He was like the stallions that passed through his hands, their hearts hungry for freedom. Once she had believed it possible to ground him with responsibility; but it had been a foolish fancy to try and curb the natural wildness of a creature that refused to be tamed.

Sage kicked at a rusty chain that lay beside the dying pond and mud sprayed up, leaving its stink on the hem of her skirt. The chain had moved sluggishly and not far, and she chased it to kick again. It twisted as it rose and crashed against the chopping block, ringing once with a heaviness that made the day seem bleaker. Sage wanted to attack it until it screamed and gasped and all life had gone, but it was already dull and useless. Just another piece of garbage that needed clearing away, along with everything else.

Along with the man she loved. The man she had trusted to love her in return – until he gave that love to another woman.

The air seemed unusually close, as though the day had grown warmer. Or maybe Wolf was on his way back, and he was bringing the heat with him. Sage looked over her shoulder. She didn't notice Emmett Hockaday urging his piebald through the outer yard because she was searching for a pale-haired rider on a black stallion. And the snarl in the words that Emmett had come there to say got caught in his throat when he saw her.

The Sage he knew was a tidy young woman, neatly clothed in garments that while workaday had always been clean; but this Sage was different. She was shabby and her attire was chaotic, as if she had reached for her clothes in the dark. Her hair, that had once sparkled like spun glass, was rough-gathered and straggling. She was peering out through its strands as though she couldn't find her way.

Emmett dismounted, cursing Wolf Shadow silently and roundly – and not for the first time. He took Sage's arm, feeling more bone than flesh through the thin sleeve. She allowed him to lead her towards the house, stepping inside as though that was just the next thing to do.

The window had been blinded with a curtain, as if out of respect for a death, and it took a while for eyes to adjust to the darkness. It was cold as well, for the hearth was bare, and although the stove in the corner glowed red it was a weak light, and there was no sign of any firewood nearby apart from a nest of slivers.

'Let me bring in some wood for the fire,' Emmett said, but too heartily, for he only wanted an excuse to get away from the strangeness that reached out from the walls, threatening to wrap him in its gloom.

When Sage answered he thought it odd that her voice should have altered as drastically as her appearance, until he realised that it was Martha Madison who had spoken. She had come into the room as silently as a ghost and he had not noticed.

'There is very little wood left,' Martha said, as though this was an acceptable fact. 'I believe that Colt will find more for us later, once he is home from school.'

Emmett didn't know what to say and Martha nodded as if she understood. 'I should like to offer you some refreshment, Mr Hockaday, but we are also very low on coffee and suchlike.'

He stared at her. 'What on earth has been going on here?'

The old woman laughed, for maybe she found it an amusing question. 'Sage's man has gone,' she said. 'And he seems to have taken with him everything that was keeping us together.'

'Yes, I know he's gone!'

Hockaday remembered the palomino galloping from his enclosure with Wolf Shadow clinging to its back; and the dog that barked a warning just too late to stop it happening.

'I know he's gone,' he said again, sealing his mouth before he could add – And so does Sheriff Parnell.

'Once a miscreant, always a miscreant,' Parnell had

declared, with some relish, after Emmett had ridden to town with news of the crime. 'That man first tasted jail back in Clay Russett's day, and when I've caught him, he shall have a chance to taste it all over again.'

Emmett turned to where Sage was still standing by the door. She seemed so brittle that he dared not take her arm in case it should snap. But Martha had no such compunction, coming forward with her own protection until the two women had merged into one darkness.

He felt pity for them both, but he was also feeling exasperation, and an overriding anger towards the man he had hitherto been glad to call friend.

But at least there would be no mercy for the horse thief once the lawman had tracked him down; despite the trade-off of the black stallion that Wolf had left behind, its reins tossed over the broken fence of his neighbour's corral.

'Do you have any idea where he is now, Sage?'

Emmett wondered if she had heard him, but she swallowed before she could speak. 'I told him to go. And so he did.'

He shook his head. 'Why has this happened?'

'Do you not know, Mr Hockaday?' Martha's voice came from the gloom. It was too eerie, and Emmett shivered. 'Have you not heard the news?' she said.

For the last few days wrath had kept him at his own homestead, shoring up the damage that Wolf had left behind, cursing the man's name and pointlessly asking himself why.

Asking the sheriff the same thing when he reported the theft.

'That man has brought mischief into my town,' Parnell had said. 'From all accounts he has been trouble for nigh on twenty years, and you shouldn't have to dig too deeply into his miserable past to learn the reason why.'

Emmett stood in the darkness waiting for the news that he hadn't heard, but Martha had closed her mouth to a tight line, as if it wasn't really her place to tell him.

And then he realised that the little girl was there as well; it was as though she had materialised through the wall. She was holding him with eyes that seemed too knowledgeable for a child of six.

Something tugged the back of his head; it felt like his mind was being manipulated. He dragged his eyes away and the tugging ceased, but it had left an echo of a dark form, and with it came the impression of danger.

Emmett felt a shiver go through his whole body. He didn't want to be standing in that haunted room with the three silent figures, but he was their neighbour and he was a good man. He had helped them when Wolf Shadow took himself away that other time, and now he had to help them again. He had to get light into their lives, warmth into their hearts and food into their stomachs.

'You are all coming back with me,' he said, fitting the hat to his head. 'Joanie would welcome it. She will have a stew waiting on the stove, bread from the oven – you know how she is.'

'Joanie is a good person,' Sage said, but wistfully, as though that was something she herself could never be.

'She sure is,' Emmett said, herding the two women to the door, the little girl floating behind like a shadow.

He could bring them wood for the fire and oil for the lamps, and the glut of produce that his wife would no doubt have stored away in her cupboards. He could lend them the dog to keep the homestead healthy at night and help them to sew their lives back together.

But he could not promise a happy ending for the spineless coward who had left them to face a pitiful future alone, because Andy Parnell was already on his tail. And with the scent of prey in his nostrils the sheriff of Oasis was a hound with a ferocious bite.

TWENTY-THREE

NIGHT FELL abruptly and lasted too long. Wolf lay shuddering under Shev Deeley's blanket. Worms were crawling over his head, he could feel them rippling through his skull, but it was the scorch of Colt's hatred that had kept him from sleep. Soon the branding would scar, leaving a reminder of his son's dismissal, like the silver lines that still remained of the final beating the cub had taken from Haine Madison's hands. Wolf Shadow's history was inscribed on his back, but he was the only one who would never read it.

Emmett's rare wild beast was feeding from the ground; it came closer and snuffled at his face. Its breath flooded his skin, receded, flooded once more, and then the animal's tongue rasped him from cheek to brow, taking in his sweat as though he was a salt lick.

Wolf gripped the rough rope halter and the fall of mane, and the horse raised its head and lifted him to his feet. His ribs were mending, they did not scream so much; but the wound in his thigh throbbed with fury, for the palomino's bite had been deep. He gritted his teeth and climbed to the stallion's back, wrapping the blanket around his waist.

Another day's ride had begun – leaving behind what used to be for what was to come. And every minute of it was going to be a challenge.

This landscape was as grey as cloud, broken with splashes of colour where green stuff grew bravely from deep roots, or where fresh rainfall reunited water courses like a meeting of old friends. The sun was a phoenix rising through fire, warm enough at least to allay the shuddering. Wolf took shaky breaths to feed his strength, but for days now there had been little to eat, and his stomach felt brutalised.

Morning passed very slowly, ending by a shallow pool where the stallion stopped to drink. Fresh droppings and ravaged earth gave evidence of other animals that had also stopped to take their fill; big creatures that had killed and left fear hanging like a mist above the water.

Wolf slid from the horse's back and his legs would not hold him; he slumped to the ground, crawled to the poolside and drank from the cup of his hands. But he drank too quickly and his belly was repulsed. He vomited it back, voiding all the gathered strength with it, and then he stretched out beside the mess and stared at the sky.

It was a good day and small clouds were up there, drifting along on their own breeze, changing from shape to shape as they passed, as if they couldn't make up their minds what they wanted to be.

Everything that Wolf had wanted to be seemed irrelevant now. He had destroyed with the fire in his blood all that he had achieved over the past ten years. The woman he lived for no longer needed him, his brave son had rejected him, his special daughter had closed her mind to him – he knew that as if she had told him herself.

When Clove was barely a week old he had ridden off with her on the back of a half-tamed stallion, cradling her tiny body in the crook of his arm, his head resting beside hers as he whispered magic to both his horse and his baby daughter. On their return, Martha had bruised him with a cooking spoon for his recklessness. Just as she had done after he'd quenched his lust with the doctor's wife.

Lucy Ryker. There she was again, the woman whose obsessions had brought him to the edge of starvation, alone in the hills with a wild stallion that had licked his face to keep him alive for one more day. A day that would soon be over. He knew it and cared little. All he wanted to do was wait for the darkness.

Although that wouldn't be what Lucy wanted. He could see her face in the clouds and her mouth moving. There was no sound, for the words were in his head.

'I didn't struggle to save a brave boy's life so that a foolish man should allow it to slip away,' she might have been saying. 'You have to get up, Wolf Shadow. Find Liberation. Find the red-haired girl who nursed you back to health and watched you ride away. She took charge of your future once and she will do it again.'

You have to get up. Directions as restless as the little pool, its surface wrinkling with sunlight when the wind blew. The glare was blinding; he closed his eyes. Loose stones rattled by his head.

At first he was only aware of the ground where he lay, and then he found himself on the stallion's back. He had no idea how it had happened, even getting to his feet had felt impossible, but now he knew how far he had come and how much further he had to travel.

What he didn't yet know was whether he had enough time to get there.

Clove was standing stone-still in the Hockaday yard. Her mother could see her through the window's feathering of dusky pink drapes. Drapes that Joanie had sewn for the house that Emmett had built.

Joanie watched Sage watching Clove. She crossed the

room and put her arm around the young woman's shoulders. 'I believe that everything is going to be all right,' she said. 'And I know that you believe it also.'

Sage patted the hand that held her. 'Maybe, but that does not make it easy to believe.'

'I have only known you for a few years, but you have already taught me the skill of perseverance.' Joanie squeezed, but too tightly; she could feel the woman's bones through her skin. 'You are a fighter, Sage. And that little girl out there is a fighter also.'

'And what about Colt?'

Too much life had happened to Colt, and too quickly. Joanie could read nothing from the boy's eyes; it was as though they were hidden behind shutters. He rose in the morning and took himself to school, and she admitted the relief of his absence only to herself.

'His body is a child's, but it carries a man's head,' she said, and with surprise that she had spoken her thoughts out loud.

Sage nodded, as though Joanie had taken the words from her own mouth. 'When I look at Colt I see an echo of his father,' she said, growing taller as she lifted her head. 'Wolf Shadow was brought to our steading when he was Colt's age; when he was known as Cub, for the sake of a proper name.'

She glanced up. 'Do you know Wolf's story, Joanie?'

'I know a little of it.'

Only what she had overheard in the town: the rumours, the back-of-hand mutterings, the insinuations. Gossip was unbridled in Kendall's store and some of it violent, but Joanie suspected that colour had been added to enhance the entertainment, for Kester Kendall was nothing if not a glorified showman.

Sage's eyes were still fixed on the little girl standing in

the yard, as though she was loath to release the child from her care. 'My pa was a hard man and there was never any ease to Cub's life,' she said. 'But Wolf Shadow is just as strong now as he was then.'

Joanie felt heat rising in her chest, but only knew that it was anger when the muscles clenched and there was pain. The strong boy who had become a strong man had helped Emmett with the building of their home, helped him with the fencing of their land, and then days ago he had helped himself to the stallion in Emmett's corral.

She didn't know how long it would take her to pardon Wolf's duplicity, but for her husband the betrayal was unforgivable.

'Well now,' she said, biting the words to make them crisp. 'We shall have to start thinking about the coming celebration instead. You will aid me won't you, Sage? And Clove too. And maybe Colt might be persuaded to lend a hand.'

Sage stared at her, breaking the connection with her daughter so that the little girl was free to wander across the yard, the big dog following at her heels.

Joanie had her attention now; the iron was hot and she struck. 'The ladies of the church are rehearsing their voices for a concert, and I know how much you love to sing. We would be delighted if you would join us with the revelry, Sage.'

'What need have I for revelry?'

'Why, we all have much to give thanks for. The summer has been fine and the crops have excelled. Over the year the town has prospered with development and business…'

'Why should I care about the town?'

Sage pushed the woman aside and walked to the door that led to the yard. 'A town where no Madison has ever been made welcome,' she said. 'The people of Oasis turn their backs when my son is bullied, they give my daughter vile labels because they are blind to her fascination. They condemn Wolf Shadow because of his Indian father.'

She seemed to suspend herself from the handle when she opened the door. 'The only person who has ever seen past the barriers that Oasis built for us is the doctor's wife. I used to honour that woman and all she stood for, but now I curse her for bringing us to this state.'

Joanie hurried over, seizing the door before it should be slammed in her face. 'Mrs Ryker is in the past; you must discount her. But you are only seeing the winter, Sage, when there is so much summer in Oasis; so many people who will stand by your side.'

Joanie cupped her mouth to funnel the final words before the woman vanished around the corner. 'Please think about it, Sage. Please help us, if only to return the help we are giving you.'

Clove was in sight again and Sage walked quickly. The dog turned around as she approached, growling at the back of its throat, and its eyes were mean. The child was holding her hand in the air, inches away from the animal's fangs, and Sage felt sick.

'There's nothing to fear, Ma. The dog will protect us,' Clove said. 'And so will he.'

She spread an arm to encompass the tidy yard, all the way to the neat barn where Sage could see Emmett Hockaday working. He was at the open doorway, making the last repairs to the wheel of the cart that had once caused Wolf so much trouble. The man was wielding a heavy hammer, his face shiny with sweat and good nature, and the back of his neck prickled when he felt the eyes upon him. He nodded to them across the space.

He will protect us now that we have no one else. Sage

saw the words in her mind, and they tumbled around the image of Wolf Shadow as he rode the black stallion from the homestead with blood on his shirt. Hatless, feckless and worthless; still bearing the stink of Lucy Ryker's perfume across his chest and the imprint of her husband's fist across his face.

Clove put her arms around the dog's neck. 'If you help Mrs Hockaday with the singing, it will be like saying thank you,' she said, staring up at her mother. 'Won't it?'

TWENTY-FOUR

THINGS WERE coming apart. He was drifting across a dismantled landscape, little more than a mess of outlines that someone had lifted into the air and let drop. Oasis had worn the same face on the day of his disgrace, but his subsequent eviction from the saloon had been directed by whisky and Andy Parnell. Now another power had hold of his body, and it was not letting go.

His mind left him and after a while it trickled back again, poorer than before, but he could still discern how far he and the horse had travelled. The hills were behind them and the plains stretched away, directionless in their swathes and tangles.

This land was a heartless companion. It had been like that before, when he was Cub and the snake had struck; when fever had purged his senses and a sheriff's daughter had wiped it away with a damp cloth.

He was hungry for the memory of water. He licked his lips, but the skin was cracked and there wasn't enough saliva to make an impression. He and the horse had gone dry for too long, but there would be water aplenty in the town of Liberation – over the next rise, or the one after that. He would know when they had reached the place where the rough land settled to a civilised road. He could wait.

But the stallion could not.

Thirst had shrivelled Wolf Shadow's tongue; his voice was dying and the strangeness with it. Over empty days the language that was tethering the palomino had stretched thin and flimsy, and once again the horse was feeling the pull of the wild. Belligerent since the night Wolf had broken it free of Emmett's corral, it was as strong as a devil – and the young man had grown too weak to fight.

He only knew that the animal had reared when he slipped from its back and met the rocky ground. His mind went away for a moment, somewhere peaceful and painless that didn't last long enough. When he came to himself the horse was heading for oblivion, and the dust of its running had already settled.

The sky was benign, as blue as a pool and laced with clouds. If it was to be the last thing he saw it would at least be a good thing. Wolf thought that perhaps he could just close his eyes and lie there for as long as it took, but the wound in his leg was yelling and he would never find peace. If he could manage to stand then perhaps the pain would shut up long enough for him to walk in the quiet of the land.

Walking was easy because his feet felt nothing. The ground dissolved and there was just air. But the world was turning too fast and he couldn't keep up. The sun slid across the sky and shadows blessed the path, and he just had to keep moving until he wasn't able to move any more.

And then it was no longer a path but a flat road. His ears were filled with sounds and his eyes with buildings, and he could smell woodgrain and wheat, cattle and milk, leather boots and perfume that came from a bottle.

Time had passed since this town was a new build, gangly as a foal fresh from birth, alive with hammers and saws. There had been a main street of stamped mud, worn in places to bare rock like flesh that had fallen from bone. But the memory that prevailed, as sharp still as if it had been tattooed into Wolf's brain, was of sunlight knocking back like angels' wings from the white boards of the sidewalk. That was where the wolf cub had once fallen, and the image of a man wearing calf-hide had fallen with him.

There were different people now; some pushed him away with raised voices as though he was unspeakable. He caught the edge of a face, the weave of a jacket, a wave of hair, and then they were gone. He was left with a sour shadow in his mind, but the reproach of their mouths remained. All he wanted was to feel the lick of water between his lips and the gentle touch of a damp cloth on his face. If he walked far enough perhaps he would find it…

His legs gave way and the road greeted him; grit rose over his head and his eyes burned. Too weak to cough, he was drowning in dust, but there were strong hands gripping him now, hauling him to his feet. Road muck fell from his shirt and left its stain there, as rusty as dried blood.

Voices were sharp, snapping like bullets. He wanted to surrender to the ground again, but the hands holding him out of the dirt were insistent. They drew him away from the cacophony of questions, and when the voices faded Wolf could hear his rescuer asking questions of his own as he helped the young man down the street.

The words bounced off Wolf's skull and meant nothing. After a while he could see nothing as well, until the walking stopped and he was standing outside a tall building, its walls painted with uneven white strokes, and a porch where an arched door opened to shadows and closed to hush. His sight came back to a wide room, rows of chairs facing a table, an unadorned wooden cross in the corner.

He was taken to one of the chairs and ordered to sit; his body obeyed but his mind had nothing to do with it. The hands set him free and he floated, listening to the pulse of silence and the surge of blood behind his ears, but then the hands returned with a wet cloth for his brow. Water trickled down Wolf's face. The hairs rose on the back of his neck and he gasped, reaching out his tongue to collect the drops as they passed his mouth. The man who had brought him there was speaking again, and his voice echoed in this quiet place, as though it had a double.

'You are thirsty. Remiss of me. Wait here, I shall fetch you a drink.'

He offered the cloth and Wolf held cool water to his face until his skin was gasping. The hall swayed in and out of focus with its high windows and its throng of chairs, and he saw a priest coming towards him in a black gown, as voluminous as a woman's dress. He was holding a tall glass that he filled, with agonising slowness, from a chipped china pitcher.

Wolf made a grab for it but the man held back. 'Not too fast; drink with care.'

It was difficult not to pour the water down his throat, but he did as he was told. It tasted miraculous, filling his body like rainfall feeding a desert. When the glass was empty the priest filled it again.

'You have gone without for a while, my friend,' he said. 'And you have suffered.'

A gentle voice, with a rough edge to it that might never be smoothed. Wolf's eyes were closed and he couldn't see the man's frown. He took the glass and drained it, but the rage of thirst had been quietened and he drank for pleasure, not raw need. And by the end he had drunk enough, so that even his eyeballs felt plumped and refreshed.

The hall had settled now, and its colours were clearer. And the priest's face was clearer too: angular, as clean shaven as possible, and honest with kindness.

Wolf tried to thank him but there was a blockage in his throat, as though the water had turned road dust to cement. When he spoke, the words broke in half and faded to nothing, but the priest was nodding as if he understood. He left the pitcher on the floor and raised Wolf from the seat, his hands under the young man's elbows as though he was presenting him to the high ceiling with its wooden beams. Sparked with new life, Wolf could walk without help, and the man led him to a door at the back of the hall, and through to a small room with a table and chairs and not much else besides the smell of damp.

'Sit yourself down,' the priest said, 'and take off your shirt.' And he did so, leaving the puddle of cotton on the floor.

The priest filled a bowl from a spout in the corner and began to wash the young man's body – tidying away the dirt of the ride, the ghost of the trail, the dried blood.

'I can let you have some pants and a shirt,' he said. 'I can't promise they'll fit, but that is no matter.' He looked up. 'I can let you have a jacket too. I kept such garments from the dark time when I was known as Tom Brophy. I have no need for them now that I have become Father Thomas, but I knew they would be of use to a deserving cause one day.'

'Is that what I am?' The water had finally washed away the detritus in Wolf's throat and the words were whole.

'Forgive me, but yes, I believe that you are.'

'Maybe you have too much belief.'

The priest leaned back and studied Wolf's face. The kindness in his eyes was shining, it shimmered above his head like a halo, but that was probably the effect of fatigue faltering in the young man's brain.

'I believe that you have come across trouble, and that it may have followed you here,' the man said. 'But I can see more than that when I look at you.'

'Can you see into my soul?'

'Indeed, I have that ability.'

Wolf shook his head. 'I think you should keep away from me.'

'Why should I keep away from someone who needs my help?'

'I don't need your preaching.' The young man stood up abruptly, wincing as he put his weight on the injured leg.

'I would not preach to one who goes his own way.' The priest stood back with his head cocked to one side, like an inquisitive bird. 'But right now I suspect you are too damaged to go anywhere.'

'You have helped me enough.'

'Not nearly enough.'

'Get me the shirt, and I will take my leave.'

'Don't be such a fool. Sit down and let me see what you've done to your leg.'

'No need. It is nearly healed…'

Father Thomas sighed. And then he pushed Wolf backwards, with surprising strength. The young man was unprepared and sprawled on the chair, half falling as it skidded across the floor. On impulse he reached for the knife at his belt, but the priest had got there first, lifting the weapon swiftly from its sheath. He brandished it as if he had a mind to use it, then almost reverently he laid it on the table and turned back with a smile trying to come to his lips.

'Now will you let me see to your leg?'

Father Thomas took the bowl of rusty water outside and poured it on the ground, rather like a libation of blood for an earthen god, he thought before signing a cross over his chest. He shook out the drops and returned to the little room where the young man was sitting, the ruined leg of his pants split up to the thigh, and the wound bandaged with a white cloth that seemed too dazzling against his brown skin.

'What kind of horse would take such a bite out of a man?' the priest said, grabbing a towel from a square cupboard and wiping his hands before pressing them against his cassock; spreading it out like a crow's wings.

Wolf made a smile that fell short of his eyes. 'One that wanted freedom above all else,' he said, stretching his leg to feel the pull of the bandage.

'And did the horse find its freedom, or did you use your knife on it?'

Wolf fidgeted as if the priest's words were causing discomfort. 'He is free now,' he said, standing from the table and checking his leg for weakness. When he turned from the window the half-light carved shallows in his cheeks.

'You are hungry,' Father Thomas said, and Wolf shook his head as if that had been a question, but he had hesitated first. His thoughts were palpable, the urge to get away was so strong that the priest felt uneasy for the first time, and unsure of his own belief in the young man's wholeness.

And a second later he was infuriated. 'I have never

before met anyone so self-destructive,' he snapped. 'Just admit that you are hungry, damn you.'

Wolf picked the knife off the table and slid it back into the sheath. The belt was loose; hanging off his waist. 'It has been a day or two since I last ate,' he said.

The priest twitched a nod. 'I will bring you the clothes I promised. I shall not be long.' He opened the door to the church, and the smell of fresh wood floated towards them as though in their absence someone had been whittling curlicues out of the rough-cut beams. Thomas sniffed and looked up to the vault of the roof as if he thought that as well, and then turned with a flap of his cassock to thrust his head back into the room. 'Do not move!'

Wolf did not move. He waited beside the table in the little room and felt the descent of peace. His skin was being stroked by feathers, as delicate as fingertips. Sage used to touch him like that. In the past. Before the journey he had taken with Daniel Ryker, from which he had returned sickened by his own depravity. She had touched him with feathers when he loved her at night in their bed under the roof, and she had loved him back, moving above his body to the music in her soul until they were both soaring.

Father Thomas returned; the church door opened and closed on a sigh, but Wolf was too far away to notice. 'Try these on,' the priest said, handing over what he had brought.

The young man was lean and the borrowed clothes hung off him like a disconnected skin. When he was a boy escaping from Madison, he had been given clothes made for a man; just a few months later he had all but grown to fit them. Come the time of a return to his family would his wisdom have grown to fit as well?

197

If such a return could ever be possible.

Wolf Shadow left the church for the street, walking cleanly dressed by the priest's side as though he was a decent man. They were heading for the hotel – a tall, narrow building with a proud façade, that had only recently been erected. The space where it sat had been empty in the days before, when he had been the wolf cub riding Leo Fletcher's storm-grey back to the sheriff's house. Another stolen horse and another escape. Not a lot had changed.

He climbed the sidewalk and imagined the scent of calf-hide, but it was the aroma of hot food that was clinging to the back of his throat as they entered the building. He swallowed automatically, and after they had found seats and a table by the wall where the curious might leave them undisturbed, he swallowed the real food as soon as it was set before him.

The priest ate economically but watched the young man with interest. 'In my estimation there have been more than just a couple of days that you've gone without food – Mr...'

He tilted his head to one side. 'We have already been acquainted for a while, yet I am still to learn your name.'

'My name is Wolf Shadow.'

'I knew there was Indian in your background.' It was evident in the colour of his skin, in hair that the sun had not bleached and the brown gaze sparked with gold. 'Would this be the motivation behind your injuries?'

Wolf looked up, and his eyes deepened as the light in them was extinguished. 'I am obliged to you, Priest.'

'I hunt out deserving causes; I told you that.'

'Then you must be obliged to me also,' Wolf said, staring around the room.

It was cavernous with its high ceiling and inadequate

furniture, the long bar by the wall with shelves of bottles that gleamed under the lights. 'This place is new,' he said. 'And the street outside has changed a great deal.'

'You've been in Liberation before?'

The young man turned swiftly and met the priest's scrutiny. 'Yes, I have been in this town before.'

'And yet I can see from your face that it was not a pleasant experience.'

'I knew very little of that ten years ago.'

'You would have been very young ten years ago.'

'I do not remember much about being young.'

Father Thomas waited for more, but Wolf had drawn back, taking some of the air with him, so that there was a sudden draught; too cold for the muggy interior where they were sitting.

'Do you wish to talk about it, Wolf Shadow?'

Wolf stared at him. 'I wish to talk about someone who lived here back then.'

'I myself have lived here for only five of those years, but I will help you in any way that I can,' the priest said, and his voice dropped as though he wanted to keep what he was about to say only to himself.

'Ten years ago I was another person in another town. I was a drunkard, and from necessity also a thief, for I had to pay for my drinking, and I chose to do so from the pockets of others.'

He paused, one hand going to the front of his cassock as though checking that he was still wearing the black gown of Father Thomas and not the reeking rags of Tom Brophy.

'I was a piece of garbage and treated as such,' he said. 'Until one day a new priest came to that town and scraped me off the street and taught me to release my soul to the glory of God.'

Wolf nodded. 'It must be under the skin of the brotherhood; the hunt for deserving causes.'

'So who got under your skin ten years ago?' The priest waited, and for a while there was nothing from the misplaced young man wearing clothing borrowed from one who had once known how it felt to be so lost. Then Wolf told him.

'Her name is Reyna. She is the daughter of Sheriff Norgate.'

'Ah, yes.' The priest sat back in his chair. 'I know of them.'

TWENTY-FIVE

NEATLY FOLDED bedding had opened up a little more space in the lean-to where they were sleeping. The nook was small for the four of them, but there was still room for Sage to change into her blue dress with its bead-trimmed bodice. She tucked as much hair as she could under the matching bonnet and draped a shawl over her shoulders, tying the ends, adding a bow. She felt like a tidy package; falsely wrapped. There should be something more beneath the finery than a fearful woman who clutched air when she reached for her daughter, and followed empty footprints to her son.

'Tell me the truth, honey,' she said. 'Will I pass as a lady?'

Clove was pressed against the wall, tightly enough to meld flesh with wood. She gave no reply. Maybe she hadn't heard. Skirts rustling, Sage crouched beside her.

'I am going to town for a while with Mrs Hockaday, and Grandma will look out for you,' she said, urging some lightness into her voice. 'Shall I bring back candy sticks? Would you like that, Clove?'

There was no reaction, but none was expected, although Sage tried hard not to care. The little girl was staring at nothing as if there was plenty to see, and her mother kissed the air above her head, hoping the child would understand that the kiss had been meant for her.

Locked inside her own world, Clove was unaware of anything else. But even her own world had shrunk after her father had ridden away on Night Dancer. She had searched for him since early that morning, but now the hours were slipping past noon and there was still no sign. How was she going to find him, when each time she closed her eyes she found the dark man instead?

Joanie was out in the yard, drawing on gloves, and the two women climbed up to the bench of the buggy that Emmett was holding steady. There was a gash on the back of his hand and an uncompromising look on his face, and he moved away before the buggy horse had reached the road.

Sage turned to watch him heading for the barn, walking too heavily. 'Is something amiss with Emmett?'

Joanie flicked the reins and the horse began to trot. 'The black stallion is amiss.' She grimaced, glancing at the woman beside her. 'I regret that when Wolf Shadow took the palomino, he took away something of Emmett as well.'

The young woman stared out at the land that was rolling past, just as familiar as her own face. She had known this view all her life, and her man's actions had turned it into an alien country.

'Perhaps Wolf Shadow thought that leaving Dancer in the palomino's place was payment enough.'

'The creature bites and kicks and cannot be ridden.' Joanie snapped the words as though she didn't like the taste. 'That horse is poor exchange.'

Sage had seen enough of the distant hills. She glared down at the hands clasped tightly at her waist as though she would have liked nothing more than to rip the skin from her own fingers. 'If I could undo the harm that Wolf has done then I would, and in an instant.'

'None of this is your fault, honey.' Joanie covered the young woman's fists with her own gloved hand. It felt comforting, and Sage battled self-pity.

'But I trusted him also.'

'He must have had a good reason for behaving as he did,' Joanie said. 'I have always believed Wolf Shadow to be a fine young man.'

That may have been so once, but did she still believe it? She fiddled with her conscience as well as the reins, and the horse chewed the bit as the Wellerson house came into view, smoke reaching up from the chimney like a righteous spirit.

Sage stiffened. This was the home of the boy Jonah, who had heaped the trouble on Colt's shoulders that his father had tried to rectify. The confrontation with Moses, the showdown with Kester Kendall – they must have tapped into Wolf's wild side and changed him. Wasn't that a good enough reason for what he had done?

But what he had done with the doctor's wife was not so easy to forgive.

Maria Wellerson was out in her yard; she looked up at the sound of the buggy as it passed on the higher ground, and Joanie raised a hand in greeting. The woman below signalled a grudging reply, but when she caught sight of Joanie's passenger she changed the acknowledgement to a cross signed over her well-buttoned bodice. She called out to her husband, who was as yet hidden behind the house. Beckoned into view he followed her pointing finger and lifted cupped hands to his lips.

'When you have associations with an Indian's whore, Mrs Hockaday, that makes you a whore yourself.'

Joanie drove at speed along the road until the farm had been swallowed up by rising land. The bitterness was left behind, but the air still tasted foul.

'I have brought insults on your head, Mrs Hockaday. You must take me back,' Sage shouted over wheel clatter, gripping the bench to keep from falling.

'I most certainly will not take you back.' Joanie tugged the horse to a stop so abruptly that its head was jerked sideways. All noise lifted, but the buggy still shuddered. 'I lived a colourful life before Emmett Hockaday came into it, and that is not the first time that I have been called a whore,' she said. 'But it is the first time that it has made me angry enough to want to inflict pain.'

She was holding the reins so tightly her arms were shaking. 'I am truly sorry.'

'I have always been proud to be an Indian's whore, if that is what I am,' Sage said, even though her skin felt as thin as beaten parchment. 'And it is not for you to be sorry.'

'Well, I am. I am sorry for you as well as for the state of Moses Wellerson's miserable soul. But most of all…' The woman paused, and then she chortled. 'Most of all, I am sorry that you have just uncovered the secret of my dubious past.'

'I have changed my mind,' Sage said. 'We shall not go back. And by the time we reach town I want to have learned much more about your dubious past. I want to see the church sizzle when we step into it on our sinful feet…'

'The air itself shall burn…'

'And the ladies of the choir shall swoon.'

It struck Joanie that she had never before heard the young woman laugh. The sound was lifting like birds and washing the day clean, and under its propulsion the journey to Oasis was swiftly accomplished.

Joanie halted the buggy by the church, shaking dust from her dress as she descended. Sage settled the shawl like body armour around her shoulders. A generous slide of notes ballooned in pitch as they opened the door, to a view of ladies gathering before the altar. They seemed to be preparing the harmonium for celebration, but the blare of the instrument hinted at armies readying their weapons rather than the rejoicing of angels.

One member of the battalion disengaged herself and bustled over. 'Mrs Hockaday, how kind of you to come,' she said, offering a hand as though Joanie was expected to kiss the ruby in her ring. 'And am I right in thinking that you have brought along a fellow enthusiast?'

She tilted her head at Sage, who was standing just behind, and it was obvious from the pinched nostrils that she recognised her as the woman whose husband had instigated recent upheaval amongst the good people of the town.

'Indeed, I have, Mrs Hetherington.' Joanie stared her in the eye, ignoring the hand that was still raised for homage. 'When you hear her sing I'm sure you will agree that Miss Madison has a very fine voice.'

Mrs Hetherington turned towards Sage, plump face rounded even further by a smile that could have been one of greeting, but was losing the battle with pursed lips to be anything but grudging.

'I don't believe we have met before, Miss Madison, and yet I have heard a little about your recent calamities,' she said, very sweetly. 'Tell me, how are you managing now that your wayward – spouse – has finally exhibited his true colours?'

The woman's voice was loud enough to overwhelm the musical end of the church, where it brought greater discord to the harmonium and a lull to the twittering. But all that Sage could think about were her odd-coloured eyes; one blue and the other hazel. It was difficult to decide which one to stare at, even more so because of the judgements that lurked behind them both.

And Mrs Hetherington had not finished. 'Brawling in the street, disturbing the peace. It was the behaviour of a savage,' she said. 'Luckily I was not around to witness it myself, but I understand that he even threatened the Kendall boy.'

The harmonium, and everything else, fell silent. Sage glanced across to where the ladies' dresses were bumping together, like full-bellied chickens in a henhouse. She saw apologetic faces amongst the blatantly agog.

She saw Korky Kendall's mother standing beside the altar.

'Wolf Shadow is not a savage, Mrs Hetherington,' she said. 'He is a man who will do all in his power to protect his family. How can you see that as being anything but honourable?'

She heard the lie in her own words. Wolf had slaked his lust and left his family in pieces. He had forfeited all honour and disappeared on a stolen horse, but it was apparent that those choice nuggets had not yet reached the ears of the church ladies.

There was a scattering of skirts in the henhouse and, obviously at risk of Mrs Hetherington's dissatisfaction, a couple of the women beckoned to the newcomers. Sage followed Joanie along the aisle. Blessed by intermittent light from the high windows, it felt like wading through puddles of purity. She wondered whether that might help to shield her from the wrath of Korky's mother.

When she drew closer, however, Sage could see that Mrs Kendall was shaking. She was not a young woman, but the wear and tear of life had accelerated the years and flattened the planes of her face. All animation had retreated to her eyes.

'My husband…' the lady began, swallowing before she could continue. 'My husband is also a protective father, Miss Madison, and Korky is our only child, gifted to us after many years of marriage.'

She reached forward suddenly and grabbed Sage's elbow, and the young woman reacted before she realised that it was not intended as a blow. Mrs Kendall's gaze was wild with fervour now and she hadn't noticed the flinch. 'Let me reassure you that I do not endorse the blame that Kester has laid on Mr Shadow.'

She had said what she wanted to say and her body slumped, the passion fading just as quickly, leaving her eyes fatigued and slightly bloodshot. Her hand slipped from Sage's arm and the fire went with it. The young woman reached out as if to hold her up. 'My name is Sage,' she said.

'Oh, my dear, thank you,' the woman breathed. 'My own name was Margharita until my marriage, after which my husband trimmed it to Rita, which maybe he found easier to pronounce.'

'Our Mrs Kendall has a sublime contralto voice.' Mrs Hetherington pounced from behind, and Margharita jumped. 'And I understand from Mrs Hockaday that you have a voice of your own, Miss Madison.'

'Well, I'm not sure. It might not hold the power you require.'

'Don't believe a word of it, Mrs Hetherington,' Joanie Hockaday said, appearing suddenly beside them. 'If you want to know about the power of Sage's voice you just need to stand in my yard and listen, for her singing crosses the land between our houses like some exotic bird.' She linked arms with her young neighbour. 'I guarantee that once you've experienced that ethereal sound, you'll think you've died and gone to heaven.'

Her eyes crinkled when she grinned. There was too much mischief there, a by-product of her dubious past no doubt, and Sage wanted to laugh again. Rolling along the valley road that afternoon she had been like a young girl giggling her way to a dance, but now her face was starting to ache from previously unused muscles.

Everything felt new. Her good friend was extolling her virtues beside the harmonium to the ladies of the church, and for the first time since his desertion Wolf Shadow had been pushed into the background. For a few minutes he had been forgotten.

One day she might forget him completely.

As if he had never existed.

TWENTY-SIX

A MAN wearing calf-hide had spooked his horse and threatened his liberty; that was all he could remember of his arrival in Liberation ten years before. His mind crazed by snake venom, the wolf cub had understood little of what followed, until the red-haired girl touched his face with water. A guardian angel in a house of strong-minded men, the sheriff's daughter had given him back his life, and in return he had saved her father from the guns of thieves.

Reyna Norgate was no longer just a daughter, but a wife and mother besides. That was how Father Thomas described her, and Wolf felt unsettled, as though he was still suffering from the malaise that had once benefited from her nursing. Had she chosen the man she married, or had he been chosen for her? Wolf didn't realise he had actually spoken the words until the priest answered.

'It has been a mystery that the women of the town still find enthralling when they huddle together on the sidewalk.'

'Just tell me!'

Father Thomas jerked in his chair as though a power had knocked him backwards. 'I'll tell you after you tell me why it matters so much.'

Wolf looked around at the faces that had turned to stare at his outburst; he took a breath and when he spoke again it was for the priest alone. 'I would like to think that she followed the right path.'

'Well, that is debatable, and fodder for the gossips as I have said. Reyna had already left Liberation by the time I was given my chance, only to return about three years ago with a baby and a ring on her finger.'

'And a husband?'

'None that I know of,' the priest said. 'She left him behind, and maybe he is still there.'

Wolf was quiet, and the hotel sounds fell to hush. Father Thomas tried to see what he was thinking, but his eyes appeared obstructed, as though a veil had been dropped. It could be that the young man who had arrived at a priest's door with his story hidden might become another mystery for the folk of Liberation to chew on around their supper tables. And it might bring them to his church on a Sunday to discover the truth from the priest himself. That is, if he could learn it first.

'How do you know her, Wolf Shadow?'

'She cared for me once when I was in fever.' The veil lifted and gold shone in Wolf's eyes. 'I had been bitten by a snake. Reyna's uncle took me in, and she saved my life.'

'You must have been directed to her house by the hand of God.'

'I was brought to the sheriff's house by a man called Thackeray Dart.'

'And I see by your face that the story does not end there.' The priest waited; and after a while he probed again. 'The trouble that has followed you here today, is it the same trouble that brought you ten years ago?'

Wolf sat far back in his chair, so that the priest and the hotel and everybody in it might recede. Maybe he felt safer there, where nothing could touch him.

'Where is she now?' he said. 'And her father. Tell me about Sheriff Norgate.'

'Reyna is close by, but the sheriff of Liberation is called Maxwell, not Norgate.'

'You told me you know them.'

'I told you I know of them.'

'I need to see her.'

Agitated, his eyes blazing above the injuries that someone's fist had cut into his face, the young man looked too vulnerable in the overlarge shirt. But Father Thomas lifted his head and nodded towards the back of the room. 'She is over there, Wolf Shadow. She has been there all this time.'

Wolf hesitated, and then he turned around to see a woman leaning against the bar as though she was using it to hold her upright. Once her hair had been a gentle red-brown, fluffing around her face like kitten fur; now it was copper, as metallic as the word and with little heart in its shine. Her soft round face had been carved away and the bones were protuberant above the hollows in her cheeks. All her natural blushes had been starved by white powder that gave her a cadaverous air, superseded by rouge, and when she smiled across the room at him her eyes disappeared behind shadows that might have made her shy if the invitation hadn't been so blatant.

Reyna pushed away from the bar and came towards them, weaving between tables that were inhabited and others that were still empty but ready for the evening to come. Hands helped her pass with a squeeze at the waist or a slap on the rear, and she bestowed the smile as though she was being honoured instead of manhandled.

She came up to Wolf's table with a sway of hips that had once been plump beneath dowdy dresses but were now accentuated by the tight bodice of her green gown.

There was no glint of recognition in her eyes, but he thought he could discern the honesty of the young girl lying dormant beneath the paint.

'I see a stranger with an interesting face,' she said, and touched the stone-gash at his temple with her fingertips. 'Even though it is obvious that some have disagreed.'

'Reyna,' he said, and her eyes widened.

'Well, I guess the clergyman has told you my name.'

Father Thomas nodded. 'We will both be praying for your soul, Reyna.'

'Both of you?' She looked Wolf Shadow over, from the length of his hair to the ill-fitting pants, and back to his battered face. 'This one doesn't look much like a holy man to me.'

'Neither did I, five years ago,' the priest said, standing up from his chair. He held it out and invited the woman to sit. 'Keep him company for a while, Reyna. I have something to see to in the church.'

'Don't pray too long, Father,' she said as she sat. 'You will wear out your knees.'

The priest smiled as though he had heard it before. 'Come and see me later, Wolf Shadow.'

'Well now,' Reyna drew the lacy shawl from her shoulders and leaned forwards to exaggerate the depth of her cleavage. 'Wolf Shadow is an Indian name. And are you an Indian boy?'

'I was once a boy…'

'But now you are a man.'

'Once I was a boy with not much name at all.'

'I spend more time with men than I do with boys, Wolf Shadow, particularly those who buy me drinks.'

It was a line she had spoken before, many times and much practised. The weight of womanhood had stripped away the innocence, but he could still remember it in the face of the girl who had nursed him as protectively as a child would a doll.

'I have no money, Reyna.'

'Well.' She sat up straight and stared at him, her face even more gaunt once the smile had slipped. 'At least that's honest. But don't you fret,' she leaned over and patted his wrist, 'because the bartender and I have an understanding.'

She waved a hand in the air, and the message was indeed understood. The barman brought a bottle and two glasses and left them on the table with a wink that could have been meant for either of them, and Reyna poured the drinks with dexterity. She raised her glass to Wolf before tossing the liquor to the back of her throat, but he made no move towards his share.

'Drink,' she said. 'Come on and drink. How will you keep up with me otherwise?'

'I have no wish to drink, Reyna.'

'Well, you should.' She poured another glassful for herself, and raised it in salute as before. 'We all need to drink.'

'Why?'

She swallowed the whisky, but put the glass down carefully, studying him for a moment. 'Because it stops us having to think. That's why.'

Wolf pushed his glass away and watched her. She shuddered.

'You are unnerving, Wolf Shadow. I don't know what to make of you.'

'Maybe I remind you of something.'

'Maybe you do; and maybe it's something I have no desire to remember.'

She grabbed the bottle and poured fiercely, splashing the table with whisky that soaked into the wood and merged with all the other stains. 'How well do you know the priest, Wolf Shadow? Did he tell you how often I have tried to lead him into sin with me? He is a man, he has needs like any other man, but he has never satisfied them with me. Although I shall keep trying, for I relish a challenge.'

She swallowed the liquor, misjudging the height from the table when she brought the glass down, so that it banged on the wood with a short echo that made her blink.

'Wolf Shadow, you are forcing me to drink too fast,' she said, looking up at him with the smile back on her face. 'But you know how to make me slow down, don't you? If you don't know then I can show you.'

She moved the glass aside, without caring whether it might fall to the floor, and leaned towards him. She held his head between both hands and kissed him, sliding her tongue into his mouth. He could hear her breathing change to something lighter, caught in the back of her throat. She slid her fingers into his hair and tugged him closer, and when she kissed him now it was with little butterfly touches on his lips.

Wolf reached up and took her hands, squeezing them gently before setting himself free, feeling the air fresh on his wet skin as he pushed her away. She gazed at him with new eyes and he could see the young Reyna, he could see her father's daughter, diminutive but strong.

'Who are you?' she said. 'What is it about you?'

'It is about ten years ago,' he said. 'When your uncle brought you a boy from the street and you nursed him back to life, in a bedroom with blue drapes at the window.'

She jerked backwards, but he still had hold of her. She was fastened to him by more than hands now, and as she stared at him her face seemed plumper, her eyes clearer, her hair a soft red-brown. 'You are Cub,' she said; and then again as if she liked the sound of it. 'Cub.'

Wolf smiled, although the rough places on his face twisted and told him that it was painful to smile. Reyna was looking at him; not in the way she had looked before but as if she hadn't really seen the man who had been sitting at a table with her and a bottle of whisky, like any other potential client. She was devouring him with her eyes, wide and blue and still astonished.

'Cub.' She was relishing the name. 'Why are you here?'

'I could ask the same of you, Reyna.'

'Oh.' She broke his hold on her hands and pulled away, gazing around the room with eyes that had dulled a little. 'Where else should I be?'

He waited for more but she was silent now, her shoulders cradled by the back of the chair. She reached out for her glass as though the solid feel of it might bring some comfort, and the taste of its contents more comfort still. There was nothing to learn from her face.

'What happened, Reyna?' Wolf said, quietly.

'That's a big question, Cub, and I don't think I have enough time to answer it.'

She glanced over at him, a damaged man dressed in another's clothes, hard muscles in his arms that told of long hours of physical work. His hair was still the colour of corn, but there was darkness beneath; that was new, as were the lines that hollowed his cheeks. But his eyes were the same: deep brown, touched with gold where the light struck.

'You are a man now, with a man's name, and yet you bear the signs of rough-handling much as you bore when I last saw you,' she said. 'So I shall ask it of you also. What happened?'

They sat at the table with the questions hanging over their heads. They sat very still, buffeted gently by sounds from the street; and in a sudden lull they heard the ponderous ticking of a clock as more time passed.

Reyna stood up; the green gown ruffled by her sudden movement. 'Come along with me,' she said, gathering her shawl with one hand and the half empty bottle with the other. Wolf Shadow followed, bombarded by smirking encouragement from the men at the tables.

'Have a good time, fella.'

'Give her one for me.'

'Watch out for the teeth; she's got one hell of a bite.'

Reyna climbed the stairs at the back of the room, playing to her audience with a flounce of petticoats and a slide of leg showing above her pointy little boots. She used to be a shy young girl whose only purpose in life was to care; now she didn't seem to care at all. She led Wolf through a curtained archway and the noise died down behind them, and everything was as bland as the door where they stopped. She felt inside her cleavage for the key.

It was not a large room. The main piece of furniture was the bed: spread with glossy coverings and a number of pillows, topped and tailed by scuffed ironwork. There was still space for a drawer chest, a small stuffed chair, a tall mirror standing in the corner. A miasma of cheap scent thickened the air, blending with the memory of cigar smoke.

'Welcome to my humble abode,' Reyna slapped the shawl on the bed and the bottle on the chest. Then she changed her mind and swallowed a slug of whisky before dumping the bottle again. The liquor rocked from side to side like a disturbed sea.

'Take a seat, Cub,' she said. 'Whichever one you like.'

He chose the chair and she spread herself on the bed. She slid her skirt up to mid-thigh, pausing by a red lace garter to pout a kiss in his direction. 'If you want to take the opportunity, you're welcome to join me.'

'That's not why I'm here, Nugget.'

She frowned and threw the skirt back over her legs. 'Nobody has called me Nugget for years, ever since my father…' She stopped suddenly and shook her head, as though to chase the words away; and there were no more words to follow.

'Did Cochrane kill him?'

That was the reason why he was here, in a Liberation that had taken ten years to grow from the new town it had been then, busy under carpenters' hands. A lot had changed since those days, although the older buildings were still standing despite having been thrown up at random on bare foundations. The sidewalks were grey now, when once they had been freshly cut and as white as sun-dazzle, burning like the fire in Cub's brain when he rode Wolf Wind down the valley dip of the main street.

Wolf Shadow was here to learn what had happened to Ralf Norgate, whom he had left behind in the robber's cabin, bleeding from a bullet wound and at the mercy of a man who had little of it to offer.

'Did the sheriff die, Reyna?'

She sat up straight and put her feet to the floor, smoothing the dress over her knees, sober now.

'My father died five years ago. He'd ridden out with a deputy on a hunt for cattle thieves. The rustlers were holed up in a canyon by the river. Father climbed the overhang above them but it wasn't solid. It gave way and he fell in. He couldn't swim; he'd never learned. He drowned before the deputy could get him out of the water.' She looked up. 'The rustlers got clean away.'

'I am sorry. He was a good man.'

'Do you think so?' She stood up, went to the window, gazing out at nothing. Her shoulders were high, angled like wings. 'Even though he locked you in his jail cell? Even though he was taking you back to that terrible life you were living before you went looking for freedom?'

'Even though.'

She turned around and stared at him. 'I told you I would never forget what you did for us; for him. I told you that when you left for the final time. And I never have forgotten. And when my uncle and my cousin brought him back from the cabin, I told Father that he owed you his life. And then he went and threw it away.'

'And now you are doing the same.'

'What do you mean by that?' She took a step towards him, and he stood up from the chair to meet any blows, for her face was hard and her fists were knotted.

'What do you think I mean?'

'When you came into our lives I was a nineteen-year-old drudge in a house filled with men, and none of them was my husband. I had no chance of finding a husband living the life I did.' She looked down at herself; looked up again with her eyes staring. 'Now I can have as many husbands as I wish, on as many nights of the week.'

'Other women's husbands.'

'It's better that way.'

He remembered a young girl unpinning laundry from a clothes line, straightening up to ease the ache in her back like a middle-aged woman. He wondered if maybe she was right.

'But you did have a husband of your own.'

She shrugged. 'Did I?'

'You came back here three years ago with a baby and

a ring on your finger.'

She shook her head and smiled, with no mirth behind it. 'Father Thomas allows his tongue to run away by itself.'

'Did you marry your cousin?'

'Clement?'

Why was she so shocked? Didn't she remember how her uncle was manipulating a Dart and Norgate marriage in order to keep a roof over his own head? And the warning that the wolf cub had given her. 'Your uncle is not a worthy man, and he has power over your cousin,' he had said. Didn't she remember any of it?

'There was no husband, Wolf Shadow. There was a man who loved himself more than me and left me with a baby. I wore the wedding ring so that the decent people of the town would accept me, that is all.'

'And the ba…?'

'The baby died, before you ask. Not long after I came back. Another fever, like yours, only you were stronger.' Reyna looked at him, but she would have seen nothing through the tears until they began to slip down her cheeks.

'If I'd had a girl I would have called her Rosie, after my mother,' she said. 'But I gave birth to a boy instead. And I called him Cub.'

The priest was at the far end of the church, gazing upwards. He turned slightly at the noise the door made as Wolf Shadow slammed it behind him, and then resumed searching heavenward.

'Some boys were playing with a ball outside; threw it too fast. I reckon they might have clipped the glass.' He pointed up to the high window. 'Can you see a crack up there?'

Wolf Shadow grabbed his arm and spun him around. 'You told me she had a baby.'

'Well, yes she did.'

'But the baby died; why didn't you tell me that?'

Father Thomas looked at the young man, the stance of him, trying hard not to raise his fists to a priest. 'Maybe I reckoned it was none of your business, Wolf Shadow.'

Wolf stepped away, pain in his face. 'She named him after me.'

'She called him Cub.'

'That was the name I was known by when I was a boy. When I came here ten years ago, running away from a man to whom I was little more than an animal. Reyna's father was going to return me to that man, and a life of eating dirt. Did you know that? But Ralf Norgate was a good man, and she was her father's daughter.'

'Well, I reckon she still is, deep down; underneath what life has made of her.'

'She is. She will be again.'

'First she needs to find another occupation.' Father Thomas snorted and slapped Wolf on the shoulder. 'She's even tried to persuade me into her bed. And if she'd approached me about it a few years earlier then she may well have succeeded. I feel a sense of aggravation about that.'

Lucy Ryker had tried the same with Wolf, but just the once. Her success was another of the reasons why he had come to Liberation. And now he had the answers to questions there was nothing to keep him in the town. He was no longer a boy searching for freedom, he was a man with obligations.

The priest was studying him closely, as though he could read everything that was written on his face.

'The man who treated you as an animal, is he the one

who gave you those scars on your back?'

Wolf flinched as though Haine Madison was standing behind him.

'And might it be his whip you are running from, Wolf Shadow?'

'Not any more.' Wolf looked up. 'I have no wish to run any more.'

'In which case you must return,' the priest said, 'and put right whatever wrongs you have left behind.'

'I left a woman and two children on their own. I left them like a coward.'

'I don't see a coward when I look at you. A man who is willing to head back into the trouble that may be waiting for him needs a certain courage.'

The wounds on Wolf's face still twinged when he smiled, but not so much, as if the muscles were growing accustomed. 'You were wasted as a thief and a drunkard,' he said. 'You are better as a priest.'

'I think so too.'

The young man turned, took steps towards the door and faltered, staring at the wall as though there was something missing. 'I had a horse but it ran,' he said.

'And then you had to walk instead,' Father Thomas said. 'But you cannot walk any more, and so I shall find a horse for you.' He hesitated, tapping his head as though testing its hollowness. 'And before I forget, this also is yours.'

He reached down between the rows of chairs and brought out the blanket that Shev Deeley, the blind man, had offered to keep out the cold.

Wolf pulled at the pants he was wearing, the shirt and the jacket. 'You have given me your clothes, the blanket was a gift from another, and now I am to receive a horse. I should say no, I should refuse, but I shall take them.

And I am grateful.'

'I tell you what,' the priest said. 'Perhaps one day you will bring them back.'

'If it is in my power,' Wolf turned to face him, 'then I promise you that one day I shall bring them back.'

TWENTY-SEVEN

LIBERATION WAS a dark hole behind him, reduced to a pattern of lighted windows and silenced by sleep. The rest of the world was ahead, where it was too indistinct to see anything at all.

The night had turned angry and hailstones punched the ground. Some found their way inside the borrowed jacket and Wolf sought shelter by a broken wall – the remains of a hovel that had once housed pioneers before crumbling in the wake of their desertion.

Thomas's piebald was complaining. Stubborn and self-opinionated, the priest's horse was an inadequate substitute for Emmett's stallion. Once Wolf Shadow had been that palomino's jailer, twisting its mind with captivations. But now it was running free somewhere, a rare wild beast in its natural state, and Wolf held nothing in his hands but dishonour.

Did he really think he could return to the man he used to be? Perhaps, like the sleeping town, that was behind him also. Perhaps everything he had built up in his life, since the day that Judge Hopgood had granted him liberty, had been a fantasy.

A stronger wind found him, chilling his skin, and he stepped away from the hovel's false protection. The piebald was disinclined to follow. Infrequently exercised and out of condition, the priest's companion had already spent a few years in dotage by the time it was acquired by Tom Brophy, and Father Thomas had been keeping it more as a reminder of their shared history than out of necessity. But Wolf Shadow had been grateful for the offer of the horse and its saddle.

He had also been keen to take his leave, and the evening had fallen too quickly while his host was still trying to persuade him to stay a while longer.

'At least until daybreak,' Thomas had urged. 'There is no sense in riding through strange country in the dark.'

But sense didn't come into it. The impulse to reach the homestead was strong now, tugging at his gut, despite the discord he would find at the end of the ride. Going back meant facing Emmett's wrath and Daniel's punishment, both of which he deserved. But most of all, it meant returning to the woman he loved – for Sage was the other half of him and without her he was hollow.

Fighting the bit, the horse followed the man through scrubland, high-walled gullies and a commotion of stones, and when the ground was as smooth as it was ever going to be, Wolf pulled himself into the saddle. But the piebald tossed and jounced and flattened evil ears.

'You will not throw me, painted beast,' Wolf shouted above the yowling. 'You will carry me over those hills.'

The night sky was pale where the wind had moved clouds and the hills Wolf spoke of were a crust on the horizon. After a while the wind dropped away like something sucked into slumber; there was a slick of moonlight on the ground, and the crazy shape of shadows. Wolf kicked the piebald to a jerky lope and the animal squawked its displeasure.

Coyotes called in the distance; one cry followed by another; the unearthly sound of ghosts in the night. The horse's withers quivered as though an insect had alighted, and the man held it steady with his legs as they moved across the land.

There was something moving across the land, and the dog raised its head and growled. The sky was silent with stars, but the animal didn't know about that and didn't like the other sounds it could hear. It scented the air and barked, and after a while it barked again.

Emmett Hockaday snapped out of sleep as noise crashed into the room. Joanie was unaffected, still heavy in slumber with one arm trapped beneath her pillow. He eased himself from the covers and went to the window that overlooked the yard. Woken like him by the dog, horses were shuffling in the corral, but it was too dark to see if anything else was moving.

Eventually the hound was satisfied. It lay down again as heavily as a dropped rug, and became just another hump of something or nothing in the blackness. Emmett knew the prick of envy. He had been sleeping badly for hours and expected the situation to stay that way for what was left of the night. He spent a weary moment listening to his slumbering wife, lost in her own sweet oblivion. He felt rejected because she was in another world and had no need of him. A world of music, perhaps, for recently the farmhouse had become buoyant with song. The plod of daily life had been lifted by Sage Madison's voice, and every murky corner felt washed clean after she had passed.

It was good to see the young woman shine, her soul in her eyes when she opened her mouth. She was growing stronger, thanks to the attentions of his Joanie and the ladies of the church. Emmett had no truck with the church in general – the preacher was too openly pious for his liking; but his neighbour had found support inside its doors, and for that he was grateful.

He settled down again, pulling bedcovers to his chin. He could have been a corpse spread out under a shroud, waiting to be laid to rest. It would feel good to rest, for his body was still aching after the toil of the day – of many days, in fact. Emmett was not a young man and he had a farm of his own to manage, as well as all the work he had shouldered for his neighbour and her children, to counteract the drudgery that had taken over their lives after the thief absconded. The man who had helped himself to a prime stallion and broken the bond of friendship.

The farmer felt the familiar surge of wrath. Hot blood coursing through his body would only keep him awake, and so he breathed for calm instead. Wolf Shadow was good for nothing, and it was the traitor's family that Emmett cared about now. He had cut and sawn and hammered and tarred and glued and adjusted until he was pretty well worked out, but at last the steading was almost ready for them to move back in.

He would let them have the hound at night to keep them safe, of course, even though it was too sensitive, reacting to wind-blown leaves as though they were a pack of marauding killers. But it would bring Sage Madison some peace. And that singing would help also, for nobody who could sing as sweetly as she should ever suffer desperation.

Joanie turned over, facing him now but still sound asleep. She gabbled some words that made little sense. The discourse ended on a raised note, as though she was asking a question, and Emmett shook his head.

'I can't answer that one, honey,' he said. 'Because I just don't know.'

*

It had recognised the scent of affection even before the boy appeared from the porch. Treated with gruffness, thrown scraps for the most part and only fed richly on a Sunday, the dog had never before known how it felt to be petted. It barked once with excitement, and then once again at the something that may or may not have been moving across the land.

The boy said nothing but he spoke well enough with his hands, stroking the soft hair on the hound's head, calming any further sounds before they began. The dog relaxed, a satisfied growl comforting its throat, and Colt hefted the strap of the bag higher on his shoulder and crossed silently to the fidget of horses in the corral.

A little later and Vixen was carrying him away from the yard; boy and pony melding a darker shadow in the darkness of the night. As soon as it grew accustomed to what was under its hooves, the red mare fell into a fast trot, the rider tight to its back. The bag on the boy's shoulder bounced, knocking air from his lungs, his breathing short and sharp with awe at what he had done, and what he was about to do.

There was triumph as well, the feeling of bonds loosened and left behind. Bonds of anxiety and the dread of persecution that had chained him to the school where the master and his wife wallowed in indifference.

Bristling with authority, the Jacksons had taken up their stance in the porch that very afternoon, too busy overseeing the exodus of pupils to notice Colt standing on his own by the school wall. The boy hid well in shadows, but he was close enough to hear every word they said.

'Walk properly, Jonah. Do not slouch, Tarlow. Stop giggling, Silvie. Straight home, Sara. Take care, Marietta, or I shall have no choice but to speak to your mother.'

Mrs Jackson had tidied hair ribbons and straightened collars, and when all the children had been overhauled and dismissed, she smoothed the folds of her skirt instead.

'The end of another day's tuition and we are finally back to normality, Mr Jackson,' she said, brushing chalk dust from the man's sleeve. 'Untarnished by tomfoolery or hullabaloo now that the boy's dreadful father has removed himself.'

'A misplaced savage and a criminal,' her husband had replied. 'A disruptive influence.'

Mrs Jackson's nod was vehement, but her hair had been rolled so tightly to the back of her head that it was in no danger of becoming unclipped. 'I do so hope that none of the father's ways will rub off on the son.'

Mr Jackson had pursed his tight mouth, eyes narrowing between folds of skin. 'I assure you, my dear, that any indication of waywardness shall be beaten out of the boy immediately.'

'Perhaps it would have been judicious if such wilfulness had been beaten out of the father when he too was a boy,' his wife had decreed. 'A few whippings might have made him respectable.'

'The half-breed?' The schoolmaster had snorted as they went back into the building. 'Nothing could make that sort respectable. Blood will out, my dear; blood will out.'

Blood will out. Colt gripped Vixen's flanks tighter at the memory and the pony squealed. The master's words were merciless, for blood had been spilled already through schoolyard torments carried out under the teachers' noses. But the Jacksons had failed to put an end to the attacks, maybe because they had always expected the bullies to take things into their own hands.

And this they had done, for not a day went by without Colt receiving some attention from his tormentors. And the pain from each bony fist and booted foot had plugged the boy's heart with hatred. A loathing that wasn't just for Jonah Wellerson or Korky Kendall, or the Jacksons themselves. It was also for the man. The father who had left his son broken on the ground, and hadn't stayed behind long enough to gather up the pieces.

Which was why the boy was riding away on the red pony, leaving his mother sleeping in the Hockadays' house, tumbling into music that was helping her to fly. Leaving his grandma snoring, hearing nothing through ears blocked by age. Leaving his sister, wide awake.

The little girl in the lean-to knew that Sage was dreaming, for the noises that trilled from her mouth sounded like birds in the early morning. Clove's mother had found song and her soul had grown wings; but the space where her brother had been lying was already cold. Colt was sinking into the dark, and his sister wondered if she would ever see him again.

'Pa!'

Clove mouthed the word, but inside she was screaming.

'Pa, Colt has gone. And the other one is coming, Pa. The dark man is coming!'

TWENTY-EIGHT

THIS WAS a murky land under a meagre counterpane of stars. The depth of space reduced the wide plains to an outline, and Wolf rode into the void with all senses buzzing, reins sinuous between his fingers as though the leather was still alive.

The tempo of the piebald's hooves beat inside his chest, the scent of horse flared at the back of his nose. He opened his mouth and tasted the wilderness; it was the same on his tongue as it had been in the time before, when he was a boy running the gauntlet of danger and destination. But in those days his body had buzzed with the thrill of escape; ten years later he was aching from healing cuts, grinding bones, the pain in his thigh where the palomino had taken its bite.

Emmett's horse had been too full of fury to be calmed by the message in Wolf's words. The beast had found freedom, and he needed its swiftness now like never before, for the piebald was making hard work of the ride. Unfamiliar with exercise, it had started to wheeze – the sound was the rhythmic creaking of saddle leather, and it was getting louder.

Wolf didn't know how much longer he could keep going. His ribs were sore, he was fogged by pain, but if the old horse failed he was prepared to run until even his brain was hurting. The lope he had learned from his father would carry him over the miles, but it would never be fast enough to get him back in time. The spot where Colt had been lying in the night was already growing cold, the hound in the yard was restless and Vixen had been taken from the corral. He knew these things as though his daughter was there with him, whispering the words in his ear.

Time passed. The new day was a smear in the east but Wolf still had his eyes to the night. The hills were rising from the earth and coming towards him, and all he had to do was cross them to the other side where Clove's strange darkness was waiting. And something unnerving was waiting with it.

Father Thomas's steed had done its best, but it was dwindling. The old horse had borne him with a courage that had been hidden under its preference for idleness, and the young man was walking by its side now, helping it forward with dry words and promises. Instinct was to leave it unharnessed in the scrubland to find its own way, but Wolf had an obligation to the priest who had succoured him, and if he was to return the man's loan then it would be best that he bring the piebald itself and not just the saddle and an apology.

He was very tired. The sky was growing clearer by the minute but a grey lake spread before him, bothered by unearthly creatures. Things were beginning to float; they drifted closer and trickled away, and he could no longer judge distances. He stumbled frequently, crashing into obstacles that should not have been there, misjudging others that pulled back before he could reach them. It was easier to stare at the ground, weeds and mud swimming in surface water that wet his legs when he missed a step.

As the day bloomed so did the puddles, reflecting the

rising land, contours rippling as if the rocks themselves were on the move. And that wasn't all that was moving. Wolf shook his head to dispel the nonsense but when he peered up the aberration was still there, under the remnants of stars – a shimmer-shape encroaching from the hillside.

The shape split into two – a cloudy grey and a stiff-necked silver crest, gilded by the new light.

Shev Deeley's cloudy grey.

Emmett Hockaday's palomino.

Nothing was making sense.

Wolf tried to call out, just a few words, anything at all, but his throat was too clogged with dust to produce more than a whimper. He rubbed his lips with sweat because he didn't have spit for the job, dragged in a breath and tried again. It wasn't working. And now the two horses had split further. The palomino was breaking away; making for the top of the hill.

Wolf Shadow dropped the reins and left the piebald standing. He threw himself up the rise, all muscles straining, feet digging clods from the earth. He overreached, skidding on stone-debris, and the land spat him aside. He sprawled, face down, dragged himself up and climbed again, faint and fighting for air. Fighting the gradient with every sinew. He could see the horse, it hadn't gone far, there was still a chance. He filled his lungs, coughed them empty, filled them again and held the breath inside. The words jerked and cleared and surged, louder and sharper as Wolf found his voice; and the language took hold. Emmett's stallion faltered, yowling, mane scattering as it tried to shake away the trickery.

Light-headed, his ears singing, Wolf knew he was about to fall, tried not to fall, tried to keep going. He stumbled and the ground seemed to move under his feet, but the dawn wind lifted, it eased him up the slope until he had the strength to walk unaided.

Slowly the gap narrowed, the words spiralled, the relentless language drilling into the stallion's brain. Spitting foam the animal struggled, white mane leaping, shaking screams down the hill, but it was already in thrall; legs pinioned, it could barely move.

It tried to rear as the young man came closer, as though that might weaken his power. The halter rope was in frenzy, and the second before he grabbed it Wolf wondered whether he was about to find himself standing on a hillside holding nothing but a memory…

No memory; not a dream. The rope was rough and very real, and the rare beast from the Hockaday corral was raging at the end of it. Wolf jerked away from snapping teeth; he collected the last of his strength and clambered to the tawny back, fists full of mane, words silky on his tongue.

He could see further from this greater height. He searched from one side. He twisted around to search from the other, and there was the grey picking its way across the distant terrain; sedately, as befitted an old horse. There was the man leaning comfortably to its sway. Wolf kicked the stallion forward, calling his name, but Shev Deeley had already come to a stop. He was waiting for the palomino and its rider as though he had all the time in the world.

Daylight was strong now, the sun fully born but still in hiding, although some of the cloud curtain was opening to the blue beyond. Everything was clearer. If the blind man astride the grey was a vision from Wolf's hot brain then there was an unusual solidity about him, but the young man was being carried by a living horse, and that at least was no sick delirium.

As he came closer to the smell of saddle leather he could see that Shev Deeley was alive as well, his mouth puffing vapour. It didn't take long to reach the grey horse, to grab the arm of the man on its back and feel the pulse of coursing blood.

'You told me to remember your name,' Wolf said.

'It is not an easy name to forget.' Deeley's smile made the skin paler where his face was in shade. 'Maybe that is why I chose it.'

'How did this happen?'

'Happenings happen as a matter of course, Wolf Shadow. Would it not be better if you just accept?'

Wolf's head was thumping with the questions he wanted to ask. But perhaps the man was right and it was better to just accept, when delving too deeply might disturb a fragile reality, and he would wake to an empty hill with a piebald that had travelled as far as it could, and the cry of his daughter fading even further from his mind.

Shev Deeley was studying his face as if he could see again. There was a rise of heat at the back of Wolf's skull, and it fell away like comfort and took the banging pain with it. The young man felt his muscles relax; he sucked a breath and Shev seemed to flicker as though he was not an actual man at all.

'Your wounds are healing.' The voice came from a distance; somewhere up in the sky maybe. 'You have been cared for and you are on your way.'

Wolf slumped. A hand had been laid over his head and lifted suddenly, and all the strings holding him up had been sheared. His eyes wore a blind man's mist, and the cloudy grey was just a grey cloud with slits where the blue seeped through. He was gripping the stallion's mane with fingers that were too numb to feel. Nobody was speaking but he could still hear a voice. He held on to its last words for as long as possible.

'Rest now, Wolf Shadow. And then you will be ready.'

TWENTY-NINE

SAGE WOKE from desperate dreams to the gap where her son had once lain on the floor of the sleeping space. A whole day had passed since Colt's disappearance, another night following, and she entered the new morning with furious questions on her lips.

'Hush, daughter,' Martha said, holding Sage as though she was still a child herself, not yet bowed down by her father's regime. 'You will wake the little one.'

Clove was a small shape in the darkness. She was lying in the same position she had chosen the evening before, when there had been enough light pushing through from the room beyond to show that even though her eyes were closed, the fear in them was not yet extinguished.

'If only Clove would wake.' Sage's voice rose. 'If only she would talk to me.'

'Come now.' Martha flustered, a hand to her mouth, her gaze to the thin partition behind which the Hockaday couple had been trying to sleep. 'If you steal everyone's slumber, then who will be strong enough to search for Colt?'

'I should be the one to do that.' Sage pushed the meagre cover from her pallet bed and struggled to her feet. 'Colt is my son and he has need of me.'

'Heavens, child!' Martha tried to grab her as she went towards the entrance, where the privacy curtain that

Joanie had fixed for them was already moving, and Emmett stood there like a blacker shape carved out of the early shadows.

'Stay where you are, Sage,' he said, raising his arm to stop the woman pushing past. 'Stay here with your family. If anyone is going out again to look for your son, it will have to be me…'

It was the scream that stopped his words. Stopped everybody's words for shock as they stared at Clove, standing rigid by a scuffle of bedding. Pointing past Emmett Hockaday as he hovered on the threshold, his hand still raised as though he was about to bring it down on her mother's skull.

'He is here!' The child's voice was almost impossibly shrill. 'The dark man is here!'

He was dozing on the stallion's back, his last recollection before sleep took hold was that it would be better if he could just accept. It was the scream that jerked him awake; he thought there had been words behind it, something about a dark man.

A dark man? Maybe he had been thinking of Daniel Ryker, the cuckold, the friend. But the words that had woken him had been full of fear; not worthy of an acquaintance of many years, unless the Oasis doctor now had murder in mind.

The new day was growing and Wolf had not even noticed the passing of night. The land seemed different; something had smoothed away the higher peaks that he had seen before falling asleep. Maybe he recognised it. Maybe the steading was no longer so far away.

He shivered, pulling the priest's jacket firmly across his chest. Shev Deeley's blanket felt tight around his waist, but incomplete, as though a shredding wind had scattered most of it across the trail already travelled. But when he looked down the blanket had gone and it was his belt that was tight, knotted with the reins of Father Thomas's piebald.

The old horse was at a canter by the stallion's side, easier on its legs than the last time Wolf had seen it. The time when exhaustion had levitated the young man to another plane, and everything had changed.

It changed again, for finally he remembered how the blind man had appeared to him in the early morning through a crash of hills, bringing the stallion from the wilderness. Even so, there were still holes in his memory, and places where fatigue had contorted reality and left him with fading dreams.

Maybe Wolf had simply imagined that Emmett's rare beast had carried him all this way, as biddable as a palfrey under an enchantment. Although of all the wild stallions he had ever tamed to bear a rider, the palomino that bore him now was the most perverse. The no-name horse that was as flawed as the man who rode it.

'I believe that you have found trouble, Wolf Shadow.'

That is what the priest of Liberation had said, but he had also seen the young man as a cause, one that deserved salvation. Out here on the last slopes of hills that would lead him back to the problems left behind, Wolf wondered if there was to be any salvation for him, or whether he was entitled to nothing more than the expected retribution.

But he was still free, riding a pig-headed horse over rocks that surged above him in frozen waves, ready to plunge until all was smothered. Trouble had found his family in his absence, just as it had found him, and he was to blame. He had to put things right again. Nothing was going to get in the way of that.

The screaming that had woken him, however, had been difficult to hear.

Just as difficult as it was for everyone at the Hockaday homestead.

Joanie and her husband stood together at the opening, staring at Clove – the hysterical child who was fighting in her mother's arms. Martha tried to grab her hands but the little girl was strong and her claws indiscriminate. She tugged her grandma's braids, freeing strands of hair that floated like silver ghosts. Joanie collected her senses and went forward to help, until Clove was outnumbered – a six-year-old child held firm by three women.

The small room laboured with breathing, but the little girl had gone into a trance. And then she started to sob, a sound as wretched as the shrieks that were still fading from the air, even though it would take a lot longer for them to fade from Emmett Hockaday's memory.

'What does she mean?' He leaned on the wall, his shoulder cloaked by the door hanging. 'What dark man is here?'

Joanie felt his exasperation. 'The maid is distressed, Emmett.'

'I can see that.' He spoke through his teeth. 'I think we are all distressed.'

He left before he could say more, and the curtain flumped back in the space he had occupied. His wife sighed; her chest shuddered with the power of it. She felt Sage's hand on her arm. The young mother's face was hollow.

'Your cheek is bleeding,' Joanie said, touching the marks left by the little girl's nails.

'My daughter's heart is bleeding,' Sage said. 'And I do not know how to heal her.'

Joanie Hockaday took a glance at the child as though anything more obtrusive might start the devastation all over again, but the little girl was gentle now, allowing her grandma to rock her as though she was still an infant.

'Clove is a singular soul,' Joanie said. 'She needs care. Perhaps more care than you and Martha can give.'

'I hear what you are saying.' Sage looked across at the tear trails glittering her daughter's face. 'But no one else could understand her like we do.'

'If you understand her, then tell us what she means by the dark man!'

Sage took a breath, collarbones sharp at the neck of her nightgown. 'Clove knows things, Joanie,' she said. 'She knows something bad is coming, but she cannot tell us what it is.'

The doorway was interrupted. Emmett stood there once more, fully dressed and buckling a gun belt around his waist. 'I am going out to search for Colt,' he said. 'And this time I shall not return without him.

'And if I should stumble across a dark man,' he spoke for his wife alone, 'I'll kick his ass all the way to kingdom come.'

He left through the main door, whistling for the dog, and some of the early morning crept in after him, spreading a little freshness through the house.

The big stallion loped ahead as if sure of its destination, but Wolf was riding blind. The land around him was vast, and void of all but the echoes of hooves, clattering like falling rocks through gaps and gullies as they left the hills behind. The urgency increased as fast as the ground was covered, and with it the sense that he was heading in the wrong direction.

Teeth primed, the horse fought back when he pulled

it to a halt. The piebald bumped past for as long as the fastened reins allowed, as though the enforced exertions over the past couple of days had given it a taste for action.

Wolf slipped from the palomino's back and left the rope hanging from its muzzle like an anchor. He untied the piebald's reins from his belt and set the patchwork horse loose. It fanned his face with its breath and went to nose the rocks for morsels.

The young man sat on the ground between a straggle of tree roots and emptied his mind, waiting to see what lay beyond; and some miles away in the Hockaday house, the little girl opened her eyes.

Her grandma was still holding her, but she needed to be alone now. She wriggled, and Martha held her tighter for there must not be a repeat of the outburst, then tighter still because it wasn't working.

And Clove, the singular child, touched the woman's cheek with a soft palm that felt like a kiss. Her grandma opened her arms, because the little girl had told her it was all right to let go.

Clove clambered to her feet and bounced, wanting to jump high, wanting to hear. She ran to the door of the strange house where her mother had brought her to live when her father had vanished. She wrestled with the handle so urgently that Mrs Hockaday rushed forward, to protect whatever was about to be broken. Clove wanted to tell her that her heart would be broken if the door didn't open and set her free.

Sage held Mrs Hockaday still, as though she knew how important it was that the child should have her wish. 'All is well, Joanie,' she said. 'Just let my daughter go.'

The girl ran straight to the corral. The horses bunched together at her approach, then scattered like creatures that didn't know which way to turn before bunching again, but Clove meant them no harm. She never meant any harm, as long as she was allowed, just allowed.

She climbed the fence, right up to the final rung of its ladder; she lifted her head and tasted the air, and sighed the deepest sigh. Her mother stood below with arms raised, ready to catch should the child fall. But Clove was not there to fall. She was there to open the link. Her mother knew this because everything her daughter did was special. And nobody else would ever understand just how special.

Together they waited – the child above the fence and the mother beneath. And although still distant, it didn't take long for the connection to be made.

Wolf's eyes were shut but he could see his daughter's face. He opened his mind and she filled it with hers, and there was his son. He was riding Vixen towards the hills, his heart so burdened that even the little mare was suffering under the weight. Colt was alone in the wild, just as his father had been years before. The land was sucking the boy down into shadows, and Wolf had to find him before he disappeared.

And then his mind was filled with the greater shadow of a dark figure. It was swallowing up his bright daughter, his lonely son. It was swallowing Sage and the Madison farm; all that was past and all that had yet to come. A dark figure, blocking out the light until only blackness remained.

Emptiness.

Death.

He opened his eyes; he got to his feet, startling the piebald that flustered a little before returning to the crevices where grass was hiding. He left it there, snuffling at the juicy blades. He grabbed the palomino's rope and swung up on its back. He went inside his head to listen; shut his eyes to bring sound closer. He could hear the rumble of burrowing animals, the snap of twigs, the howl of wind blowing across a breach in the rocks. He could hear the piebald chewing and the palomino ploughing the ground with impatient hooves. And just above that, slightly discordant, he could hear a distant tapping that might have been a carrion bird pecking at the carcass of a rat. Or the jogging of a red pony with a boy on its back.

His face whipped by mane, Wolf Shadow dug heels into the stallion's flanks and the horse reared, leaping into a gallop before its legs had reached the ground.

THIRTY

OASIS WAS growing dull with the drawing in of the year, and Sheriff Andy Parnell was adding to the general atmosphere with that thickset face of his. This was what Clay Russett considered from his vantage point on the sidewalk, balancing on the hind legs of a chair outside the Misses Elsey Dress Shop for Dainty Ladies.

The curtains at the tall bay window had been flickering for a while, the two proprietresses taking turns to check on the white-haired man outside, flaunting gravity in his precarious seat. He was doing no harm from what they could see, as they fluttered together in their taffeta and lace (direct from Paris, France), but he was likely to deter customers if he should stay there much longer.

It was all irrelevant to the former sheriff of Oasis, who had eyes only for the officious meddler prancing around in the office just across the street. The man had a lot to learn, but very little in his head to learn it with, Russett decided, projecting a judgemental globule of spit towards the road, before touching the brim of his hat to a speechless woman who had adroitly avoided being splattered on her way to make a Dainty Ladies purchase. Just as adroitly she turned on her heel, changing her mind about the length of pink satin that was to add a touch of daring to the hem of an outgrown skirt. But Russett didn't know anything about that.

'By all that's eternal, what has that monkey been up to?' he muttered, glaring through the sheriff's window as Parnell balanced a rifle on his desk and slipped off his jacket.

'Erm… Mr Russett.' Angelica Elsey peered around the open door of her emporium just to the fore of her younger sister, her hair so expertly curled that the ringlets bounced like wire springs. 'Might I enquire as to whether you intend to spend much more of your day sitting out here?'

He glanced over at the intrusion and saw a concerned citizen. 'That man enforces the law in this town as if he was a private army of one,' he said.

'Well, I'm sorry to hear that, but with regard to our clientele…'

'He's been tangling with something.' Russett wagged a finger in the seamstress's face. 'And I've a good mind to find out just what it is.' He stood up suddenly, and his chair skidded backwards. 'Are you with me?'

Without waiting for a reply, he stepped down from the sidewalk and marched across the road, passing the hitching post and the well-ridden horse that Parnell had left to steam in the cool air.

Miss Elsey watched him go with relief. 'In spirit, Mr Russett, only in spirit,' she said, adjusting the cuffs of her blouse before shooing her sister back inside the store.

Russett marched into the sheriff's office, as if it was still his territory, and Andy Parnell turned as the door creaked open, before replacing the rifle in the rack on the wall. His deputy took no notice, too busy opening drawers – maybe looking for a length of rope, Clay reflected, to tie up that sallow-faced wiseacre and make certain he kept his nose out of innocent people's affairs.

Parnell brushed down his vest with tired hands. Trail dust scattered, but the creases from a heavy ride stayed put. 'Anything I can do for you, Mr Russett?'

'That's just what I was about to ask you, Parnell.'

The sheriff half-closed his eyes. 'Make it quick if you want to speak to me. I have work to get on with.'

Clay Russett leaned back against the wall and made himself comfortable. Parnell's audible sigh raised a little smile. 'Where in blazes have you been, Sheriff, with your arms full of fire power?'

'I've been out minding my own business, old man, and I suggest that you do the same.'

Parnell offered a set of handcuffs for the deputy to replace in his drawer and turned back to find Russett standing in front of him; too much bulk to push aside, even though the younger man was obviously thinking about it.

'From one law officer to another, Andy, why don't you tell me who the manacles were for?'

Parnell studied the man from his matted hair to his cracked boots, and for once there was a twisted smile on his face, as though he might even have a little respect for the tenacity of this thorn in his side.

'They were for a particular lowlife who helped himself to someone else's horse a few days ago and bolted to the hills.'

'Then he's already had a few days' head start.' Clay chuckled and his shoulders bounced. 'He isn't likely to have waited for you to find him, Sheriff.'

'Well, I know that!' Parnell bristled. 'But Emmett Hockaday was a touch tardy in reporting the crime.' He adjusted the gun belt around his hips until he was satisfied with its weight. 'Seems he's been too busy attending to the needs of the thief's family.'

Russett sucked in his mouth and stood straight. 'Exactly who is this thief?'

'A troublemaker of your acquaintance.' The sheriff lifted off his hat, exposing lines of dirt and flattened hair. He nodded at the unease that was creasing the other man's face. 'And I don't think you need me to tell you who that might be.'

He slapped the hat against his leg and tossed it on the desk. The dust followed, turning to grit and falling to the floor as he took his seat. 'Is there anything else I can help you with?' he said, but Clay didn't hear. He was too busy remembering Wolf Shadow on the day that he had been flung out of the Rykers' place with his clothes torn and blood in his hair.

The old man had been disturbed by the raucous group gathering near the doctor's house and its guard of tall trees; he had seen the missile flying and Wolf stumbling to the ground like so much fodder for amusement. And Russett had been ashamed of himself, because he too had stood amongst the jeering citizens who cast stones and passed judgements, as though they had a right.

Wolf Shadow had needed friends that day and none had been forthcoming. Clay Russett didn't want to know what sin the young man had committed to merit Daniel Ryker's disapproval, but now he'd gone way beyond sin. He'd broken the boundaries by stealing his neighbour's horse.

That was stupid, and unforgivable.

What the hell was wrong with him?

THIRTY-ONE

DARKNESS HAD been building up in the sky and now there was a power behind it. Colt lifted his chin and felt the first drops on his face, like something that may only be gentle to start with. Unwisely he had left the homestead without preparing for rain, and he was going to get so wet.

He had left without preparing for anything much at all, not least for where the journey would lead him. He had set Vixen on the path and now she seemed to have taken control of the route, as if she knew where she was going. At least Colt hoped that the little mare knew where she was going. He had gone astray a while since, wasting time by winding in pointless circles, and now he was miserably adrift, and ashamed.

He had been raised on the story of his father's escape from tyranny. When just a few years older than Colt was now, Wolf Shadow had scouted this land on foot; he had found a horse to ride, dealt with people standing in his way, and nearly reached his destination. He had known which direction to take. It sounded so easy when he described it in that bare bones way of his, skimming the bad bits and dwelling on the good.

Wolf had transformed his own ride to freedom into an adventure, so why should it be any different for his son? What's more, Colt had begun this quest with every intention of making it to the end. Unlike his father and a weakened horse, no ill fortune was going to drag him back to the Madison farm. Such brave determinations; nonsense hatched under cover in the Hockadays' lean-to. He wasn't going to make it to the end now, because he was lost – chasing his tail and rummaging for bearings. The grandson of an Indian and he did not even know the lie of his own landscape.

For a while the wetness on his face was only due in part to the downpour. Which was growing heavier, batting against his head like something that had an urge to get inside. His jacket was offering little resistance and it didn't take long for the rain to find his skin.

This land was far too open; easy terrain for a gathering of water. Although there was a group of trees over the way; outlines misted behind the pewter-grey weather, but still canopied by a weave of branches that may protect him from the worst of the deluge. Colt was about to guide Vixen in that direction before he realised that the pony was heading that way by herself. She really did know where she was going, and her rider was grateful. And humbled. He was feeling very small out in the wide world beyond, and his nine years sounded like a short length of time that stood for nothing.

The bag he had brought with him was sucking up a great deal of water. It lay against his side as cumbersome as a damp dead animal. He tried to remember what it contained – some items he thought he couldn't do without, swiftly garnered from prized possessions he had arranged by his bed. Not his own bed, just a truckle on the floor of a borrowed space in someone else's home. Everything in Colt's life had shrunk; even his family was reduced in size on account of the father who had fled like a coward in the night.

Rainwater had soaked right through the boy's clothes, as greedy as a hungry bear with a nose for warm flesh. Colt sat upright on Vixen's back and tried not to shiver, but even so his bones were bumping together as the pony climbed the slopes that were rolling down from the wooded place.

Now the trees were nearer, reaching out to collect the boy and his pony with twisted branches that would stem the weather for a while. If Colt should find any that were dry enough maybe he could put together a sulphur-match fire for his comfort. And he could eat what remained of the food he had gleaned from Mrs Hockaday's kitchen, even though there had been more gaps on the shelves than he remembered, and not much to take. In his hunger he would be strong, just as Wolf Shadow had taught him.

Colt shook his head to rid himself of that memory, and it fell away and left him empty. He couldn't think about his father; there was too much hatred crossing that path. He thought instead about finding shelter on the green hill that was coming very close now that Vixen had risen to a canter. She splashed his legs with water from the ground, but he was too cold to feel it, until he was gathered in by trees. Suddenly it seemed warmer, and the wetness was lifting, way up into the sky beyond the stretch of canopies that were clasped like the linked arms of friends.

He didn't have to pull Vixen to a halt, she halted by herself and began to nose the earth for nourishment. The boy slid from her back, his legs buckling, and stood like someone on the deck of a boat for a few moments before he could think of walking. The ground did not appear welcoming enough to light a fire, or even to sit down. But at least, and at last, he could eat.

Colt pulled open the neck of the bag with fingers that were too numb for the pain of torn nails. He found the nub end of a loaf in there and a shard of sweet pastry, and that was all. The bread was sopping, like a sponge, and the pastry fell apart before he could lift it clear of the bag, but he stuffed what he could into his mouth and swallowed without satisfaction.

And then he chose a tree with an accommodating trunk and began to climb, leaving the wetness below for the wetness above, that seemed somehow less. He got halfway up before the handholds finished and the tree was smooth and straight, rising above him with lowered branches that could have formed an umbrella if there had been silk stretched between them. Branches that still bore a thickness of summer leaves; maybe thick enough to keep the worst of the rain away.

He picked one and put it in his mouth, because it was green and looked juicy and he was still hungry. He spat it out before it could leave its bitter taste on his tongue, and settled back as comfortably as possible, wedging himself in a knobbled fork. He tried to huddle inside his jacket, as though that might afford some warmth and protection. He could always pretend that it did. For a boy familiar with the schoolmaster's callous treatment, and who had fooled his own mother into believing stuff that wasn't as true as it might be, Colt had learned a lot about pretending.

But why worry about any of that now? He was finally on his way, wasn't he? Following the paths that his father would have followed all those times he had ridden out alone on Night Dancer, or on the horse before Night Dancer, or the one before that.

For all of his young life Colt had watched Wolf Shadow riding away. His first ever sight of the man had probably been of his back, as he left for yet another trip into the wild. Left his son behind, just as he always did. Colt had grown up wishing that one day he would be allowed to ride beside him, sleeping under the stars, brewing up the morning coffee on a friendly fire. Seeing the land through his father's eyes, speaking with his tongue, learning about his life. It had never happened, and now it never would. There was no point in wishing for attention from someone who didn't even know he existed.

It was easy to relax in the arms of the tree, with all the other trees standing sentinel. The grove was a slice of calm cut out of the turmoil beyond; that which wasn't required had been kept away. The atmosphere was almost holy, prayers may once have been said beneath the leaves and eyes closed to everything that was hurtful. And that is why Colt thought it would be okay to close his own eyes for a minute or two, or at least until the rain had done its worst and retreated back into the sky.

He slept in peace and deeply, building up the hours that he had lost since riding away from the Hockaday farm. He was not aware that Vixen had stopped chewing, lifting her head from the ground to search for the sound she had heard. She made a noise in her throat that might have been warning or threat; or it might have been a welcome, for her ears ceased their flicking and settled, and the grass blades became interesting again.

She took no notice of the shadowy man who was moving closer, so quietly that it was as if he was floating above the floor of leaves and vegetation. She didn't feel the touch of his hand on her neck, although her skin had quivered where his fingers stroked.

The little red mare thought nothing of it when the stranger looked up to the fork in the tree where Colt was sleeping. Or that when he saw the boy huddling like a child curled in his bed, the dark man raised his fist in the air and held it there, as straight and strong as an arrow.

THIRTY-TWO

EMMETT HOCKADAY eased backwards until his spine clicked into place. The resultant twinge of pain didn't help to minimise the frown that had been gouging a deeper furrow during the lengthening expedition.

A number of hours had passed since he had ridden away from his farmyard as keenly as a young man, with his gun in its holster and his dog skimming an eager nose across the ground. Now Emmett was feeling all of his fifty years, and the keenness had died and been carried up in the air, to fall again as dispiriting rain. But the words he had voiced back in the house were still rattling inside his head as if there was nothing else up there to stop them, and he scowled at the fool who had spoken them.

'I am going to search for Colt and I shall not return without him.'

Rash words from a numbskull who thought the trail of a mere child would be easy to follow. The trouble was that there was no trail to follow. Neither were there any tracks, or at least none that showed much logic. The dog had picked up a scent, that was true, but it had passed into another scent and somewhere along the line it had come to an end. There was no accounting for it, unless the kid had actually been going in circles.

By this time Emmett knew quite a bit about going in circles. But he had spent too long chasing a falsehood, and now the farm was calling him home. For a few moments the idea of breaking loose and riding away completely was overwhelming – in fact, doing just what Colt's father had done without qualm or reason. Escape appeared as second nature to the likes of Wolf Shadow, and the good folk of Oasis had had plenty to say about that over the few years that the Hockadays had lived above the valley road. Emmett had taken little notice of it before but he knew better now, and this saddened him, because it meant that the trusted and respected young man whom he had once considered a friend was in truth nothing but a liar and a thief. And that made Emmett a bigger fool.

Mindful of the need to feel more masterful, his hand closed on the gun at his waist. For a moment he savagely relished the notion of pointing it at Wolf Shadow's head. But it was only a moment, quickly pacified when Joanie came into his mind. The kindest woman that ever lived, she had always believed in the young man and – to her credit and Emmett's incredulity – probably still did.

Then he thought of the last time he had seen Sage Madison, standing in that cluttered lean-to with the reckless child in her arms. She had been staring at him, eyes wide with trust. Sage believed that her neighbour was going to do what he promised and bring her son back – it was as simple as that.

Emmett sighed loudly enough to spook his horse, and the hound gazed up at him with its tongue lolling, catching rain. Rain that was swaying as it fell, with gaps in the sway through which he could see a rise of ground some way ahead, crowned with a bird's nest of trees by the look of it. He had nowhere in particular to go, so why not head for a place where he may gain some respite from the water that was trickling down his back? And anyway, he might be able to see further from that small hill, which could decide where he should aim for next.

The rain kept them company as they travelled. Soon it had grown familiar and Hockaday hardly noticed it, except when overspill from the hat brim distorted his sight, so that for a while everything which should have been still was in motion, and everything which moved was in hiding. Like the distant figures of horse and rider that had been darkened to smudge by the weather. That grew darker still as they drew nearer to the trees.

By now the rain had become a cloak, and Wolf Shadow wore it like a second skin. The palomino's hide was the colour of bronze, glossy as polish and just as slippery. Wolf had to grip tighter, until every muscle in his legs was hard and he and the stallion had merged into one wet creature.

He had been riding since dawn, after taking a halt for some of the night so that the horse should be sufficiently rested for whatever might be asked of it in the coming day. Despite closing his own eyes, any hope Wolf had of sleep had been frustrated by the clamouring in his head. But that was no matter, for it meant that his daughter was still with him. His mind and heart were filled with Clove's image, his ears with a fall of sound. It might have been the clatter of the land, the drub of the stallion's hooves, the drone of fatigue in his brain. But Wolf Shadow knew that it was the child calling to him through the susurration of rain.

However, there was more to Clove's message than just a welcome; there was fear lurking beneath, sharp as a lightning flash. She knew something was coming, that it was surrounded by the dark, and her father was still too far away to help.

This territory was bleak under the rain, as though dissolving down to the colour of steel. The ground was riven with drifts of water, and sometimes dangerous hollows where the depth was hidden beneath false levels. Hollows where an unwary animal might step too hard, maybe stumbling, maybe snapping a leg. It was risky to gallop when vision was poor, and so Wolf and the stallion loped. The landscape rose and fell with them as smoothly as waves on a gentle sea, and the journey was shortened by every passing minute. Every interminable minute of what was left of the day.

THIRTY-THREE

COLT SLUMBERED on, and the man beneath his tree stood motionless, almost like a tree himself, rough and rugged and caped in black. The rain washed his face, seeking the grooves in his cheeks and making a winding river of his long hair. He looked up at the sleeping boy, and then he stepped away to where the horses had flocked – his dun and the little bay standing close enough to share the same breath. The dun shook its tail like a dusky skirt around the mare's hindquarters but didn't move when the man came forward, reaching into a saddle bag for the oiled cloth and the rabbit's leg that he had roasted the day before.

Returning to the tree he held the leg aloft, freeing cowhide fringes to ripple down the sleeves of his jacket. The smell of cooked meat was not strong, but in this thicket where tree leaned against tree and what was left between them was funnel, it lifted towards the boy, filling his dreams with saliva until he woke to the grind of hunger.

Colt couldn't remember where he was, and when he found that he was balancing over terra firma on a narrow branch, he couldn't remember what had brought him there. The rain, however, was a constant, in and out of his dreams, its tang filling his nostrils and barely leaving enough room for the scent of food. It was when he looked down that he knew what had woken him – and by that time, he was too frozen to move. It wasn't due to the numbness creeping inside to still his heart, for the beating was fierce now, and loud enough to send echoes into his throat. The reason he couldn't move was because of the Indian who was standing below, raising a rabbit's leg like a lure.

The boy opened his mouth to silence; his teeth were chattering too hard to allow space for speech. After a moment his whole body began to chatter and the tree jolted, knocking him off kilter.

He slipped down the trunk. Slowly at first, his hands too dazed by cold to grab at the wet lichen, but then with speed, until he couldn't help himself. He cried out as he fell, knowing that the landing would be unforgiving. But instead the landing was kind, and it took a second to understand that his body was in suspension, and another second to realise what was holding him up.

The man appeared to be balancing the boy in his arms, as though deciding where it might be safe to set him down. The scent of wet leather mingled with cooked rabbit in Colt's nostrils, and there was another smell that he thought he recognised, before a sudden gust of air swept it away. There was no sensation in his legs. He wallowed when he tried to stand, as though he was being sucked into the mulch of mud and old leaves. Something dark was thrown over his head. He was surrounded by noises – a scraping and a flapping and wind in his face. It was as if the world was coming to an end.

Unmindful of the marshy ground, the man had sunk to his haunches, his leather tunic patched by rain. Colt was wearing the black cape now. The water ran down its slopes and couldn't get to him. The rabbit's leg was held out again and he snatched it and filled his mouth. He had never in his young life tasted anything so delicious. It fed all his senses for the short time it lasted, and even that small amount of food sent his blood coursing. He felt stronger now, more awake now, ready to fight for his life if fighting was needed.

The burst of fierceness was a swift one; it flared inside him and fell back depleted, leaving the impression that all was well. An oddness had entered the group of trees with the dark man, as though what had been real a minute earlier had stepped away from itself and was floating in the air. Colt thought he could hear words. Perhaps they were in the wind that was battling with the mesh of branches. He tried to listen, but the clatter of sound was too distant to make any sense. Although that didn't seem to matter; it was the listening that was important, not the hearing.

He lifted his head with some difficulty to look at the stranger beside him, crouching on a root of the boy's tree. The man was staring out at something that might be coming towards him through the foliage; his hand on the knife at his belt as if he was preparing to use it. Even though he appeared to be old, he had the posture of a younger man. The bones of his face had been sculpted by the wind and the weather and the tides of life, the grooves ploughing deeper shadows under the light. His skin was the colour of earth, and the sight of him seemed to flicker as though he had learned how to conceal himself in this earthen place. His hair was dark in the rain but grey as iron at the temples, and a coil of marks snaked across his forehead and partway down his cheeks in a design that didn't make any sense.

The rain was washing in and out of the man's open eyes, but Colt was untouched, thanks to the covering that had been wrapped around his body. The familiar scent was stronger now, and he strained hard to remember where he had smelled it before. The man blinked as though the boy's concentration had broken his own. He looked down, and Colt jolted when their eyes met.

'Who are you?' he said. Or at least that is what he wanted to say, but the power of speech needed time to grow. He cleared his throat and tried again, although it sounded more hog-like than human.

'No trying to speak.' The voice was as dry as gravel and so quiet it seemed to reside in Colt's mind. The man shook his head, and the markings on his brow were pale, silvered like old scarring. They made the boy think of the lines that crossed his father's back and painted their own silver when the summer browned his skin.

The man returned to the bag that had held the rabbit's leg. There was more of the animal still inside. He pulled out a second limb, also wrapped in oiled cloth, and the boy took it without hesitation, chewing the meat and sucking the bone until all the edges of his hunger had been smoothed. Like something sneaking up on him he realised that feeling had crept back into his fingers, and his toes were almost whole again. He recollected his manners as well and offered thanks for the food before getting to his feet. There was nothing beyond the blank look on the man's face, but Colt could feel a tugging in his head as though he was being investigated.

He started to unravel himself from the black cape, to hand it over with more thanks. 'I have to leave now,' he said.

Vixen was sheltering at the place where the thinner trees made way for the empty land, and the dun was close beside her, its hide as pallid as a ghost horse. The rain was stopping, the clouds ripping apart like soft grey cotton. The ground would be easier to ride now for the distance Colt had to travel, whatever that might be.

He was holding out the waterproof, but the man wasn't taking it. He took the boy's arm instead, his grip too hard to ignore. 'No. You stay,' he said. 'Together we wait for what is coming.'

Colt couldn't move. There was a rushing in his head like a dam bursting, and the strange scent that he knew from somewhere became a smell he had lived with all his life in the house at the Madison steading.

He stared up at the dark man; and his father's eyes stared back at him.

The black cape fell to the earth like something that had died.

THIRTY-FOUR

MORNING HAD bloomed early, the sun ripping sheets of clouds apart as if there were muscles in the sky. But now its potency was hiding behind a lamentation of pewter-grey, and a wall of rain was coming their way. The air was heavy; the three women at the farmstead were heavy as well, and there was nothing much they could do about it.

Joanie had been outdoors for some time, winding through her chores as if ticking them off a list. Martha had watched her through the window, before donning a shawl for the cold and offering assistance. And then after a while of helping she stepped away from the neat, sweet-scented yard where hens were glossy and everything was in order, and started walking down the hollow road that led into the valley.

Oasis pulled back in the opposite direction, a town much like any other – such as the one where she had lived as a child, even though she hardly thought about it any more. Or about the parents who had so despised her husband. Maybe they'd had an inkling of the monster he would become, his blood curdled by drink. But their daughter had chosen love over kin, for Haine Madison had once been a handsome young man. Just as she had once been a foolish young woman. Now he was dead, and she was older. If that meant wiser – Martha decided as she reached the walls of her house – well then it did not amount to much.

She had expected to be greeted by scenes of neglect and anarchy, hungry animals and tools damaged beyond salvage; but the homestead came as a surprise. Even though it had been a matter of days since the place was abandoned, in all the hours he could spare from his own steading, Emmett had re-erected the toppled fences, patched up what was cracked, brought fodder for the beasts and an axe to the wood pile. And he also had a plan to bring Night Dancer back to the empty corral, as if that might encourage the black stallion's master to return – if only to reunite with his broken family, which was more than he deserved.

Emmett was a good man and he had done his best, but there were jobs that only a woman might consider important. Martha spat on her hands before taking a broom to the floor of the house, and wound her palms with dusting rags in order to brighten up the pictures on the walls.

She swept and brushed and sang as she cleaned, and Joanie Hockaday toiled in her yard just along the road. The older women were easing their minds with work, but Sage's mind was cluttered and her legs were aching as she stood by her neighbour's corral fence, where Clove had been since early light, balancing as near to the top as she could get. At times the child's arms were raised and at times her head was bowed, but the brightness in her eyes was steadfast. Her lips moved, although there were no words to hear. The message in her silence, however, was eloquent.

Peace had returned to the Hockaday home. Clove had climbed the fence in the yard and a connection had been made. Sage stood below her now and wondered what it meant. She wanted to feel the same serenity she could see in the little girl's face, but the sinister prophecy had stabbed a ragged hole in the young woman's heart that refused to close.

'Please tell me what you see. What dark man is here? Daughter, why will you not speak to me?'

It was no use begging. The child had not spoken since the night that hell had arrived in the sleeping house. The night that three women had struggled to restrain her, and Emmett had gone outside to disappear.

Clove was waiting, and so they all had to wait. But Sage couldn't bear it. Sometimes she just wanted to scream.

That morning Martha had had words with her.

'There is only one who can see inside that little maid's mind, daughter, but he has left us and taken the secret with him.'

'He left because I made him go.'

'No one forced him to lie with the doctor's wife, Sage. Like any man who acts upon his urges, he earned the outcome…'

'But did I do the right thing?'

Martha had lifted her hands as though she wished nothing more than to fill them with cooking pots, spoons and ladles, the chopping of onions to brown for a stew. But those mundane actions were things of the past, along with everything else that had once made sense of her existence. Her present consisted entirely of memories. She longed to go back in time to when the family was complete and there was not even a suspicion of the shattering that was to come.

Her arms had begun to shake. She was weary to the bone, but her daughter was expecting an answer that would make sense of the question.

'Did Wolf Shadow do the right thing when he chose another woman's body over yours?' Martha said, and Sage had flinched from the barb's bite, a small movement that brought a blood-spot of colour to her cheek.

'That must be what he believed, Ma.'

'Then we have no further use for such a sinner,' Martha had declared, wondering if she really meant it.

She thought about that again on her return from the Madison farm, bones aching after the effort to restore some tidiness to the home that the sinner had worked so hard to rebuild. Rain had taken charge of the sky by then, and the shawl wrapped over her head was sopping. The wet restricted her sight, even though there was nothing to see, for the Hockaday yard had been buried under a lethargy that hugged the ground like fog.

Joanie was sheltering by the porch. Martha's skirts wept water as she passed inside to find towels and dry garments, but the other woman scarcely felt the drops. It was quiet out there, the steady pattering drowning all other sound. Birds huddled under the eaves, the animals in the fields lowered heads and clumped together, horses were bumping the corral fence as though they had a mind to break through and gallop away.

Captivity had been creeping up on Joanie Hockaday for a number of days now, binding her with weighty chains, and she recognised the horses' desire to escape. Her beloved homestead had made roots of her shoes, burrowing deep in the ground. But even so it was better to be outside the house where the air at least smelled of freedom, for the mood inside was almost solid.

Nobody's fault. Blame the weather, blame the lack of sleep and the lack of space. Blame the absence of the men, and the boy who was lost to himself in some wilderness that not even the nose of Emmett's dog had yet been able to infiltrate.

She took a breath and held it until her head buzzed. The rain was skipping across the yard, scouring holes in the mud and varnishing the barn walls; but it didn't seem to have affected the something or other that was floating from the corral fence, where Clove had been at her strange vigil before the weather drove her indoors. What could it be? A banner, maybe? A scrap of blanket playing in the downpour?

Or was it a fragment of enchantment that the child had conjured over evenings spent knitting with her grandma? Stretching in the air as though a breeze had given it wings, and shimmering like a rainbow.

Joanie lifted her feet, snapping the greedy roots. She marched into the house, disturbing the woman who was sitting by the stove. Sitting so close it looked as if she was about to feed herself to the golden glow – a flare up of energy before she crumpled to ash.

Sage stared up at the intruder, and Joanie saw age pull at her face as though she was coming back from a past that had not been easy. But it was a moment's anomaly, swiftly dispersed, and Sage was young again, despite the shadows that made hollows of her eyes. Joanie touched her hand; it was nothing but a collection of bones.

'Gather your shawl, honey, for you and I are going into town.'

As she had expected, Sage made gestures of refusal, turning back to the stove as though something inanimate was preferable to the older woman's vigour. She tried to speak but the words were too deep in her throat to be heard. However, the gist was understood.

'Sorry, Miss Madison, but I will brook no argument,' Joanie said. 'So go and fetch your shawl.'

The young woman's back straightened, as narrow as

a spearhead. Joanie was glad to see it, although she readied herself for a skirmish.

'I cannot leave.'

'Oh, for certain you can.'

Sage turned at that, staring up at her friend with sharp eyes. 'And what if my son comes back to me and I am not here to receive him?'

'Then he will just have to wait patiently until you return.'

'No, Joanie. You go to town if you wish it but I need to stay put.'

Joanie Hockaday crouched beside the woman's chair, bringing their heads so close together that hair mingled.

'Listen to me, sweetheart,' she said quietly, every word precise. 'You have been locked inside yourself for so long that you have started to shrink. Tell me what will happen to Colt and Clove when you have disappeared altogether?'

'Ma will take care of them.' Sage sighed; it was an eerie sound, and although she was surrounded by warmth, Joanie still shivered.

'Yes, Martha will do that for sure,' she said. 'But right now it is I who must take care of you.'

'Once Wolf Shadow had a mind to that.'

Wolf Shadow. Joanie felt a surge of animosity that took her by surprise, but she relished this burn of anger. The power of it was invigorating.

'That may have been so, Sage, but I am here and he is not. I understand that there is no comparison between the two of us, and I realise what a paltry replacement I am for the man who turned his back on his own family. But the ladies of the church are waiting for us, and you know well how much it hurts to be disappointed.'

Sage didn't speak for a moment or two, smoothing

away creases from her skirt as if allowing herself time to decide. And then she got to her feet with a suddenness that Joanie saw as admirable.

'Let me make some adjustment to my hair and I shall be with you shortly,' she said, going towards the alcove at the back of the room; the place where her daughter was charming new life to the yarn on her needles.

Sage stood at the entrance, halted by the colours between the child's hands. She spoke without turning. 'It may be that I shall not find my singing voice today, so you will have to make the music happen for us both, Mrs Hockaday.'

'In which case,' Joanie said quietly to the space where she had been, 'I shall try to be like Clove, and make magic happen as well.'

THIRTY-FIVE

JOANIE HOCKADAY recalled those words as she and Sage were racketing along the valley road a while later, the buggy wheel's creak berating her for its lack of a good greasing. In fact, there had been a lack of interest in anything to do with the farm since the whirlwind had carried off three well-loved people in quick succession, and during moments alone in the room that she and Emmett normally shared Joanie had questioned the reason behind it all. Perhaps she had been infected by the same lethargy as the young woman beside her, gripping the narrow seat as they juddered over obstacles hiding in the puddles.

As far as Joanie could tell Sage had tidied her hair, twisting it anew under clips until it was higher on her head, revealing her achingly narrow neck and the fragility of her shoulders. A mother of two children but looking more like a child herself inside her waterproof cape, Sage was staring through the rain as though she couldn't wait for the town to come closer. That was how it seemed to her companion, but both women were keeping their own counsel and neither one could know what the other was thinking.

Sage was thinking of Clove, and how earlier that day she had been persuaded back indoors when the rain showed no sign of lessening. The little girl had obeyed immediately, clambering from the fence with a rush that spoke of an ending. And now she was busy knitting in the lean-to, the curtain across the opening hiding her from the rest of the house.

A small space to begin with, the alcove shrank even further under the murky light, but the atmosphere had been far from bleak when Sage went in to collect her shawl and twist her hair.

Martha was resting on folds of bedding and Clove had been sitting on the floor with her back against the wall, all her concentration centred on the needles and the ragged bundle of yarn. And it seemed to Sage that the threads had been re-dyed with their original hues of rose pink and spring green, the blue of an evening sky and sun-yellow bright enough to sting. She had shut her eyes to the dazzle, opening them once again to the washed-out grey of elderly garments that her mother had unravelled and rolled into balls.

Martha had looked up at her standing by the opening, the curtain in her hand, and she answered the question even before it had been asked – as though she had read it from her daughter's face.

'Don't worry, Sage. Everything will be all right.'

'But how can I go out and leave you alone, Ma?'

'I shan't be alone; I have this little maid for company.' She waved a hand at Clove. 'A maid with enchanted fingers. Just look at what she can do with two sticks and a hank of old wool.'

Sage had crouched down beside the child, smelling the garden scent that rose from her hair.

'Be a good girl for your grandma, Clove, and when Mrs Hockaday and I return maybe we can…' She searched her mind for the rest of the sentence. 'We can sing together. Would you like that?'

There had been no response, and Sage thought of how easy it was for Wolf, communicating with his daughter in the way that he did; a way without words that she could never share. She had felt rebuffed. But then Clove had smiled at her, a sudden transformation that would have brought sunshine through a storm-pocked window, and the young woman had come away with the image in her heart.

The memory of that smile was travelling with her now, and not even the rain could wash it away. It was keeping at bay the chill of bedraggled townsfolk and their pinched faces as Joanie drove down the main street towards the church.

The two women left the buggy for the pale building, its bell tower dripping as though weeping tears for sinners. The door was partly open, but there was no emergence of harmonium or song, just an agitation of voices striving for precedence. The ladies of the choir had collected below the altar, pecking away at each other like starlings, and nobody noticed the newcomers.

Joanie Hockaday slipped off her waterproof and shook it gently, wet spots blessing the polished floor. And then she shook it with more emphasis, until the movement disturbed the conference, and the voices clipped off one by one. The ladies stared, accompanied in their silence by the rain knocking on the roof as though demanding access.

'I trust that Miss Madison and I are not too late to join in the practice,' Joanie said, laying her damp garment on the nearest chair.

There was a moment's hush, and then a flurry of feet came towards them, tapping echoes from the high rafters. A few choristers had remained by the altar cloth, their humble dresses severely outlined by its embroidery;

the others brought welcome to the two by the door.

'We didn't know whether we might see you today.'

'But here you are now. And looking so… so well.'

The words tailed off to an embarrassed silence, by which time the two women had been accompanied all the way to the dais, where the harmonium was primed and ready. Where Margharita Kendall was waiting to enfold Sage to her bosom, wet shawl and all.

'My dear, you have been suffering; to me it is obvious although not so much to others.' Mrs Kendall glanced pointedly at the ladies by the altar. There was some muttering, to which she paid little attention.

She gripped Sage's hands. 'I regret to tell you that Mr Kendall has been leading the hullabaloo that has resulted from your husband's expulsion.'

'Expulsion?' Sage pulled back from the word, but the other woman kept her hold.

'Forgive my bluntness,' she said, quietly now, 'but the news has filtered through that Sheriff Parnell had to… persuade Mr Shadow to leave town.'

Sage slid her hands free. 'That ought not to be of interest to anyone, except of course as the subject of gossip.'

'In a predictable world,' Margharita said, 'I am afraid it is the unpredictable that excite curiosity.'

So Wolf was unpredictable, was he? It was a good label for a man like him. Life with Wolf Shadow had been surprising, disconcerting, infuriating. And wonderful.

Would she have wanted it any other way?

Sage gazed up at the tall window where the day seemed paler. The rain was ceasing. She remembered Clove's remarkable smile, and realised that there might, after all, be blue sky beyond the cloud.

The church was full of light, and Margharita didn't

273

believe it was because the door had just opened to deliver Mrs Hetherington in from the street.

'My husband is the leader of fools who hang on his every word,' she said. 'And if I aspired to even a quarter of your mettle, Miss Madison, I would ask the sheriff to expel him as well.'

'Margharita.' Sage spoke quickly before the heavy footsteps could reach the end of the aisle. 'I want all my family together again. I want Wolf Shadow back.'

It was only after she had voiced the words that she knew them to be true.

There was a rustle of song sheets behind her, followed by a discordant shriek from the harmonium as Mrs Hetherington brought them to order.

'As always, ladies, you must do your best to achieve perfection with your performance,' she declared. 'But today I am feeling unusually benevolent, and willing to show mercy for your mistakes.'

She raised a hand, ready to strike the first note. 'You are, after all,' she said, 'only human.'

THIRTY-SIX

EMMETT HOCKADAY didn't realise the rain had finished until he perceived that it was no longer disturbing his hat. He removed it to shake collected water from the brim, and coolness lay like a hand over his hair.

The sky was clearing swiftly, as though losing patience with the grey matter that had blocked out the light, and the gathering of lofty trees on the slight hill ahead appeared to be waving, like friends preparing to greet the weary traveller and his weary horse.

Emmett flung back the flaps of his waterproof, but it was an old garment suffering from weak seams, and he felt slovenly in his damp clothes. As the hours had passed so had his thoughts, and with increasing frequency since the rain began. The roof of his house came to mind and the protection it afforded to everyone inside; and how much he would like to be home again with black coffee scalding his gullet and the scent of Joanie's cooking teasing the back of his nose.

The dog, its coat as wet as sealskin, seemed to agree, uttering an eloquent howl that rumbled from its chest like a banshee cry.

'It is a welcome thought, hound,' Hockaday muttered. 'And we will be back there before nightfall, with or without the boy.' For promise or no promise, he was swiftly losing patience with this foolhardy errand.

The dog made the ghoulish howl again, but this time with an edge to the sound. The animal had slunk lower to the ground as if afraid that something with teeth was about to make a grab for its throat.

'What has got into you, crazy beast?'

Emmett stared from the cowering dog to the way ahead. He felt a shiver of unease. There was an unnatural darkness about the hill which seemed more noticeable now that light had fought clear of the clouds. And whether he liked it or not – and he definitely did not – he was going to have to investigate.

The piebald moved forward, lifting fetlocks clear of the wet ground. Its mottled flanks had been richly marked by the mud, as had the man's pants – spattered with brown slurry that given time and a warming sun should dry to a grey crust. The dog was indistinguishable from the mire by now, but it was trailing behind the horse and its rider, as bowed as a beaten cur.

Emmett didn't like that either; it was making his back crawl.

'You are as much use as a cart with one wheel,' he called out.

The hound paid him no heed but that mattered little. Hockaday had only wanted to hear the sound of his own voice, for there was not much else to share that felt friendly. He was alone and near the end of his endurance in this troubled place.

New and enriched, the sun left strange shadow patterns on the ground, of things that might have claws. Emmett reached for the butt of his firearm – smooth, clawless itself, but still capable of doing business with anything untoward. He was glad now that he had thought to wrap it around his waist.

He searched for a more verdant area of ground for the piebald's hooves and the pace picked up as the horse began to trot. It was a long loping stride, and Emmett settled in his seat as the mounted trees came closer. He would have a hunt around, and if the dog could be persuaded perhaps it might put its nose to the earth. They would pursue Colt through the twigs and roots and wild plants, and anything else lying under branches that still bore colour, despite the leaf-fall.

That is what he had in mind – a thorough, and final, hunt around. There may well be nothing to discover, but he would put off worrying about that until later, once he was on his way home again.

Home. The word alone caused his spirits to rise. He was looking forward to getting back, divesting himself of rain-soaked boots, sitting beside the stove and making inroads into whatever meal Joanie had prepared. Easing out the rest of the day in a chair instead of a saddle – or at least as much of it as he could manage before the clamour of chores grew too loud to ignore. Just thoughts, but even so, they were good ones, and as he relaxed into them the piebald ate up the distance, and after a while the little hill was almost upon them.

The closer they came to the mound the larger it grew. The trees were thicker, some erect, some bending, some stooping low. The small wood was all-encompassing and filled with a silence that didn't feel right. Emmett's horse had halted without waiting for a tug on the reins, and its ears flicked backwards and forwards as though it was following two conversations. But there was nothing to hear, for the tree canopies were motionless and if there was a wind it had already bypassed this place.

Emmett stood in the stirrups to look around. All he could see were trees. Shaped by the seasons, the weather and hardship, they had turned into souls transformed; furred in green, too static, watching him as he watched them. He didn't like the idea of turning his back because of what might be happening behind him.

This then must be the reason for the darkness he thought he had seen from open land where the rain had been normal; it was just the all-pervading strangeness of compressed trees. But perhaps he was wrong. Perhaps it was something else.

He started to shake. He lifted the gun from its holster. And that was when the man pounced.

The farmer would have been knocked to the ground if his horse hadn't moved, stepping sideways, throwing up its head with a scream when the assailant collided with its shoulder. Emmett juddered in the saddle but stayed put, a loose stirrup dangling and the reins scattered. The piebald thought to turn in a tight circle, blanking out its rider's view for a few moments when anything might have happened, but didn't.

By the time he had twisted round again the man had gone, almost as if he had never really been there. Emmett Hockaday heard a groan and only realised a moment later that he had made the sound himself.

His scalp was crawling, his mind filled with the tales of evil wraiths that had scared him witless when he was a child. He waved the gun around, searching for ghosts; but there was nothing supernatural about the adversary. He had been flesh and blood, and for a moment Emmett was elated to know that he was at least human. But not to know that he had also disappeared.

No, he had not disappeared. He was still there by the trees, his colouring and his garb a perfect camouflage against the peat-brown bark. There was a boy beside him, far too close to the knife in the man's hand.

'Is that you, Colt?' Emmett blurted, stupidly, because it could not be anyone else. The runaway he thought he would never find was standing a few feet away, eyes wide in a pale face, clothes caked with trail dirt.

The shade inside the huddle of trees was thick, and everything it surrounded was solid with darkness, just like the man who had hold of the boy's arm. The dark man, raw-boned and gaunt, long hair caught back by a band of leather, marks like strange writing across his face. For an unhinged moment Emmett wondered what story had been etched into the dark man's skin, and who would want to get close enough to read it. Perhaps even as close as Colt was right now.

Hockaday pointed the weapon and shouted. 'Let the child go!' The piebald bounced with the shrillness of it.

There was no reaction from the man, as if he could only hear what was inside his head. But Colt had heard, and he tried to speak. His voice was weak and the words were lost, but it seemed to Emmett that he was reaching out for help.

The farmer didn't mean to jerk the trigger, firing a premature bullet that crashed between the trees, missing both boy and man. The sky exploded with noise. The piebald shrieked and Emmett's ears sang. He pointed the weapon again, but the horse was as agitated as the tremor in his hand and he had trouble holding it level.

Colt shook his head. 'No, Mr Hockaday!' His voice was stronger now, practically hysterical. 'Please. You do not understand!'

But he thought he understood only too well.

The dark man had not moved; it was as though none of this had anything to do with him. Frantic now, the piebald lurched and twisted. Hockaday slapped its rump and swore, and then he lifted the gun once again, pinning its sight on the man's chest. The motionless man who had been staring at something over the top of Emmett's head – and that was making the farmer madder than anything.

He yelled, 'Let the boy go!'

And tightened his finger on the trigger.

THIRTY-SEVEN

THE PALOMINO had reared, a split second before the air was cracked by gunshot.

Wolf Shadow was unprepared. He clamped legs to the horse's belly and they wheeled around together until the animal was once more under control. He heard the explosion again in his mind, so loud it seemed to echo. The blast faded but its residue remained, muddled with hidden images and his daughter's fear.

This was the culmination of a slow journey on an unruly horse, accompanied by warnings and confusion and the sense of blackness. Sometimes so black that he wondered whether anything might exist beyond it. He was on his way home, riding over mantraps towards something that had already been determined. There was a threshold ahead that he knew he must cross, trusting that he would make it to the other side. Hoping that he would make it to the other side.

A single gunshot, not repeated. It was difficult to tell where it had come from in a landscape that allowed very little space between clumps of rock, and vegetation thick enough to swallow sound, but Wolf knew that the hand which had fired the gun was only a short ride away.

He was calmer now. Injuries and fatigue set aside, he lay across the stallion's neck and breathed to its ears. The horse leaped forwards, mane spreading like wings in the slam of air, and the young man's hair rose in response.

The land reared up and tumbled down as the horizon changed, and over the thunder of hooves Wolf heard a dog bark; a deep sound, urgent and hoarse, and coming from the same area as the shot. The stallion's stride lengthened, as though obeying some urgency of its own. Wolf tried to pull it back to the lope that had already eaten up the miles, but the animal fought him, following its head as long as it could before being restrained.

As quietly as possible they approached the small hill in the distance where the trees were crowded and plentiful, showing that maybe something greater than normal nourishment might be found under that simple mound of earth. Smooth and secretive beneath its greenery, the hill grew taller the closer they got. It seemed impenetrable. It seemed like a very dark place.

Still from the distance, Wolf brought the stallion to a halt and dismounted. Leaving the animal tethered to words and whispers he moved on alone, sheltering from sight where shelter was possible – a swathe of tall grass, a tumble of rocks, a bush scrubbed clear of growth by harsh winds. Although if anyone had a view of him from those trees no amount of hiding would keep him safe should they choose to turn the gun in his direction.

But there was nothing coming out of the thicket: no confrontation, no reception; only a sprinkling of sound as though a breeze had brewed up from somewhere and was playing its music with sticks and tightly-skinned drums.

Trees teetered above him now, and all around was an upheaval of land taking on many shapes, as though the maker had been undecided over its design. Wispy clouds as grey as ash were lifting from the swells and hollows like smoke from dying fires. The sky was streaked and uncertain, and a bulbous gathering proclaimed that new rain was on its way.

It crossed Wolf's mind that he would like to be mounted and gone by the time it fell, with nothing but easy riding between this place and the home he had helped to build, when the future had been secured and his newborn son was weightless in his arms.

He stood on the outskirts of the knoll and its bank of trees, listening to the strange music that seemed to be playing inside. Maybe it held a message for him. Maybe it meant that the line was still open and his daughter was at the other end, refusing to let him go.

Even thinking about Clove had brought her nearer. Wolf could feel her mind knocking sense into his own. But it was more than that, she had led him to this place and now she was tugging him further. He could almost hear her inside the wood – her voice shrill and insistent, but falling lower and deeper as he listened until it became the staccato call of a man, cautious but valiant, trying to be someone he had never been before.

Once again, the dog barked. The animal seemed so close that if Wolf Shadow stretched out a hand, he might have been able to touch its pelt. He could virtually feel soft fur on his fingertips as he stepped between the trees, his gut tightening as though there was a rope around his waist. But this time it was not his daughter doing the tugging. It was his son.

He could hear other voices now, muffled when the branches bunched together and free flowing where they parted; raised and lowered, appealing and rejecting. The small wooded area was peopled by many, or few – it was not easy to decipher. There was the sound of horses as well, stamping the ground and snorting with fear.

Wolf was in a puzzle; words came at him from behind

and then from beyond. He turned his head and it was no different. He did not recognise what was being said, but the further he moved through crowded trees, the easier it was to separate the three people who were speaking. One was strident and panicked; one was soft, barely distinguishable, mesmerising. And one was Colt.

Wolf started to run but he was hampered by tree limbs as thin as fingers, with sharpened nails that reached for his eyes. He crouched low, the mulch of dead leaves disappearing behind him as he tried to reach the voices.

The dog began an intermittent spate of barking. Wolf wondered if it had picked up the sound of him straining to be silent as he crossed the undergrowth, following lessons taught by the Indian who had been his father. He discerned anger, and sudden movement. He heard a command with a break in it. He queried the voice when he recognised it, because there was no reason for Emmett Hockaday to be in the middle of a situation like this.

Its hollering cut short, the dog had begun to whimper. In the quiet that followed Wolf heard his son, calling out words that sent a steel rod up his spine.

'Don't shoot, Mr Hockaday! Please, don't shoot!'

Wolf leaped forwards, slashing at everything that got in his way. He didn't care about the noise he was making or the boughs that snagged his face. He stopped caring about anything at all, except that his boy was in danger from a man he had respected and trusted. A man from whom he had stolen something irreplaceable, and who would maybe take his revenge for that from whatever source he could, as long as the thief's blood ran in its veins.

The trees opened up for Wolf as though they had been waiting for this moment; a curtain had been drawn back and there in front of him was Emmett Hockaday, sending startled glances in his direction as if searching for the wild animal he believed was heading his way. He was holding the gun as though it was something noxious but necessary, and it was shaking in the air and ready to explode by itself.

Which was one frightening thing.

The other was Colt's proximity to the danger, from where he was standing beside an earth-coloured stranger with a knife in his hand. Standing close enough for their arms to be touching. Colt's hair, wild and disordered, the man's long and straight – mingling so completely that it was difficult to tell which was the boy's and which the intruder's.

Even though the fringing on his sleeves was rippling, the man himself was utterly motionless. It was as if he was alone in this closely-packed wood filled with noises: whispers in the wind that had lifted again from somewhere outside; the creak of harness from the three horses that were sharing the same patch of grass, where perhaps the pickings were easy.

Wolf could see Colt's red mare, as sturdy and familiar as a friend; he could also see Emmett's piebald and a pale dun with a dusky mane, but it was only Vixen he wanted. Somehow, he would make the pony run with the boy on its back, out from the encompassing trees to where the palomino was waiting. Not long now and not far – there would be little distance to cover when the time came to move.

All this Wolf Shadow saw in the second it took to blink, and by then he had already thrown himself at the man who was holding the firearm as though he had no idea how it had got into his hand, and yet had every intention of using it.

His vigilance dulled by fatigue, Emmett's reactions were sluggish; he only managed a half-turn before Wolf crashed into him, trapping his arms and shaking the weapon to the ground. They careered together through scrub and low bushes until the momentum was halted by trees; and then they split apart.

Wolf made a grab for the gun and rose to his feet, and Hockaday made no attempt to stop him. He was lying where he had fallen, his head averted, his cheek scraped ragged by rough bark. The brindled dog was snuffling by his feet. Wolf looked around for Colt and the stranger. They were still there, joined together by a float of hair. The boy's eyes were wide but there was little to sense from the dark man. He was gazing into the distance, the band around his forehead failing to hide the patterns engraved on his face.

From this proximity it was apparent that these marks were not the characters of some outlandish language but the winding trails of old tattoos that told a story of their own. The whole thing struck a chord in Wolf's mind, but it was like trying to seize a memory that didn't want to be caught. And he had no time for guesswork.

The gun felt too warm, as though Hockaday had been gripping it so tightly that some of his life had flowed into the weapon. Maybe it had been what was left of his life, because he was very still in that huddle on the ground. The dog had flopped down beside him, its whole body bouncing as it panted. Its breathing animated the flap of Emmett's waxed coat, but nothing else about the man was stirring.

Wolf's fire began to cool as he stared at the friend he had wronged, and something settled down inside him. It was as if he had stepped into a lull like the few moments of half-dream before sleep. He shook his head to clear the stupor, because it felt wrong to be so tranquil in this unnerving place.

Emmett hadn't moved, and neither had the dark man, the boy standing by his side as though he had been trapped by more than just his hair. By some kind of electricity maybe, sending sparks into the air above their heads.

'Come to me, Colt.' Wolf raised a hand and beckoned, but the boy was transfixed, staring at his father with eyes that could make no sense of what was happening. Wolf realised he still had the gun in his hand. He flexed it and began to step forwards and Colt shrieked like an animal in a trap. The young man winced. He had never before heard such a sound from his son's mouth. It seemed to echo back from the mass of trees as though they too were screaming.

The dark man was unperturbed, but only on the surface, for Wolf could feel an insistent tugging in his chest, as though it came from inside those black eyes. He forced himself to break the contact, and strength surged back into his body, together with an anger fierce enough to burn.

'Let my son go,' he said, quietly, the warning behind the command vibrating the back of his throat.

There was no reply, but when the dark man closed his eyes Wolf felt a cluster of words gathering like wind-moan inside his skull. His body shrivelled as if he was under attack. He stepped forwards, wavering like a drunkard, his fingers white with strain around the gun's grip.

'Let him go,' he said again, 'or I swear I will kill you.'

The dark man shook his head, a wave of emotions passing over his face so quickly that it may only have been a change in the air, but wretchedness remained in

287

the tightness of his lips and hollows outlining the bones beneath his skin. And something happened when he opened his eyes, something compelling, a message to Wolf that didn't make any sense, that nudged a memory that was inconceivable, but that fell into place when the man finally spoke.

'The wolf cub remembers what was taught,' he said, his voice cracked by the passing of years. 'But he has yet to learn.'

Wolf Shadow found that he couldn't breathe; he felt himself dissolving. For a moment the gun hung useless from his trigger finger, and then he let it fall. 'You call me wolf cub,' he said when he could speak again.

The dark man glanced at him, grimacing as though he was in pain. He shook his head like a horse would chase off flies and the movement snapped the bond between his hair and the hair of the boy who hadn't moved from his side.

Colt stumbled as if that union had been all that was keeping him upright, and then he saw what was about to happen. His mouth opened but it was too late to cry warning, for Emmett Hockaday was already there.

The farmer barged into Wolf's body and knocked him off his feet. He skidded blind across the ground, failing to see Hockaday scooping up the dropped gun, and turning on them all with the weapon raised. The man's face was deathly white and shockingly marred by blood and he was growling, an inhuman sound that sent the dog crazy with barking.

The noise ricocheted from the tree trunks. Vixen and the piebald fought to escape it, but were trapped by a net of low-hanging branches. The stranger's dun stood still, as though it was obeying some instruction, but the ears were flat to its skull. Wolf could hear its teeth grinding, clashing the bit, and above that he caught the click of the gun's hammer.

In one movement, he rose from where he had fallen and sprang forward, colliding with Emmett's solid body and deterring the bullet's flight. The two men tackled the air before landing, heavily. Lying winded and still for the short moment before the dark man and the boy could react, slowly at first as though their legs needed time to work again, and then each at their own speed.

Emmett turned over, groaning as the bruising began to hurt. He lay frowning up through the canopy, as though he had no idea how he had come to be there. He could hear horses racketing and a dog whining and voices as well, and then he closed his eyes because maybe it would be better just to rest.

Colt reached his father first and then the other man was there, crouching down beside him. Wolf Shadow was absolutely still; lying on his stomach over broken branches. His head had pushed away some of the debris to make a shallow nest, and there were scraps of vegetation in his hair. Carefully and gently, the dark man began to pick them out.

'Get up, Pa,' Colt said. And then he shouted it. 'Get up, Pa!'

He pushed at Wolf's shoulder hard enough to jolt him awake from that unearthly slumber, but the dark man put his hand out for him to stop. And then, just as carefully and gently, he turned the young man over, lifting him away from the snapped wood, and the profuse amount of blood that had already leaked from the ragged hole in his side.

The stranger bent to listen at Wolf's chest. There was nothing to hear, not even the lonely sigh of the final breath fading from his lungs. His spirit had gone.

But not too far; not yet.

With sudden force, the dark man slammed the heel of his hand into Wolf Shadow's breast bone. The young man bounced back from the impact, and lay still again.

Claws for fingers, Colt went for the monster who was murdering his father. The dark man shrugged the boy off and hit Wolf again and then again, almost hard enough to break bones. Colt came back at him, punching and kicking; and when he saw what was going on, Emmett Hockaday finally understood.

The farmer scrambled to his feet, ignoring his own hurts for the sake of the boy. He pulled Colt away from the long-haired man and held him tightly, until the struggles had eased and the sobbing began. But the pity of it was lost beneath the rhythmic crump of the fist that was hammering the body of a silent man.

Time seemed to slow as the assault continued, until the dark man eventually ceased what he was doing; gulping deep breaths before putting his ear again to Wolf Shadow's chest. He listened for a while, and everything in the little wood seemed to be listening as well, it felt so quiet. When he straightened up his face was an empty mask.

That was when Emmett set the boy free.

THIRTY-EIGHT

THE CHURCH was filled with voices, reaching as high as the roof, knocking back from the walls. The space reverberated, and calm took a while to settle once the singing had ceased, dust motes blessing the women who were grouped around the harmonium.

Mrs Hetherington lifted her hands with a flourish from the instrument and brushed particles from the shoulders of her blue dress. She was breathing quickly, along with the other ladies of the choir, some of whom were already rearranging their music in readiness for the next piece. Others were simply mouthing the words they had just produced as though they had no desire to let them go quite yet.

'I believe that is one of the best renditions of "To Heaven Above" that we have ever delivered,' proclaimed Livvy Seneschall, a neat woman clothed in black and white and probably the poorest singer in the company. She nodded vehemently at the sheets in her hand and failed to see the sour look on the face of the woman at the harmonium.

'That may be so,' said Mrs Hetherington. 'However, it should not prevent a certain number of us from trying even harder next time, Mrs Seneschall.'

Livvy blushed. The snub pushed her to the back of the group where she struggled to collect herself, together with the pages of music that she had dropped in her agitation.

Joanie Hockaday allowed her voice to be heard over the hubbub. 'It seems to me, Mrs Hetherington, that the whole choir should try even harder.' She lifted her head and met the woman's disconcerting eyes. 'Would that not benefit us all?'

Without waiting for a response, she turned to the disarray of women by the altar and flapped her hands as though herding geese.

'Come along, ladies; our musical director is waiting to bring us in,' she said. 'Isn't that right, Matilda?' She stood erect with the twitch of a smile and met the woman's indignation full on.

Mrs Hetherington took a moment to recover from the illicit use of her Christian name by a subordinate. Her mouth nearly disappeared inside her suck of disapproval, and she stabbed the harmonium until her fingers hurt.

The organ's discord was swallowed by shadows under the rafters, and the grey sky beyond. But the clouds were clearing properly now; shreds of blue brightening the tall casements. Albeit pale and struggling, at least some heart was coming back to the day. Which was more than Sage could say for herself as she stood by the dais, mangling music between her fists.

'I want my family together again. I want Wolf Shadow back.' Wasn't that what she had told Margharita Kendall? An easy thing to say, but what was the chance of it ever happening – now that her daughter was lost inside her own mind, and her son was lost in the wilderness? And Wolf Shadow was lost completely.

That last thought struck her without warning, and a sudden darkness came with it.

The church was blessed by a rise and fall of chatter

and the rustling of skirts. Friendly sounds, such as the young woman had never before experienced in a life spent on the outskirts of fellowship. But she was in the wrong place with this gathering of ladies. She needed to be on her own to feel the fear; the something bad that was coming.

Clove felt it as well. Sage knew this, almost as if the spirit of the child was with her now, floating above the altar. Clove should have been sitting with her grandma in the Hockaday house, busy with needles and wool, but she had brought those neat stitches into the church. And she had also brought a message.

It was for her mother to listen. Just to listen.

But Matilda Hetherington heard it first, her sharp ears on the lookout for dissension in the choir's ranks. She frowned and stared at the door, her mouth chewing on disapproval, as though she would not tolerate any more interference to her musical afternoon.

Perplexed by her strange behaviour the other ladies grew silent, which made it easier for them to pick up the disturbance in the street. People yelling; the rush of hooves; a woman's sudden laugh, too manic for humour.

There was pandemonium in the house of God. Sheets of music fell like petals, a disjointed pathway across the floor.

'Is it a stampede?'

'Or a riot?'

'It's the end of the world!'

'Don't be ridiculous,' the musical director demanded.

All eyes were fixed on the door as though it was about to be rent asunder by mayhem. And then Matilda sprang into action, marching past the rows of seats and flinging wide the portal, ready to give this interruption a piece of her mind.

At first Sage couldn't see what was going on, her view of the street obliterated by the woman's grandiloquence; but she only needed one glimpse to recognise the little red mare as it trotted by, her son clamped to its back and her neighbour's guard dog loping at its side. She lifted her skirt and ran along the aisle, polished wood clipping under her feet; clipping under the echo as well, of Joanie Hockaday running behind.

Sage pushed Mrs Hetherington out of the way, too fixated on what she could see to give a damn about the woman's umbrage. At first it appeared to be only Vixen jogging through the standing water, but the pony was followed by Emmett Hockaday's piebald, its rider smeared by mud and something unfathomable that was adding years to his posture.

And after them both came a high-tailed dun bearing a figure with tassels to his sleeves and a marked face framed by long hair. A dark stranger sitting upright, one arm tightly wrapped around the body of the man he was holding to the front of his saddle.

They were accompanied by a sea of people keeping pace on the sidewalk. Citizens of Oasis, straight-backed and respectable, pointing fingers and braying like mules. Slightly ahead of them and pink-faced with sanctimony rolled Kester Kendall, cresting the waves with his belly.

He drew level with the church door, faltering when he caught sight of the young woman who was standing in its frame with the ladies in waiting behind her. He smirked some words that were lost in the uproar, he gripped his suspenders and flexed muscles hidden in his portly arms. It was all wasted on Sage, who knocked him aside as she ran into the street, careless of the puddles that fringed her hem with mud. Careless of everything but the pale horse that was carrying the stranger and the broken figure of Wolf Shadow, his arm swinging with the animal's pace, fingers curled as though he had been holding something and now it was gone.

Sage ran until she had caught up with them, the horse and its double-load. Wolf's head was bent low, hair smothering his face so that she couldn't see if those brown eyes were open; if there was still gold inside. His hand was cold to the touch, like a carving made of stone instead of flesh. She jerked at the chill, but didn't let go. She squeezed his fingers, forcing everything that was keeping her alive to pass into Wolf Shadow. She squeezed until her whole arm was pulsing.

The three riders made their way down the street and those who pursued them called out what they needed to call, and after that was done they grew tired of the parade and disbanded. The short cavalcade came to a halt outside the post and rail fence; the hound gave one mournful howl and sat back on its haunches, and then only the everyday sounds of the town remained.

Frail and bare, the trees were no longer bushy enough to protect the doctor's house. It was easy to see the little girl who was peering out of the upstairs window, and the face of the woman who had come to join her.

Lucy Ryker started back from the glass with a hand to her neck as though she had been caught off guard. But Sage didn't notice the woman who had noticed her. Neither was she aware that Joanie Hockaday had also been hastening along the street beside her husband's horse, and it was she who went up to the bell pull near the Rykers' door.

All Sage knew was that warmth seemed to be returning to Wolf Shadow's hand, and she told herself that for sure she had felt his fingers twitch. It made it easier to give him up to Emmett Hockaday and the long-haired man as between them they lifted him to the ground.

She didn't see Emmett slipping away with the dog, his back hunched like someone who needed to hide, she only had eyes for the dark stranger who had gathered Wolf up as if he was carrying a child. He stood waiting for the door to open, and it seemed to Sage that maybe he would wait for ever, as long as he could cradle Wolf Shadow in his arms.

There was a touch on her shoulder and the familiar scent of her good friend. She turned towards the comfort. Joanie held her until her own warmth had reached the places in Sage's body that had grown as cold as Wolf's fingers. When Sage opened her eyes she realised she could see clearly again, and that although Emmett had disappeared, Colt hadn't moved from Vixen's back.

She reached for her son's hand in the way that she had reached for his father's, and it was a warm child's hand, calloused and rough and achingly young. He slipped from the red pony and clung to her; his arms glued around her waist in the way that she remembered from when he was little.

But even now he was not much more than little, as if he was shrinking back into the happier days of his childhood. She rocked him and allowed him to cry. His tears were hot, seeping through her dress and burning her skin, but that only made her hold him closer because he was her son and he had come home with stories to tell. She would have the chance to ask him to recount what in God's name had happened, but now was not the time. Now belonged to the man who had also come home, but not as whole as when he had left.

Sage had recoiled from the blood. So much blood,

making an insult of his shirt. She had heard his pain as he struggled to breathe. Wolf Shadow had been brought to this house to be mended by a man he had wronged and in the presence of a woman who had been the cause of it. Sage needed to be there as well to make sure the mending took place.

'Is he going to die, Ma?'

Colt was looking up at her face, drinking in everything he could see there. 'Is Pa going to die?' he said again, and his voice tore on the jagged words.

His mother shook her head, and only stopped once she realised that she was shaking her son with the effort.

'No, Colt, your pa is going to live.' She had said it and therefore it would be. 'And right this minute I must be with him.'

Joanie Hockaday understood. She put her arm around the boy's shoulder and Sage eased herself away and went towards the house that she had hoped never to enter again.

'Have no fear, Colt,' she heard Joanie telling the boy as they turned to go. 'Dr Ryker will take good care of your pa. Wolf Shadow could not be in safer hands.'

THIRTY-NINE

IT WAS sombre inside the Ryker house, and not just because the lamps had yet to be lighted. The windows were still draped from the night before and dust lay on surfaces like shakings from a pepper pot. There was no evidence left of Esme's employment. The little maid had been returned to her impoverished family, abandoning the rooms to a stagnant chill.

Sage followed the trail of blood that was staining the floor. It led her to the doctor's dark office; made even darker by the silent men who had collected in the gloom. She barely saw them; her eyes were for the one who had been laid out on the couch by the wall, the man whose face was the palest.

She went straight to him, touching his legs and his arms and his chest; trying not to touch the ravage of blood or the ghastly wound above his waistband. She only knew that Daniel Ryker was beside her because he was blocking out even more light. Sage felt a rush of air when the doctor crossed the room to draw back the drapes, and everything was clearer when he turned around, not least the sight of him.

He had aged since the day of her last visit to the house, his wife's gifts bundled in a bag that she had upended on the floor. Grey hair wild, beard untrimmed, shadows under his eyes that might have been drawn by dirt – Daniel had suffered. They had all suffered. And the woman standing awkwardly at the doorway, so that half of her was inside the room and half had still to emerge, she was the reason why.

But even Lucy seemed to have been afflicted by her husband's ague; tendrils of hair were hanging like spiders' threads around her neck, and the lack of cosmetics had added years to her appearance. Sage realised that despite its muddied hem, her own dress was far prettier than that woman's plain black skirt and simple blouse. It gave her a flush of pleasure, quickly doused but strong while it lasted.

Ryker caught sight of his wife as he went back to the couch, but he turned away as though it pained him to look at her. Her eyes flickered from her husband to Sage and back again, before coming to rest on Wolf Shadow. One hand crept up to fiddle with the collar of her blouse, the other one worried at a fold of her skirt. Once Lucy Ryker had been steeped with such spirit that it had blazed from her face, but there was no evidence of that left. Sage felt the push of sympathy, but that was only for the children, for Dulcie and Bella, having to live in this dead house with parents who had given up caring.

It was then that she picked up the crying. A wrenching sound that might have been continuing for some time, except that her mind had been fixed in another direction. The twins' distress pulled at her belly as though she was their mother, but Lucy seemed unaffected. Sage went up to her; she had to drag herself away from the couch to do so, but that dismal sound was too heavy to ignore.

'Mrs Ryker.' The formal address felt awkward in her throat, although she would have found anything more familiar too difficult to pronounce. 'Your children are calling for you.'

It took a while for the other woman to meet her eyes. 'My husband has a patient to treat,' she said. 'It is my job to assist him.'

'This time it is I who will assist him.'

Lucy stared. Pushing Sage out of the way she stepped further into the room. Sage took her arms and shook her, just once, but hard enough to set more of her hair free from its clips.

'Can you not hear your little ones' tears?' she said, before letting the woman go and returning to the couch where the doctor had already pulled away Wolf's shirt to expose devastation at the curve of his waist.

Dr Ryker turned Wolf over to examine his back, and when he rested him down again it was with some gentleness. 'The bullet passed straight through,' he said. 'Two openings to deal with but the wound should be clean, thank God.'

He called for lights and boiled water and Sage tried her best to collect what was required. It took more time than usual to bring heat to the stove and flame to the lamps when all she could see was the shadow of Wolf, so inert on the couch that he seemed to have fallen into another dimension. She didn't notice Lucy Ryker leaving the room or the hushing of her children. Neither did she notice when the stranger left as well, for he was too ensconced in his own darkness to have made any difference to the atmosphere.

The doctor had shucked off his jacket and rolled up his sleeves. There was a slop of stains on the front of his shirt but his hands were clean and his nails trimmed, as if he had been prepared for the clamour of horses that were heading for his door, and the townspeople bawling judgements in their wake. He was wearing a different face now: the man had retreated and the physician had come to the fore. Perhaps Joanie had been right with what she had told Colt out in the road, and it was true that Wolf Shadow could not be in safer hands. Sage wanted him to know that, but he was lying so peaceful and still that maybe he already did.

A tumble of hair had fallen across his face; Sage stroked it back, relieved to feel the grit and the knot of wind-tangles that made him real. As though her touch had been the stimulus, Wolf opened his eyes; it was barely more than a crack but enough for a sliver of his fire to burn in the lamplight. Enough for her to learn what was in his mind – the regrets, the sorrows, the hope.

She tried to smile, to pass him messages from her own eyes, but there were too many tears distorting her vision of what the doctor was preparing to do. And when Ryker picked up his instruments and set to work Wolf was already somewhere else.

Emmett hadn't gone far, even though it had been his intention to ride out of the town and away from what was taking place at the doctor's house. He had slunk off because his trigger finger was the reason why it was taking place, but in the cold light of realisation, there was nowhere left for him to go without dragging the guilt along with him.

That is why he had ended up outside the hardware store, warming his hands on the hound's pelt. Pans and pots and buckets were hanging over the sidewalk, rolling on sways of wind, and he found the movement soothing. The knock and clatter were like music, growing more distant as his ease increased. Until he saw himself again: damp and ragged and weary of just about everything, knowing that he could have killed Wolf Shadow in that strange bundle of trees. Knowing that there had been times over the nightmare that had travelled with him since discovering the theft of the stallion when he had wanted to do just that.

Emmett shut his eyes, tight enough to hurt, but the thought was still there when he opened them again. And he was still here, hiding in the shadows while the young man who used to be his friend was growing weaker from blood loss, maybe weak enough to disappear altogether. What would happen to that hopeless family then? Could they ever forgive him for what he had done?

And Joanie, his generous, open-hearted wife; would she be able to forgive him as well?

Emmett wanted to curse, but he was too exhausted. Blaspheming took effort and cut away a piece of the curser's heart, and it was all he could do to balance on his feet in the twinkle of dancing stew pans. He barely heard the gruff bark of the hound when the sheriff came to a halt in front of him, accompanied by his usual ill-temper.

'I have been searching for you, Mr Hockaday, but it looks like you've been otherwise engaged.' Andy Parnell settled back, hands on his hips, as though all he wanted was a friendly chat on a cool afternoon in a town where nothing much happened.

Emmett couldn't think what to say. His silence seemed to rattle the other man, who moved his hands from hips to gun belt and stood just a little bit straighter.

'I have been particularly busy lately, on the hunt for a horse thief,' Parnell said. 'And so, it seems, have you.'

He pushed his face forward; Emmett stepped back to avoid the intrusion and shadows drew closer behind him. He felt safer under their shroud, as though they would make him invisible; he could do what he wished and say what he wanted.

I am the one who shot Wolf Shadow – that was what he wanted to say. I took a man's life and need to be punished for it.

He opened his mouth for the words to escape, but they fell away behind the growl, the menace of it that rose from the dog as sharply as the hairs on its neck. The animal stood quivering, ears flat, long teeth like ivory daggers. And the dark man from the unearthly clump of trees materialised before them, as if he had been magicked up through the sidewalk. He laid a hand on the dog's head, taking little notice of the vicious jaws that were just a bite away; and the growling ceased, as suddenly as the man had appeared.

The hound sat back on its haunches and gazed up at him, its tail busy with contentment. The sheriff's reaction to the stranger, however, was not as accepting.

'I am informed that you are the one who came back with the lawbreaker,' he said. His eyes made judgements as he took in the marked face and long hair, the splay of beadwork across the man's tunic, the weapon at his waist. 'If you found trouble with him, don't think you can bring it to my town.'

'I bring no trouble.'

'I would be prepared to believe that,' said Parnell, 'if it were not for the look of you.'

The dark man lifted his hand as though to push away the lawman's prejudice. 'I have travelled far in peace, Sheriff, and I wish to remain in peace.'

Parnell stepped away from the raised palm as if it was some sort of threat. He reached for his gun. The stranger didn't react, not even when the weapon was up and aiming, other than to drop his hand to his side.

Emmett Hockaday looked from the harmless man to the sheriff's gun, and then he looked down at the guard dog that was squatting as serenely as a family pet merely because the stranger had laid a hand on its head. And that is what decided him.

'You are pointing that weapon at the wrong person, Andy,' he said. 'I am the one who brought the trouble. This man is not to blame.'

Parnell hesitated; his thoughts printed on his face. He just wanted an excuse to squeeze the trigger, Emmett could see by the way his hand was twitching. Without thinking what he was doing the farmer stepped in front of the dark man. The gun barrel nudged his ribcage, and then it was lifted away.

'You have no quarrel with this man, Andy,' he said. 'No quarrel with me, or with Wolf Shadow either, for I retract my complaint.'

'I went hunting a horse thief on your accusation, Hockaday. Have you been wasting my time?'

'Wolf had no intention of taking anything that belonged to me,' Emmett said, staring the sheriff in the eye. 'I know that now.'

'And you trust him to return it?' Parnell slid the gun back in its holster with a flourish that smacked of exasperation.

'I trust him.' Emmett blinked as he thought back through the four years that he had known Wolf Shadow; known and liked him as a good neighbour, a good friend, a good man. 'I have always trusted him.'

The dark man behind him winced, blinking slowly to cover it, but Emmett couldn't know that, and Andy Parnell was too busy turning his back on them both and storming across the road to his office. Stamping the hard-packed ground as though he needed to leave an impression.

Emmett paused before looking around, but the dark

man's attention had left the scene. He was staring towards the post and rail fence, swaying on his feet as though he was being pulled back to the Ryker house.

'Who on earth are you?' Hockaday said. 'Why are you here?' But the questions were lost on the stranger.

'The cub was strong and the wolf will recover.' He was speaking as if to himself. Reassuring words that accompanied him along the street.

Emmett stood watching him go. The hound stood up to watch as well. It whined and took a step forward as though to follow. Its master laid a hand on its head, just as the dark man had done; but the dog wasn't interested in Emmett Hockaday.

It was the woman who opened the door, dressed as though there were things she had forgotten. Everything about her was in disarray, and yet at sight of him she made herself straighter and began to tuck dangles of hair beneath the clasp on her head. Maybe it was because of his own straightness, his stillness; maybe it was because of a nudge of recognition, for this was the guardian who had carried Wolf Shadow so gently to her husband's couch.

Lucy stepped aside, allowing the dark man to enter. There were two little girls peering down from the top of the stairs; like frightened rabbits they shied away when he lifted his head, too young to understand. Too pampered to be able to cope with the pain that permeated this unhappy place.

These children had never been given the opportunity to grow strong; not like his own child in the days when all weakness was punished by the weariness of life.

He moved into the next room where the bearded man and the young woman were not quite at rest, but more restful than when he had last seen them. The lamplight made the room kinder despite the disorder, but it was shining with too much vehemence on the heap of blood-sodden rags beneath the leather couch. The doctor was wiping his hands on another one, long muscles in his forearms clenched as though in spasm. He dropped it to join the pile, red with red.

Sage saw him coming over – Clove's dark man, the harbinger of danger and death. He was the one who had brought Wolf Shadow back to her. She had seen the way he hesitated as he laid the young man on the couch, his hands raised as though it had been in his mind to grip the patient's shoulders, leaving his warmth behind. She had seen the flicker of emotion crossing his face before it could be contained.

She didn't yet know how Wolf had received the wounds that Dr Ryker had been working on, frowning in concentration, swearing in consternation because the bleeding would not be stemmed. She recalled that Emmett had been reluctant to look her in the eye, even to acknowledge that she was there when he helped to lift Wolf from the stranger's horse. He had still been wearing the gun that he'd holstered before leaving his homestead to search for Colt. He had touched it, perhaps by accident, and she had seen him flinch. It was as though it was contaminated. As though it was still hot from the firing.

Firing the bullet that had ripped open Wolf Shadow's body.

Sage whimpered, but she couldn't weaken. She had everything to learn but too much to do. The knowing must wait until she could breathe properly. When Daniel had finally staunched the flow of precious blood and Wolf could breathe properly as well.

But he was so unnaturally still. His chest rose slightly and fell, and after far too long it rose again. It was as if his spirit had already left him and was waiting in limbo. Maybe he would grow strong enough for it to return, or maybe there would be no return. Maybe, after all that had happened, he didn't think it was worth returning at all.

No! He had to come back! She would fight for him. She grabbed his hand, squeezing hard enough to hurt. Wanting it to hurt so that his eyes would open like they did before, showing his golden fire. She squeezed until his bones rubbed together, but there was no reaction.

Sage had never learned how to pray, but now she pleaded. She was unaware that Dr Ryker had brought a chair and ordered her to sit, or that Lucy had appeared again in the doorway. She didn't see the doctor busying his wife away but she smelled the lemon and lavender the woman left behind, like an unpleasant taste.

Neither did she ask herself what the dark man was doing in the room. He had gone to the head of the couch as though to preside over the operation. He reached out, maybe to hold Wolf down so that the doctor could work on the wounds, but his hands were hovering in the air just above the patient's body. It was as if touch was not needed. The Indian's eyes were closed and his mouth was moving with incantations; the marks across his face like an exotic script, telling the story of his life.

He and Sage were joined together, praying for the bleeding to stop. Calling their own gods down to where Wolf Shadow lay like someone who was already dead.

FORTY

AFTERNOON WAS drawing to a close and an early evening chill had already risen above the Hockaday steading, but it didn't seem to bother the little girl who was waiting in the yard.

Clove had known the buggy was coming before it appeared because she'd seen it inside her head, jouncing over ruts in the track. Mrs Hockaday was driving the horse, just as she had driven it earlier on the way to do the singing in Oasis, but there was no Ma sitting beside her, glorious and bright in her beaded dress. Colt was sitting in her place, neither glorious nor bright, and Vixen followed behind the wheels, her red coat dulled by travel dirt. Both boy and pony were stooping low as though the ground had sucked their strength.

Clove hardly noticed when her grandma came from the house, wrapping herself against the air's sharp bite. She had brought out a spare shawl for the child's shoulders, but it was shrugged away. There were fiery roses in the little girl's cheeks and her skin was too warm. Martha thought that maybe she was sickening for a malady. Maybe it was all that could be expected in a place where nothing had been right for far too long.

At least the boy was back, praise the Lord for that. But where was his mother? What had been happening in that empty space beyond the Hockaday farmstead where people could be taken away and returned on a whim?

Joanie brought the buggy around in a slow arc. She didn't want to face the old woman and the child for she had no answers to give them, too full of questions herself. But Martha's questions remained unvoiced as she stepped forwards, reaching for her grandson even before the vehicle had stopped travelling. Colt took a while to move from his seat, as though having to accept that he'd been brought back to the place he had wanted to escape, before clambering to the ground and his grandma's arms.

'You are in need of food and warm clothes, child,' Martha muttered, wrapping him in the shawl that Clove had discarded, squeezing his shoulders to keep the comfort inside. 'Come along now; I have prepared a tasty stew.'

Bending her head to speak, she drew the boy towards the house, her hair stark and grey next to his tousled darkness. Joanie had heard her words, but she realised with a pang that the tasty stew was probably only bubbling away inside Martha's mind. She felt a crushing sorrow, but it was just another layer on top of the sorrows that had already been stacked in her heart.

The little girl standing in the yard stared up at the woman on the buggy seat, but when Joanie had climbed down the child's stare had shifted along the track to Oasis. Clove Shadow, wan-faced, almost ethereal; a mere child but with too much knowledge in her eyes. Joanie reached out to lead her into the house, where her grandma and her brother had gone, but the girl recoiled from her aid and walked by herself.

Joanie felt relieved, and then ashamed; and finally, resolved. It had been a tough day that was only going to get tougher, but she could cope with that. A sturdy woman who had faced many hardships, Joanie Hockaday would always be ready to face more if need be. And even if Martha Madison had only imagined that stew, she would get the real thing on the go as soon as she could find a knife and some vegetables to chop.

Indeed, there was nothing tasty simmering on the stove, although Martha seemed to have forgotten about that already, too engrossed with wrapping the boy in blankets. And rugs as well. So many warming things that Colt had already started to disappear behind folds of roughhewn and scratchy. He sat quietly, crouching inside his grandma's comforters. His sister came to sit beside him and they leaned against each other, seeking some comfort of their own.

Joanie set to work with the preparation of food, keeping out of the way as Martha warmed milk for the children. Maybe she thought they were still babies requiring coddling. Maybe she thought she was in her own kitchen. It was just another strange situation, made even stranger by the fact that no one had spoken since entering the house.

The stove began to crackle, and a while later the small room was warm again, painting a pretty scene through the window, with lamplight jumping merrily around the four people who had collected there. Emmett was glad to see it as he rode the weary piebald along the track, accompanied by the whisper of wind, the crunch of hooves, the occasional grunt of the hound as it loped by the horse's side.

Night had fallen like a cloak and the stars hid behind a billow of clouds. He had relished the peace that surrounded him on the journey back from Oasis, but it cracked a little when he arrived to find the buggy abandoned in the yard, the chestnut and the little mare still hitched and harnessed. Joanie and the boy had been remiss, but that was of no matter for Emmett welcomed more time alone, trying to inject some sense into the day before the questioning began.

He unsaddled and rubbed down, fed the steeds and secured the brindled dog. He buried his thoughts under labour; but it wasn't working. His mind refused to co-operate, replaying what had taken place through the rain by the trees on the hill, until his skull was throbbing from the gunshot blast, the heat of the weapon in his hand. Wolf Shadow making that sound in his throat as the bullet tore him apart – a compressed agony that would stay in Emmett's memory for a long time to come.

Enough was enough. Near to collapse, he tossed bridles over a hook and made it to the house. Joanie glanced up from the stove as he came inside, her dear face rounding with pleasure at the sight of him.

There was a pile of blankets by the table that at second glance became the boy. His grandma fussed nearby, crooning a cradle song, but the little girl had moved into her own separation at the side of the room. Hers was the face that Emmett saw first, for she had been staring at the door before he opened it. Clove's eyes were fixed on his. Eyes too old for a young child. Too knowing.

She could see right through him. There was nowhere to hide – until his wife came over and kissed his cheek. It was a spontaneous gesture straight from her heart, and it meant that Joanie believed in him. Maybe that was all he needed to be strong when it was time to speak of what had transpired.

'That stew smells good,' he said, and even his voice sounded false. 'I sure hope you've made enough for me as well.'

Martha turned around as though his words had set off

her mechanism. 'Tell me, Emmett Hockaday, have you come across my daughter on your travels?'

Joanie looked up at the sudden disruption. 'Sage is still in Oasis, Martha.'

'She should be here caring of her children and yet for a while there has been no sign of her,' the old woman continued.

Wiping her hands on her apron, Joanie went over to the table. 'I have something to tell you, Martha,' she said, helping her into a chair. 'It concerns Wolf Shadow.' She took a breath; it stuttered in her throat when the woman clutched her arm.

'It is all that boy's fault.' She spat the words. Joanie pulled away from her stale breath and met the shock in Colt's eyes.

'Colt is certainly not to blame,' she said loudly, feeling too weary to take on this extra mantle.

'The boy has been a curse on this house ever since the day that my husband brought him here.' Martha banged the table with her fist. 'He fathered him on a whore and told me to treat him as my own child.'

She grabbed Joanie's arm again, dragging her closer. There was fever in her gaze. 'But how could I, Mrs Hockaday? Try as I might, I was never able to bear a boy myself, and so Haine Madison found another willing to birth his son.'

Joanie recoiled and stepped away, her skin prickling with an eerie chill as the old woman fell suddenly quiet, hardships dripping through the hole in her memory.

Martha was back in the present, but the past had scratched her grandson, hard enough to hurt. Colt stared at the floor, tracing pathways along wood grain, but seeing only the father who had grown from that boy. Fearless, strong, protective of words, Wolf Shadow was the man that Colt wanted to be when he grew into a man himself. He was the man who had always returned, no matter how many times he went away. But he was in Oasis now, and maybe he was about to go away again, except that this time he would not be coming back at all. And his son didn't want to think what life would be like without him.

The last view Colt had of his father was linked to the colour red. His shirt had been red, Mr Hockaday's hands were still stained with it. There was red across the tunic of the dark man who had carried Colt's father into Dr Ryker's house. And although barely conscious, at that time he had still been alive.

Colt fought for the words, and they were sharp and shrill.

'Pa is coming home!'

It was a demand, not a question, and Hockaday jerked as it smashed into his skull. He wanted to tell the boy that for sure his father was coming home; even if too much of his blood was to be left behind on the doctor's floor. He wanted to say it, but the words were prevented by what he had seen through the Rykers' window that evening as he untied the piebald from the hitching post. Sage and the dark stranger in a position of last resort, so motionless in prayer that they might have been carved from wood. They were preparing to mourn the man on the couch as he took his final breath.

Emmett looked over to where his wife was carefully stirring the stew. He looked at Martha, who had settled at the table with her knitting and a formless humming that followed the swish of Joanie's spoon. At Colt who had relinquished the stifling blankets with the same fortitude that the farmer had always recognised in Wolf.

And then he looked at Clove, standing at her own

distance, staring back at him. Her face was glowing. The child appeared as bright as a silver moon on a calm and magical night.

'Pa is coming home,' she whispered, perhaps unaware that she was repeating her brother's words. But this was no demand, it was pure and sure and definite.

Clove knew things; Emmett had heard Sage speak of it. She knew of the confrontation on that strange tree-hoarded hill where four people had come together in search of the same ending. She knew of the fracas of wind and rain and heat and rage. She knew the hand that had fired the bullet and betrayed her father's lifeblood. Maybe she even knew why.

She was the barometer, this remarkable child, this frightening child. She could see the future. It was shining in her face.

Later that night Emmett would admit culpability to his wife as they lay together in bed and spoke of everything that had happened. And Joanie would forgive him; he was sure of it. But that was for a time to come, and what was important now was the present.

'That's right, Clove honey,' he said. 'Wolf Shadow is coming home.'

FORTY-ONE

NIGHT LINGERED, and day was a long time arriving for Emmett Hockaday, lying awake with darkness like a living thing pressing on his eyes. With nothing to see there was little need to see at all, and he welcomed that oblivion.

Even in the dark it had not been easy to offload his blame. His wife had lain silently on her side of the bed while he spoke of what had taken place inside the strange clump of trees, of his own wrongdoings and how he may never forgive his wayward finger on the trigger. He told Joanie everything, and when he finished she was still silent. For those few seconds Emmett had felt very alone, until she began to speak, saying all the right things, forgiving him, reminding him of her love. She held him tightly until she fell asleep, and only then did she let him go.

But even so there was little peace to be found. The wind rose and sorrowed in the yard, moans crept from the corners of the room and footsteps tapped across the floor, bringing horrors to Emmett's bedside. For hours he lay as still as possible so that his wife should rest easy, unaware that foreboding had already interrupted her thin slumber, and she too was lying as still as possible. She caught friction in his breathing, felt his heartbeat through the mattress. She could hear thoughts tumble in his head, but she kept her mouth closed because words were useless. She was glad when he gave up pretending and slipped from the bed.

Emmett was pleased that he hadn't woken her, or so he thought. When he left the room, Joanie stretched cramp from her legs and turned to face the window. A lighter rectangle in the blanket of night, it framed her memory of the afternoon; of Wolf Shadow, unable to walk, unable to speak, carried from the dark man's saddle into the Rykers' house. He had turned into a dark man himself. The gold in his eyes was hidden, and it made her sad to think that she might never see that life-light again, or his fine-looking face as he rode past her home on the black stallion.

Joanie stared at the pale block of window until it seemed to shine. The glow might be construed as a sign of hope, but Joanie saw it as the final flare. Despite the children's brave words of the evening before, she recognised that their father was unlikely to return to the valley dip. He had been hurt too much. Soon he would be gone, and after his arrest and a short trial her husband could be gone also, laid in a murderer's grave. She, and the little family that shared the alcove on the other side of the wall, were going to be left alone in a house built for her by two dead men.

Emmett Hockaday went out into the yard. The night was cold and he collected warmth inside his jacket. The wind was playing games; when it heard him coming it urged him to play as well, like the hound had been wont to do when it was growing out of puppyhood. Emmett ignored the urging, just as he had ignored the young dog, and pretty soon it settled down again.

The farmer followed the path to the corral and leaned

his weight on the topmost rails. There was nothing much to see, but still he stared in that direction as he might in the daytime when it was all he could see, and he set free the thoughts that had thickened through the long night. Powerful thoughts; they swirled around his head like hornets, lifting into the air and filling the darkness.

From where she was lying under blankets in the sleeping space, Clove felt the first jab of insect stings, and then the onslaught as thoughts were released from the man by the corral. For a while she lay buffeted. The words in Emmett's head fell over themselves; they were too loud for the small space, and Clove was the only one to hear. Her brother slept on, his breath faltering as his mind rode jagged dreams, and her grandma lay muffled by snores.

Clove was quiet as she left the house, and those in the lean-to remained undisturbed. The darkness outside was extreme, but the child tracked Emmett's thoughts as though he had laid a trail.

It was her bed-warmth that alerted the farmer to the little girl who had followed him into the yard. She was standing close by the fence and he welcomed her company, and the chance to talk to a living creature that wasn't likely to neigh or bark in reply. He suspected that Clove would make no sound at all and he welcomed that too, because he had things to say that didn't require any comment. Although he wondered if perhaps it was unwise to speak of what was in his mind, since she was only little and Wolf Shadow was her father. But there would always be something different about this girl.

'I found Colt up by a stand of trees on top of a small hill. They were strange trees, Clove, bent and wary like they were listening. Like they were joining in with us; me and Colt and your pa. And the dark man.'

Emmett peered at the child. She was very still; just a black shape in the general gloom.

'How did you know about him, Clove? How did you know the dark man was coming, and bringing trouble with him? He must be a bad man, because it's all down to him that your pa is spending the night in the doctor's house. It's the dark man who is accountable.'

He faltered. The little girl was staring at him with burning eyes. He knew that because of the extra heat that had risen in his face.

'The dark man brought that trouble to your brother,' the farmer told the air as it swirled over the corral, scented with horse and old hay, and he hoped that the words were reaching the ears of his silent companion.

'Colt could not get away from him.' But maybe Colt hadn't wanted to get away from him. 'He was frightened.' But what was it that had frightened the boy?

'The dark man was threatening Colt's life,' Emmett said. 'I had to do something, didn't I?'

His voice had risen as though he was accusing the night for judging him. But it wasn't the night. It might have been the little girl, but she was very still, as she had been all along; waiting to hear what he was about to tell her.

'Wolf Shadow tried to stop me, Clove. Your pa was in the way and the gun went off too soon. There was nothing I could do to prevent it.'

Emmett looked down at her. She was a little clearer now. Maybe it was closer to dawn. He thought he could see a gleam of light in the sky.

'Wolf was protecting the dark man. Can you believe that? He was protecting the Indian from me!'

And the only reason he would do that was because...

'I think your pa knows who he is, Clove. And I believe

318

you might know as well.'

She blinked, at least that was his impression; it was still too murky to be sure of anything in this strange otherworld where two disparate people were standing in the middle of a farmyard at night.

But that wasn't the end of it; Emmett had just one more thing to say before he could be released from her judgement.

'It was me who shot your pa,' he said, appalled by his own words. 'But it was an accident. I am truly sorry. Please will you forgive me?'

Forgive me for what I did. And for what I wanted to do.

Something was touching his hand: the start of a grip that was withdrawn too soon, leaving a residue of warmth on his skin. The imprint of a child's fingers that vanished as quickly as it had appeared.

FORTY-TWO

SHE SPENT what was left of the night in the little chamber where her brother and her grandma were still asleep. She slept as well, dreaming that her father was lying on a leather bed with a hole in his side. He was fighting for his life. She told him not to be frightened; she told him to let go. And when he heard what she said he fell into a peace that was as endless as space.

Dawn had passed, and now Clove was standing by the corral beneath the widening sky, dressed for daytime. She was the first to hear the sound of the buggy horse and the wheels scattering stones on the track, and she knew it meant that once again everything was changing.

Half-hidden from the valley road, the Wellerson house sloped into its own dip. Daniel Ryker drove past without noticing Maria's pale face appear at a window; without hearing her gasps of righteousness that misted the glass at sight of the buggy and its passengers. Sitting upright on the bench, the doctor gripped reins and stared ahead. Maybe he was trying not to think of the woman beside him, or the man she was holding in her arms. Or the other man, riding the dun behind the vehicle where all sound was muted.

The doctor's horse grumbled at the bit, fighting the morning chill and the hard ground. It was more than ready to be brought to a halt in the Hockaday yard where the hound was pulling at the leash and adding its own voice to the complaints of bay and buggy. And then the house door was flung open, followed by exclamations as Joanie Hockaday ran outside, aware only of what had arrived.

She noticed the small girl by the corral a moment later and made to call to her, but Martha Madison was there first, shaking out a dark green rug and swaddling the child until she became a baby again; just as strange and just as special.

Colt was battling indecision. He lingered by the open door so that he would reach it in time if flight should become a necessity, and Emmett Hockaday had to push the boy aside in order to find out what was going on in his yard that morning. He saw Daniel Ryker climbing down from the buggy, stepping around the bay's head to reach up for Sage Madison's burden. He saw them lowering Wolf Shadow to the ground, and it was like a silent ballet of movement, bringing the dead man home to his final resting place.

Except that Wolf was not dead. He was standing sandwiched between the man and the woman, fighting to stay upright until he had sought out and connected with the farmer's eyes. He nodded, and Emmett stood by his house wall and nodded in return; two men passing silent messages of regret and forgiveness from one to the other. But that small effort had taken all of Wolf's strength and he started to shake. He would have crumpled if the dark man hadn't reached him first, cradling him as if he was still the wolf cub. As if, after a long time out of kilter, everything was clicking into place.

Colt edged out of the dark man's way as though fearing contagion, but everyone followed the stranger who was carrying Wolf into the house. He took the young man to the sleeping space and laid him on a bundle of blankets that Martha had relinquished minutes before. They were still warm from her night's rest, and the Indian wrapped them around Wolf Shadow's body as carefully as a father tending his child.

Eyes closed, Wolf was fighting pain. He was wearing the same shirt from the day before, now tattered and stained and crusted dry, but the bandages beneath were stunningly white in the gloomy room. They showed no sign of the haemorrhaging that Emmett had seen before returning home at the fall of night, heavy in his heart and already in mourning. For surely no normal man should have emerged in one piece from such blood loss?

That is what he would have asked Daniel Ryker if it hadn't been for the fatigue etched across the doctor's face. It was as though he had spent the night in a crazy dance: the dance to save the life of a traitor, or a friend; or both.

Sage entered, smoothing down her crumpled dress. The dark man moved back to allow her space and the house shrank for the tallness of him. Sage took his hand and pressed it to her heart, and everything she wanted to say was in her eyes as they kneeled together beside the man on the ground. She took Wolf's hand as well and pressed it to her heart, joining young man to old, joining herself to them both. It was a gesture of great intimacy that broke Colt's shackles.

Grief and guilt battled with love as he looked down at his father. His mother rose, cupping the boy's face with hands that the two men had warmed. She glanced up as Clove came into the little space, so quietly that she might have been a ghost. Still bundled in her grandma's rug, the small girl was like a flower growing in a nest of moss. She touched her mother with a gaze, she touched her father, and finally she looked up and understood the long-haired man who was gazing back at her.

They had no need of anyone else; not even Sage's mother – but Martha didn't care about that, she was too busy with pans in Mrs Hockaday's kitchen, a thousand miles away from what was happening at the end of the room. Joanie was with her, directing her attention from this to that, as if she knew what to do with the personality that had taken possession of Martha's mind.

Her strangeness was a recent development, but now was not its time. Now belonged to the people in the lean-to, bonded together by their own shadows. Emmett thought he could hear muttered words. They sounded a little like a call to arms, or maybe it was the dark man making an invocation to his gods, just as he had done in the doctor's house.

This was nothing but a small farm steading with everyday chores and responsibilities, but a change had taken place and it was overwhelming. It even touched Daniel Ryker as he climbed to the buggy seat and set the bay in motion. He raised his head and the wind made wings of his hair. Joanie Hockaday, watching from the door, saw a hint of the young man he used to be in the smoother skin of his face. She sent up a prayer that some of the doctor's new hope would filter down to his troubled wife and those poor, bewildered children who were waiting for him back in Oasis. For it was only fair that everybody should be given a second chance.

Following up her prayer with the sign of the cross, Joanie returned to the kitchen. She wondered whether someone had scented the air with perfume; she tried to find it, but there was no direction to follow. The freshness seemed to come from all around, as if windows had been opened to a spring morning. The whole house smelled of release. Joanie smiled to herself and started to sing as she fed the stove and pondered on what might happen next.

She didn't have long to wait. Sage was there when she turned around, delight giving plumpness to a face that had grown too gaunt too quickly. The young woman's eyes were eloquent, and so were the arms that embraced the farmer's wife. She was still drum-hollow, for it would take more than a while for her to regain the person she had been before, when her ordeal had yet to be suffered, but she seemed somehow taller.

'Thank you for being my good neighbour,' she breathed by Joanie's ear. The soft words tickled the other woman and made her laugh like a child, but that may have had something to do with the changes, the perfume in the air, the wholeness that was filling every corner of the house.

'Thank you for being my good friend,' Sage said. And it was then that Joanie realised she was really saying goodbye.

FORTY-THREE

THE MADISON homestead was closed up and as silent as a tomb. Wolf Shadow recoiled from the sight of it, but only for a moment, and after that he wanted to take an axe to the logs waiting by the wood pile; he wanted to collect the hammer and nails and ride Night Dancer out to check the fences.

He wanted to dig out the hollow in the yard that was a history of the pond which used to lap there, reflecting back drifting clouds and the moon's twin on silvered nights. But now it was a black smear that allowed no reflections. Sheriff Russett had once released him from jail to find the same smear of black water where there used to be pond, and the first thing the wolf cub had done on the day of freedom had been to dig out the hollow and begin again.

Challenged by hard work and commitments, the life that followed that freedom had not been easy. Coping with the widow who had so virulently despised him; facing fatherhood when he was still a boy; lifting the farmstead from the mire – the past confronted Wolf Shadow again as his neighbour drove the buggy into the yard. His body torn by Emmett's bullet, still too weak to climb down unaided, Wolf looked around him and didn't like what he was seeing. But it had been his decision to bring his family back to the home that he had broken, along with the ties that had once held them together. His short-lived pleasure with Lucy Ryker had been followed by the near loss of the woman who was with him now, watching as the dark man helped him to the ground.

The long-haired Indian who had started as a fearsome stranger half-carried Wolf Shadow into the house. And after they had paved the way, Sage climbed down as well, tucking back her hair with stiff fingers before she gathered her children and followed. Behind her came Martha, rheumy eyes greedy for the garden with its rampage of dried stalks and sodden leaves, and the poor soil that needed a coating of good fertiliser. She would make a start on that in the morning, once she had hunted out her straw hat and her cotton dress, for the sun was sure to be high and hot that day. She drew the shawl tighter around her chest, but the motion was merely habit for she didn't notice the chill. Her mind was warm with summer and she could only see blue skies and flowers.

The dark man had already relinquished Wolf to a chair beside the stove, and he sat there shivering, as though he had aged many years since the shooting. The stove was cold and dusty and Wolf felt the same. He leaned towards the small pile of kindling but it wasn't close enough and so he stretched out further. The wound screamed like the stab of a knife, and he must have cried out for Sage was with him so quickly she might have been forewarned.

'Are you a fool, Wolf Shadow? You will shear the stitches and open the bleeding!'

She laid hands on him as though they were blessed with healing. Her heat spread through his body and it was a while before she pulled away.

'You must give yourself time to mend, husband,' she

said, gathering the kindling herself and preparing the stove. Her movements were practised and swift, and Wolf watched the thatch of sticks grow into a nest that flared from the flame like a phoenix reborn and whole again. He wondered how long it would take for that to happen for him, but the injury's throb was already receding. The holes that Emmett's bullet had opened through his body had been sutured meticulously by Daniel Ryker; he had given to Wolf Shadow the same care that in another time he had given to a boy called Cub who had come to his house with a flayed back. It was as strong as the friendship that had since grown between them.

But throughout the operation and his long fight to staunch the bleeding, Daniel had never once looked him straight in the eye, too aware of his wife walking the boards of the rooms upstairs. So maybe forgiveness also needed time to mend.

Time was elastic, this is what Wolf was learning. Through the dust-frosted window he could see Emmett Hockaday unloading the family's belongings from the buggy. The farmer was smiling, probably because at last he and Joanie had their house to themselves. He had already brought Night Dancer back to the Madison corral, but the stolen palomino was still running free in the wilderness. Emmett's rare wild beast belonged in the Hockaday enclosure; it was not a replacement for Wolf Wind and never had been. Wolf Shadow had simply been struck by a lunacy that had overturned reality; he had just wanted what he could not have. Sage had been right all along and he was a fool. Perhaps the biggest fool of all.

The dark man would have told him that. Wolf watched him through the glass, lifting heavy boxes from the buggy as though they weighed little. He watched his son carrying a rolled rug that his grandma had brought to adorn the floor of their temporary home. It was the same one she had laid across the floor of this house after her husband's death had cleared the way for colour in spaces that had once been dark and doleful. Colt was at ease with the weight of the rug. On the cusp of ten he was taller now, as narrow-hipped and straight-backed as his father had been as a child.

Colt was standing beside the stranger, and the only thing they couldn't share was age. Eyes just as black, hair as dark and straight and sheened even though the sun was hidden. Their shoulders were square and capable of weights that Colt had yet to bear and the Indian had borne over years. The few years when he and a small boy may have sat together on flat-topped rocks making enchantments for the sky and the land, for the health of jugglers and tumblers and clowns. Years that had passed too quickly, leaving the boy to fend for himself. Teaching him that no one could be trusted. Not even his own father.

By early evening the house was once again a home, filled with warmth and the aroma of cooking. Joanie had added some of her own provisions to the belongings piled on the back of the buggy, but the cupboards in the Madison kitchen space were practically bare. Sage could foresee a journey to Kester Kendall's store, tolerating sight of his smug face for the sake of Margharita's welcome.

Colt was in the barn, grooming Vixen for the third time that day. After all the strange and chilly months the boy was warm again, wearing happiness like an extra coat. The pony's hide was a gleam of copper, and she was as content as her young master.

Clove had taken herself away from the table early,

forsaking the bright stove for half-light in the room she shared with her grandma. She sat on the floor with her back against the wall, string cradles busy in her hands, messages busy in her mind. She too was warm, but not yet content; a crowd of thoughts allowing little space for happiness.

Light was already waning when Wolf Shadow donned a coat and left the house, dusk stealing away the day's balm and leaving chill behind. He was still too weak to walk unaided – that was what Sage told him. She went on to ask whether he realised what a stubborn fool he was, and he nodded before kissing the mouth he'd thought he might never kiss again. She touched the kiss as she watched him easing his way to the corral, limping for the healing wound in his thigh, not to mention the other hurts that afflicted his body.

The dark man was there already, leaning into the fence, gazing at the black horse like someone who was making up his mind. He didn't turn until Wolf had reached him.

'That stallion will not bend easily to your will,' he said, watching Night Dancer's self-assured swagger across the enclosure.

'The stallion still has much to learn,' Wolf said, and shrugged the coat higher up his shoulders. It used to fit him well, but recent privations had diminished him so much he could have been a different man. The wounds in his side shrieked and taught him that it was wiser to keep still.

The dark man nodded. 'Men must learn also, wolf cub. Just like horses.'

They rested in silence, watching the black stallion until it grew tired of parading, and snaffled the ground for snippets of fodder that might have been missed before. A breeze lifted the animal's mane and played it like a musical instrument, but there was no sound, except for the pulse that began to throb inside Wolf's ear.

'I once knew a man who carried me as a child on his shoulders,' he said. 'I was so high I thought I could see what was about to happen before it did.'

The Indian made a sound in his throat; maybe he was agreeing, maybe it was something else. He stared out at the corral and the night that had risen up to swallow the black horse.

'And then the man disappeared,' Wolf said. 'But I was not high enough to see it about to happen.' His voice was louder, as though his throat had gathered the strength he was searching for. 'They told me he had been killed, and that is what I grew up believing to be true.'

Breezes wound around the house chimney. Smoke escaped in pale ribbons that filled Wolf's nostrils and he coughed, cringing from the explosion of pain in his side.

'And now you want me to believe that you are that man; that you lived and they lied.' The smoke reached his eyes and they started to water. 'The man who did not come back. Who deserted Ma, and she died. Who deserted me, and I was sold. If you are that man, then I have a right to hate you.'

The smoke was strong; his eyes were stinging now, and his face was wet. He wanted to take his knife to the one who was standing next to him, but knew he would fall if he let go of the fence.

'They told you lies because they needed me gone,' the dark man said. 'I would not have left you there, Cub. I would not have left your ma. I loved you both…'

'My name is Wolf Shadow! Once I was Cub but now I have become Wolf Shadow, because my father was the Indian called…'

'Dark Wolf. Your father is the Indian, Dark Wolf.'

Wolf stared at the man's face; the marks written there like a message that should have meant something. He stared hard enough for his eyes to glisten. 'Do you know what happened to him?'

There was a whistling from the chimney, an ache of sorrow as the wind moaned. The dark man shifted his weight and the wood creaked. 'The circus people did not want an Indian for a white woman's mate,' he said. 'Five of the men came in the night to attack. They beat me with clubs; left me for dead. The circus moved away, leaving lies and taking you with them. A travelling tinker found me, healed me. It took a while.'

He was silent, as though that was his story and there was nothing to follow, and then he spoke again, but quieter now.

'Memory had gone. I no longer had a woman, I no longer had a son. For years I was in darkness, but there was always a shadow in my mind; something I had to learn. One day I heard a cowhand remembering a pale-haired boy he had once met, walking hungry over hills. A boy who had used language from his throat to tame a stallion into bearing a rider.'

He looked down at the young man who was gripping the corral fence to stay upright and staring out at nothing – because there was nothing to see in the night, only the pictures crowding his mind.

'I learned of a boy who had spoken to horses. A boy who by then would have grown into a man, still with the language in his throat,' the Indian said. 'For I taught him well in the days when I carried a child on my shoulders and loved the mother who had birthed him.'

His voice cracked like a twig in the ice and it was a while before he could speak again. 'The mother died, but the child lived. It has taken a long time looking but now I have found the boy who talks to horses.'

The wind rose once more, before falling to earth and disappearing. The Indian filled his lungs in the hush and his breath escaped on a white cloud. 'I am the one who gave you life, Wolf Shadow,' he said. 'I am Dark Wolf, and you are my son.'

Wolf waited for the pain to lessen, and then he shook his head. A slight movement; but an ending.

'No. You are not Dark Wolf,' he said. 'And I am not your son.'

FORTY-FOUR

RECOVERY WAS grudging. A battle fought over two handfuls of days that could only be won by courage, along with the blood of the father flowing through the son's veins.

For the length of the fight the dark man remained at the Madison farmstead, taking up residence in the hayloft of the barn. That was his choice, but it was not Sage's.

'I cannot allow him to sleep up there like a farmhand,' she said. 'If he is your father, Wolf Shadow, he is also part of the family.' Although it felt odd to say such a thing about a stranger who had come to life as a frightening phantom in her daughter's mind.

It made Wolf angry to hear her say it. 'Not part of my family,' he claimed. 'Soon he will be on his way.'

The Indian, however, appeared to be going nowhere, and Wolf Shadow kept his distance because of it. As his strength grew he found himself spending more time beyond the Madison place, riding the grey mare since Night Dancer was too fiery for the mending of wounds. The black stallion was still in need of tuition, to replace the sense that had been wiped out by indolence and overfeeding on the Hockaday steading.

The grey was more obliging, albeit with a sedate pace that made its rider feel elderly. But Sage would tolerate no argument whatsoever and he knew she was right.

After all, she had nearly lost him. Colt and Clove had nearly lost him. And he had nearly died and lost the chance to be anyone's son.

At times Wolf Shadow rode away to the edge of the wild, and against his wishes he was at times accompanied by the broad-beamed dun and the one who called himself Dark Wolf. The young man learned how to ride in silence and the dark man learned not to speak until speaking was required.

'We had love, your ma and I,' he said once, when they had stopped to rest in the place where the land curved and rocks formed natural seating. The sentence had come from nowhere, but it had the power to scrape Wolf's spine. He shuddered, and it wasn't just for the chill.

He waited for the Indian to say more, and he did, but not before watching a flock of birds in flight. He pointed upwards after they had passed, as though the birds were returning to pass again.

'I called her Dove,' he said.

'Her name was Minta,' said Wolf, too quickly, keeping hold of his own history.

'Minta was her name,' the Indian said. 'But for me she was a dove.'

Wolf Shadow was silent. This was a life that did not belong to him. There was too much of the unknown about his past and that bothered him, even though it was of little matter. The mother he could remember had been no dove. There had been nothing sweet or peaceful about the woman who sold her body so freely and gave her son hell when she wasn't otherwise engaged in her bed.

'You must be speaking of her twin,' he said.

The dark man glanced over. There was a battle taking

place in that young man's soul, spitting fire from his eyes.

The Indian nodded. 'She could be fierce.'

'To me she was little else.'

'You have the same fierceness, Wolf Shadow. And Clove also. She has her grandmother's heart.'

'My daughter has only ever had one grandmother and her name is Martha, not Minta and not Dove. Clove has no one else's heart but her own.'

'She has your mother's…'

'I have no mother! For longer than I can remember I had no father either.'

Wolf stood up, too suddenly for his injuries. 'I must have died from Emmett's bullet, for I do not recognise this afterlife,' he shouted; and stumbled.

The Indian rose swiftly to support him. The young man pushed him away.

'I don't want any help from you.' Gruff and cranky, he went to the grey. It was an effort to mount, but the dark man stood and watched and did not help. Wolf settled in the saddle, glanced down and glanced away. The pain in his eyes was more than physical.

The Indian climbed to the dun's back and gathered reins. 'The stallion of your neighbour that is lost,' he said.

Wolf's head jerked. 'What of it?'

'It must be brought back.'

'Soon. I will hunt for it soon.'

'You will go alone?'

'I lost it alone, I will bring it back alone.'

'You are a fool, Wolf Shadow.'

'Oh, am I?' He twisted around, abruptly and unwisely, but this time the pain didn't meet his face. 'Maybe that is because I am the son of fools, and blood will out.'

He swung the mare towards the pathway, and she shuddered at the rough handling as he set her running.

The dark man watched him leave, and only then did he make as if to follow. For a while at least.

Sage found Wolf in the barn where he was stripping the grey, bending to the ground with the saddle in his arms. She had to stop herself from rushing forward to help, for he would not have welcomed that – she could tell from the ring of gold blazing from his eyes.

Wolf lifted the saddle to the rail and turned, a hand to his side where the wound was clamouring. He saw his woman framed in the doorway. It reminded him of the time she had brought to the barn a vision of men with sticks, but then stayed with him until the dawn on a ruffle of straw. The memory was good; strong enough to ease his wretchedness, clear enough for him to realise that he was feeling wretched.

He went to unbuckle the bridle and Sage came over, unravelling burrs from the grey mare's mane. 'There is food ready,' she said. 'Soup and a wedge of my mother's bread. Come into the house and settle for a while.'

Wolf touched her arm, to show that he had heard her words and recognised the concern that was behind them.

Sage pressed further. 'Will your father be eating with us?'

Wolf Shadow faltered, bridle in one hand, the other moving to the knife at his waist. 'My father?'

'Dark Wolf.' She had seen the movement. 'Did you not ride out together?'

'And since we did not come back together, Sage, how should I know where the Indian is now?'

She waited a moment for him to settle his spleen, and another to settle her own.

'You lived for seven years with a man who whipped you raw and spat salt into your wounds, and now another arrives with gentleness in his soul, and when you are dying he makes deals with his gods for your life.'

She pushed past him, striding into the yard; showing him her back because her face was too furious. 'Which man would you prefer to call "father"?' she shouted.

The words hung in the barn for a while after she had disappeared, and although the grey fretted in their sour echo, Wolf Shadow had not moved.

He didn't appear for the soup and the bread, and neither did the dark man. The gaps they left at the table were huge and eloquent, and Sage swallowed ire along with the seeds in Martha's loaf. And then she cast them from her mind and went about her business.

Towards the end of the afternoon she ventured once more to the barn. The door was closed, and no reply came from within to acknowledge her knock. When she pushed it open, to the usual rise of must and floating chaff, a chain stirred from one of the wall hooks and a hidden creature scuttled across the floor. They made the only sounds. The storeroom, and the hayloft above where the Indian had set up his bed space, were empty.

She felt the nudge of concern but refused to rise to its challenge. She had suffered from concern too often and too recently and she'd had enough of it. Let them be missing, let them be gone. Let Wolf Shadow slink away and lick his wounds, real and imaginary. He will return; he had been through too much not to.

But if he was to return, it must be as an adult and not a whining child!

Sage marched back to the house, only staring once at the lowering sky which was promising rain, and maybe wind gusts to go with it. Her mind flitted over the waterproofs by the porch that were keeping nobody dry, and then it flirted with the disquiet that would always appear in the space left by her man's absence. Just for a moment she could see the doctor's house behind its thinning trees, and triumph in Lucy Ryker's face.

It was only a moment, but it weighed heavy and left a vile taste and the seed of doubt. Sage struggled past it and through the door, and there was Clove. The child was sitting at the table, weaving miracles from a pair of needles and a pile of yarn. She wasn't looking at the knitting in her hands, it was as though body was separate from mind. She was looking instead through the wall, out into the yard and beyond the farmstead, perhaps all the way to the distant wild. There was such contentment in her eyes that no one seeing her could feel anything but peace.

Clove was telling her mother that there was nothing to worry about. And Clove knew things, didn't she?

Night fell, bringing unkind weather and eventually Wolf Shadow as well.

He came through the door on a squall; it was as if the wind had lifted him up and deposited him on the floorboards, skidding the rugs from under his feet. Wolf shook off the rain like a dog; it scattered across the walls and spotted the nightgown of Sage's mother who had been ejected from her room by the intrusion, broom ready in her hand. At first glance it seemed that she was there to sweep him away with the rest of the rubbish, brandishing the handle like a spear that had lost its warhead.

Sage was there to take the broom away, storing it in the corner by the dresser. It had felt like a relief to climb down from the roof space, for lying awake until the early hours had allowed the young woman no rest. Now she looked from her mother, hesitating by the side of the room as though she was neither coming nor going, to the man who was making the floor very wet.

'All is well, Ma,' she said. 'Get yourself back to bed.'

Martha's face brightened as if she had made up her mind, and she followed that decision and left the room. Sage listened for her door to close before turning to Wolf. He was squeezing rain from his hair, lifting it away from his face. The injuries old and new that marked his skin were highlighted by wetness. She recognised the similarity with the Indian's scrolling tattoos.

'Welcome home, husband,' she said, 'and have you brought Dark Wolf with you?'

Wolf glanced at her. 'If the man who claims to be my father is not in the barn, then no, I have not brought him.'

'Did you not think to look?'

'No, Sage, I did not think to look.'

'Well I think you should.'

He let his hands drop, made to walk past her, but she was fixed firmly in his path. They stood face to face, the man looking down on the woman who was outstaring him in a way he'd never seen before.

'I cannot be responsible for someone who might once have denied responsibility for me.'

Sage lifted a hand, then held it tight with the other so that no, she would not slap him.

'He has explained the reasons why…'

'He has told me a story.'

'He explained it to me, as well as to you.'

Wolf faltered, knocked back by her ferocity. Her power was taking away his own and leaving him with something that felt like stupidity.

'He lied.' Even as he spoke the words, Wolf wondered whether he actually believed them.

Sage had stepped close, the scent of flowers rising from her clean skin. 'He has the look of you, Wolf Shadow. He has the look of Colt. It is up to you whether you seal your mind to it or not. But…'

She was even closer now, touching his body with hers, his wetness soaking through her nightgown. 'But if you deny him you are denying your birthright, and that I cannot understand.'

The last word disappeared on a sigh, she spoke it so quietly. Wolf's jacket muttered when he held her, the squeak of leather was soothed by her arms when she held him back. Their lips met and slipped apart. And when they met again she breathed into his mouth.

'Come upstairs with me, husband. Come and help me chase away the storm.'

I have ways to bring you back to me, Wolf Shadow. I have ways to make you see sense.

They left the floor to its puddles and climbed the ladder to where the bed cover that had been pushed aside was pushed aside again. And Sage pushed aside questions about the past few hours. He would tell her where he had been when he was ready, she was sure of it. As sure as she was that the doctor's wife had nothing to do with it, because there was no evidence of her purple-yellow scent anywhere on his body.

More of Wolf Shadow than his wounds were healing as they joined together in their bed, as sweetly as before, when they had been almost too young for a night of love. And just like the first time that Wolf had entered her and arched his back, Sage felt the thrust of his seed reach her womb.

FORTY-FIVE

THE NEXT day the barn was as empty as before, all evidence of its occupant removed from the hayloft platform.

The Indian had gone, proving that he had not been the person he claimed. Wolf felt justified, but Sage was disappointed in a man who appeared to have been little more than the dark invader of her daughter's psyche. She had envisaged something better from him. Something better for Wolf Shadow.

'I knew him for a liar,' he said.

'He gave you back your life on the mound with the trees,' she reminded him. 'He bullied your heart into beating again.'

'That is what Emmett has told us.'

'You only need to look at the bruises his fist left on your chest. There is your proof.'

Wolf smacked the barn door with a palm. 'Enough. It is over. The imposter is gone and I am glad of it.'

But he didn't appear glad as he moved across to the enclosure where Night Dancer was standing idle and apathetic. The man was restless in comparison, and if he had chosen to ignore his hurts and take a foolish saddle to the crazy stallion then Sage would not have been surprised.

Wolf had been crushed and rebuilt and crushed again

so many times over the years that he had learned the senselessness of hope. Maybe in truth he had expected more from the stranger who claimed to have twice given him life – once when he was born, and once when he was about to die. Maybe there was more of the dark man to come?

That, at least, was what Colt wanted to believe.

The arrival of the tattooed Indian had swiftly aroused excitement throughout the school, and Korky Kendall's bullies were keeping careful distance from the one who shared space with that dangerous devil. Where once he had been ostracised for being a filthy Indian whore bastard, now the midday recess brought an audience eager to hear Colt's tales of the dark man who had materialised from beyond the plains where the land grew craggy.

The land where mustangs roamed, herds overseen by long-tailed stallions breathing fire. It was such country that the Indian knew from his youth, where he claimed to have hunted his first horse with the aid of his father, just as his father's father had done when he too was a boy. It was a tradition that should have continued to the next in line if life had been kinder and the chain had not broken.

This was what Colt had learned the day before the Indian followed Wolf Shadow from the yard, and Wolf had come back alone. The day before he vanished, the dark man and the boy had been sitting together in the barn, rubbing suppleness into the dun's harness. No longer the frightening vision from his sister's mind, or the entity who had tried to murder his father on that strange hill with the trees, the familiarity of the dark man had grown as strong as the scent Colt had known since childhood. As strong as the clean straw he had piled up to make a seat on the hard-packed floor.

'Would you have gone with my pa when it was his turn to hunt a wild horse?' the boy had asked.

'That is what I would have done,' the dark man had said. 'If my mind and my son had not been lost to me.'

'Pa hunted his first stallion alone,' Colt told him, soothed by the swish of burnished leather, 'in the time when he was called Cub.'

The Indian had stopped polishing, the cloth held steady in the air. It took a while for him to speak again.

'Your father was just a cub when last I saw him and now he has grown into a wolf.' He had collected himself, nodding at the boy who was leaning forward to catch every word. 'You are still a cub.'

'I am a colt.'

The script across the dark man's face leaped into life when he smiled. 'And when you too are a man you will be a stallion.'

Colt had swaggered. 'I like the sound of that.'

'But when that time comes you must submit to your father's teachings, for it is in a wolf's nature to overcome a stallion.'

'Not if the stallion tramples the wolf first.'

The Indian had been quiet for a moment, one of those moments that seemed to be a part of what made him who he was.

'Your father's first horse was the golden one the cowhand spoke of.'

'Wolf Wind. That was the name Pa gave him.'

The burnishing had begun once again, the dark man working with his head on one side. 'And the stallion of the neighbour that is lost, it is also a golden horse.'

'Mr Hockaday's palomino.' Colt had been searching around for a juicy piece of straw to chew, paying more attention to that than to the dark man's face; missing the decision in his eyes. 'Pa… borrowed him. That is all.'

'What is borrowed must be returned.' The Indian had got to his feet, settling the saddle back on the rail. 'Until then nothing will heal.'

Not quite nothing, for it was thanks to the appearance of the dark man that schoolmaster Jackson and his wife had the sense to keep the strap in their desk drawer, and their concerns about Colt Shadow's dubious bloodline mostly to themselves.

Apart from a swift detour into the sheriff's office to bring the matter to the law's attention.

'A full-blood Indian, brazen and bold as brass.'

'Strutting the street as though he owns it.'

'Who can tell what trouble is brewing as a result?'

'Where is he from…?'

'What does he want…?'

'How safe are we in our beds?'

Andy Parnell started to speak, but the couple had not yet finished.

'And the man, dragged half-dead through the town.'

'Bleeding like a pig.'

'My poor wife was most upset.'

'I cannot venture from home without my smelling salts.'

'The Madison place is a den of tribulation…'

'Sin and crime…'

'What do you intend to do about it, Mr Parnell?'

And so it went on, until Mrs Jackson had worked herself into such a state that the sheriff had to relinquish his chair to her, while her husband fanned her with his sharp black hat.

Her moans had drifted through the door into the

street and pricked at Clay Russett's ears where he was hovering nearby on the sidewalk. He had seen the couple scampering to Parnell's side with their tales of woe and woe betide. Although absent from town at the time, he had since learned from the thrill of gossip and rumour how Wolf Shadow had been returned more dead than alive with his body rent by bullets from a mystery gun, and of the stranger who had carried him into the Rykers' house. A stranger who, by all accounts from those agog on the day that it happened, was at least seven feet tall with black snakes for hair, his face gouged by outlandish markings that were probably unhealthy, unwholesome and altogether unholy.

The old man wiped his brow with a handkerchief that had seen cleaner days. And then he smiled. If it weren't for Wolf Shadow and his exploits over the years, and especially these latest dark deeds and fascinations, Oasis would be a colourless place to live.

Spate and spitefulness temporarily lulled, the Jacksons had left the sheriff's office, the husband holding up the wife with an arm around her waist. An arm that seemed unaccustomed to close association with the woman's body; which made Russett smile again. He tapped them the brim of his hat and watched as they bustled back to the schoolhouse, to carry on teaching purity, obedience and the three Rs, assisted by the frequent and severe encouragement of a length of knotted leather. And they had the audacity to speak of another's savagery.

Parnell was sitting with his head in his hands. Clay could see him through the window. He experienced a tug of sympathy for his arch-enemy, and it was so rare a feeling that he left well enough alone and walked away, pleased for once that resolution of the town's problems was balanced on another's shoulders.

Sounds of joyfulness joined him as he passed the church front – demanding hands on the harmonium and the singing of ladies, some of whom were actually hitting the right notes. There was a certain rhythm to the general exultation, and Clay Russett skipped along to it as he made his way to the saloon.

FORTY-SIX

JOANIE HOCKADAY tossed the basket from one hand to the other, glaring up at the weather that had bared its teeth as soon as she left her house. She lamented the swift passing of summer and the fleeting dispersal of autumn leaves. There had been too many other trials taking her attention and the seasons had died unnoticed, bringing winter closer than she would have liked.

The wind was lying in wait, and she was ambushed as she followed the track to the hollow in the valley. Now it seemed even hollower, as though the Madison farm had been sinking slowly through the years, and would eventually disappear altogether. When that time came, she would mourn the troubled family that had lived in this haunted place. She would mourn especially the loss of the young man who had created such upheaval for Emmett.

It was a sudden realisation that gave her pause; the wind tussled with her hair when she stood and considered it. Something to do with her dubious past, maybe. She'd had associations with bad boys before; she often thought about them when Emmett was asleep and sonorous beside her, and although she would never renounce the life she spent with her gentle husband, she could still recall what it felt like to be wild and reckless.

Much as Wolf Shadow was wild and reckless, and always had been.

Joanie shook herself back to sense and everyday predicaments, such as the weeds that were cultivating Emmett's corral. He spent too much time leaning on the fence, glooming at the empty space where the palomino had once paraded. In his generosity he had retracted his complaint against Wolf and Andy Parnell no longer had reason to drag the horse thief into a backroom cell, but Joanie knew that her husband was hurting.

As she came closer to her neighbour's property now she could see the offender in the yard. Aping Emmett's despondency, consciously or not, Wolf was leaning on the corral fence, but he was staring at a black stallion instead of a horseless void. His hand pressed his side as he straightened up, the discomfort clear in his eyes. For a moment it slowed Joanie's feet, because it was her husband's careless trigger finger that had caused the young man's pain.

Wolf had noticed her coming from the direction of the Hockaday farmstead. He watched as she approached, but there was nothing to read from his face – neither welcome nor rebuke.

'Good morning to you, Wolf Shadow.' She might have been acknowledging the shell of him, for his life spark had retreated inside. The creases in his cheeks were more pronounced and his brown eyes had faded so much it was difficult to believe that they had once sheltered a bright core.

He was wearing leather, thick enough to keep the chill at bay, but even so he shivered. There was no sign of flush or fever so it was not a sickness. She recognised the affliction because she had seen it already, in the man she had left at home.

Wolf and her husband were both grieving.

Smoke was rising from the roof of the rough wooden house. It was warm inside, and Joanie was growing cold. She tucked her hand around Wolf Shadow's arm and took up a position by his side. Jaunty, like two people heading out for a walk.

'Escort me indoors to visit your wife,' she said, tilting her head and smiling at him. Trying to restore some youth to his battered face. 'I apologise for my intrusion,' she lifted the basket, 'but I come bearing gifts.'

Through the window Sage watched the odd couple approaching, the middle-aged woman clutching the young man's arm as if he was her beau; even though in his reluctance to move she might have been propelling him forward instead. Joanie was still smiling, but maybe her mouth had become fixed in that position, because there was little jollity in her eyes.

Sage had already opened the door, and Joanie set Wolf free as she crossed the threshold, but he didn't move any further into the room. 'I need to…' he said, searching for a suitable ending to the sentence. '… To deal with – something in the barn.'

He nodded, but his sight had dropped to the floor and he didn't notice the flash of vexation in Sage's eyes. He began to wander away and she closed the door quickly so that she didn't have to watch. She waved her neighbour further into the room, rubbing the furrow from her forehead when Joanie's back was turned, but the frown had not been missed.

'I have coffee on the stove,' Sage muttered and went to see to it.

'I have brought little cakes to go with it,' Joanie said. 'And a request.'

The door was opened again, and Joanie noticed how

swiftly Sage turned towards it, and how the expectation fell from her face when it was Martha who came inside, tugging off boots and clapping them together at the entrance so that some of the thick earth was scattered into the yard. The floorboards had received the rest, but the old woman took little notice. Clove slipped through the door after her, hopping delicately between the blobs of mud as though joining dots and forming a picture.

Martha drew something from under her coat flap and held it out to Sage with a smile that split her face with wrinkles. It was a bunch of stalks, brown and slimy and headed with the corpses of flowers, already drooping towards their resting place over the woven rugs.

Sage started backwards, raising a hand to her mouth, and it was Joanie who reached for the dead blooms. She watched as Clove gently took her grandma's hand and led her away to their shared bedroom. It was like seeing ages change, the young in charge of the old.

The yard was the best place to deposit Martha's gift, it gave Joanie time to collect herself. She was calmer on her return to the table, but the old woman's deterioration had been shocking.

Sage had set out the coffee and the cakes as though this was just an ordinary day free from the peculiar. She indicated for her neighbour to take a seat, but Joanie bypassed the chair and headed for her host instead.

'I am sorry,' she said, holding the young woman tightly, for quite a while; at least until her stiffness had softened.

Sage Madison had too much on her plate; coping with a mother who appeared to have lost all reason, as well as a husband who had tossed his away. Wrong. She was just about coping. It was obvious from the set of her head.

Joanie took a seat. 'That is why I am here,' she said,

as though carrying on a one-sided conversation. 'To ask if you will come back to the choir.'

'The choir?' Sage spoke as if she had never heard the word before.

'Is bereft without you.'

'I hardly think so.'

'Listen, Sage,' Joanie shifted in her chair, taking hold of the woman's hands so that she could not escape. 'The choir needs you, your voice and your magic. Without it we are but an unaccomplished group of ladies with no sense of direction.'

'You have Mrs Hetherington's direction.'

'Mrs Hetherington has Mrs Hetherington,' Joanie said. 'She exists in her own world of baton-bashing and stridency, but we cannot work like that. We need purity and rhythm and the ability to sing the right notes in the right order from the right pages.'

The corners of Sage's mouth began to wriggle. The other woman was pleased to see it.

'You do not realise, because you still cannot believe in yourself, how much our singing has improved since you came to join us,' she said. 'Neither will you realise that the day of the concert is creeping ever closer, and we are in turmoil. Half of the group is still following the words with a finger and losing the notes at the back of their teeth, while the other half have been confused by the very fact that we are being required to sing to a congregation of music lovers in just a few weeks' time.'

Sage turned away. 'I can't…'

Joanie raised her voice. 'We are falling apart, and only you can save us. You can put us back together again.'

'No, Mrs Hockaday, I cannot.'

'Yes, Miss Madison, you surely can.'

There was a hush in the room. Joanie hoped it was a

sign that Sage was making up her mind, but the young woman's attention had been snapped. She was staring at the little girl who had appeared silently in the doorway, arm raised and finger pointing.

'The dark man,' Clove said, and that was all. But those three words were still enough to send a shiver down Joanie Hockaday's spine.

There was upheaval outside, rising like a storm, the racket of hooves and squealing of horses, and someone was shouting. The women left their seats, hesitating for just a second before heading for the door. Sage had flung it open before Joanie could stop her. They were buffeted by noise, the fury of movement, the two horses in the yard, the two men.

Arms stiff by his sides, Wolf Shadow was staring at the mustang – rearing, black mud to the belly, tail stringy with filth and hooves gouging holes from the ground. Wild with rage, the stallion was throttling itself from the noose around its neck, the hands that gripped the end of the rope belonging to the rider of the sturdy dun. Sturdy himself, muscles taut across his shoulders as he bore the weight of the animal's fury. As if carved from agate his face showed no expression, a line of blood from a cut over his eye stuttering through the markings on his skin like punctuation.

Wolf Shadow stepped forward, offering his hand to the stallion. The horse stamped, rearing as far as it could at the end of the rope. The rider's muscles clenched further and the dun juddered, snarling. Sage ran out into the yard, she seized Wolf's arm and tried to haul him away from the slash of hooves and the danger. He turned as if surprised to find her there, and Joanie could see him saying something that appeared to paralyse the young woman. She let him go and stepped back, and Wolf went forward again calling out words that no human would understand.

The man on the dun began to speak as well, the strange language that Sage knew from experience would chase the wild from a mustang. Wolf and the dark man – two speaking as one. The curious harmony grabbed hold of the frenzied horse and wove a strangeness through the women's minds, and time passed unnoticed until everything, and everyone, was at rest.

Rain had started, spitting up crud that had been scored from the ground by the animal's gyrations. The horse was standing quiet, tail washed white under the downpour that rinsed its flanks and replaced the dirt with gold. Joanie could not quite believe what she was seeing, but she didn't need to say the words, because Sage had said them first.

'Emmett's stallion. Dark Wolf has brought it back.'

FORTY-SEVEN

WHAT SAGE remembered most about that evening was a bowl of water turned rusty-red by the dark man's blood.

She had cleaned the cut over his eye as well as she could, but there was no guarantee that the bleeding would stop. Even so, he had refused the offer of a bandage, which reminded her of Colt's stubbornness after once cutting himself on a piece of flint. But her son had been six years old at the time, his head crammed with the family history of bravado and deprivation, and the Indian was a full adult.

He was also Wolf Shadow's father, beyond any doubt. Although Wolf had been keeping his thoughts to himself since the stallion's return.

After he and the dark man had joined their voices the palomino had conceded a semblance of defeat. It had no choice when there was nothing in its armoury to fight the magic that had addled its brain. Meek as a foal it was coerced along the track between steadings, its hide more copper than gold now under the dogged rainfall.

Wolf and his father walked alongside with ropes and the unyielding power of words, and Joanie walked ahead in order to be the first to bring news to the man who was about to regain what he had lost. There was a similarity between Emmett's situation and a parable she had once learned at Sunday school, but that notion was left behind when she reached the barn, and her husband who was sheltering inside.

Hockaday hugged his wife before stepping into the rain, his eyes alight under the onslaught. He saw the young man limping, the older man steadying his own pace; he saw the allegiance between them that was more than just familial resemblance. Most of all he saw the rare wild beast, normally as ornery as hell but right then on its best behaviour, being led like a child's mount into the corral. Gentle until the gate was closed and the spell was broken, and the creature woke suddenly and didn't much care for where it found itself.

Like old friends, all three men leaned on the fence together, watching the hoodwinked horse searching for a way out and attacking the wooden posts when none was found. They were outside in the rain for some time, long enough for Joanie and her stove to have rustled up something tasty for when she and Emmett were alone once again.

When next she peered from the window the Indian and Wolf Shadow had started to move away, the rain scampering ahead of them like puppies at play. The sight made her smile. She would have smiled even more if she'd looked out moments earlier to see Emmett shaking the father's hand, and then the son's – healing one wounded friendship and securing another.

Sage had been peering from her own window at the very same time, but there was still no sign of them. She had a while to wait before husband and father-in-law appeared at the entrance to the yard. There was not much land to measure between the homesteads, but for Wolf and the dark man it was an inestimable distance. A distance that encompassed pasts, shared and yet to learn;

wrongs, righted and discarded; bonds, realised and accepted. A lot of ground was covered over a splintered mile, and time had to be allowed. And when they finally appeared it was getting on for evening and they were both wet to the skin. But that was of no concern, because they had come through the torrent together.

It rained until the early hours. The house lay at rest, ticking over with the fire that still glowed in the hearth. Awake in bed, Sage told herself she could hear the subdued crump of shifting fuel, but it was probably something else moving in the empty room downstairs – maybe little feet that had yet to settle for the night, or larger ones that were looking for where they were meant to be. Clove or her grandma, grasping for sleep when there had been too much keeping them awake.

Sage knew how that felt. The night was lying heavy, the passing hours had not been kind and sleep had evaded her. She lay supine, her soul flitting through the house, tickled by the light of the night fire, easing into the spaces where the children should be in slumber – Clove lying to attention on her back, and Colt wallowing in his pillow.

Colt indeed was asleep in bed, but wallowing instead in a slurry of excited dreams. His mind was too busy trying to make sense of the noises he had heard coming from his neighbours' yard that afternoon. No angry horse had beleaguered the Hockaday fences since the day Emmett had returned Night Dancer to the Madison enclosure, but the sound of fury and stricken wood had been unmistakable to the boy riding home from school.

He had taken Vixen to the edge of the track, and that was when he saw the palomino in Emmett Hockaday's corral. Like a tornado under the rain, it was kicking up a storm of its own, and Mr Hockaday had been watching it from the gate, misshapen under a waterproof. He'd been laughing, mouth wide, as if the stallion's tantrum was the cheeriest thing he had ever witnessed.

Colt had ridden the rest of the journey at speed, and he and the little mare were sleek with wet by the time they scrambled into the Madison yard. The first thing the boy had seen was the big dun, taking its ease under the animal shelter. Then through the window he'd caught sight of Clove's dark man, sitting at the table with his mother, and she was wiping his head with a bloody cloth.

Everyone had started at the noise as the door burst open, and Colt stood dripping on the threshold, rain melting from his oiled poncho and stress melting from his body. There had been something in the air, a lack of restraint that seemed to be rollicking over the place where his sister and grandma were weaving rainbows in a click of needles.

His mother had smiled at him, squeezing the cloth over a bowl of water. Colt had seen no smile on his father's face from where he was standing at the far side of the room, but there had been such fire in his eyes that the boy could almost feel the heat from the doorway.

'Go back outside, Colt. Take care of Vixen,' his father had said. 'When that is done you can come and get dry.'

A command, but not harsh, almost with humour behind it. The boy had grinned, and his father's mouth seemed to twist in reply. And over at the table was the stranger with his father's eyes, and his father's gentleness when he wasn't keeping it hidden behind a scowl. Then all was quiet as the big man spoke.

'I will help with the caring,' he'd said, looking over at Colt's father as if to seek his permission, and Colt's father had returned the look, and nodded.

Snippets of the unforgettable evening were replaying in the boy's dreams that night. Dark Wolf with Vixen's saddle in his arms, almost weightless the way he was holding it; Dark Wolf with enchantments at the back of his throat, stroking water from the mare's flanks with his wide, firm hand. The same enchantments that he had cast over the mound with the trees where runaway Colt had once sought shelter between branches, what seemed now like a hundred years ago.

Thus had the Indian helped with the caring, and the boy had stood beside him, invoking sorcery of his own. The words slipped into his mouth with ease, for they were a language he knew well from his father's tongue. And when he spoke them the dark man had raised his eyebrows, the marks on his face rising to meet them.

'You have been learning from the wolf,' he said.

'Pa taught me young, just like his pa taught him,' the boy had replied, too busy rubbing down the red pony to see the look on the man's face.

Then after a moment the Indian had asked how many years he had, which Colt thought might be something to do with his age.

'I'm nine now, but soon I'll be ten.'

He had stood tall, and as straight as possible. 'Pa was about my age when he was brought here by Grandpa Madison.'

'It is nearly time for you to hunt your own stallion.'

The boy had stared, the towel hanging from his hand.

'You are the son of my son,' Dark Wolf had said, with a twist to his voice. 'I lost him too early for his own hunt, but chance has come again with you.'

Son of my son. Still asleep, Colt mimed the words as though he had only just heard them. He began to dream about school the next day, imagining the looks on the faces of his friends when he told them he was going out with his grandpa to hunt down a stallion.

The same sort of words were running through Sage's mind as she lay awake that dark night. Sleep had flown away long before and she had given up waiting for its return. The bed was warm and comfortable, and Wolf Shadow was an extra darkness beside her. She could hear him breathing, too lightly for the drag of slumber. He was awake also, lost in his own reverie.

She turned on her side, her breasts against his back. His breathing faltered at her movement, and when she reached a hand to his chest she could feel it settling again.

'He wants to take Colt out to hunt a stallion,' she said, voicing her thoughts.

Wolf Shadow sighed. 'Yes.'

She paused. 'Does that worry you?'

He opened his mouth, and closed it without speaking. The bed rocked when he shook his head. Sage waited and the words followed soon after.

'But not a stallion; he is too young,' he said. 'A colt will be enough.'

'A colt will grow into a stallion.'

'Just as the boy will grow into a man.'

It kept her quiet for a while – the image of her son standing tall, with a man's shoulders, and a beard. Maybe with a son himself.

Would Dark Wolf still be around when the time came for Colt to take his own son out to hunt a stallion? Would the Indian have moved in with them by then?

'It does not feel right that your father should still be sleeping in a barn,' she said. 'We can make room for him in the house, I have told him this, but he is stubborn.'

'Stubbornness runs high in the family line,' Wolf said,

and when she chuckled he turned on his side as well, facing her darkness as she was facing his. His hand drifted to her hair, lifting it, letting it flicker through his fingers. The breeze of it falling was fanning her cheek.

'I am thinking that Dark Wolf finds wellbeing in a place where his son can only find ghosts and sour memories,' she said, stroking his chest, feeling his growl beneath the skin.

'Not always,' he said. 'There are good memories in the barn, at night when the straw is thick and the moon creeps in between broken boards.'

He combed her hair back with his fingertips. She took his hand and kissed it, just as she would do in the barn after they had made love and the horror of the dawn was too far away to care. And then she kissed his mouth, and his eyes, and all the sore places on his face that had yet to scar.

Martha Madison heard movement from the floor above. She stopped roaming the downstairs room just long enough to recognise the beginning of lovemaking. The sounds reminded her of when she was young and romantic. She thought of the hill in its distance from the house, the covering of trees that were spiked like dog fur, and smiled on her way back to the room where a little girl was sleeping.

She wondered whose child it was. She hoped that her parents would remember to collect her in the morning.

FORTY-EIGHT

JOANIE ENTREATED until Sage succumbed, and the choir was enriched, even though the church was growing chill as winter encroached, its gables and tall windows laced by ice. Mrs Hetherington took to wearing gloves, directing the singing with sweeping movements of fleece-lined leather, and many of the ladies were comforted by wool. Living on the edge of the wild and accustomed to the unkindness of elements, Sage and Joanie found that the addition of thicker shawls sufficed.

'There is talk of installing extra stoves for the evening of the performance,' Joanie told Emmett as the event drew closer. 'It seems that townsfolk feel the cold.'

Despite their fullness of girth, Emmett disputed, thinking of Kester Kendall and others of his ilk. He shook his head and whisked himself out into the yard before his misguided wife could suggest that his own attendance at the concert would be a good idea.

Sage had been blessed with easier persuasion. The event would be Wolf Shadow's first appearance in town since his near-death resurrection under Dr Ryker's hands. It would also be Dark Wolf's induction into the town's righteousness, and further proof of his kinship with the half-blood from the valley dip. Tales were already being woven of the Indian and the horse whisperer, and the audience that evening was to be swelled by the curious of Oasis.

Wolf Shadow's wounds were knitting and his limp was merely a reminder. If he felt any ill effects he was keeping them hidden from Sage, who seemed to have developed a liking for coddling – only natural for a woman with a baby set fast and safe in her belly. A baby that would be filling her more tightly by the time of kinder weather and Wolf's ride to Liberation, taking Colt along with him to return what had been borrowed from Father Thomas. Even though the loaned garments were by now shredded and unwearable. Even though the lost piebald was probably sheltering in another corral, loved by its new owner's young children and settling back into idleness. But Wolf had made a promise to a priest, and with another horse and another shirt, he intended to honour it.

Each day he grew stronger. He had already been to the Hockaday steading to work with the palomino. And when he was freed from the engrossment of chores, Emmett would watch from the perimeter's safety as the young man steered the stallion around the enclosure, reminding it of the time at leaf fall when it had obeyed the pull of words and carried a thief across the land.

Joanie watched them both from the doorway of the house, wondering at the speed with which done could be dusted and ills forgotten. Shuddering more than once at the thought of how close Daniel Ryker must have been to forgetting that he was a doctor, on the night that his wife's lover had lain at his mercy on the couch.

And what would have happened to the dark man if he had failed to start Wolf's heart with his fist? Would he still be making his home in the hayloft? Because despite Sage's urgings Dark Wolf chose to remain in the barn. It offered him the solitude to invoke the spirits and lay the ghosts of the farm to rest, for he too felt them in that haunted place, instilled by the skull-faced one who had died bequeathing the reek of whisky and the creak of the coiled whip. Although it had been a while since Haine Madison's release from the earth, his wraith remained like an indelible stain. The Indian felt it heavy when the night was dark and windy; when the barn was tormented by storms that found entry through gaps in the walls.

He understood that Wolf Shadow felt it also; that the past had clung to him over the years he had grown from child to adult. The young man never spoke of it, but the Indian was learning about Wolf from what was hidden in his eyes. The stories that Dark Wolf unearthed he kept to himself, in the same way that he concealed the journey he had made to the wooded mound to hunt down Hockaday's rare beast, on the day that he and his son had cemented their kinship.

Although it had run from the gunshots, the palomino had not wandered far from the place where Wolf Shadow's blood and Emmett's bullets were buried under tree roots. The horse had been easy to track, and after a day's chasing it had been firmly snagged on enticements from Dark Wolf's tongue. As a result, its capture had been comparatively straightforward, as the capture of the boy's colt would be once the winter had passed and the wild horses were kicking their heels through spring's pastureland, too stupefied by rich grass to free their minds from the dark man's language.

His language, and his son's – for Wolf Shadow would be there as well on the day of Colt's initiation.

And the little maid? A strange one, brimming with magic but yet to master its power. That was to be the grandfather's job as well, and Clove was already a willing pupil. Just see how quickly she had created earth music from the hollow-wood pipe Dark Wolf had whittled for her. She played well enough to accompany her mother's singing that was helping to lift melancholy from the homestead.

But the child was still very young, and if she wished to keep her own counsel then allow it of her. And if when she spoke it was only to her grandma and the knitting she held, now growing in length and colour like a kaleidoscope tumbling from her hands, then be grateful that at least she spoke, and that the old woman appeared to understand despite the mystifying spaces in her mind.

All seemed calm on the surface, but no one was aware that there were mystifying spaces in the child's mind as well. Back in the time of the troubles she had known of a dark figure, but the man he had become had brought peace to the steading, and not the danger and the death that Clove had expected. Danger had passed and death had been averted, and there should have been a shining golden light to follow.

But the light had not appeared and the darkness had not faded. The little girl still fell asleep with it weighing on her mind. And since the forthcoming of winter it had grown thicker. There were times when she could feel it leaking from her ears.

There was no reason for it. Danger had arrived with the dark man, that is true, but instead of bringing death he had brought her father back to life.

And yet... And yet...

And yet while she hummed and knitted and wove music in the air with her grandfather's pipe, Clove Shadow still knew things.

But she didn't know why, or when. Or who.

FORTY-NINE

THE DAY of the concert was sharp with cold. Puddles iced and shone in the yard and frost covered the grass as beautifully as crushed crystals. But as the afternoon drew on, the bitterness increased.

Sage had no wish to see her mother suffering in the buggy to town, or quaking in the chill of the church. For despite the extra stoves, their puny heat was likely to rise straight to heaven, instead of reaching the sinners who would have welcomed it more.

By evening she was convinced.

'The concert will not last long, Ma,' she said. 'We shall be back as soon as the singing is over.'

Be sure of it and know it will be so, she thought as she stepped out into the biting air and was glad that the house was cosy and her mother was safe and sound in her chair by the stove.

Nobody saw Martha buttoning up her cotton dress and taking her bonnet and leaving the house. No one noticed her standing by the wall where the garden was waiting for the spring to magic new growth.

Clove did not see her grandma beginning her walk towards the far hill and its crown of trees, because if she had the little girl would have wanted to go on the journey as well, and perhaps she would have brought blankets to protect them from the chill. Clove did not see because she was sitting in the church with her grandpa and her brother. And her father, dressed in leather, fair hair brushed back from the scars on his face that told the story of his life.

Silent and still, Wolf Shadow's eyes were shining like spots of gold on the woman by the altar cloth. Sage Madison – young and strong, radiant with her unborn child and the music in her throat. Mrs Hockaday was standing to one side of her, Mrs Kendall to the other. The three of them could have linked arms they were so close together.

It was the power of lasting friendship. Clove reached out to touch it, until Dark Wolf caught her hand and held it in his.

The land that day was all shades of green; just as it had been when she was a bride, naïve enough to think that she would eventually soften her fierce new spouse. Gentle enough to see the colour and beauty that surrounded her before life with Haine Madison became the hammer that crushed her into the ground.

It was the middle of July, the hottest month of the summer. Martha was young and strong and radiant with a baby in her womb. A daughter, maybe; and in a few years, God willing, she might also be blessed with a son.

It was just a short walk to the wonderful hill, crowned by trees as tender as grass. Not far to go now. She should be there and back before twilight, meadow flowers filling the lap of her skirt. And her handsome husband might take her to bed and show her how much he loved her.

The evening was pitching towards night. It was dark and raw and beginning to snow. The distant hill was ghastly with stunted trees. Martha's cotton dress flapped in the wind. Icy water had plastered the thin bonnet to her skull but still she smiled, her eyes full of purple and green, and the golden rays of the sun.

After a while the home she left behind was swallowed up by blizzard, but Martha kept on walking through the black curtain that had fallen across the world. Until finally all she knew were the folds of land beneath her feet, undulating like the back of a worn-out mare.

47746936R00221

Printed in Poland
by Amazon Fulfillment
Poland Sp. z o.o., Wrocław